TALL IN THE SIGHT OF GOD

TALL
IN THE
SIGHT
OF
GOD

ROBERT A. BOWEN

JOHN F. BLAIR, *Publisher*
Winston-Salem

1958

THE AUTHOR WISHES TO THANK THE PERSONNEL OF PACK MEMO-rial Library in Asheville for their efficient and generous help in his research. Especial thanks are due Miss Myra Champion. Others whose encouragement and criticisms were of inestimable value are Julius Parker, Bernard Szold, Clarence Sumner, Hubert Hayes, Betsy Lindau, Sam and Mickey Greene, Isaac Northup and, of course, Bessie Collins Bowen, who has valiantly put up with the writer, lo, these many years.

D. Hiden Ramsey, whose journalistic vineyard the author helped tend for more than a quarter-century, is due a special ac-knowledgment for his critical analysis, along with that of his wife, Mary Ramsey.

ROBERT A. BOWEN

Whatsoever things are true,
Whatsoever things are honest,
Whatsoever things are just,
Whatsoever things are pure,
Whatsoever things are lovely,
Whatsoever things are of good report—
If there be any virtue,
And if there be any praise—
Think on these things.

St. Paul

TALL IN THE SIGHT OF GOD

CHAPTER ONE

PETER GHERKIM

1795-1832

A hero of the battle of New Orleans
Who repented his sins and prepared
For eternal life in Heaven before he
Was hanged by his Christian neighbors
For stealing a poor widow's sheep

LOFE LAGERMANN'S CHISEL MADE A FINAL FLOURISH AT THE LAST letter on the Gherkim epitaph. He tapped it lightly with his hammer, then stepped back and squinted pridefully at his handiwork. The tombstone was a natural outcropping of blue granite three feet wide and about two feet in height. It sloped away from the new-made grave at a forty-five degree angle. Lofe had chiseled a smooth spot large enough to hold the lettering. The calluses on his hands were sore from days of patient chipping and handsanding the stone.

Each day as Lofe had worked Ajax Arvane and Zebulon Cedric had dropped by and sat around stolidly, sometimes arguing back and forth between themselves for hours while Lofe sweated with the stone.

"I figure," Lofe said, "as somebody owes me about five dollars for this here job, an' I don't figure the job wu'th a damn to nobody but the man as pays for it." He snorted. "Whoever heard of puttin' up a monument to the memory of a damned sheep-stealer. Now wuz it a stone tellin' folks how Ajax Arvane

and Zebulon Cedric come inter this here valley fifty year ago an'
done so much f'r it, I mought work for a mite less. I ain't sayin'
I would, but I ain't sayin' I wouldn't, neither."

He dropped his chisel and hammer into the front of his mason's apron.

Zebulon rose quickly from his seat despite a twinge of rheu-
matiz in creaky joints. He almost danced a jig in his indignation
as he shook his fist at Ajax. "Again, you was a-tryin' to trick me,
wasn't you, Ajax? You said you could get this writin' on that
there rock for practically nothin'. By grannies, where I come
fr'm practically nothin' means nothin' a-tall. If you'd a-had the
brains of a hummin' bird with his head chopped off you'd a-
knowed I wasn't a-gonna pay no money to see no writin' on no
stone for no Peter Gherkim as ever lived."

Ajax smiled through his beard at Zebulon, extracted a pouch,
handed Lofe a gold piece. "Didn't expect you to pay none
of it," he told Zebulon placidly. "Knowed for more'n fifty years
you was too stingy to pay a copper cent to see Moses climb down
Jacob's ladder an' dive into Modesty Creek. I knowed I'd have to
pay all—if it got paid."

"You did, did you?" Zebulon growled. "Lemme tell you
somethin'. When I said no money, I meant no money. If Lofe'll
drap by my house he can pick his-self up the biggest middlin'
o' meat in my smokehouse. An' I figure that'd be mighty generous pay f'r a little bitty piddlin' job like he done on that there
rock. Shucks, iffen Lofe had a-knowed anythin' about what he
was a-doin', he coulda done that there little bitty rock-writin'
in a hour, or a hour an' a half. No call to take a month peckin'
on one rock."

Lofe's youthful face clouded over. He threw back his powerful blacksmith's shoulders, shoulders and sinews made powerful
by the operation of his small home-grown iron forge and smithy.
"Looky here, Mr. Zebulon," he said, "at your age it won't be too
long afore I'll be a-fixin' a stone for your head. Iffen you want
a middlin'-o'-meat stone, say so now. I'm the man as can give it
to you."

"Don't want none iffen it's gonna cost. What good's a stone to me after I'm dead? Take one o' them stones over to Anserville an' try to buy a barrel of flour with it." He snorted, derisively, and started down the footpath.

"When you're dead, Zeb," Ajax called after Cedric, "you can spend a headstone just as easy as you can spot cash. Trouble with you is you're just the stingiest man in Modesty, an' ever'body knows it, an' ever'body says so."

"Ain't nobody said no such to my face," Zebulon called back. "I'm a-sayin' so now."

Zebulon snickered gleefully. "You ain't nobody," he called back.

Ajax followed Zeb down the steep footpath that led off the brow of the small hillock where Modesty graveyard sat peacefully in the sunlight. Lofe, in the hurried impatience of youth, passed him, walking rapidly, swerved around Zebulon. By fast walking he could make Anserville in time to make the rounds before closing time.

Ajax let his eyes wander up the valley to where Modesty Cove dropped off the ridge at the foot of Mount Acacia; up where it fanned out to begin Modesty Valley and spewed forth the cold clear waters of Modesty Creek, which went cussing and clawing at the boulders in the cove, then surrendered to a more sedate ten-mile stretch of happy gurgling before it again went berserk in Big Tom Gorge, getting ready to slosh into Elk River. Ajax tried to be an humble man, but he couldn't let his sight sweep up and down the valley, as he did from the promontory of the graveyard, without a feeling that in some way he, personally, was akin to the Almighty.

He quickened his pace, caught up with Zeb. "Zeb," he said kindly, "Doctor Rob Arvane brung me a jug o' bilin's, fr'm out Cat Creek way, which-as, he says, is the best you ever sampled. Wish you'd come by an' give me your opinion on it."

"Don't keer if I do," Zebulon said.

A few minutes later the two old men sat on the front porch at Ajax's. They had just drunk lustily from a medium-sized dipper gourd, and the clear distillate of corn was beginning to assert its authority as it seeped mellowly through their innards.

"You know, Zeb," Ajax observed philosophically, "me an' you've done a damn good job o' fixin' up this here valley an' makin' it fitten for folks to live in. Makes me kind o' proud when I think about it."

"Ever' time I'm about to git proud about that I git mad at the way you run our chillun outen the valley just as it was about to git ready for 'em to start pleasurin' from livin' in it." Zeb was emphatic.

"I ain't run nobody nowhere," Ajax said mildly. "I ain't never told nobody he had to do nothin' in my life," Ajax reminded Zebulon.

"More'n one way to do anythin'," Zebulon rejoined sullenly. "All o' my life, an' you know it, I was a-lookin' forward to my gals marryin' up with your men an' settlin' down here in Modesty Valley where I could pleasure myself with my own grandchillun. But you wan't satisfied. You couldn't wait for them boys to find out they was men in their own good time. Fast's they got some size to they bodies, bones a little meat on 'em, you'd take 'em out to the barn an' let 'em wet down some straw. If you was satisfied with the amount o' foam, then you'd make 'em take down their pants so's you could take a look at their hair. Now don't go a-callin' me no liar on this, 'cause your own boys said you done it. They said if you could find a fair smidgen o' hair on their bellies you'd r'ar back an' snort like a wild bull. It went somethin' like this: 'God Almighty, here you air, hairy as a mountain b'ar, an' still playin' around like a child. You better start a-courtin' that little Samanthy Cedric 'fore somebody else runs off with her!' And blest if he wouldn't be a-courtin' my gal that very same day." Zebulon filled his cheek with black hillside tobacco, rolled it on his tongue for a moment, clamped his old teeth into it, then spat disgustedly over the porch railing.

"I'm damned glad my last gal didn't marry up with your last boy an' my last boy didn't take your last gal," he told Ajax, grumpily, as he went clumping down the steps toward the road.

Ajax watched his oldest friend going down the creek road in the slouching shuffle of elderly mountain people the world over, and his lips twitched in a smile of benign affection. "Old Zeb shore pleasures his-self with grousin' an' growlin'. Been doin' it so long now I almost think he thinks he means it, sometimes," Ajax mumbled to himself.

It had been more than a half century since the Regulators, of Alamance, had attempted to stand against the North Carolina militia and wound up with a large number of their ranks either killed in the short battle, hanging at the end of ropes, or on their way, escaping to the mountains. Ajax and Zebulon had been too young to take part in the fight, but they had helped bury their fathers, who had both fallen in the first burst of musketry. The massacre had left such bad tastes in both his and Zebulon's mouths that when the Revolution came they determined to remain neutral and forthwith denounced both sides, saying it wouldn't make any difference to honest hard-working folks who won; a poor man wouldn't have a chance either way.

They were mature settled men, past twenty years old, with wives and families getting started, when the realization came that, while they had managed to stay out of the fighting, they had also become very unpopular with both Tories and patriots alike. In fact, so unpopular that their lives were in actual danger, and they found themselves not only working their cleared patches together, with guns near at hand, but also sleeping out in the woods at night.

So one night, right after first dark, Ajax Arvane and Zebulon Cedric told their families good-bye and left the Alamance country with the goods they needed to make a new settlement in the mountains to the west lashed to the backs of an even-tempered old ox and a frisky, yet balky, young bull, while a spotted cow, with widespread horns and sorrowful eyes, brought up the rear. A couple of work steers, and enough provender to last a year, had been left with their women.

"I swear to God, Ajax, I'm so wore out fr'm beatin' on that

there bull's back end with hickory sprouts I'm a-gonna bed down
at the next waterin' place we find an' stay right there to it comes
another day. Then, if this bull don't git along better I'm a-gonna
have me some bull meat." Zebulon sounded disgusted.

"We have to keep our bull," Ajax told Zeb placatingly. "Else,
how we gonna git us a herd of cows started in our rich valley?"

"Rich valley, hell! How do I know they's any valley of any
kind over them there mountains? Nor you neither? All you
know is what you heard Dan'l Boone say, an' I'd bet he was
drunk when he said it."

"The valley's there all right," Ajax said, "but there is one little
bitty pint I forgot to mention. It was sort of set up as a dividin'
line betwixt the white settlements and the Injuns. Boone said
Sevier signed a paper with the Injuns that no white could ever
take it away fr'm 'em except by a fair and square trade, and the
Injuns wasn't to cross over th' ridge an' bother no whites. Like
I told you, Boone says this valley's eight-ten miles long and
more'n a mile wide at some places on its floor. He says it's a-
workin' alive with game, an' that the fish in the creek as runs
down its middle is plumb vicious they want to be caught an' et
so bad."

Zebulon cussed for five minutes. First, loudly and eloquently;
then, more slowly, but vehemently; finally in a low mumble. "I
might a-knowed," he groaned, "they was a big hitch in it if you
was interested. 'It's a big, rich valley, just a-waitin' for us, Zeb,'
you said. But you failed to say we had to trade it away from a
passel of fightin' Injuns. If Dan'l Boone couldn't git it away
fr'm 'em, how th' hell you think you can? You ain't got nothin'
to trade but your big mouth, an' I don't allow as how even a Injun'd want that."

"It don't take much to trade with Injuns if you know how
to make medicine. I know we ain't got much in trade goods but
I got mighty strong medicine. Th' kind a Injun can understand."
Ajax's voice had a positive ring.

"You got the kind as'll git a hatchet sunk into your thick skull.
I just hope I ain't around when it happens." Zebulon groaned.

"This is powerful medicine," Ajax argued. "I got it fr'm a doctor. Told him I wanted to git a painter as was a-killin' my sheep. I meant to use it agin them prowlin' patriots and Tories was they to come around, an' I got a chance." He waited for Zebulon to ask for more details, but Zeb was too angry to ask any questions.

Their stewpot was bubbling when they heard the loud clear notes of a bugle sounding retreat. They had crossed the first, and lowest, ridge and were ready to head toward the backbone of the sky-pointing North Carolina portion of the Appalachians.

"British bugle blowing retreat; must be the Old Fort over the hill," Ajax said. "I hear it's King's men there, so they won't give us no trouble."

As he spoke, an officer and three soldiers burst through the bushes. "Whence came ye, my hearties?" the officer asked. "And where do you go?"

"We are," Ajax told the officer, "runnin' away from the Alamance country, headin' for the Watauga to make settlement."

"H-m-m-m," the officer mused. "The Watauga. A veritable hotbed of renegades, from what I can learn. Men with their feet planted firmly in both camps, waiting to see which way the tree falls. Search them and their packs, men."

As Ajax and Zebulon rose slowly, the officer shouted, pulling his pistol. "On your feet, scum, and show proper respect for the King's uniforms."

A soldier searched them rapidly, looked into their packs and possible bags, scattering their contents on the ground. "Nothing here," he said.

"Put them things back where you found 'em," Ajax told the sergeant, testily.

The young officer whirled. "Use a civil tongue and soft words when you address a soldier of the King. By rights you should both be hanged for trying to escape to the Watauga, but I'll show you the King's mercy. I shall requisition your ox to feed our troops and let you be on your way. You should thank me for being so lenient."

Ajax leaned over his pot of boiling and bubbling stew. "We want the King to fare well," he said, dejectedly, "but it ain't right to take our ox when we need him so bad."

"Who are you, to put your needs before the King's?" the officer asked. "For your arrogance we shall take all three of your cattle to teach you a lesson in good manners, and give you a good flogging besides if I hear one more word out of you."

"To hell with you and the King, too!" Ajax yelled, deftly swishing the pot of boiling stew into the faces of the officer and his sergeant. As the scalded men sat down suddenly, hands over faces, screaming in agony, the two soldiers stood stupified for a moment before they dropped their guns and made a break to run. The break was too late. One hadn't gone two steps before Ajax crushed his skull with a rock thrown at six feet and Zebulon had the other on the ground tightening a huge paw on his windpipe. When Zebulon knew his man had breathed his last, and loosed his grasp, he was just in time to see Ajax dispatching the officer and sergeant with an axe.

"Hate to have to do a thing like that to a man already blind, but we couldn't leave 'em here to tell on us." For once Zebulon didn't argue the point.

CHAPTER TWO

In a matter of minutes they had stripped the king's men of arms, ammunition, clothing, along with everything else of any possible future value to them, thrown the bodies into a dry wash, covered them with stones, trailed some vines over the spot, and were ready to move on.

The remainder of the night was spent making a wide circle around the fort. A thin moon outlined the worst of the thickets and kept them from the more precipitous of ledges. When morning came, Ajax found that by climbing a tall chestnut he could almost look down into the fortified area to their rear, although it was some miles behind. "Guess them soldiers not gittin' back last night didn't cause no excitement," he told Zebulon. "Reckon we can keep on a-movin' all day."

"I reckon you can," Zebulon said. "Me, I'm a-gonna rest myself to th' sun's noon-high 'fore I move a inch." He sat down heavily.

Three days later, and sunset, found them encamped on the western slope of the ridge that butts so bluntly against Mount Acacia. A few miles below they could see their valley. The valley they had left the Alamance country to conquer, to seize for themselves and their descendants forever. Ajax climbed a tall tree, studied the valley. "I can see," he told Zebulon, "smoke from three campfires, which means the Injuns have three huntin' parties in our valley now. After I have a good feed I'll slip down there an' git 'em in a trading mood." Zebulon grunted, noncommittally.

It was still light enough for Ajax to cut an elegant figure before Zebulon when he decked himself out in the British officer's uniform with its gold braid, lacy sleeves and collar. He pulled the gold-hilted sword from its scabbard, spat on the blade, and tested its cutting edge with his thumb. Among the soldiers' effects he had found a hundred feet of punk roping, of the type used in starting a fire, which had been drenched in a solution of tar and gunpowder, then allowed to dry out. It was coiled neatly under his coat along with the officer's gold-mounted pistol. He felt in his pocket a last time to be sure he had his medicine powder wrapped tightly in a piece of buckskin. "If I don't come back by mornin'," he told Zebulon, "don't come a-lookin' f'r me. Amble round t'other way an' find white men. Tell 'em I went down to see them Injuns on a peaceful visit, an' you think they done kilt me. Maybe they'll help you run them Injuns out an' give you an' my family the valley to pay for me."

"I don't reckon you're a-goin' down there by yourself," Zebulon said, morosely. "I'll be a-layin' back in the bushes, and the first Injun as picks up a hatchet'll git one a-twixt th' eyes."

"Zeb," Ajax said, "don't be a damn fool. You go off an' leave these critters up here an' the b'ars won't leave nothin' but horns come mornin'. I'll be a-comin' back, an' you know it good as I do."

The Indians' nearest hunting party was encamped at the mouth of the cove. They had a large rock with a pan-shaped hollow in it filled with fresh venison and meal. It was covered with a flat stone on which a fire roared. Ajax's mouth watered sickeningly as he came within smelling distance of the feast. No sentries were out, and Ajax was standing among the Indians before they knew he was present. He spoke. "I am from the white man's king. Who speaks English?"

The Indians were startled, but not enough to keep them from seizing weapons and standing ready.

A tall brave whose ornaments and bearing branded him the leader of the party stepped forward. "I speak English good and better. Better I unnerstan', better I speak. What brings our white

brother? Knives, maybe? Gooder and better guns for kill more
game?"

"I bring not guns, not knives, not things that can be used in
war. But I bring you sad tidings from the medicine men of the
white man's king from across the big water. My king sends me
flying across the water to warn his red brothers, to save your
lives and the lives of your people."

"Talk more, king's messenger," the Indian leader spoke.

"The king has learned from his wise medicine men that evil
spirits are abroad in this valley, that they are now making their
way into the bodies of the game so that all who eat of the game
so entered shall surely die. The evil has not entered into all the
game but in a few moons it will and no man who eats of game
killed in the valley shall live. And as the game is killed the
spirits will enter into the bodies of other wild things of the forest
so that whosoever shall eat of them will surely die."

"I hear the king's messenger, but I cannot tell if he is speaking with one or many tongues. Can he make a medicine to prove
what he tells?"

"I am not a medicine man," Ajax told the Indian. "I am only
an humble messenger. I will be pleased to try, oh Chief, to try
and detect if there be evil spirits in the meat on the fire. If the
spirits have not entered into it you can fill your belly with it an'
no hurt. But if it's there, and you eat one little taste, you will
surely die."

Silently the Indian pushed the cover from his pot, reached in
with a piece of curved willow bark, and brought out a small
helping. Ajax took the food, began walking around in widening
circles, describing a figure eight, all the while muttering an un-
intelligible singsong as he whiffed the food. Each time, as his back
was to his audience, he dropped a pinch of his magic powder into
the food. Finally, he brought it back, dumped it into the pot,
stirred the stew vigorously with a handy stick. He turned to the
Indians' leader; said, apologetically, "My brothers, my medicine
seems to be weak. I cannot tell if there be any evil in this food.
Try your medicine and see iffen you can find anything in it."

The leader was no fool. He was not the leader of the hunting party because he was lacking in brains. He took some of the food, whiffed it snortingly. "I can," he said, gravely, "smell spirits in it, but I cannot say it is not the harmless spirit of the deer." He tossed it back into the pot and stirred it all together briskly. "We can," he said, reasonably, "let one of our braves eat of it, and if he does not die, we would know you came, not as a friend, and that you must perish."

"I did not say," Ajax cried out, as though fearful, "that this food was so beset. And I will not allow one of my brothers to take so great a risk. Have you not an animal we can let eat of it?"

The leader sneered. "Everyone, even the children, know that animals cannot be killed by evil spirits."

"I speak with truth," Ajax argued. "These spirits are powerful. They can kill anything. Even the trees, the maize, the flowers."

A young and strapping brave stepped forward, dipped a willow paddle into the stew, piled a helping on a slab of willow bark, and began eating gustily. Ajax halfheartedly tried to prevent the young brave from eating the stew and was jerked away by others in the party, roughly and unceremoniously. The youth had taken only a few bites when with a half-scream he clutched his stomach, fell backward from his squatting position. He was dead by the time they reached his body.

The hunting party looked loweringly at the dead man, then turned to their leader, who had walked to face Ajax. "What now, oh powerful messenger of the most powerful white king?"

"First," Ajax said, "send runners to other hunting parties and tell them not to eat of any game taken between the ridges of this valley unless you have a medicine man powerful enough to smell out that in which the spirits are resting."

The leader spoke and three braves left in a fast run. He then turned to Ajax and tried to make conversation, but was cut off abruptly. "I wait," Ajax said, "for your chief." He needed a few minutes to plot his next move.

The chief was old, wrinkled, but withal had a sharp eye in

his gnomelike face. He couldn't, or more likely wouldn't, speak a word of English. When things had been explained to him he scooped some of the stew from the pot and threw it to a couple of mangy dogs skulking around the edges of the camp. As the dogs kicked their last the chief nodded his belief in the potency of the evil spirits. Through an interpreter he asked what the messenger of the white king would advise.

Ajax said it was not his business to give advice. He was only a messenger from one reigning sovereign to another. But he assured them the valley was not ruined by the presence of the spirits. The king's medicine men had found that the spirits were unable to leave the valley, and that game driven over the ridges before it was killed would be free of poison. Thus, it was believed, the chief should make an effort to drive the game out of the valley, then put his people to clearing it of all forests and setting the land to crops. Thus he could make good use of the valley in feeding his people while, at the same time, the mere clearing of the land would cause the game to seek other places to live. It was that simple.

The chief demurred. His people, he stated proudly, would never, so long as the sun and moon coursed through the skies, stoop to so menial a task as back-breaking toil after the ways of the white man, and clearing so large a plot would be too much for their women and children. Could it be, the old chief leered cunningly, that the king's messenger wanted to purchase the valley?

Ajax rose and stood dignifiedly before the chief. The messenger, he said, was not interested in the purchase of the valley, not even so much as one willow switch. He would, however, he said, like to extract one promise from the chief. That should he, at any time in the future, sell the valley to his white brothers, he would tell them about the poisoned game, so they would not die from eating it. The chief promised. "I go now," Ajax said, "back to the top of the great mountain, where just before the coming of dawn a huge bird will swoop down and carry me back to my king with the news that his message has been delivered."

Because Ajax had about the same faith in the veracity and honesty of Indians as he had in white men, he expected to be followed. He eased along a game trail as silently as he could, climbing the ridge at an angle that would miss their camp by a mile. Halfway up the ridge he took out the punk rope, dropped one end on the path, and began uncoiling it. When he had reached the end, he took it around a tree to shade the light, used his flint, and lit the end of the rope. A moment later the powder-coated punk was on fire and the flame racing back down the mountain, hissing and popping. As the fire went down the hill, Ajax, standing hidden behind a tree, threw back his head and laughed loud and insanely three times. Then, he stood for a few seconds more chuckling to himself as he heard the Indian braves running, falling, screaming out terrifiedly to each other as they raced back down the slope.

"That," Ajax told himself, "should convince the old bastard the Good Lord is on our side."

It was a week before Ajax and Zebulon finally reached the valley. The British officer's uniform had been taken off and cached along with the sword. Ajax had practically bathed in sassafras root tea until he was as brown as an Indian. He was back in his woodsmen's clothes. "Shucks," he told Zebulon, "they won't know me outen that fancy git-up, but just in case, I want you to do all the talkin'."

They came down off East Ridge at about the middle of the valley, forded the creek, and made camp. Ajax got a fire started, then piled green wood on it to make it smoke. "That old chief, he ain't so far away he can't come a-runnin' soon's that smoke gits a-goin'," he told Zebulon.

Again Ajax was right. Soon the chief, with his interpreter and two medicine men, was with them. He made a long palaver. "He asks," the interpreter explained, "if you are from the king's messenger."

"Didn't know he had a messenger. We're a-headin' over that

way, lookin' for a place to make settlement." Zebulon waved
an arm haphazardly toward the west.

It was explained that the land to the west was reserved for
a hunting ground by the Indians. But to accomodate his white
brothers the chief might be willing to sell the entire valley they
now occupied, for settlement. The valley, Zebulon said, was
larger than they wanted. Too much work to clear. He thought
they should push further, find a smaller valley.

The chief explained politely his people would frown mightily
on further settlements to the west, but the valley was definitely
up for sale with all of its rich land and abundance of game. Besides, it wouldn't be necessary to clear more land than they actually needed. Zebulon agreed that the valley must be worth
a great deal, but he had only a small amount of trade goods. He
was, he explained, a very poor man. In fact, about all he could
spare was three complete uniforms taken from the king's soldiers.

That, the chief argued, would be a mighty niggardly price
to pay for a prize so rich. The offer would have to be stiffened.
With a gesture of finality Zebulon laid one of the guns taken
from the British soldiers on the pile and brought out two fish-
hooks, which he presented to the chief as a personal gift from
him. That, he explained sadly, was the limit to which he could
go. He knew the valley was worth more, but he was out of trade
goods. He walked disconsolately away. The chief accepted and
began powwowing with his fellow tribesmen. Without understanding a word, Ajax could tell the chief was accepting congratulations for a job of super-salesmanship.

The talking over, Ajax extracted from their pack a quill, ink,
and paper, and began writing under the caption, A TREATY
OF TRANSFER, with which he boldly headed the title transfer
contract. Under the terms of the transfer, as Zebulon explained
to the chief, the Indians freely admitted they had ample payment
for the valley and agreed never to hunt or fish within its confines
again, nor were they to enter its boundaries at any time in the
future in numbers of more than five at the same time. The chief
agreed it was a fair contract and made his mark at the bottom.

He then wished them good hunting for the present, and later, good crops in the valley.

A few hours later, as they munched pone and broiled trout, Ajax observed, "This is about the middle of the valley. Let's divide her up here an' now. You take one end an' I'll take t'other-un." He picked up a chip, spat on it, tossed it whirling into the air. "Wet or dry?" he called.

"Wet," said Zebulon.

"Dry she falls," Ajax said, picking up the chip. "I'll take the upper half. Not as much farmin' land, but more'n I can ever use, and prettier lookin' scenes, an' I 'spect a mite better fishin'."

"I think, Ajax," Zebulon said, "you done more to git it than I done. Seems to me you're a-bein' a mite too modest."

Ajax slapped his skinny thigh. "That's what we'll call our holdin's, Zeb. Modesty Valley. We'll start us a city right here and name it Modesty. The creek is Modesty Creek. An' my end of the valley is Upper Modesty, and your end is Lower Modesty. Right now, we're rich in good land, and good wives, and healthy chillun, an' some day we'll be rich in money an' worldly goods. Think of it, Zeb! Ours, all ours, miles and miles of it. Bought honestly, signed and sealed, fair and square."

"I ain't goin' to blow that honesty horn too loud," Zebulon said, wryly. "We mought a-cheated them Injuns a tiny bit. Seemed like their chief was awful trustin' to me."

"What do you mean by cheated?" Ajax was emphatic. "Didn't the low-down red bastard sell us a valley full o' poisoned game and never tell us one word about it?"

Zebulon frowned, thought the last over a minute. He stomped a foot down, hard. "The lyin', cheatin' heathen! Do I ever git th' chance, Ajax, God so help me, an' I'll cut his throat!"

CHAPTER THREE

As soon as varmint-proof housing could be provided for the stock Ajax and Zebulon began building their own single-pen log houses. Puncheon boards made the roofs, and cracks were sealed with puncheons and clay. Ajax found enough flat stones in the creek to make a rough floor in his. Zebulon looked at it and sneered. "My old woman never had nothin' but a good packed clay floor in her life. I don't aim to change it now."

"That's what you're a-sayin' now," Ajax laughed. "Wait'll she sees what kind o' floor Nancy Arvane's gonna have before you make any long promises."

For the next few months Ajax hunted and trapped while Zeb's axe made an ever-widening cleared spot for them to begin farming come another spring. Zeb had managed a few acres of late corn and some beans, now already dried into leather britches. Too, he had cut enough wild hay to get the critters through the winter with some to spare. It was only a matter of six miles over East Ridge to Anser's store, where they could sometimes find the possibles they needed and sell the furs Ajax brought in.

In those days the Watauga was wild country, but not so wild that men didn't still talk about wars and rumors of wars, Indian trouble, and the outlandish prices a man had to pay for anything worth while. The settlers took their rumors in full stride, with little rancor or resentment toward a man who expressed an honest opinion either way. So, while the Revolution blazed, flared, and exploded up and down the coastal areas, the back-country folks of the Watauga maintained a watchful neutrality. Mostly it was sort of a tacit sympathy for the patriots, but not quite strong enough to cause them to shoulder their long rifles and rush off looking for a redcoat to shoot.

Ajax and Zebulon sat talking while they washed down a mess of food at their midday meal. "I can't see how we'd be any better off, no matter which side wins, nor no worse off, but I c'n tell you one thing, let one side or t'other do me like them Britishers tried out by Old Fort again, an' I'll grab my gun an' go a-runnin' to jine with t'other." Zeb was speaking.

"If I could see, fair an' square, where one side's winnin' would affect me or my fambly I'd be in there a-shootin', jinin' up with 'em." Ajax said it honestly, frankly.

They were still talking when John Sevier and five of his rough-and-ready boys rode into the valley. Sevier went straight to the point. "The Indians have reported to me that you men cheated them out of this valley. Led them to believe the game was poisoned, then traded them out of their land."

"I'm damned," Ajax swore. "Did that Injun say we told him a fool thing like that?"

"Well, no," Sevier admitted, "he didn't. He said you sent a British Officer who said the game in the valley was poisoned by evil spirits and they took his word for it. Said you came along shortly after that, while they were still believing what the officer said, and bought the valley from them."

"We don't know no British officers an' don't want to know none," Ajax said emphatically.

The treaty of transfer was duly inspected by Sevier. He read it over carefully. "That's the chief's signature mark, all right. Know it in a million. Seems legal enough to me. But how did the Britishers get mixed up in the deal?"

"Damned iffen I know. I expect they was in here tryin' to stir up trouble 'fore we come along. I'd like to git my gun sight on a few of them lobsterbacks, for shore. Bet they'd like to git them Injuns so riled up they'd come down offen th' hill and massacre me and Zebulon Cedric."

Sevier looked at them quizzically. "If it's a little fightin' you want, I'm here to sign you up right now."

"Wouldn't mind one or two good fights, but me an' Zeb can't spare th' time for no long spell of soljerin' for nobody," Ajax said.

"You won't be in but one campaign, and there won't be any pay except the loot we'll divide if we win. We rendezvous a week from today under a big linn tree up on the main ridge. That's all I can tell you now, except that we'll need you. Comin'?"

"We'll be with you," Ajax said.

"Good," Sevier came back. "You can leave your animals at Anser's, and I'll get word to the old chief to see that his people don't bother anything here at your settlement while you're gone. He'll do what I say. Leastwise, he'd better."

As Sevier straddled his horse and trotted away, Ajax heard Zebulon muttering to himself as much as to him, "Ain't nobody, nowhere in the world, got as good a partner as me. Also, they ain't nobody else got a partner as can make up our minds to run off to a war as don't mean nothin' to us as quick, neither."

It wasn't much of a climb getting up the slopes of King's Mountain for the men from the hills. They straggled up and scattered to surround the British bivouac. Ajax and Zebulon, staying close together, loaded and shot from behind trees at anything wearing a red coat that came into range.

Lieutenant Colonel Ferguson, British regular in command of the twelve-hundred-odd English and Tory soldiers on the mountain, had set the scene perfectly for the men of the mountains to excel in the only battle they knew how to fight. Outnumbered, by about two hundred, the mountaineers soon knocked almost four hundred of Ferguson's force out of the fight before the remainder surrendered. The doughty Ferguson was one of the first killed, along with most of his officers. The mountain men lost their first in command; duly elected Colonel Williams, the colorful Virginian. At Williams' death, Sevier took over the command, assisted by what was probably the largest ratio of colonels to enlisted men ever assembled by Americans in battle.

The battle over, word was passed along that there would be no looting of the dead, no robbing of prisoners, no confiscation of military supplies until a complete stock-taking had been completed. After that, purely military supplies would be sent to the Continental army, with the men's pay coming from a division of the remaining loot. Sentries were posted to see that orders were obeyed.

"I wish," Zebulon said wistfully, "we had a couple of them teams and wagons to take back to Modesty with us. But I reckon in th' war business it's just like ever'thing else, the little feller gits left out."

"Tell you what, Zeb," Ajax said. "I didn't dang nigh walk my legs off an' waste ammunition a-shootin' at no redcoats for nothin'. Let's git us a couple of them wagons." He started toward the teamsters' bivouac.

"We've got to git the borry of two teams and wagons to bring some of Colonel Sevier's stuff up th' mountain," Ajax grumbled to a sentry. "Don't see why th' ol' toot-box can't bring up his own stuff."

"I don't nuther," the sentry agreed. "You c'n tell 'im for me, don't he git me some vittles up here right soon, he's gonna be a-lookin' for a new man to hold down this God-damn post. Help yourself to hosses and wagons. I'll help you hitch."

Ajax waved gaily to Colonel Sevier as they drove past the officers' quarters. The colonel returned the salute with an airy hand gesture. A couple of hours later, with Ajax leading, they left the main road and followed a little-traveled trail around a bend behind some heavy woods. From there Ajax went back and erased their tracks where they had left the main road. "We'll head," he explained to Zebulon, "a little east of northeast and miss every town we can, just to play it safe."

"We'll find it a hell of a long ways to Modesty headin' in that direction, to my way o' thinkin'." Zebulon was sarcastic.

"Zeb," Ajax said severely, "was we to go straight back to Modesty, we'd be there when the troops git back, an' John Sevier'd come down so hard on us it wouldn't be nothin' left but two tiny grease spots. We aim to head for Alamance. Stick around there awhile pickin' up a few things we need, then take our families back to Modesty with us."

"That's what I was tryin' to say when you popped your mouth open," Zebulon said testily. Ajax happily left it there. He knew his partner.

"But," Zeb went on, "it just happens that the gold I got in my pocket adds up to the same amount you got in yours; exactly none, right down to the last pence. These hosses has to eat if we don't."

"Zeb," Ajax said, "I looked around inside the wagons whilst you was a-pickin' out th' hosses. 'Twouldn't harm you none to do the same."

Zebulon peeked under his wagon's canvas cover stretched over a hickory bow-frame. "Uh-h-h-h. Looks like some sacks o' oats, two brass one-pounders, an' a heap o' ammunition."

"Git inside mine and take a good look," Ajax urged.

"A passel o' blankets, a sack o' dried beans, an' three big slabs o' salt pork. We're just plumb lucky, Ajax."

"You ain't picked up that blanket over there in the corner." Ajax smiled broadly. "It's a-coverin' some o' the finest meat as a man ever saw."

Zeb picked up the blanket, stepped back. Two curly heads popped up. One of the girls had jet-black hair, the other dark brown. They were both sparklingly beautiful, both crinolined in the height of fashion. Zebulon suspected they were just as sparklingly senseless. "Well, he observed, awesomely, "this beats all hell with a short axe helve. Where'd you git 'em, Ajax?"

"They come with th' wagons," Ajax answered, modestly virtuous.

"We have decide zat we stay wiz ze wagons, mais oui," the brown hair butted in. "When ze bad mens start shootin' ze guns, an' swearin' ze swears, we hide in ze wagon. Our mens was killed, dead killed. Zey was handsom' officers, an' now, we mus' ride ze wagons wiz you back to Charlestown."

The black hair, who had kept silent up until now, looked at

Ajax and dimpled, her eyes eloquent and promising. "Well," Zebulon said, a note of generosity creeping into his voice, "I don't see nothin' wrong with givin' two helpless females a lift along th' road. O' course, you'll have to climb out an' hit it t'other way a-fore we git to Alamance, lessen I want to hear my old woman a-yappin' forever."

The girls were Charlestown Frenchies who had been camp followers with Ferguson's men. "Not ze kin' what go to bushes and wait for soldat to line up. We belonged to ze Captain Bobbitt and ze Lieutenant Jonas. Now zey are dead killed, an' we," the black hair rolled her eyes disconsolately, "'ave no one to sleep wiz. Always, since I am sixteen, zese long two year, I am sleep ever' night wiz ze comfortable mans to keep me warm. Is not ze truth, Lois?"

Lois giggled. "Zat Celeste," she rocked in glee, "she say ze leetlest, thinnest mans ees warmer on top of ze belly zan ze thickest blanket."

Ajax was in such a hurry to accommodate the ladies that he served the beans and bacon when they were only about half cooked. He and Zebulon, who were accustomed to their kind of cooking, ate without giving much thought to what they put in their mouths, but the girls only picked at theirs.

"An' ze brave mans from ze mountains, zay 'ave ze gold, but no?" Celeste asked the question.

"Gold?" Ajax said softly. "Not nary a rusty ol' copper penny. I was figgerin' on doin' you as much good as you c'n do me. If it's gold you have to git, you better hit the road. Maybe if you walk real fast all night you might meet up with somebody as has some gold he don't care nothin' about."

"Is not gold for pay Celeste and Lois. Is to buy ze food. We do not like ze bean, but raw they was cook."

"I'll put some on a slow fire an' let 'em simmer-cook all night," Ajax told her. "They'll be real good come mornin'."

"For breakfast, but yes," she murmured softly, slipped her arms around his neck, turned her lips to his.

They crossed the Catawba by floating their wagons between

logs lashed to the sides and swimming the horses. With Ajax leading the way, they kept to the back roads for a couple of days.

It was midafternoon when they topped a rise and saw in the distance a crossroad with what appeared to be a large trade store sitting in one corner. A farmer back down the road had told them about the store. Said its owner was thought to be in sympathy with the Tories if he wasn't actually one of them, although he would rob one side or the other with equal gusto if he thought he could get away with it. Ajax presented his informant with a blanket for the news and drove ahead. He stopped at the top of the rise and eyed the store, then turned off into the woods, driving slowly and carefully, after beckoning Zebulon to follow.

Well hidden from the road by trees, they tied their teams, hefted a one-pounder from the wagon, and took it forward to within a hundred yards of the store, loaded it, and laid out ten additional charges.

"I'll go in an' see how the land lies," Ajax said. "If I don't come out in about fifteen minutes slam two shots into the roof. Wait a minute after that, an' then if I don't show up, shoot the damn buildin' to pieces."

"Go on," Zebulon urged, "git it over with." Secretly he was hoping for a chance to try out the little gun on the roof.

Ajax examined a stack of blankets on a table in the store, asked the price. "I've got," he said, "a hundred and fifty, twice as good, I'll sell you for half that price."

"If you have any just that good I'll give you half the price for 'em," the proprietor, a large man with a scowling, scarred-up face, said.

"Can't use Continental money. Have to be gold or nothin'," Ajax said.

The proprietor began questioning Ajax. He wanted to know where the blankets were, where they came from, how they came into his possession. Finally, Ajax told the man, "I've got th' blankets, you've got the gold. We can trade, or we can't trade. Say which you want right here an' now."

Ajax had noticed when he stepped into the store two rough-looking fellows playing at cards in the back of the store. They had a pair of long rifles within easy reach. Now they had stopped their game and were listening intently. He knew the minutes were ticking by rapidly and that Zebulon was itching to try out the one-pounder. Not being sure how well Zebulon could aim the piece, he decided he would rather be on the outside when the first shot slammed into the roof. He started out. The proprietor moved between him and the doors. "Not so fast, my bully," he said. "My boys here figger on goin' with you to see that nothin' bad happens to you 'til we see them blankets you was braggin' about so loud. They'll know what to do if you're lyin'."

"You don't treat me right," Ajax told the storekeeper softly, "an' my men'll turn a artillery piece on this damn shack."

By that time the two toughs had moved up on each side of Ajax. They caught him roughly by his arms. "Le's go, Bully-Boy," one of them said, as they guided Ajax toward the door.

As they stepped out on the ground Ajax yelled, "Let 'em have it, boys." A moment later the one-pounder coughed and a ball ripped through the building, just below the eaves. Sound reverberations were still coming out of the building after the roughs had dropped their guns and, with screams of anguished fear, taken to their heels at top speed down the middle of the road. The next moment the proprietor came out with a wild leap, grunting in fear. Ajax threw out a foot, tripped him, and before he could regain his feet, clubbed him with one of the rifles the toughs had abandoned. Inside, the store was being well messed up as Zebulon sent one shot after another into it. Ajax stood over the storekeeper, the rifle pointed at his head. One of the shots had landed in the vicinity of the fireplace, scattered burning embers, and set the building ablaze.

"Next time," Ajax told the storekeeper, sternly, "you won't question the word of one of Colonel Sevier's officers."

The man sitting on the ground looked at Ajax and trembled with fear. "Captain," he whined, "I'm as much for th' patriots as any man alive. If it's for Colonel Sevier's use help yourself to anything you need and tell him it was a gift from Rinko Braun."

"Work fast, then," Ajax commanded. "Git ever'thing you can outen th' store 'fore it goes up in smoke, and rustle up all the gold you can. I'll give you a receipt for it so you can be paid off by the Congress after we win the war."

The man darted back into the store and began tossing out merchandise as the flames ate slowly along the floor and the wall on one side. The roof would soon be on fire, after which it would be too late to bring out much merchandise.

When as much of the store's goods were outside as the owner could safely bring out before the roof fell in, Ajax searched his host and found exactly one hundred and four English gold guineas. He then made a snap estimate of the value of the merchandise, told the proprietor to write out a receipt for the goods and money and he would sign it. "Better write yourself a safe conduct pass in case you run up on some of our men, an' let me sign that, too. Some of our hotheads might not be as charitable as I am," Ajax told his prisoner.

"Notice that sign over there says it's only forty-five miles to Charlotte. You better head in that direction. Have less chance of meetin' up with our fellers that way. I would advise you not to let it be knowed around that we had to shoot your place to hell and burn it down to get you to help out Sevier's men. Keep your mouth shut 'til after th' war, then look me up in th' town of Anserville an' I'll see that you git paid back."

Ajax signed the receipt and safe conduct pass "Captain Ajax Arvane." "Got damn tired o' bein' a ragged-ass private and promoted myself's what I done," he told Zebulon facetiously.

After the store's loot had been loaded, Ajax showed the girls the little sign with a finger pointing toward Charlotte. He handed each of them a gold piece. "You can use this to help you git back to Charlestown, if you want to use it that way. If not, what you got under your dresses will take you anywhere, there an' back."

"We don't want to go anywhere, an' back. We want to stay wiz you." Celeste was ready to pucker up.

"Can't be did, can it, Zeb?" Ajax turned to his partner while at the same time he pointed down the road. Zebulon shook his head sadly, resignedly.

They reached their Alamance homes late at night and were told immediately by their wives that it would be dangerous to be seen in the community, what with the peevishness both sides felt toward them. Better to hide in a nearby swamp, with their wagons, until they could make ready to leave. While they were hid out in the swamp, the women took Zebulon's rickety old cart, journeyed to a mill, and purchased two barrels of flour. The next day they took whatever things they didn't want to take with them and drove to the nearest market place and sold out lock, stock, and barrel. That midnight's stillness, along the road to the west, was sharply broken by the rattle of the harness chains and groaning clunks of their heavily loaded wagons going home to the Watauga.

It had been good to be with their families. Just like being freshly married again, except for having to stay hidden out in the daytime. Nancy and Lucy had been so happy to have their men with them they had blabbed and chattered away like two mating magpies until Lucy was able to get enough of her old-time wind back to remind Zebulon that if he had as much get-up-and-go as Ajax, he'd have more of this world's goods. The mere fact that Zebulon had exactly the same amount of worldly assets as Ajax made no difference to Lucy, once she got wound up, as Zebulon bitterly reminded her.

The two families, after taking it leisurely so the militia would have plenty of time to disband before they arrived in Modesty Village, were encamped for the night on the road between Morgantown and Anser's store, when Ajax spoke up. "I been a-settin' here a-thinkin', Zeb. With them hosses we can finish our clearin's in no time. Then this summer we c'n ditch us a still pond outen th' creek an' hew us out a ice cave where we got our things hid, all durin' our spare time. Come fall we c'n have that ox rollin' fat. Come a good freeze an' we c'n cut us enough ice to last a year, butcher th' ox, an' spread 'im out with the ice. I c'n see that there cave right now, all piled with beef, b'ar meat, venison, an' other good eatin' critters, all a-waitin' for us to step up an' whack us off a slab."

"God dammit, Ajax," Zebulon broke in angrily, "I swear to God if you don't quit a-figgerin' up work for me 'way ahead, just to pester me, when I'm tryin' to git some rest, I'm a-goin' to shoot you."

CHAPTER FOUR

"Spittin' image of ol' Ajax, ain't he?" were familiar words to Robin Arvane by the time he began bursting out of childhood into puberty. He habitually threw out his chest and went into an unconscious swagger at the thought that he might resemble his great-grandpa. For the years of Ajax and Zebulon had become a legend in the valley and, for Robin, Ajax Arvane was ancestor, miracle man, and demigod rolled into one.

A little undersized for a twelve-year-old and slightly on the skinny side, Robin was nevertheless hard and muscular. His advanced years had given him a sobering sense of his masculinity; a masculinity, however, deeply grained with streaks of tolerance for others not so strong as himself, such as his mother, Pamela, who he had to admit could be sympathetic, stern, fair-minded, and sensible all at the same time, or his younger sister, Cecily, who considered him the epitome of intelligence and gallantry.

Love, respect, and a certain amount of physical fear were co-mingled in Robin's heart for Pless Arvane, his pa. Then there was Zack, his oldest brother, full-grown and married, starting a family of his own, clearing more land every year. And Minter, who was next to Zack, a grown man, too, seventeen, and just before running away to marry up with Malvina Crewes, only daughter of old lawyer Crewes, who considered himself Anserville's chief legal light. Like older brothers everywhere Zack and Minter enjoyed pestering Robin.

He stood their childish antics up to a point, but sometimes they were impatient because they couldn't rouse his ire with verbal teasing and knuckled his hair, not too hard, but hard enough to sting; then they would chuckle happily when they saw him eye a rock and laugh goodnaturedly when his accurately-thrown missiles clipped them. "Little booger sure can throw rocks," Zack was wont to say pridefully of his small-fry brother. When the going got too tough, Robin had already learned he could slip up the ridge to a laurel thicket, light up a pipeful of strong, black, mountain tobacco, and settle his nerves in no time at all.

He liked to take Cecily with him as a lookout, but most of all as an audience. In his opinion she qualified as an expert because she always agreed with him. After a good smoke Robin found it easier to formulate plans for besting Josh Todd, assistant headmaster at Modesty Academy. Robin found it a little hard really to hate Josh except in a sportsmanlike manner. Not so with Phil Cogle, whom Robin detested with a hatred based on his flat belief that Phil was a blow-hard, a coward, and a sneak.

Unfortunately for Phil, the folks in Modesty Valley believed that every tub should stand on its own bottom. That fair and square was not an empty phrase. Phil acted as though he believed the fact that his pa, Jarrett Cogle, had spent a great deal of his substance sending him to the State University made him something special. He had become automatically too good to do productive work of any kind, though he had tried very hard to have Josh Todd ousted from the school so that he might take his place. When he hadn't succeeded, he turned sour against the folks in the valley and made it a point to sneer at his mountain kin and neighbors and to bully all who would let him. More than once he threatened to turn Robin over his knee, as much, he said, to teach the Arvanes they were not so high and mighty as to give Robin a much-needed lesson in good manners toward his superiors. Each time he made these threats Robin stood up to him, calling him names not usually acceptable to a man of the mountains, and dared him to lay a hand on his hind-end. More than once Robin had quietly told Cessie, "I expect when I get a little bigger, I will have to kill Phil Cogle."

His love for Phil wasn't enhanced after that July afternoon

when Pless had sent him and his cousin, Walt Cedric, across the creek and up the ridge to Lofe Lagerman's blacksmith shop to have some plows sharpened.

Lofe had long since closed down his little home-grown foundry, but he still was able to make a good living blacksmithing, despite the fact that weeds and grass usually captured whatever field he might plant. Robin, like everyone else in the valley, knew there was no love lost between Phil Cogle and Lofe. The two boys, with their plows sharpened and slung over their shoulders in a couple of cloth pokes, had come back down the ridge and were crossing the Modesty Creek bridge when they met Phil, riding his skittish roan mare. The little horse, with proper training, would have been a good and lovable animal but under the tutelage of Phil was a well-trained, vicious little devil. Phil reined to a stop. "Say, Arvane," he said harshly, "what's this I hear about you saying you would like to knock my head off?" Robin unloosened his poke from over his shoulder. "Didn't say anything like that," he told Phil Cogle.

"Well, I heard you did. So, I'm telling you, just keep good and quiet when you think about me, unless you can say something good. Even an Arvane should have sense enough, by now, to know how I feel about any criticism from Modesty Valley yokels."

"I didn't say anything of the kind. I said I was going to knock your head off as soon as I grow big enough. Want a written guarantee on it?" Robin answered.

"Mighty big talker for a mighty little kid, isn't it?" Phil sneered. "It will probably save you some later trouble if I give you the pants-warming you got coming, right now."

"I dare you to get off that horse so's I can knock your brains out with this bull-tongue shovel." Robin's hand reached into the poke.

Suddenly Phil turned the mare's rear toward Robin, sawing the bit. The mare backed rapidly, kicked with both heels with every step. Robin stepped to one side, loosed the bull tongue at Phil's head. If its sharpened point had struck Phil around the neck or head, it probably would have been his last day on earth. As it was, the shovel caught him on the back of his shoulder flatways and almost knocked him from the saddle. In pain and surprise, Phil involuntarily lammed a spur deep into the mare's flank. She made a wild plunge and lit a shuck up the hill, Phil hanging on with both hands, one stirrup swinging crazily. The two boys messed around on the bridge, watching a large and sassy trout minnow-fishing among the rocks, while they discussed and cussed Phil Cogle. About twenty minutes after Phil went up the ridge he came back by. They heard his horse's hooves pounding several seconds before he came into sight, the mare in a dead run. Robin hopped up on the bridge bannister and watched Phil pull up in front of the house of his grandpa, Dr. Rob Arvane.

"Maybe you hurt Phil's shoulder worse than you thought with that plow," Walt said.

"I hope so," Robin answered.

A few minutes later, the doctor, driving two horses at a fast trot in front of his two-seated buggy, slowed down and called to the boys, "Hop in. Perhaps you can help me." He told them that Phil had reported Lofe Lagerman was hurt, bad. Seemed he was trying to shoe Phil's horse and got kicked in the head. His grandpa looked quizzically at Robin. "Couldn't get Phil to come with me. Said he had to hurry home and doctor his own shoulder where you hit him from behind with a plow. Did you do that, young fellow?"

"Yes, Sir," Robin told his grandpa. "I hit him on the shoulder with the bull tongue, but I didn't go to do it. I was throwing at his head. He started it."

Robin's grandpa chuckled amusedly. "I don't doubt you had a good reason. Seems to me like Phil's working mighty hard to make everybody hate him. Hope poor old Lofe isn't hurt very much."

Lofe was hurt. Unto death. He lay at the side of the forge with the front of his skull bashed in where the neat print of the horse's hoof came down against one eye. As they picked up Lofe's body to take it into the house, the doctor looked down into the sand which Lofe always kept spread cleanly in front, and on the floor of his shop. "The horse," he said, more to himself than to the boys, "seems to have been backing and kicking as he went. U-m-m-m, horses don't usually go into a shop for shoeing backwards."

Dr. Arvane spread a sheet over the body and told the boys to remain at the house until he could get someone else, older, to relieve them.

Robin went to the nearby woods and picked an armload of wild blossoms, brought them in, and spread them neatly over the bed. Then, with his face white and the small muscles working across the points of his jaws, he told Walt, "Phil Cogle will say he was fighting the horse to keep her from kicking Lofe when Grandpa tells folks the mare backed into the shop, but you an' me, Walt, we'll know Phil backed her in, trying to give Lofe a scare, and we'll know that he didn't care if Lofe got kicked." Robin's words were slow, deliberate.

"I'll swear to you, Walt, I've changed my mind about knocking Phil's head off when I grow big enough. Just as soon as I'm old enough for folks to say I'm responsible, I'm going to shoot the son-of-a-bitch dead!"

CHAPTER FIVE

Robin was fourteen a short time before that spring morning when he lay on his bed half-dreaming and half-imagining, his thoughts leaping from one pinnacle of fantasy to another. On that particular morning he half-felt and half-imagined he was fleeing the length of the valley, or circling the hills, on a huge white stud horse, the stallion speeding like the wind by day, racing against time, as though each minute of daylight was a morsel that had to be seized on approach and discarded in passing, never to be thought of again. Then, he allowed his imagination to take him into that timeless time when day fades into dusk and darkness spreads a gentle mantle of obscurity over the earth so that man may take his rest, or whatever, in utmost privacy. Then, as the darkness intensified, the horse changed from white to black, shrank smaller by the minute, until he disappeared from under his rider completely, leaving Robin to find his way home from some wild remote section he had never seen before.

It is natural that Robin kept such fantastic dreams to himself, which in the true sense are not dreams at all, but only half-dreams, fed by a boy's attempt to understand the process of growing up. It never occurred to him to talk with his grandpa, whose wisdom was as unassailable as Robin's faith in God. However, if he was bothered too much, he would sneak out of bed and rap on the door for Cessie, who would climb drowsily out of her bed, throw a quilt around her shoulders, and follow him quietly to their talking place on the big poplar log at the springhouse. Once there, Robin never told Cessie of his fantasies, but launched into a discussion of his hopes and ambitions for Modesty Valley and its people. It was such a morning when he was fighting his consciousness to the surface through a mass of dreams that his pa came into the room and shook his shoulder until he was awake, after which Pless Arvane said softly, "Grandma passed last night." Here was something Robin could not fight, not even with a good throwing rock. His grandma was dead and that was that. It brought home to him the finality of death. For many years afterwards, Robin could not think of death without, in some way, remembering the mingled odors of iodoform, camphor, turpentine spirits, and a thousand and one other exotic smells which forever had permeated the air in his grandma's house as they seeped through the walls from the good doctor's office.

"I shall," Dr. Rob said a few days later, "close the house here in the valley and move my residence and office into Anserville so that I will have a better chance to keep up with my calls, and as soon as possible, I intend to bring in a younger doctor to take over my practice as rapidly as it can be shifted. Of course, those that insist that I doctor them can count on me as long as I'm able to go to their side."

It was only a short time since affable Joshua Todd, twenty-six, slightly on the portly side, a graduate of West Point and assistant to Preacher Arch Barnes, headmaster of Modesty Academy, had met his big test in the eyes of the people of Modesty Valley. Josh had a better education than Arch, so he had been assigned to teach the more advanced subjects while Arch called tunes for the smaller fry. Todd was an honest disciplinarian, eloquent and good-natured. As a result, many of his students had developed the idea among themselves that he was soft to the point of cowardice. The showdown came the day the largest of the Calhern boys challenged Josh for a fight in the classroom and had it explained to him that, while Calhern was almost as large as his teacher, there was a difference of ages in favor of Josh, but since anything can be weighted in one direction enough to make it fair for both sides, Josh would be glad to tie his right hand behind him and go on from there. When it was over, Josh helped young Calhern stop the blood pouring from his nose, patched up his contusions, and expelled him from school. He thought he was walking into trouble when he found old man Calhern and the boy waiting for him the next day. He was most pleasantly surprised when old man Calhern asked if he would accept the boy back if he apologized to him and the classroom, as well as to Mr. Barnes.

Josh, of course, did, and Calhern left after shaking hands and admonishing his youngster, "Next time you have to raise a quick fight, come on home an' keep it in the family. I like you good enough to accommodate you any time." This exhibition finished winning the friendship of practically everyone in the valley, with the exception of Phil Cogle, who was home again after his final expulsion from the State University, and who was heard to say, "I would never have thought anybody in Modesty Valley would not be game enough to stand up to that damned Yankee schoolmaster."

Phil's sister, Ellen, who was close to being an old maid in years, but far from it in looks, thought, or deed, was frankly and emphatically on Josh Todd's side.

She flared at her brother, "Why don't you, and see what happens?"

"There you go," Phil sneered, "taking up for a nigger-loving Yankee! I have never had an iota of faith in a single soul born north of Mason's and Dixon's line until he proved himself, and Josh Todd hasn't done a damned thing to make me want to change that opinion."

Ellen gave a derisive laugh. "Talk, big talk!"

Robin was crowding seventeen in 1861, and war-clouds were creating a nimbus over democracy from Maine to Texas. However, if the imminence of war bothered Robin or his cousin, Walt, in the least, they didn't show it. While the older men were wont to gather in front of Modesty Church and discuss the seriousness of the political situation, Robin and Walt would more likely be found straddling their horses, a pack of hounds strung out in front, riding the ridges, ears a-tingle to the bugling of the big redbone hounds as they chased foxes through the laurel thickets. Once in a while, Cessie would saddle the old family buggy horse and follow them, but she soon stopped that, as she could see no sense in chasing a fox for miles, and then calling off the dogs once he was treed.

It was after such a foray that the boys came by Molly Regnar's house a few minutes after good dark. As there were no stock hitched in front, they presumed nobody was visiting Molly that night. Robin had seen Molly and her two daughters many times, but he had never spoken to one of them. He had heard his elders say that Molly ran her organization in a very businesslike manner, considering the business that it was. She took no insults from anyone and treated everybody right. Her word was as good as the next when she gave her promise.

Robin guided his horse up to the Regnar gate, swung down, threw the rein over a fence post, and said to Walt, "Let's go in. Visit awhile. " He jerked his head toward the door. Walt, feeling trembly inside, but without a word, dropped off his horse and followed Robin. Molly loosened the lock chain on her front door enough to open it a crack and peer out.

"Howdy, Molly," Robin said. "Just passing; thought we'd drop by to offer compliments of the day and other small favors."

"Scat," said Molly, "an' come back when you are few years older. Pless Arvane found out I let you chillun go to bed here, he'd take the last bit of skin offen my behind." She closed the door and they heard a lock click.

As the boys' horses plodded up West Ridge, and on into the gap, Robin observed, "How'd that bitch get the idea we wanted to go to bed in her filthy hovel? I just wanted to see how it looked inside."

"Me, too." Walt lied as bravely as Robin.

Picnic Ledge is a large flat monolith with an overthrust and a sheer drop of a hundred feet to the mountainside below. For four generations it had been the private picnic ground of the Arvanes. A rock wall around the drop-off side of the ledge, put there by Ajax Arvane himself, precluded small children from the risk of pitching over. From its vantage point, one could look up or down the valley from end to end or study the contour of ridges and peaks for miles and miles around. It was a spot which the Arvanes considered strictly private family property, not to be shared by others except on extraordinary occasions. Dr. Rob was sitting on the sunny side of the ledge. He had tamped his pipeful of tobacco and leaned back against a convenient rock. "I'm worried, Robin, about the way things are going in Washington," he told his grandson.

"Do you think it's all in Washington?" Robin asked.

"Well, yes and no. In a way, you might say the trouble is actually in Kansas, Illinois, Ohio, Pennsylvania, and all of New England; and, of course, the entire South. But, our leaders in Washington could head it off if they wanted to. They won't, of course, because that would be damned poor politics. Right now, the big scream is about States' rights, but when the fighting starts, slavery will be jerked in as the big issue. Personally, I have always felt slavery is wrong, but to what degree I have not been able to decide. Of course, the cheapest thing to do would be to free all the niggers and pay off the owners for the loss of their property. But that would still leave the South in a hell of a fix." Robin was deeply impressed and said so. The doctor waved an impatient hand. "Wait a minute," he said, "you and I know that wouldn't be done. It would be called compromising with the devil by the ministers, politicians, and old-maid sewing circles up North who are, by-and-large, honest people according to their own words. I don't believe the South wants to fight, but I think it is willing if it comes to that. I don't think the rank and file of the North wants to fight either, but on a showdown, they will follow their leaders.

"One thing is certain, a showdown is coming, and if the South wins, and it has a good chance, it will be hurt almost unto death. Within ten years, most of the slave population will have escaped to the North and the remainder will be freed as a matter of economic expediency. Do you follow me?"

Robin nodded that he did, though he wasn't certain.

The doctor went on, musingly, "It will be something to remember for those who live through it. It is highly probable that
more white men will die than there are male adult slaves in the
South. That, to my way of thinking, is a damned poor swap. I
suppose you will be going when it starts?" The latter was a direct question.

"I don't know," said Robin. "I haven't given it much thought,
Grandpa. I have done a lot of book reading, but I haven't done
much with the newspapers. I thought up until now it was mostly people just talking big." Robin was slightly apologetic.

"There is," his grandpa said, "a powerful lot of big talk. But,
in this case, it happens the people doing the big talk are in dead
earnest. I am sixty-one, but a pretty tough old turkey for my age.
When it breaks, I am trying for a cavalry command. Don't like
walking. Been reading up on cavalry tactics lately."

"Yes, sir," agreed Robin, "it's a certain thing they can't fight
a war without surgeons."

"Who said anything about doctoring?" The old man snorted.
"I'll go as a fighting man or not at all. Naturally, I couldn't refuse to help out the surgeons in case of emergency. Hell, boy, you
ought to read the papers more. When Minter joined the guards
and went off to Wilmington last month to train with the State
Militia, I told him he would soon need all the training he could
get. He agreed with me but said not to tell Malvina, as she
thinks he will be home after the usual training period. He told
me he wanted her to go back to Anserville and live with her pa
until he got back, but she wouldn't do it. She was bound to stay
where she is and have the house ready for him when he gets back.
I hope, pray, and believe he will get back, but, of course, there
will be some who never will. Naturally, I think Malvina would
rather be out here in Modesty with little Minter than with her
pa, the old lawyer Crewes being the tight-reined bastard that he
is."

"Malvina is all right," Robin said. "She has lots of courage
for a woman."

"Never said she had anything wrong with her courage, but, for a mature woman of twenty, she damned sure shows she is touched when it comes to the kind of folks she makes friends with. She was in town the other day, riding with Phil Cogle. There's nothing wrong with her riding to town with any young gentleman in the community, only, Phil Cogle is not a gentleman, if I know what it takes to make one. I couldn't afford to do it, but you have always been mighty close to Malvina. Suppose you drop her a hint. She wouldn't resent it from you."

"No," Robin said. "I'd rather speak to Phil."

"Handle it your way," his grandpa said. "But handle it."

CHAPTER SIX

T HE WEATHER WAS ZIPPERY COLD THAT SPRING AFTERNOON WHEN Robin and his grandpa came off Picnic Ledge and made their way slaunchwise across the ridge, aiming at coming out at Modesty graveyard. As they passed the grave of Peter Gherkim, Robin asked, "What actually happened the night Peter was lynched? You should know, Grandpa."

"I know exactly what's on that stone, and I believe that's as much as any living soul knows, or ever will know for a certainty," the doctor said.

"Seems to me it was a pretty big penalty for one little sheep," Robin said slowly.

The doctor said, "Beyond what's on the stone, I can only surmise." The doctor sat down on the granite headstone for a moment of rest.

"When it happened, I was so busy getting my practice started I didn't pay a lot of attention," the doctor said. "I got to know Peter pretty well right after he came among us. He was a Swiss, or German, or some sort of nationality from the old country. At least, he had enough of a trace of an accent to leave that impression with me. He never told anyone his real business in the valley, which of course was a mistake on his part. He had a little girl, beautiful child, and said he was a widower. He rented a little shack down by the creek, and every day after that he could be seen wading the creek, studying its bottom, or out tramping the mountains. It wouldn't have taken a Philadelphia lawyer to figure he was prospecting for something, but he actually never said so. Naturally, he was not popular. When he wasn't out tramping around, or looking after the wants of his daughter, he was courting the widow Cedric, who, as you know, had lost her husband a year or so before. I didn't know her very well then, but since, after she married Jarrett Cogle, I took her through childbirth a few times. I wouldn't trust her."

"I still can't understand," Robin argued, "why they would lynch a man for stealing one little sheep."

"I can't either," the doctor said, "but one thing's sure. Whatever was inflicted on Peter was dished out by two of the oldest men in Modesty, Ajax Arvane and Zebulon Cedric, without any help from anyone. I did overhear the widow tell Pa that Peter Gherkim had stolen one of her sheep and asked him to visit Peter and see for himself. I also overheard Pa advise her to go home, keep her mouth shut, and let him and Zeb handle the matter. Beyond that point everything is strictly guesswork. I know Pa wasn't the kind of man that raced up and down the valley looking for small things to pin a lynching to. The tombstone says Peter was baptized after repenting. Arch Barnes' old daddy, who was our preacher then, said if he was baptized it wasn't by him. That he knew nothing whatever about the affair."

"But you think there was more to it than people knew?"

"Much more. The widow must have told, and proved to Pa, a lot more than I overheard. The execution of Peter, who, as I have said, had made himself very unpopular, was a nine-day sensation here in the valley; then folks found something else to talk about. Mostly, everybody thought the proposition had been handled perfectly."

"Then that tombstone tells all anyone'll ever know about the death of Peter Gherkim."

"I'm afraid so. We'd better be moseying back. Your ma'll be calling supper pretty soon."

At the grave of his grandma, Robin bowed his head while the doctor recited a brief prayer for the loved ones his mate had left behind.

Supper over, Robin slipped his pa's smallest six-shooter under the waistband of his pants, covered it with his shirt, and told his folks he might spend the night out. His pa admonished, "Don't you and Walt prowl too late. We might have a job of work for tomorrow."

Robin went up the road toward Malvina's on the small chance that Phil Cogle might be hanging around. He wanted to deal with Phil in such a way as to keep it from ever getting back to Minter. He admitted to himself, but not without argument, that he was a little bit in love with Malvina himself. He had to admit that she was a sprightly morsel of womanhood, flirtatious and capricious, but he believed that was mostly because she was so full of life, so enjoyably fond of lively company. Anyway, he meant to see that nothing befell her that would cause Minter a moment's humiliation.

He didn't feel a sense of surprise, only shock, when he found Phil's little mare tied at the gate. "The bastard could, at least, keep his horse out of sight when he comes to see her," he breathed to himself, after which he felt a sense of shame for the implication behind the thought.

Malvina and Phil were seated at the table in the kitchen. A partly empty bottle sat between them. Malvina's two-year-old, little Minter, was playing about the house. It was almost bedtime. Malvina told him to pull up a chair, and her catchy little giggle told him she had taken more than one helping from the bottle. Phil hardly spoke but sat poutingly staring into his almost empty glass.

"I'll just take Phil's chair, since he's fixing to go," Robin said.

"Who said I was leaving now?" Phil threw the words straight out.

"Well, Phil," Robin said mildly, "I thought you might want to go now so you'll be fresh and physically fit for a private discussion with me tomorrow morning. It's something we can't talk about in the presence of a lady."

"Arvane," Phil flared, "I've got nothing to discuss with you, or any of your kind. I'll give you sixty seconds to get out of the front door before I throw you out and kick you all the way back to your roost." Phil almost cracked the table slamming his fist down on it by way of emphasis.

"It's always been a rule with the Arvanes never to allow anybody to work faster than they do, Phil. So, in that case, I give you just ten seconds to be out the front door before I shoot you and drag you out." He pulled the gun from under his shirt, cocked and aimed it at Phil. "Furthermore, I'm staying here tonight to see that you don't come messing around here again. Tomorrow morning I'm coming down the lane by your house, and I expect you to come out and meet me. When you get close enough you better start shooting. This fight's going to be a killing matter. For your information, you'd better make it fair unless you want to take on the job of killing Grandpa, Pa, Zack, and Minter.

"There's only one thing you can do to keep me from killing you tomorrow morning, Phil, and that's to be somewhere else besides in Modesty Valley. You've been blowing off steam about how you'll fight with the Yankees if war comes. I wouldn't try to tell you how to run your business, but you'll be safer in the Union Army, fighting a pitched battle every day, than you'll be in Modesty Valley after tonight. Now get for home." He waved the cocked pistol at Phil again.

His jaws set tight and trembling all over, Phil reached for his hat, went out the door.

Robin sat at the table lost in thought. He was trying to decide whether it would be better to try and shoot Phil Cogle in the head or try for the easier body shot, a larger target. He decided on the body shot and felt better.

Malvina put little Minter to bed, then came and stood behind Robin. Her arms dropped down around his neck. She kissed the top of his head lightly. "You know," she said softly, "I'm so glad you came and chased him away. He told me tonight that if I didn't start treating him better he would tell Minter he spent practically every night in the house while he was away." She spoke slowly, hesitantly.

"You should have known better than to take any stock in that. Phil's not loaded down with sense, but he knows too much to commit suicide by telling Minter a thing like that. Besides, how do I know you're telling the truth?"

"You don't believe me?" she asked incredulously.

"According to Grandpa, you've been seen in too many places, riding around with Phil, to hold a lot of hatred for him."

"So, you don't believe me?" she asked.

"What would you think in my place?" Robin answered.

Malvina whirled away from him. "You can believe anything you damn well please," she said airily. "I'm going to bed. Lock the door as you go out, or you can stay and guard my virtue from the likes of Phil Cogle. Don't wake little Minter when you go to bed."

A few minutes after Robin shucked his outer clothes and crawled into bed with little Minter he could hear Malvina stirring restlessly. He was almost asleep when he heard her call, softly. "Come here please, Robin. I don't feel good. Don't make a light; then you won't need to put on any more clothes.

"Robin darling, get me a glass of water, then talk to me," she whispered.

Malvina drank the water. "Robin," she whispered, "I'm frightened, I'm depressed, and I'm lonesome. Sounds silly, but that's the way it is. You're too good for me, Robin, and too good to me." She reached up, caught his hand and pulled it against her naked breast and lay stroking the bare skin on his arm. The strokes went higher and higher up Robin's arm as she pulled his hand harder against her breast.

Robin felt his breath shorten as a wave of righteous shame welled over him. Then, the wave of shame was melted in a great fire that had him trembling delightfully. He could hear Malvina's rapid breathing. He heard her whisper urgently. "You're all trembly. Get under my covers and warm yourself before you come down with a cold."

He slipped out of bed while she still slept, went to the kitchen, and started breakfast. Then, he called her, suggested she get little Minter ready to eat. A few moments later he heard her singing as she roused Minter and dressed him. When she came into the kitchen she was wearing an extremely décolleté white silk robe. She whirled around in front of him. "Like me?" She asked. Robin didn't answer, but his woebegone, saddened expression was as eloquent as a hell-fire revival sermon.

Suddenly Malvina sat down to the table, put her face in her hands, and began sobbing bitterly. "Robin," she wept, "I'm so ashamed. I didn't mean for it to happen that way. We couldn't help it, but what are we going to do?"

"Nothing we can do," Robin said, sadly. "I've done the worst thing a man can do to his brother. If I was half the man I should be, I'd confess it all to Minter and let him take it out on me in any way he might wish. To do that would hurt him in the worst way. I'd harm little Minter, and I'd be doing you dirt, though you and I don't deserve anything but dirt."

They picked at breakfast, little Minter looking from one to the other, trying to piece out what was wrong. She followed Robin to the door, caught his face between her two hands, pulled it forward, and kissed his forehead softly. "Try to forget it, Robin, and forgive me. It was my fault. Let's try and blank it out of our minds."

"I will," he told her, "on one condition. You move to your pa's place in Anserville and stay there until Minter comes home."

"I will, I will," she promised fervently.

Robin looked at Malvina and a crooked grin leaked down from one corner of his lips. "I hate to remember, I've got to shoot Phil Cogle this morning. Especially when I know I'm lower than he is."

CHAPTER SEVEN

"I SPENT THE NIGHT AT MINTER'S," ROBIN SAID WHEN HE WALKED in on the family at the breakfast table. "Malvina's scared and flustered. She's going to her pa's and stay until Minter gets back. I promised to ask Pa to take her."

"U-m-m-m," Pless Arvane ruminated, "not like Malvina to be afraid. Why don't she come up here and stay with us?"

"Malvina's hard to frighten, but I reckon it's mostly because she's afraid for Minter. Afraid he'll be sent to war, or something. Anyway, something's got her bothered. She said it wouldn't look right for her to stay with us when her pa's living in Anserville in a big house, by himself. She thinks people might think she's not welcome at her own pa's," Robin said.

"Might be something to that," Pless said, spearing a helping of fried apple and chewing reflectively. "Old Crewes can be powerful mean when he gets started, they tell me. I'll be glad to hitch up and take her to Anserville, soon's I can finish my breakfast. I'll get your ma to go with me."

In his room Robin sat with his head in his hands, feeling miserable. He was, he told himself, the lowest of the low, with only one redeeming quality he could think of. He would die, he swore to himself, before he'd let such a thing happen again. He had always been taught, without anyone ever putting it into words, that a man who betrayed his blood brother, under any circumstances, was as low as they come. Or was he? Robin grasped at the thought. After all, unless Malvina became pregnant, really nothing had happened more than a few moments of paradise.

No, he had to face it. He had made his brother a perfect cuckold. The only course left for him, he reasoned, was to keep his mouth shut, his thoughts pure when he was around Malvina, and make it up to Minter in some handsome way in the future.

Today he would start by eliminating Phil Cogle, even if he did know Phil was probably less blameworthy than he. At least, he had promised Phil he would shoot him, and in the presence of Malvina at that. There was no honorable way he could get out of his promise. If it could happen that both would be killed, that would be the height of the Good Lord's justice. The last thought made his mouth dry, swallowing difficult.

The rumbling rattle of the wagon going over the planks of the bridge across Modesty Creek told him Pless had his horses in a smart trot. He got up, put the pistol under his shirt, and started out through the hall. Cessie stopped in front of him. "What's bothering you, Robin. You look pale. Seen a ghost? You got worries?"

"Some. Not so bad," Robin told her, and wondered how he could speak so calmly. "Tell you all about it, maybe a little later."

"Good," she said, and went back to the kitchen.

Robin saddled his horse and rode down the road, past the Cogles' and on to the Cedrics'. He thought Phil might see him and come out. He decided to dismount when the shooting began so there would be less chance of the horse being hit, and, too, he would probably be able to shoot more accurately that way. Should Phil come out with a rifle, he meant to lie flat on the ground and rest the pistol over his left wrist to improve his aim.

He didn't see anything of Phil. The Cogle horses were loose in the horse lot, but Phil's little mare was not among them. He thought to himself that he must have been talking too fast when he made a definite promise to Phil to shoot him, if he was in the valley today. Oh, well, the promise was made. There was no getting around it, unless Phil would knuckle down like a coward, which Robin had no idea he would.

"Howdy, Walt," Robin hailed his cousin, as he rode up to the Cedrics' hitching post and swung to the ground. Walt came from toward the barn and leaned over the gate. "Coming in?" Walt asked conversationally.

"Can't, right now," Robin said, casually. "Want you to do me a favor."

"Name it."

"I want you to go up to Cogle's and tell Phil I'm riding back up to the crossroads, and to get his gun and come on up so we can finish what we started a few years ago. He'll know what you mean," Robin told Walt.

"What the hell are you talking about?" Walt was mystified.

"Remember the day Lofe was killed by Phil's horse? Remember, I vowed to you that as soon as I was old enough to take the responsibility, I was going to shoot Phil Cogle? That time's come." Robin's tone was still casual.

Walt came through the gate, closed and leaned back on it. "You're joking, of course, but that's a hell of a thing to joke about."

"I was," Robin said, "never more serious in my life."

"You mean," Walt asked, "that you'd shoot Phil just because his horse kicked old man Lofe, and you swore, like a little kid, that you would some day? Is that what you're trying to say?"

"That's the main gist of it."

Walt took a deep breath. "I'm damned," he breathed. "If that's what you mean to do, that's what it is. I'm telling you now, I think you're a damn fool. I know I'm one for having anything to do with it. Wait a minute till I can go back to the house and swipe Pa's pistol to tote under my shirt, and I'll go tell Phil."

In front of Cogle's, Robin climbed on his horse and trotted him toward the crossroads. Walt turned into Cogle's drive. After tying the horse to a sapling, Robin sat down by the side of the road to wait. Through the trees he could see the front porch of the Cogle house. In a little while he saw Walt come out alone, and it wasn't long before he appeared, walking up the road toward Robin. Walt took out a big blue handkerchief, wiped his face. "Phew," he said, "you won't shoot Phil today, nor tomorrow, nor any time soon. He left at midnight last night, on his horse, going north to join the army of the Union. The family's all upset. Alan says if war comes he'll join up with the South. Ellen says Phil did it to spite the rest of the family. She's boiling mad at him. Say, did you know he was leaving and put all this on as a joke on me? I sure hope it was that way."

Robin thought a minute, then laughed relievedly. "Pretty good joke on you, wasn't it? But I'm glad. I know now I can count on you all the way, if the time ever comes."

"Who said you couldn't?" Walt asked, heatedly. "I just think you picked a hell of a way to test me out. I don't like it."

"I'm sorry, Walt," Robin told his cousin, contritely. "I, well, I thought it would be a good joke. What are you doing today?"

"Pa wants me to ride over to Chafferton," Walt said, "and see what I can learn about this war everybody's talking up so hard. He thinks they'll be fighting in a few days. Anyway, he gave me a passel of silver dollars and said ride. Said if I couldn't learn what it's about in Chafferton, to get on the train and go somewhere I could. He said I ought to take you with me. How about it?"

"All right," Robin said, "go saddle up. I'll scoot down to our house and see if I can borrow some money from Cessie out of Ma's change gourd."

They hadn't reached Chafferton, nearest railroad metropolis and seat of Daniel County, when the sun disappeared, and soon a cold drizzle set in. They stayed with a farmer for the night. Next morning the road was sloppy, splashing mud in every direction. There were more horsemen going and coming on it than Robin ever remembered seeing before, the younger ones riding with a sort of debonair grace, bespeaking a feeling of high adventure; the older ones looking kind of sadly bewildered, as they rode homeward from Chafferton. They met a few men they knew who told them hell was popping all over the country, secession was a completed achievement, and the capital was moved to Richmond. Most of the men of the mountains thought the whole idea was the work of a passel of damn fools on both sides. Many of them thought the North had deliberately pushed the South into a corner and dared it to move. And, of course, as everybody knows, nobody takes a dare like that, even when he knows he'll get his head knocked off.

Chafferton was lathering all over that day, just as every other town its size, with a railroad and telegraph line, was. Men from all over the mountain section, and eastward, crowded the streets, arguing, discussing, talking peacefully. Bottles passed around, and when the train arrived, bringing the Richmond, Washington, and Raleigh papers, everyone rushed down to the station to learn the latest. A bugle sounded on a side street where, on walking over to see what it was, Robin and Walt found a large group of young men, and some not so young, doing close-order drill without guns and in civilian clothes. The proprietor of one store was auctioning off his stocks preparatory to going to war himself.

Robin and Walt read avidly from newspapers they borrowed from some men who beat them to the station. War, it was evident, was a matter of minutes, hours, days at the most. Robin folded the paper he was reading, returned it to the man who had loaned it to him, sat down by Walt on the courthouse steps. "These people are not playing. They're mad. Mad clear through. Ready, willing, and able to fight. Wonder where we can go to join up?"

"I'm not," Walt said. "Professor Todd was down to our house last night talking to Pa and me. He says Modesty doesn't stand to gain anything but suffering by getting into the war. 'We don't have,' he says, 'a single nigger in Crinshaw County to fight for.' He says if the valley will get together, and stick it out, we won't have to furnish one single fighting man to either side. He's writing a petition-pledge to that effect, and it'll soon be circulated around, he told Pa. He'll do it, too."

"Yes," Robin agreed, "if Josh Todd says he will, he will. But that won't make it the thing to do. Fact is, if the people in the valley get as stirred up as they are here today, it'll be a good way for Modesty to have an excuse for burying a fine schoolteacher. I don't believe in telling other people how to run their business, and I wish Josh wouldn't try it."

CHAPTER EIGHT

It had been almost noon when the boys reached Chafferton. It was now coming on dark. Their horses were well taken care of at a livery stable, but they hadn't looked for a place to spend the night themselves. Despite the fact that they had much better than average educations, for their day and locality, they knew practically nothing about town customs. It hadn't occurred to either boy that he couldn't just knock on any door and ask to spend the night, like anybody would in Modesty. They found a crowded eating place and had a good supper.

The first house they aproached was large and imposing looking. It sat well back from the street with a carriage drive circling through a porte-cochere. "Looks like this might be a nice place, with plenty of room. Ought to be glad to give us a place to sleep," Robin observed.

It was a nice place, but they emphatically didn't want any visitors—especially visitors they'd never seen, nor heard of, before. No, the Negro butler explained, they didn't know anybody who took strangers into their homes at any time without proper introduction. It wasn't done among the quality folks of Chafferton. The black man was slightly patronizing in his attitude. He said there were a couple of inns where, ordinarily, they could find a room, but with everybody crowding into town, making a mess of everything, so that decent people hardly dared to go on the streets, he doubted there were any rooms available for them at that time of night. He shut the door and locked it.

"Damn," Robin swore, as they went back to the street, "there's

a damn nigger don't deserve to be free. On the other hand, whoever his son-of-a-bitch master is, he's not worth fighting for,
either."

"That's what Professor Todd's trying to tell the folks in Modesty," Walt answered.

The boys were turned away, a little later, from both of Chafferton's hotels. With Robin leading, they meandered up and
down Chafferton's few streets for a few hours, killing time. For
the first time in his life Robin had that feeling of futility, of aloneness, that comes to every man trying to buck a custom he knows
nothing about. It had never occurred to him that an honest trav-
eler wouldn't be welcome in any decent place he wished to stop
for the night. They came to a small and shabby-looking saloon
on the very edge of town. There were lights inside and the sound
of men in brawling companionship. "Let's go in and have a drink
of store whiskey," Robin said to Walt. "Maybe somebody will be
gentleman enough to ask us home with him to spend the night."

"Well," Walt hesitated. "Pa didn't tell me not to." He followed Robin into the saloon.

There were half a dozen, or so, customers seated at pine
tables against the wall. Three well-set-up men in rough clothes,
and with tough faces, were at the bar. It was evident from the
conversation that they worked at a local sawmill. One of them
was suggesting to the bartender that he fill 'em again, and that
he'd see he got his money come next payday. The bartender
shook his head, stayed out of reach, and eyed his bung-starter
under the bar-top. Robin rang a gold piece on the bar and ordered two double straight ryes. In his back-country ignorance, he
believed what he had been told, that it took a large swig of store
whiskey to equal a tiny smidgen of Modesty Valley corn. He and
Walt were seized with coughing spasms the minute their drinks
hit bottom. After they had their breaths back, Robin observed,
"May not have the strength of Modesty corn, but it sure falls just
as hard."

The tallest of the three toughs at the bar looked the boys over,
tried to drape an arm over Robin's shoulder. The bartender shook

his head. Robin moved away. The man said, "Neighbor, I reckon you come in here special to buy drinks for Chafferton's three leadin' citizens—meanin', o' course, me and my friends here. I know you didn't come in lookin' for trouble, because you don't look like no troublin' man, so it'll have to be that's how come you're here." There was a hint of a threat behind his leering tone.

Robin leaned back, propped an elbow on the bar. "Way I been treated in this town today, I wouldn't give a Chafferton man the sweat off my hound dog's balls." Robin was still boiling mad about the reception they had received from the Negro butler.

The man looked Robin and Walt over, studied them for a moment. "Ain't no God-damn mountain jake gonna come to my town an' insult me by refusin' to treat when he's asked politely." The man leaned his face toward Robin and spoke over his shoulder to the bartender, "Set th' licker out, Jake."

Out of a corner of his eye Robin could see the other customers of the saloon leaving by front and back doors. He could also see the tall man's companions moving in close to him and Walt. The stubble-covered face, smudged and darkened with dirt, grease, and tobacco stains, was getting so close to his it seemed to become a blur. Robin set himself and swung his right at a jaw, putting all the punch his one hundred and forty pounds would allow into the blow. He felt his wrist sting as his right landed. He also felt a dull thud against his head, another thud, and heard a slight groan from Walt, as he dropped into a darkened pit of unconsciousness.

Later that night the drizzle had stopped, and a puny moon could be seen playing hide and seek with scudding clouds overhead. Robin's consciousness seemed to be swirling in slowly lessening circles. When it finally came to rest, he sat up, slowly, painfully. Walt was sitting beside him, all hunched over, his elbows on his knees, his head resting on them. "How long," Robin asked, "have I been asleep?"

"Asleep," Walt muttered through puffed lips; "if you call being knocked cold, sleeping, you've been having sweet dreams for about fifteen minutes since I woke up. I don't know how long I was out. We got hell knocked out of us, remember?"

"Yes, I do now," Robin said, slowly. "What'll we do now?"

"I don't know," Walt told him shortly, "but I wish I was back in Modesty."

"We can go over to the stables and sleep in the hay," Robin said, and got up shakily.

After some argument, the watchman at the livery stable told them they could sleep in the hay, but he'd have to wake them up before the proprietor appeared at nine the next morning. They agreed that would be fine with them.

Next morning after a face-wash, and combing their hair, at the stables' well, they felt better—but hungry. Suddenly Robin felt in his pocket. "My money's gone," he said.

"So's mine," Walt answered, after feeling in his pockets. "Say, Robin, I don't like this town. Let's get our horses and get out of here as soon as we can. I reckon we can wait until we get back to Modesty before we have to eat."

"Not me," Robin said. "I'm hungry now. Besides, they won't let us take our horses without paying for their keep; you know that. Let's go get our money back and eat before we start home. Lucky we left our pistols in our saddlebags. Bastards would've had them too."

The boys slipped their six-shooters under the waistbands of their pants and buttoned their coats over them. Walt followed Robin, grumbling. "We could put up my gun for security to get our horses. Seems to me like you're looking for trouble and don't care where you find it."

"I'm not," said Robin. "I'm just not running from it. You don't want to, either. I know you, Walt."

The proprietor of the saloon was there, alone, when they arrived. No, he told them, Jake didn't say anything to him about what happened the night before. He was real sorry. Didn't know if Jake was afraid of the three, who had given him plenty of troubel in the past, or in cahoots. Anyway, Jake wouldn't be working there the next time they heard from the place. He knew where the three lived, and if they'd wait until he could lock up, he'd go with them to the town marshal. Marshal might be able to scare them into giving part of their money back, but he doubted it, since nobody had seen any robbery committed.

"We don't need any help from the marshal. Folks out our way always look after themselves. Just tell us how to find them and we'll be on our way," Robin told the saloon man.

The saloon man told them the men lived in a small shack, in the alley back of his place, about a block down. They would, he said, probably be at home this early in the morning. He knew they wouldn't go back to work until their money was gone.

The shack was a dingy, one-room, dirt-floor affair, but there was smoke coming out the chimney. The door and wooden windows were closed. The two boys walked up to the house together, where Robin shoved the door open, and they stepped quickly inside. Robin had told Walt to loosen his coat so he could get at his pistol easily. There was a rough table in front of the fireplace, with the three men seated at it, with half a quart remaining in a bottle on the table among cups and dirty dishes. The tall man, who was evidently the leader of the trio, was facing the door. He jumped up when they came in. "What th' hell you want now?" he snarled. "I s'pose you got the marshal out there, an' that you been tellin' him some o' your wild tales. Beat it, an' take 'im with you. We ain't done nothin' but give you th' thumpin' you had comin' after insultin' the entire town o' Chafferton."

The two boys stood silently, eying the men as though sizing them up. The tall man advanced a step. "God damn you," he yelled, "I said git out!" He made a forward motion and Robin shot him in the stomach. For a moment the wounded man stood watching the blood spurting through his fingers as he held his hands over the bullet hole, then he gave a sighing groan and sank to the floor.

"Don't move an inch from where you are," Robin told the two remaining toughs. "I'll take the one on the right and you kill the one on the left, if they so much as move a finger," he told

Walt. Walt nodded. The two sat trembling, their eyes roving around the room like frightened animals.

"Now," Robin said, "give us all our money back, if you want to go on living."

"We can't," one of them quavered. "Runcy spent forty-five cents for that quart of licker. We—we—we couldn't stop him from robbin' you-all." The two hastily emptied their pockets.

"Where's the rest?" Robin asked gratingly.

"In Runcy's pocket."

"Get it out then, and put it with the rest. He won't need it any more. Get it out, and mind you don't get it all bloody, or I'll shoot you."

Robin held his pistol ready while Walt gathered up their money from the table where the men had laid it. "Now," Robin said, "I suppose you want to go with us to tell the marshal how it happened. Looks like your friend may not live."

"Not me," the one who had remained silent up until now spoke up. "Runcy was the one th' marshal was afraid of. Soon's he knows Runcy ain't with us no more he'll take after us an' run us all the way back to Georgia. Me, I'm a-takin' off soon's you-all git away. I'm kind o' glad. Runcy was about to git us all kilt."

"Me, too. I'm glad Runcy's dead, after he come this nigh to gittin' me kilt," the quavery one echoed.

"In that case," Robin told them, "you better dig a hole in this floor and bury Runcy deep, then set fire to the shack and start running. Let's go," he said to Walt, giving the two thugs a look of utter scorn. With that, Robin and Walt turned, walked out the door, slammed it behind them, and proceeded down the alley without once looking back.

Within an hour they had eaten a breakfast to do credit to a couple of growing lads of sixteen, settled with the stables, mounted, and started out of town. "Look, Robin," Walt cried suddenly. "A fire!" Robin stood on tiptoe in his stirrups, then climbed higher to stand upright on the saddle.

"It's their shack burning," he told Walt. "Damned if they

aren't taking our advice." He dropped his rump back to the saddle and clucked to his horse.

"Pa," Walt said, as they rode toward Anserville, "will raise un-
shirted hell when I tell him what happened."

"Your pa," Robin reasoned, "sent you to Chafferton to learn
what you could about the possibility of war. You've done that. It
would be kind of low, to my way of thinking, to give him anything else to worry about. I wouldn't have old man Pless know
I shot a man in Chafferton for anything in the world."

"I'll have to admit you're right on that score," Walt admitted.
"I'll keep my mouth shut. But it does seem to me that anybody
who goes around with you doesn't have to look for trouble. It
comes looking for him."

CHAPTER NINE

U P UNTIL WALT MADE HIS LAST REMARK ABOUT TROUBLE COMING
naturally to him, Robin had been so engrossed in leaving Chafferton behind he had not used a moment for any mental stock-taking. Walt's outburst bothered him. Perhaps, he thought, trouble
did come to him naturally—or perhaps he was a natural trouble-
maker, the same as Phil Cogle, only of another kind. At least,
he didn't think he had ever caused anybody else any trouble because of spitefulness.

Robin's horse was carrying double, for old Satan had clamped
a passel of gloom on Robin's shoulders that had sagged them forward and bowed his head over the horse's withers. He rode with
his eyes fixed on the rich, proud mane, but he was oblivious to
its existence. His troubles were riding him with the tenacity of a
family of possums clinging to their mammy's back.

He remembered, a few Sundays back, when Arch Barnes, with
his long arms waving in eloquence or his bony finger pointed
down the throats of the Modesty congregation, took the Ten
Commandments for a text. Arch had said, "Thou shalt not covet." Robin reluctantly had to admit he had begun to covet Malvina the previous summer, long before his even greater sin. He
had taken her an armload of rhododendron blossoms and she had
held him tightly in her arms, kissed him on the mouth, and told
him he was sweet. If Minter had been present when it happened
it would probably have made little, or no, impression on him.
But Minter had been away, dusk was falling fast, and she had

pulled him inside the darkened house for a tight hug and a kiss on the lips that lingered overly long.

At home, for the next few days after the return from Chafferton, Robin moped. Even a generous fall of flies did not send him to the creek, as it ordinarily would, to catch a quick mess of succulent trout. He was in the stage of moping that is accompanied by an urge to prowl—to prowl, however, over the best-known and best-loved scenes that he knew. Thus, he would seat himself in the family parlor for a minute or so. Then he would be up and off to his room, only to reappear and walk rapidly, and alone, up the path to the spring. Cessie, who really knew him better than anyone else on earth did, thought he was worried about the imminence of war. She tried to reach her sympathy out to him, but he shook it off by pulling her to him for a short, almost rib-cracking hug, then turning and walking rapidly away. She understood he wanted to walk alone through whatever Gethsemane had come his way, or whatever troubles he had cooked up for himself. If that was what he wanted, Cessie could see no reason why he shouldn't be left alone.

Early one bright June afternoon Robin went out the back door and walked up the ridge path to the Picnic Ledge. The sun was warm, but there was shade from a ragged old locust tree that had fought its way to a precarious footing among the rocks. He lay under the locust's shadow, still trying to fight his jumbled worries. He was actually, and unconsciously, trying to fasten a greater sense of guilt on himself, looking for more causes for self-recrimination. All in all, he was seeking a judgment to render against himself; some form of self-punishment that would be humbling and retributive without causing hurt or unhappiness to others. He told himself that he knew what he had done. He knew what his deed made him, and now he must come to the judgment. That, he reasoned, should be passed by another, but, try as he would, there was no other he could trust to pass such judgment as would be adequate to the occasion. In anger, puzzlement, and self-abasement, Robin lay on his face and wept great heaving sobs. Then he thought, why not examine the picture as though he were on the outside looking in?

That would do it. He would get on the outside and ask a few questions, and Robin Arvane had damn well better answer them. First, he wanted to know why Robin Arvane had betrayed his own brother? The answer: It had been done before he had time to think. Robin Arvane had not been half so much to blame as Malvina. Don't pack it off on her. That's nothing less than cowardly. Well, anyway, what was done, was done, and there wasn't much could be done about it. He could, and would, he promised, see that no such thing happened again between Robin and Malvina, and he would keep his eyes open and try to see that she wasn't exposed to temptation from others while Minter was away. It might be for the best, after all, he thought, to know she was that way, for in knowing, he was better prepared to protect Minter's interests. But did he have any right to make an effort to kill Phil Cogle? On that score he wasn't sure, but since he hadn't been able to go through with it, why worry?

That left only Runcy's death. Runcy, he had to admit, must have been a mean man. A man who must have hurt a lot of people badly, perhaps killed a few, for all he knew. A man who would have hurt some more, perhaps killed a few more. One thing he knew, Runcy was the type that would have no compunction about killing anyone who got in his way if he thought he could get away with it. So, perhaps it was for the best that Runcy was dead, though he couldn't help feeling sorry he was the one who was called to kill him. Then, in a flash, he remembered another one of Arch Barnes' sermons in which Arch stated unequivocally that everything always happens for the best; that man can never go beyond the plans of his Creator. So, whatever had happened, it had been ordained by God from the beginning, and there was nothing this side of hell could change it. Looking at it that way, he had only done what the Good Lord had put him on this earth to do. He had done, according to the best teachings of the Good Book, what he had to do, and there was nothing he could have done but just what he had, and nothing he could do now to change events that had already happened. It was all that simple.

Robin got up and followed the little path to the Picnic Ledge spring for a drink, and as he leaned on his hands and knees to get his lips into the cool water he saw the reflection of his face in the water, as his hair dropped over his forehead and trailed floating as he drank. He laughed, a more-or-less forced chuckle. The joke was on him if he would admit the truth of all the Good Book said. Anyway, whether he liked it or not, what he had done had been arranged many, many thousands of years before he was born. He felt better.

Robin went back to the Picnic Ledge, found a fine, round, throwing-size rock, picked it up, leaned back, cocked his left leg, and threw. A second later he heard the rock's sharp thud as it landed on a large stone and bounced off to go crashing into the treetops three hundreds yards down the hill. He stood for a moment as though listening. Then he took off his hat, turned his face to the sky. "Thank you, God," he said, reverently, "for straightening me out."

Robin walked down the ridge a full-grown man of almost seventeen, lacking only experience to take his place among the knowing and worldly men he knew. He had, in one short afternoon, stood on Picnic Ledge and thought his way to manhood. He had shed his adolescence without knowing it and left it a stark naked nothingness, an unseen vaporish void, to lie dormant among the laurel thickets, but always ready to seep into the minds and thoughts of future generations of Arvanes. All this he understood without knowing. And knew without understanding. What he did know, and understand, was that, as a man, he would from now on be able to face up to any responsibility that he believed was rightfully his and stick by whatever decision he made. If he made a mistake, he reasoned, it would be one made in what he believed to be the best interest of those he loved, and he would not ever again allow himself the luxury of self-condemnation. These thoughts did not, however, allow any idea of self-justifi-

cation for his seduction of Malvina. That was just another thing
he would have to watch in the future.

Cessie met him as he went through the back door of the kitch-
en. "Grandpa's here to spend the night. He's headed for the
war," she told him casually, but with a deep undertone of excitement in her voice.

CHAPTER TEN

Robin's grandpa was in the parlor with Pless and Pamela, dressed in his very finest gray broadcloth, like he was headed for a very important funeral. He wore his shiniest riding boots with silver spurs a-jingle. Robin knew his grandpa's big and vicious old roan, Jughead, was in the stable and probably at that moment kicking meanly at the partition between him and the adjoining stall. His grandpa stood up to shake hands with Robin, then resumed his seat. "I was," he told the boy, "just explaining to Pless and Pamela that I wrote Jack Hoberson, your grandma's cousin, as you know, that if war came I wanted a fling as a fighting officer in the cavalry.

"Jack wrote back that he was sure a majority could be arranged for me if that was what I wanted, and if I was as tough physically as he thought. But, he felt, I could do more good as a contract surgeon, take it easier, make more money. I wrote him back that I had spent the best years of my life chasing around, delivering babies for people who couldn't afford a doctor for such a nothing, dosing and guessing at diseases, and that if I wanted to keep on doctoring I'd stay where I was, where it would do just as much good. I think when a man gets to be sixty-one he ought to be allowed to do what he wants for once. So I wrote it was combat for me, or nothing. I got a letter back saying I could come ahead. I'll get an early start tomorrow and ride to the railroad in Tennessee.

"That's my little speech, Robin," the doctor went on. "I haven't heard much applause from my son and daughter-in-law.

All they can talk about is my chance of getting killed. I keep telling them that a man lives a complete lifetime in a war. A really fast lifetime. If he gets through a couple of campaigns he's lived a long time. If he lasts through it all, he starts on a new life. Going through a war, and coming back to a devastated country, which we are almost certain to do, will be just like being born again, starting out with a new sense of values, and precious little else to rebuild with. I think the North is right in just about every phase of this argument, except the main one, which I'm defending. That's the right to secede. I wouldn't think of trying to make a man stick around when he got tired of my company. You understand, don't you?"

Robin said he did, but he wasn't sure. He thought he might after he had time to think over what the doctor said.

"Anyway," the doctor concluded, "it'll be a mean old man and a vicious old horse that'll be riding with Johnston, if he's the man in charge, down in Tennessee."

That night the doctor slept with Robin so they could, as he put it, talk awhile in the darkness. Robin could remember the shuddery anticipation of delight he had felt when, as a small boy, he had a chance to sleep with his grandpa and they had lain murmuring, just above a whisper, as the conversation leaped from subject to subject, like a jay bird hopping from twig to twig, until one or the other had dropped off to sleep as his voice was reduced to a low throaty mumble. In the pure love of one human being for another, Robin knew he loved his grandpa next to Cessie. The knowledge, sometimes, gave him a twinge of discomfort in his conscience, because it suggested a mite of disloyalty to his parents, even though he was sure they wouldn't mind in the least if they knew. They also adored the old gentleman.

This time Robin didn't waste any time. "I reckon," he said confidently, "I'll have to load up and go with you. Seems I've heard a major has an orderly to look after him. Somebody to sort of keep him looking like an officer."

He heard his grandpa chuckle deep in his throat. "I thought you had something like that in mind. I'm glad. That's why I wanted a chance to talk with you. No grandson of mine will ever be an orderly to any God-damn officer, even if it should happen to be his own grandpa. I reckon most of the officers will have their own black boys with them, and I reckon I could, if I wanted to, buy one for my own, but I don't believe I could stand being the owner of another human being. I wouldn't feel free myself, if I did. I wouldn't feel free owning a slave, and I wouldn't feel right having a white body servant. If I can't find a free nigger, and hire him, I suppose I'll just have to orderly for myself, which of course would be just too damn bad, since I've been doing for myself the greater part of the past sixty-one years."

"I'll just go along and enlist, then," Robin said.

"No," his grandpa said. "You won't do that either. I don't want us together. I don't want too many Arvanes together in this war. Seems to me if we were all fighting in the same outfit, and it got hit pretty hard, we might lose the whole crop, which would just about ruin Modesty Valley."

"You know, Grandpa, I'm not going to stay here in the valley if fighting breaks out. Not with you somewhere in the thick of it."

"Of course you won't," the doctor said. "Much as I'd hate to see you in it, I wouldn't ask that of you. It will break out. Make no mistake about it. Our men are concentrating around Richmond now, and the Yankees are crowding into Washington. In about a week, or ten days, they'll run head on into each other somewhere between Richmond and Washington. It'll be a quick and bloody fight between raw, untrained troops."

"Do you think we'll win this first battle?" Robin wanted to know.

"I'm afraid so," the doctor said, with a note of sadness in his voice. "Much to my sorrow, I'm afraid so. If we could get a sound drubbing, in this first battle, we'd have a much better chance to win in the long run."

They talked on and on until finally Robin heard his grandpa mumble sleepily, "Let's try to doze off now. We've been blabbering here for a couple of hours, while more righteous souls under this roof are sleeping in saintly peace."

With blanket roll in place, saddlebags and holster strapped where they belonged, handshaking and kissing all taken care of, the doctor stood by old Jughead, who was pawing, twisting, and shaking his head. "Old horse," he observed, "reminds me of myself. No fool like an old one. Wants to be off and away to see what's around the next corner, and too old to profit by what he'll learn by seeing it. I don't believe in deceiving myself. I know this is going to be a long, hard war. If I live through it, I'll be too old to get much out of my memories. All I'll have will be an understanding of what the youngsters feel when they get on the subject. Anyway, I want you all to understand I'm going because I can't help myself. I don't expect to make a picnic out of it like your grandpa Ajax made out of King's Mountain. I didn't want you to know it at the time, but I spent night before last with the Cedrics. I told them I was going to be here last night and asked them to stay away so I could remember my folks best as families, with me in the center; not as a conglomeration of company, close kin though they might be."

The saddle leather creaked a merry tune as Doctor Rob Arvane settled his seat into the saddle. The doctor's head was high, and Jughead was in a fast lope by the time he turned from the driveway into the Modesty Creek Road. Pamela went back to her kitchen to shell peas and sent Cessie to the garden for more fresh vegetables, while Pless sought his room to kneel by his bed and ask the Good Lord for guidance in a situation about which he knew next to nothing. Robin peered at the ground in the road looking for some good throwing rocks. He found three, and cocking his arm, he hurled them toward the creek. Since he could remember he had thrown rocks toward the creek, hoping against hope that one day he would be man enough to reach it. He saw his third rock splash water, another evidence of his new manhood. He looked up at the new sun, coming over East Ridge, and went off down the road toward Walt's.

CHAPTER ELEVEN

T HE CEDRICS WERE UP AND EXCITED WHEN ROBIN REACHED THEIR house. They were as perturbed over Doctor Arvane's going away as Pless was.

Things had been happening while Robin was moping around, Walt told him. Everyone in the valley was running around repeating every word of news he had heard, only to have the last news killed dead as a doornail when the next newspaper came. "Grandpa says," Walt told Robin, "that the only way a man can ever know much about this war is to get into it, and then you'll know without understanding. He says it'll be at least a hundred years before the historians will be able to figure it out, if then. "Get into it," he says. "But I can't see where a hunk of lead in my head's going to make me know anything."

"I can't either," Robin said, "but I think our grandpa is the wisest man we'll ever see in this life." Walt refused to argue that point.

"Anyway," Walt said, "if you haven't heard, Professor Todd has called a mass meeting at Modesty Academy for tonight. Asked every man in the valley over twenty-one to be there. Others, not twenty-one, will be welcome, he said."

So many men and boys from the valley turned out for the professor's meeting they had to move to the church, with the permission of Arch Barnes, preacher-in-charge. Arch got up, told the assembly he knew what the meeting was for, that he had no sympathy for it, but every man had a God-given right to decide everything for himself. He said he knew all about the pledge Mr.

Todd was trying to get the men of Modesty to sign, the signing of which, he believed, would be treason in itself, no matter where a man's sympathy lay. A man, Arch declared, had to be loyal to something, loyal enough to expose his body to danger in support of that loyalty. As for himself, Arch explained, he had already written the governor and offered his services as a combat soldier, and he couldn't see why a man shouldn't be able to fight, if he had to, for what he believed was right, and still be a good preacher. But, because he did not want to be accused of influencing anyone in a final decision of what he might think was right, or wrong, he wanted to be excused from the meeting, though it was being held in church, in which he held greatest jurisdiction.

After Arch left Josh Todd took the floor. He explained that Modesty Valley had nothing to gain by mixing in with a war that it had nothing to do with starting. Crinshaw County, Josh reminded them, had tallied almost as many votes for Mr. Lincoln as it had for the other side during the recent election. There was not, he said, one single Negro in the county. Slavery was not an issue with the people of Modesty Valley. It would be, he pointed out, an intra-valley war, if it came at all, because there would be so many who would choose to fight with the North against their neighbors, their brothers, their friends. He believed, he said, if Modesty Valley would sign a pledge to have nothing to do with any hostilities, on either side, it could be an idea that might spread to other communities on both sides, thus causing cooler heads to stop, think, and seek another solution than that of force of arms. He said memorializing both sides with copies of the pledge might start the ball rolling toward peace. He hoped so. He admitted he had no signatures as yet, but he believed that the people of Modesty thought as he did, and that once they saw their neighbors signing up he'd soon have the signature of every man in the valley over twenty-one, with those who had already gone excepted.

He asked for a show of hands of those who thought as he did. A few hands were raised—not many, and most of them were folks who couldn't have carried a musket anyway, as Robin told Walt

later. It was then Josh turned on the full force of his oratory.
That was what Robin and Walt had come to hear. Josh went
back to the Children of Israel crossing the sea, to Joshua at Jeri-
cho, to Gideon and his small band winning with the help of Je-
hovah. He mentioned, in passing, the rise and fall of the Roman
Empire, the Battle of Hastings, the fight at King's Mountain. He
assured them no battle had ever been won except where the winning was the will of the Almighty. It was foolish, he contended,
to rush into a war, take a chance of leaving loved ones behind,
when the final outcome would be decided by God alone, regardless of the numbers on either side. Since the Good Lord had long
since decided who would win, there was nothing to be gained by
lining up with the winners, and even less than that for those on
the losing side.

Josh was honest in thinking he knew the people of Modesty
Valley. He didn't know he was preaching a sermon they were
enjoying immensely, but one with certain practical aspects that
were meaningless to their way of thinking. The people of Modesty Valley sincerely believed that the Good Lord ran things of
this world, both great and small, exactly as he saw fit, but they
could never understand why an enterprising believer couldn't give
the Lord's understanding a slight nudge once in a while. So,
when Josh had finished his oration, they were nodding approval
all over the church. Approval of Josh's eloquent obeisance to the
Almighty, not to his idea of signing anything. It wasn't Josh's
fault that he thought they were ripe to sign his petition at that
moment.

It is no wonder that Professor Todd was shocked, rudely,
when he asked all that felt as he did to come forward and sign up,
and only Timothy Calhern, whose legs were bent to one side from
past contact with a falling tree, got out of his seat and clumped
forward defiantly on his crutches. Timothy was followed by Uncle
Mance Calhern, who confessed to being eighty-six, and who
walked glibly down the aisle and told Josh, "Put down my name
an' lemme make my mark. By damn, I don't aim to go traipsing
after no war."

With those two signed, and no more coming forward, Josh looked very put out, as anyone would, and announced he would entertain a motion to adjourn. Pless Arvane rose to his feet and told them he would like a word before the meeting closed.

"I can," Pless said, "understand what the professor wants. I can't agree, but I can understand and admire him for it. It looks like we're goin' to fight. It looks like a fight nobody wants, which is always the worst of all fights. Pa left today to join a cavalry regiment in Tennessee. My boy Minter's already in, and ready to go when the first bugle blows. Zack, my oldest, says he won't stay home once the fightin' starts. I figure if it starts, and lasts long enough, Robin'll be in it. As for myself, I haven't made up my mind, but when I do, I'll be the one'll do the makin' up. I can tell you one thing, there ain't nobody livin' goin' to come around my house and tell me I have to go, if I think it's a thing I ought not to do. I want to say right now that I know, if it comes, like they say it will, we're goin' to have men on both sides. The side they choose will be the one they believe to be right. So, I'm here to say, I don't mean to get riled up at anybody in Modesty Valley about which side he likes. I say, if you got to fight, go on join up with the side you like, and fight it out, but don't get mad with your homefolks because they might like another idea.

"If it's a big war, it'll kill off a lot of our men, but them that are left'll be comin' back. Let 'em come back. Let's forget which side they was on, once they get back, and before they go. I, personally, wouldn't sacrifice Modesty Valley for every damn thing they both got to offer. Now, I'd like to move we adjourn."

Pless closed his speech, which was an extremely long one for him, by turning toward the door. He had said his say. He was going home and to bed. But the things Pless had said that night, about keeping the valley peaceful within itself despite which side its folks wanted to fight on, set men to talking and were believed to have been the reason families with boys in the Union Army, and families whose sons had espoused the cause of the Confederacy, remained close friends throughout the days between Manassas and Appomattox.

CHAPTER TWELVE

F OUR HORSEMEN RODE UP WEST RIDGE HALFWAY TO THE GAP, THEN sidled off slaunchwise across the slope. It was midafternoon, the seventh of July, and the east slope of the ridge was already beginning to cool off from the oppressive heat that had beset the valley lately. Pless Arvane's horse led the group as they rode loiteringly along, each one silent in speculation of the conclave that would have to come later. In the distance they could hear instinctively, but without interest, the scattering yelps of the dogs working over a cold trail of the fox they were supposed to be chasing. Pless pulled up under a massive chestnut oak, dropped his reins, found a resting place on a fallen log. Robin, Walt, and Walt's pa dismounted. Everyone made chitchat conversation of no import whatever. Pless got out his knife, found a good whittling stick.

"This is it," Robin told himself. He studied on the way Arvanes did things. He recalled that when his grandpa wanted to talk with him, or any other individual member of the clan, he suggested a walk, or a ride, or going fishing. No Arvane ever said, "Let's sit down at the table and talk it over." Any serious talk at the table would be carried on under the guise of sitting down for a few drinks of whiskey. In the book of Arvane any really serious problem had to be met casually while you did, or pretended to do, something else. In the first place, Robin knew neither Pless, nor Beamish Cedric, cared anything for chasing foxes in the hot sun. Especially when they both knew far better than he did that it would be next to impossible to raise a fox, or follow his trail, in the scorching dry woods. If you wanted to stick around until the dew could dampen the grass, the dogs could hit a trail before you knew it, but he knew they would be riding back down the ridge before it was dark enough for a horse to stumble on the rough ground. All these things Robin knew as he waited for Pless to begin.

Pless began casually. "Way I see it, the shootin' and dyin' s'posed to be startin' up Virginia way. If it has, an' I can't see how they can stop it now, we'll soon be a-tellin' a heap of the men of the valley good-bye for the last time. Some of them the valley'll miss badly in the years to come, an' some we'll be better off without.

"Bout the way I feel," Beamish Cedric observed.

"Thing we got to decide," Pless went on, "is which two of us is goin' to stay an' keep things together while the others are gone. That's the way I see it. I'll go in a minute if Robin'll promise to stay here and look after his ma, Cessie, and the other Arvane women and children. I've talked to Zack and he'll be gone soon's his crop's made. He doesn't mince any words, nor make any argument. He's goin'.

"I could just tell Robin to stay home and go on myself, but I don't know he'd do it unless I could get his faithful promise. It does seem to me that if the fightin' starts today, some of us will have to be movin' out of the valley tomorrow. This one isn't goin' to be like it was for Grandpa Ajax, who could pick out his battle, go off an' fight it, then come sailin' home with a passel of loot. Man gets in this'll have to make up his mind to stay until the last gun fires, if he's alive an' able to fight when it fires."

"I plumb agree with you," Cedric stated.

Robin got up from where he was seated, stretched his arms. "Seems to me," he said, "there isn't much more to say. I kind of feel elected. That is, I feel if they're going to do any fightin', I mean to see my share of it. I was aiming to run away and enlist tomorrow, but it looks like I won't have that to do now. Walt and I were planning to get away before day, in the morning, then write back from camp."

TWELVE

"Makes it easier on us." Walt grinned.

"That settles it, then," Pless said. His head was back, defiance in his voice. "If Robin, Minter, and Zack are all in it, I'm not goin'. Not even if they start this conscription stuff. And I'll be damn sure prayin', ever'time I think of it, that the Good Lord'll see fit, in His wisdom, to send our boys back."

There was a nod of assent from Beamish Cedric. Pless swung on his horse and started angling down the slope.

What with good-byes to both families to be said, the boys were a little late getting started next morning. It was almost eight o'clock when they crossed Modesty Creek bridge and saw Josh Todd's dark horse climbing the hill in front. They spurred up and hailed their old professor. They were traveling light, but Josh had his saddle loaded with luggage.

"I suppose," Robin said, "you are headed toward the army like we are. Reckon we can ride together if you don't mind, Professor."

"Not unless you want to turn left in Anserville," Josh told them, sadly.

"No," Robin said, "it's best to take out for Salisbury, Pa said, where Colonel Hedgewick is raising a regiment of volunteers. That way we can be in the army within a couple of days."

"Do you actually want to fight, Robin?" Todd asked.

"I don't know," Robin told him, frankly. "I think I wouldn't mind the actual fighting, but from what Minter writes, I know I won't like drilling and marching. I hate to think about them."

"You've got horses of your own. You can join the cavalry," Josh told them.

"Not us," Walt spoke up. "We don't want our horses killed, and we don't want to be killing any horses. We're sending them back home where they can't be hurt. Besides, our folks need them to work. These are plow horses before they're saddle nags."

"Professor, when did you decide to go to the war?" Robin asked.

"When the first gun was fired at Manassas yesterday. I didn't know it at the time, of course, but that's actually when I made up my mind. I'm not happy about any of it. I have to go and fight with the North, but I won't like fighting against my friends in Modesty."

The talk went on until they were ready to part with the company of Josh in Anserville. They shook hands. "Good-bye and God bless you both," Josh told the boys. "I hope to see you, as friends, again after this mess is over."

"Same to you, Professor," Robin said. "I hope I don't see you again until its over and we're all back in Modesty. Should I see you before, I might have to shoot you."

Walt and Robin rode by the Crewes home to tell Malvina good-bye. As they were leaving, Malvina told Walt, "I have some private business with Robin. I know you won't mind, Walt."

After Walt left them together, Malvina threw her arms around Robin and began to cry. "Oh, my darling," she sobbed. "Why do you have to go? Please let Walt go on ahead and stay with me until tomorrow, darling please!" She turned her mouth to his. Their lips clung; then Robin pushed her away, kissed her gently on the forehead. He opened the door, waved gaily. "Good-bye, Malvina," he called.

As Robin remounted he could see Walt sitting his horse and gazing at Malvina in the doorway. Suddenly Walt's lips trembled. He whirled his mount and took off in a wild gallop. "Oh, Lord," Robin said to himself. "Walt's crazy about her."

A few days later many of the folks in Modesty saw the first Negro they had ever beheld when a wizened little black man brought the boys' horses back from Salisbury for delivery to their fathers. The slave said he was supposed to walk back, but Pless wouldn't hear of it. He took the man to Chafferton and gave him money for passage, after he had had time to rest up and satisfy his hunger from Pless' fat stores of home-grown provender.

CHAPTER THIRTEEN

"COLONEL HEDGEWICK," ROBIN WROTE HIS FOLKS FROM CAMP, "is a little flea of a man sitting up on the tallest horse in the army. What he lacks in size he makes up for in noise. We are all convinced he screams orders in his sleep. We call him the Bull of Bashan, but not to his face."

Hedgewick was a driver. He had promised to take a raw, volunteer regiment and have it ready for battle action in six weeks. He said if men knew how to shoot, get into battle formation, and march, march, march, they were ready to take on the best the Yankees had to offer.

Hedgewick didn't get the regiment into action in six weeks, but he had it ready, and in Virginia, its head up, rearing to go, in a little over two months. "They can make me walk to the war," Robin told his comrades, "but damned if I'm going to walk home after it's over. That's a for-sure thing. No train running, I'll wait for an oxcart to come along before I'll walk one mile away from this poor benighted state."

Robin continued, "Axiom Ludlow offered to kiss a Virginian, and he was told that a good Virginian wouldn't let a Tar Heel kiss his ass, unless he first had his teeth pulled and his mouth washed clean with good Monongahela whiskey."

"Looky here, Arvane," the tall private Ludlow spoke up, heatedly, "yuh ain't heeard me say nuthin' 'bout nobody kissin' nobody, nowhere, an' yuh know it. I ain't like yuh. I don't go 'roun' talkin' 'bout folks what ain't here, like yuh, an' that there Walt. Yuh ain't never heeard me say nuthin' bad 'bout th' Yankees, even. My Pa allus said it don't pay to talk 'bout nobody, least-wise them as ain't there to defend theyselves. I oughta give yuh a argument t'other day when yuh called th' colonel a little son-of-a-bitch to his back. Yuh done it. Yuh can't deny yuh done it. I didn't like it, neither."

"I'm sorry about that," Robin said to Ludlow. "I know just how you feel. Shucks, I was aware you knew better, and I ought to have explained at the time I didn't actually mean he's a little son-of-a-bitch. What I meant was he's little in size for such a big son-of-a-bitch."

"Man can't be little an' big at th' same time," Ludlow countered.

"Colonel Hedgewick can," Robin said, solemnly. "He's thoroughly familiar with every known way there is to be a first, second, and third class, plus having some very clever secret methods of his own."

"I know what's wrong with yuh," Ludlow bellowed, furiously. "Yuh don't like our colonel. That's what it is."

Within a few months Robin and Walt were in several small brushes with the Yankee forces, and one medium-sized battle. Between times, they marched. Robin soon learned to keep his gripes to himself mostly, shooting off steam to Walt, usually in a sarcastic vein, which made him feel a little better, and which, for some reason, seemed to amuse Walt.

There were times when Robin felt some worry about Walt. It wasn't that Walt had ever shown cowardice, exactly. It was more Walt's tendency to let imaginative emotionalism get the better of him that bothered Robin. By day they marched together, fought together, ate together, and by night they spread the oilcloth from one pack on the ground, slipped between their blankets, and spread the other oilcloth on top. Come rain, come snow, come cold weather, two men thus outfitted could sleep warm and dry, and if they were smart enough to get away with a little supplemental foraging, they could eat fairly well. Confederate military regulations provided the death penalty for foraging, but carrying out the penalty was usually left to the discretion of a regimental commander. So far there was no evidence of one of Hedgewick's men being shot, but any man caught had felt the colonel's wrath so heavily that most of them had given up the gentle art, except in rare fool-proof instances.

Men of all armies, from time immemorial, have always been hungry, no matter how well they might fare in the belly-filling department. It was so of Robin Arvane and Walt Cedric in March of 1862. The regiment was temporarily encamped in a pasture not too far from Richmond. The late snow had melted away in the pastures and in sun-sprinkled spots in the woods nearby. It was, all in all, what might be called a balmy March day for that section of Virginia. Colonel Hedgewick called the regiment together, and with the men seated, crowded together in circles around him, he stood in the center and addressed his soldiers.

"You have," the doughty commander said, "performed gloriously. I assure you the entire State of North Carolina is watching us. You have been selected to join the forces of one of the finest generals in the army of the South. You are free to make your guesses. We'll be moving out soon, and I want every man under my command to remember he is a soldier from North Carolina. You will respect the rights of other regiments, the ranks of officers other than your own.

"No formations for the next two days, unless we have orders to move, and no foraging. I can promise you a very small amount of foraging, on the part of a very few men, can bring a hell of a lot of close-order drill for the entire regiment. Private Robin Arvane, report to my headquarters tent immediately."

"I wonder," Robin said to Walt in a dramatic whisper, "how he learned we put that little shoat under arrest last night."

"Maybe that isn't it," Walt answered.

"Only thing it could be," Robin said, "and I'd like to know who told on us."

Robin saluted stiffly, stood at attention. "At ease, Private Arvane, be seated, please. Have a cigar." The colonel was smiling.

Robin sat gingerly on the edge of a camp stool. The colonel

began: "I don't believe in beating around the bush, Arvane. I propose to make you a brevet lieutenant, as of now. If you turn out well, as I feel sure you will, we'll give you a permanent commission later on." The colonel beamed. "Does that sound good?"

Robin hesitated a minute. "It sounds very complimentary. It makes me proud, of course, but I wish you hadn't said it, Sir."

"And why not?"

"Sir, as sorry as I am to tell you, I can't accept."

The colonel sat for a moment, thinking. "Can you tell me why without violating a confidence?" he asked.

"I can, Sir," Robin answered. "But I will ask that you take it confidentially."

"I will."

"Before I enlisted," Robin told the colonel, "I promised my grandfather that my cousin Walt and I would always have the same rank. That we would return to Modesty Valley with neither outranking the other. Seems sort of crazy, I know, but I promised Grandpa. Besides, Walt needs me right where I am. Not that he's lacking in bravery, or anything like that; it's just to sort of steady him down. Maybe I need him too."

"What if he were transferred out of the regiment, sent to another part of the country, what would be your answer to that? It seems to me you'd be relieved of any sense of responsibility for Private Cedric then," the colonel argued.

"I might have been," Robin answered, "if it had happened before this. But if it did now, I'd know why Walt was transferred. So we'd desert, go home and hide out in the hills until the war is over. Sir, you know we could do that."

"And if I could catch you, what?" the colonel asked.

"You'd probably shoot us," said Robin.

"Oh no," the colonel said. "I would never waste powder and lead shooting a deserter. I'd have you hanged."

"Yes, Sir," Robin agreed.

"You know, Arvane," the colonel went on, "we are up against it in this regiment for officer material when promotions are available. Twenty-five per cent of my enlisted men can't read or write.

You and Cedric are two of the best educated enlisted men left in the outfit. I've been getting confidential reports on both of you for a good while. Without my saying a word, you know why we can't promote Cedric. How would you like to serve under an officer who could barely sign his name? That's what you are going to have to do if you remain an enlisted man, unless we get some outsiders transferred in to keep up our officer strength."

"I don't care in the least, Sir," Robin said, "how little education my immediate commanding officer has as long as he's fair with me, knows which direction the Yankees are, and is game enough to lead us to 'em."

The colonel stood up, offered his hand. "I think you mean that. Good evening and good luck, Private Arvane."

On his way back to his bivouac area Robin took a short cut through the woods. He hadn't gone far when a large wild house cat leaped from the bushes by the side of the path and scooted ahead for a few yards, then climbed a tall poplar to rest on one of the lower limbs. Out of an almost forgotten habit, and without thinking, Robin looked around for a good throwing rock, found one, took aim, and let go. He didn't expect to hit the cat, but he thought he might scare it enough to see it climb higher up the tree. Instead, the rock caught the cat in the center of the forehead, crushed its skull. It was almost through kicking when it hit the ground.

He was standing over the cat, feeling a little sorry for having thrown the rock, when the idea for the joke came to him. It was only a matter of a couple of minutes before he had his knife out, the cat neatly skinned, its head, feet, and tail cut off, and a small gambreling stick under the tendons of the hind legs. Then, swinging the carcass on the gambrel, he hurried in search of Walt. He found Walt sitting hunched up in front of a tiny fire gazing unhappily into the flame. Walt looked up, saw the carcass, and his face lit up, his eyes widened.

A few yards away, looking and listening covertly, Robin could see Axiom Ludlow and another member of the fourth squad, a gang notorious for successful foraging and petty theft.

"This," Robin told Walt with a sly wink, "is one of those big old Belgian hares you hear so much about. Big as a cat. Tell you what. Let's hang him out there in a tree to cool off and tender up tonight. He'll be nice for cooking tomorrow."

He walked over to a near-by tree and hung the carcass on a low limb. Then to Walt: "Little town about two miles down the road; let's mosey down that way for a while." He winked again and walked away. Walt followed.

They skirted the woods along the road for a short distance, then cut into them and circled back toward their bivouac while Robin explained to Walt. "Most of those fellows in the fourth squad wouldn't know the difference between cat meat and the hind leg of an elephant."

They parted some bushes and peeped through. A man from the fourth squad was taking the carcass off the limb. The two boys chuckled for several minutes. Suddenly, "What did the old man want with you?" Walt asked, anxiously.

"About that shoat," Robin told Walt airily. "I fixed it up. He almost apologized."

"I was afraid we were going to catch hell," Walt said.

They could see the men from the fourth squad cutting up the cat, putting it in a pot, building a fire. "It'll take two hours to boil that thing tender enough to eat. Let's mosey down to that little town and look around," Robin suggested. They got up, circled back through the woods to the road.

As they came back from town, Robin circled back into the woods, found the cat's pelt, rolled it neatly, and stuck it in his pocket. The men of the fourth squad were sitting around a nice pile of clean bones, cheerfully smacking their lips in memory of a sumptuous meal. They saw Robin go by the tree where he had left the carcass and they began whooping. Robin went over to them. "Best rabbit I ever stuck a fang in," Corporal Riddle told Robin, guffawing. The others echoed his loud bray.

"You didn't eat that danged cat I had hanging out there, did you? I was going to give it to the colonel for his dog. It was so sick it couldn't walk, down there in the woods, so I killed it for the colonel's old mutt. I was joking with Walt here about it being a Belgian hare. Didn't think you heard me." Robin's tone was contrite.

"Sour grapes, Arvane," the corporal shouted, laughingly. "If that was a cat, it was the best 'un I ever et. Bring on more o' them, an' I'll eat 'em, hide an' all."

"Here's the hide. Try frying it for your breakfast," Robin said, and tossed the cat skin at the corporal's feet.

The remainder of the members of the squad came over. They looked at the hide, pushed it around a bit with their boot tips. "You say he was sick?" one of them asked.

"So bad he couldn't even walk," Robin said.

"Go-o-o-o-p!" The soldier was disgorging the cat meat. His fellow squad members were turning a pale green around their lips. One or two had fingers down their throats to hasten the disgorging process. "Might die if we keep a sick cat inside of us," Corporal Riddle moaned between retchings. In a few minutes, half the company was crowded around while Robin and Walt explained about the sick cat. Everybody seemed to be having a fine time, except the men of the fourth squad.

Corporal Riddle, who was now sure he had no more cat meat inside, moaned in a low tone, "I thought them hind legs looked awful short for a rabbit's, but then I thought maybe them Belgian things is got short legs."

"Let this be a lesson to you," Robin told the corporal severely.

"You ain't tryin' to tell me not to forage. Not you, you ain't," Riddle said to Robin.

"Hell no," Robin answered, "I'm trying to tell you not to eat sick cat meat." He and Walt walked away, but the echo of his laughter was left hanging in the air.

CHAPTER FOURTEEN

A COUPLE OF DAYS LATER THEY WERE ON THE MOVE AGAIN, WALK-
ing with the swinging, easy slouch that made Southern troops the
fastest maneuvering foot soldiery the world has ever seen. To a
man, they knew they were headed for the Shenandoah Valley
to help out Old Jack, the man of legend, who couldn't be licked
no matter how many Yanks came against him. When it became
apparent that his men knew as much about where they were
headed as he did, Colonel Hedgewick spoke to his regiment
again.

"General Jackson," he told them, "is, I understand, a very strict
disciplinarian. He believes officers should be treated as such, and
that soldiers should behave like soldiers when they are not fighting, as well as on the battlefront. If General Jackson wants us to
be military as all hell, then we'll try to be military, as long as we
are under his command."

The next day the regiment went storming into the valley with
their diminutive colonel, straddling his tall horse, in front, and
with their guns loaded, ready for battle. The colonel's admonition
had come back down the line to keep alert: an attack might come
from any direction at any minute. To the north they could hear
the roar of cannon, interspersed with the far-off mutterings of
musketry. They were moving at an almost forced-march time,
and the officers were constantly patrolling their own lines to keep
the men from abandoning blankets and other equipment not
necessary to fighting. It was about ten o'clock that morning and
Hedgewick had just pulled his men into a close-up marching for-

mation, when a regiment of Yankee cavalry came down a side road, from what they thought was ambush, and tried to ride them down. It was a sorry fight, idiotic in its conception and suicidal in its attempt. When the Yankees who had lived through the charge had withdrawn, Hedgewick pulled his men up on a hillside to the left of the road and had them entrench, while he sent out skirmishers to ascertain the lay of the land.

It wasn't long until orders came for the Carolinians to remain where they were, covering the road, as an attack in force was expected momentarily. A smartly uniformed general, with a luxuriant brown beard, came riding by, his easy grace in the saddle bespeaking superb horsemanship. In their exuberance, after their so easy victory, the Tar Heels forgot the admonitions of the colonel. Someone started it, and as from one man the shout went down the line and echoed around the general's head: "We see you, Private Jones, an' we know you been foragin' for foxes, 'cause we see th' tail stickin' out o' yore collar."

The general stopped his horse, faced him up the hill, smiled and saluted smartly; then rode on to cheers, happy catcalls, and jeering remarks.

As night was closing in, the orders came for everyone to remain in the company area, and no man was to leave his squad without taking his gun with him. The colonel was taking no chances of a surprise night attack catching him with his Tar Heel britches down.

Robin and Walt caught sight of Private Ludlow sneaking away toward the thickets with a bulge in front of his coat that could mean only one thing. Private Ludlow had been foraging. They let him get enough start to believe he wasn't followed, then sneaked along behind. "We'll let him cook whatever it is, then step up for our share," Robin told Walt.

They saw Ludlow gathering dry sticks. Then he plunged into the thickest clump of laurel he could find. They heard a light squawk. "Chicken," Walt said.

"Yeah," said Robin, "and if the damn fool's got sense enough to use his oilcloth, he can fix it so the light can't be seen from the road."

Ludlow didn't have that kind of sense. He fixed his oilcloth to shield his light on the sides but forgot that a cook fire also reflects upward. The chicken was frying away, giving forth the little crackles that are better music to a hungry Tar Heel than the most beautiful rendition of the world's finest orchestra, when Robin heard a small cavalcade coming down the road. The horsemen paused for a second, eased their horses across the roadside ditch, and rode slowly over the fifty yards that separated the road from Ludlow's hideout. Axiom was so intent on his duties, as chef to Private Ludlow, that he didn't hear the horses until he was completely surrounded. The light showed their leader was a youthful colonel, who addressed Ludlow.

"Soldier," he said harshly, "foraging carries the death penalty in Jackson's army."

"I ain't in no Jackson's army. I work for Colonel Hedgewick, of N'th Ca'lina. Jackson ain't got nuthin' to do with me." Ludlow was defiant. He stooped and turned the thickest piece of chicken in his pan. It was about done and ready to eat.

"If they take him in he'll be shot," Robin told Walt, as he removed his hat and coat and thrust them into Walt's hands. "You wait here."

With his shirt collar open, no coat, no hat, and the fresh shave he had given himself that afternoon, Robin figured he had a good chance to get away with what he had in mind. He strode up to the puny circle of firelight and noticed that Ludlow was seated back on his heels, tearing meat off a chicken leg with his teeth. "My compliments," Robin said. "Excuse my being only partly dressed, but when I heard this man had come this way with a foraged chicken, I came after him just as I was. I'm Captain Sommersby, of C Company, North Carolina. This man is the worst forager in the army, and I aim to make an example of him."

Ludlow looked around, goggled-eyed. "Foragin', Robin . . ."

"That's right," Robin interrupted quickly. "Foraging and robbing are the same thing. Gentlemen, in my opinion the worst offense against our cause, other than cowardice, is robbing the people we came here to protect. Unless some officer here who is my senior in rank orders it otherwise, I shall have Private Woldul shot as soon as I can assemble a firing squad."

"But, but ..." Ludlow was trying to say something.

"Shut up," Robin stormed at him. "Open your mouth again and I'll shoot you myself, here and now." He called back toward Walt, "Orderly, go and assemble a firing squad and bring it here."

The tall colonel said, "I must say North Carolina believes in quick justice. I don't mind telling you, Captain, I'm Colonel Beeson, temporarily on General Jackson's staff. He sent me here tonight to sort of check up. It seems," he laughed wryly, "your regiment does have a bad reputation for foraging. I shall be happy to report that your officers have the situation well in hand. It will please the General. Of course you'll want us to witness the execution?"

"I do not," Robin told him sternly. "North Carolina prefers to wash its dirty linen in private. I don't think Colonel Hedgewick will be happy to know the General thinks so little of our discipline that he finds it necessary to send out scouts against us." Robin was enjoying himself.

"I quite understand," the colonel said. "My apologies, and you may rest assured if I am ordered on another foray of this kind I shall protest."

"Thank you," Robin said. "In that event I shall say nothing to Colonel Hedgewick about it, except to report the execution."

The young colonel reined his horse around and, with his troop, rode back down the hill.

Robin listened until he heard the horses' shod hooves on the road below. "Kick out that fire," he ordered Ludlow, "and bring the chicken. We'll have to eat it somewhere else."

Ludlow, who was just beginning to understand what had happened, whispered, "What if that officer hadda not b'lieved you? S'pose he'd arrested you an' took you back with 'im?"

"If he'd tried that I'd have shot him and then yelled for us both to run like hell. Let's find Walt and eat that chicken."

CHAPTER FIFTEEN

FIFTEEN MONTHS LATER ROBIN ARVANE AND WALT CEDRIC WERE lying stretched out in Virginia dust at the edge of an oak thicket surmounting a small ridge. Endless months of campaigning had hardened their muscles to the pliable strength of rawhide. A half-inch of brownish fuzz sprouted from their jaws and chins. Their eyes expressed the wariness of soldiers who have learned the difference between a bullet whining loudly like a banshee, in the distance, and the soft, seductive whisper of a near-miss. They were veterans. Hard. Cautious. Ready and willing to fight, but anxious to stay alive themselves. In both directions the dirt-streaked, ragged uniforms of their Tar Heel comrades stretched along the fringe of the thickets. They could hear a Roanoke Islander engaged in a lying contest with a store clerk from the sandhills, until they were told to shut up by a huge and dour mountaineer from Buncombe County, who said he wanted a few winks of sleep before he had to fight again.

They had moved into position late in the afternoon of the day before, and everyone had worked until well after dark throwing up makeshift breastworks. Robin could remember the gripes they used to put up when ordered to dig in. Now, nobody ever griped about that chore. Too many of them were alive because they had learned to dig breastworks. No cooking fires were allowed. The regiment got a few hours' sleep after a meal of cold corn pone and hog meat washed down with tepid water. Most of the day before, and all the night before that, they had marched, dragging their bodies, shifting the weight of their gear, stumbling in deep-rutted back roads, over a roundabout route, to reach a place less than seven miles from where they started. They were tired from the marrow of their bones outward.

Even the most unknowing of the men in the ranks were aware they were plugging a gap the Yankees thought was open.

Officers sat on the ground, some with their backs against trees, tired as the men, but still trying to look alert and officer-like. Periodically an officer would crawl furtively to the edge of the thicket and train his glasses across the leached-out sedge field, where clumps of sassafrass and other brush concealed their men on picket duty.

Early rising birds twittered joyfully in the woods behind them, and from far off they heard the sharp bark of a dog fox. Robin discovered a doodle-bug hole. Supported on one elbow, he blew into the hole until the little black ant-catcher at the bottom was uncovered. Then he lifted it out gently, smoothed over its sand hole, put it back, and idly watched it circling energetically backwards, creating a new trap. He shifted his face toward Walt, "If our legs hold out we'll win this damn war yet. Hey, Walt, wake up, what are you thinking about?"

"Girls," Walt said, dreamily. "All the pretty girls all over the world. I'd give a small slice of leg to be with some pretty girls again."

"If you had a big slice of leg gone, somebody else would beat you to all the pretty girls," Robin said.

"Not in Modesty, they wouldn't. No single men left in the valley that a pretty girl would spit on, and remember, I'd be a wounded hero, with more pretty girls chasing after me than I could fight off with a bushel of throwing rocks. Wish I could get a leg shot off—kind of low down—next to my foot, just enough to get out of the army on. Last letter from Ma said girls and women are doing every kind of work while their men are away. She said what we read in the papers about women saving chamber water to make ammunition for the Confederate Army is absolutely true, and that every woman in the valley who is for the Cause is actually doing just that."

"I saw it in the papers, and I've heard enough about it, but you know I never much believed it," Robin said. "Reckon if your ma says it's so, it's got to be that way.

"Damn, wouldn't I like to kill me a couple of blue bellies with a little of a Modesty gal's chamber water!" Robin went on, musingly. "Man, I'll bet a gun loaded with it would shoot a mile. Hell's delight, Walt, I'll bet they don't have to do any work on Modesty Valley gals' chamber water to have first-class ammunition. Just pour it in the gun, point it, and pull the trigger, and a whole regiment of Yankees would fall down dead. Tell you where we made a fool of ourselves. We should've stayed home, got jobs collecting chamber water. Shucks, if I were at home, at this minute, I'd be sitting by the side of some Modesty gal, like Ellen Cogle, waiting for her to fill the pot so I could rush it off to the ammunition makers." He laughed softly and turned back to inspect the progress of the doodle bug.

"Laugh, damn you," Walt said bitterly. "For some reason it isn't funny to me."

Just then the low-spoken command, passed down the line, tensed the regiment: "Prepare for action."

In less than two minutes the line had blanket rolls tied, knapsacks ready to go, guns ready to fire. Robin peered, as best he could, from a kneeling position, across the sedge field. Orders were to keep low, and he could barely see over the top of the sedge. For an hour nothing happened except that the tenseness of the men seemed to stiffen. Robin started to open his pack for a bit of left-over pone, but thought he'd better not. He stretched out and tried to remember the taste of fried chicken, but fried chicken seemed like something that had happened to him a million years ago, and his imagination kept returning to the succulence of the pone, which reason told him was within a few inches of his reach, inside his knapsack. Damn orders, anyway. Expecting a man to fight well on an empty belly was unreasonable.

He looked at Walt and noted that, as always just before action, Walt was white around the mouth and humming a little nameless tune through his teeth. He felt a little trembly, but when he held out his hand, and studied it, it was still and steady. Hell, that fluttering in his belly was because he hadn't had any breakfast. He wished the Yanks would come on and get it over with so he could eat.

Just then the stillness in the skirmish line deepened. The line seemed to freeze, holding its collective breath. It made Robin think of a fine dog on a point. He peered again over the sedge and saw a chunky Union Officer, in a resplendent uniform, leading a black horse out of the woods three hundred yards in front, and across the sedge. The officer looked intently toward them for a minute, then apparently seeing nothing of note, mounted, raised his hand, and Robin heard a voice, vaguely familiar, clear and sharp: "Advance as skirmishers."

The blue uniforms came out of the woods in a beautiful skirmish line, with the black horse dancing and tossing his head a few paces in front. From behind a stump, shielded by a clump of sassafras, a picket's rifle cracked shatteringly, and over the puff of smoke from his gun Robin saw the mounted officer sway, catch himself, then fall heavily out of the saddle. The horse turned, galloped back into the woods. Far off, to the right, Robin heard the uneven rattle of musketry. Near by he could hear the low but carrying voices of the Confederate officers, "Hold your fire, hold your fire. Damn it to hell, hold your fire."

Hedgewick's marching men had scored another perfect ambush. And Robin's stomach was churning proper, but he didn't think he would be sick like the time he went into battle right after eating a dozen foraged fried eggs.

Musketry to the right and left was getting closer. The Union troops wavered, halted, and fired a volley toward the woods. Robin could hear the almost spent bullets crashing the leaves above their heads. Green troops. He felt a little sorry for them. The Carolina pickets were scurrying back to their own lines while the Yankees were reloading, getting set for a Confederate charge, or maybe, preparing to charge themselves. Commands were being squalled up and down the Union line. The blue uniforms again fell into a skirmish formation and, with rifles at high port, came forward through the sedge at a brisk half-trot.

Tar Heel officers and non-coms were frantically urging the Carolinians to hold their fire as the Union line drew nearer and nearer. Suddenly Robin heard, or sensed, the command to fire, and a loud bellow, "Aim low and let 'em have it!" He picked out a figure, fired, and as the wind wafted the smoke back into his face, he reached for another load. The Union men wavered, spread, filled the gaps cut in their line, and kept coming. Robin fired again, and as he reached for another load he heard the bugles blaring a charge, along with the ear-splitting yell, half hysteria, half defiance, that launched uncounted Southern attacks.

With outthrust bayonets the Carolinians came out of the thickets in a wild leaping run, whooping and screaming with every step. The decimated ranks of the Union troops couldn't hope to withstand the mad rush of the wild Tar Heels. They broke and scuttled back toward the shelter of the woods across the field. A few dropped their guns, threw up their hands, but mostly, those who were able to run reached the woods, and continued through them, with the Tar Heels halting at the edge to reform ranks. The Carolinians paused to take care of their wounded, see about prisoners, while covering pickets and scouting parties were sent after the retreating Yankees. In a few minutes word came back that the Yanks were crossing the next field and entering another wooded area a thousand yards in front. Robin knew the fighting for that day was over. The Yanks wouldn't attack again, and his regiment wouldn't move until the entire line pulled up evenly so as not to expose their flanks. He opened his knapsack and fished out the hunk of pone.

He had swallowed the last bit and licked the crumbs off his fingers when he thought of Walt. He wondered why he hadn't noticed Walt was not along when he came across the field. Never before had they been separated during a fight. Robin's sergeant said he could go back for a minute to see about Walt, if he would hurry.

Walt was lying right where he had been when the first shot

was fired, his pants leg, halfway to his knee, almost blown away. He groaned and tried to sit up, then fell back prone. In a few seconds Robin had cut away the bloody cloth and cleaned up enough to see the shin-bone splinters. He bound the wound with Walt's shirt to stop the bleeding. "Seems like," he said conversationally, "you got that leg shot off you wanted. Did you do it on purpose?"

"God-damned recruit, on my left, let his gun go off," Walt gasped between his teeth. "Ask him why."

"Can't. That is, I hope I can't for a long time. He got one through the neck. Lying dead, right over there," Robin said. "Shucks, I don't care how it happened. You're plumb lucky. Just stick to what you told me, if they ask you how it happened. No time at all, and you'll be back in Modesty Valley chasing around, gathering in the chamber water." Robin joked, but he sighed wistfully, too. "Doctors'll fix you up nice and slick. Give you a big slug of licker and a leather belt to chew on while they hack it off. Next thing you know, you'll be back in the valley."

He talked on for a minute before he noticed Walt had fainted. There was only a handful of Carolina wounded, and the ambulance carts were already arriving to pick them up, the drivers swearing at the mules and cussing the Yankees.

"I wish you all would kill the Yanks dead, or give 'em time to pick up their own wounded. We've got enough God-damned work to do without havin' to cart off a passel of blue-bellies," a tall, stooped, bearded man grumbled as he helped load Walt into his cart. He cussed the mule, and the cart jostled along the fringe of the thickets to finish loading.

When Robin got back to his company he found them bringing in the Yankee wounded. "Don't fool with their dead at present. Just get their wounded into the shade, out of the hot sun," their captain told them.

Robin slipped his hands under the armpits of the wounded major he'd seen shot from his horse when the Yanks first came out of the woods. The officer's head sagged limply. Robin saw his face plainly and almost lost his hold in surprise. It was Professor Todd, whose voice had sounded familiar when he gave the forward order.

They laid Todd in the shade of a persimmon tree and Robin unbuttoned his tunic. The bullet had gone clear through, low and to the left, under the heart. He had bled some, but not too much, Robin figured. He was unconscious, but he would soon come around. Pretty badly shocked, Robin thought. "Cap'n, Sir, I know this officer. Used to be my school teacher in Modesty Valley. Comes from up Pennsylvania way. He's not bad for a Yankee."

"Then help him all you can and try to get him on an early ambulance," the captain said curtly, and turned to other business.

Robin cut Todd's coat off and made a headrest, emptied his pockets and shoulder kit and laid their contents neatly on the ground. Razor, soap, shaving brush, and comb were transferred to the Arvane knapsack. The money in Todd's wallet went into Robin's pocket. He began reading the letters found in Todd's coat pocket. They were all signed by Ellen Cogle, and promised to wait for Josh Todd, even though the war should last a million years. Robin whistled softly through his teeth, returned the letters to the major's pocket. Next, he dug the cork out of the bottle of Monongahela he found in the bottom of the kit and covertly took a long, gurgling pull, careful not to be seen. He eyed the bottle critically, took another, but shorter drink, then tilted the bottle over the major's mouth and rubbed his jaws to make him swallow. A slight spasm crept over Todd's face. He shivered, opened his eyes, gave a sighing groan, and closed his eyes again. Robin tilted the bottle again. The Monongahela began working. Todd focused his vision. "You, you look familiar."

"I'm familiar as all hell. I'm Robin Arvane. You've been wounded pretty badly, but it'll be all right, except you won't like a Confederate prison. I took your things, all except the letters from Ellen. Figure I'll need 'em more than you will. You been fighting much?"

"You're welcome to my things, and I thank you for leaving me the letters from Ellen. I've been training troops since I saw you. This was my first engagement and it seems like I bungled it. Should have sent out scouts, but I was told to advance as rapidly as possible, and that I wouldn't make contact for several miles yet. Now I may not have another chance."

"No," Robin said, "you won't have another chance, but I expect you're lucky, at that."

"I'll have another chance if I can escape," Todd gasped. "When you write home ask them to tell Ellen about me. Tell her I'll write if I can. Tell her I'll see her when this mess is over; that I love her more than ever, if such is possible. Wait and see, I'll meet you again in Modesty someday, Robin."

"If you do, I'll return the things of yours I'm borrowing for the remainder of the war," Robin answered.

An ambulance came by and they lifted Joshua Todd, not too gently, and carted him away.

By now it was past noon. Robin lay down, rested his head on his blanket roll, idly watched a buzzard in a circling glide high overhead. He wondered idly where the quartermaster's ration carts might be. He also wondered how Walt was doing. Having lately learned of Minter's death, he started concentrating on hating the Yankees, for cutting his brother down and robbing him of his chance to pay him off for the great crime he had committed against him. Try as he would he couldn't keep his thoughts on any one thing for long. Oh well, he could ask the captain to let him visit the hospital and try to get some first-hand information on Walt. That is, he would ask if they didn't have to move forward right away. "Where the hell do you reckon that quartermaster's wagon is?" he asked the man next to him. "A fighting man needs to eat three times a day."

CHAPTER SIXTEEN

Walt shared the floor of the ambulance cart with other badly wounded, while two others, less seriously hurt, rode on the seat with the driver, who cussed elegantly, but dispassionately, in a tone that showed he meant his diatribe to be cheering to his cargo. Taking first things first, the driver cussed the mule, the rough ground and jolting cart, the higher eschelon of Southern officers generally, and the entire Yankee army in particular. When he ran down he popped his whip and started over. His eloquence was nothing less than earth-shattering when he found it necessary to tell the slightly wounded, sorrowfully, they would have to walk, as he was not allowed to tote those who could navigate on their own steam.

Nerve spasms that rippled across Walt's face showed he suffered a jolting throb that shook him to his mid-gut area with every lurch of the ambulance. One wheel of the cart was crying for grease. "S-q-u-e-a-k-k-k-k," it screamed twice with each revolution. The wheel must have had two warps in it, and as it passed each it sang dolefully. " 'Gangrene,' that's what the damn wheel's hollering at me," Walt screamed to a soldier with a shattered arm, who sat placidly in a corner of the cart furiously chewing tobacco. The wheel shrieked. The cart lurched, the tobacco-chewing soldier saw Walt cram his mouth full of his sleeve's cuff and chew hard as though he were trying to bite away pain.

Then Walt was weeping bitterly. His tobacco-chomping compatriot eyed him dispassionately, not listening too closely. "Listen to that wheel," Walt sobbed. "First it says 'Gangrene,' then 'Geth-

semane.' I know all about leg wounds and gangrene. They lop
off a piece of you, trying to stay ahead of its filthy rot; then they
keep on lopping it off. When there isn't anything left to lop off,
they take you out and bury you, but that would be all right with
me, for if I had to go back to Modesty in a pine box, I wouldn't
care whether or not I went."

Perspiration rolled from his forehead and mingled with his
tears. He began mumbling the Lord's Prayer. The tobacco-chew-
er spat expertly over the tailgate. "Shucks," he said, kindly. "Me
an' you'll be a-goin' home in no time. I 'low we is jes' plumb
lucky." Walt didn't hear. He had fainted. He was being jolted
along on a stretcher when consciousness returned to Walt Cedric.
The stretcher-bearers were talking.

"Th' ol' man said take this'n straight to th' choppin' block.
After a hour o' this, each load gits heavier an' heavier for each
God-damn trip. Le's rest a minute."

They set the stretcher down and squatted by it. Walt kept his
eyes closed. After a moment the man on the back end of the
stretcher said, "Can't rest long. Too many to look after. This
pore feller ain't gonna be as heavy comin' out as he is goin' in."
They went on by the tiers of hospital tents to the surgery at the
end of the row.

The surgeon was harried, hurried, and tired. The sag in his
shoulders was partly from present fatigue and partly from thirty-
five years of Georgia piney woods country practice. The skirmish
in which Walt had been hurt had been only a single facet of a
vast, quick-flowing maneuver of armies that had developed into a
major battle, raging in three directions, and that would continue
through another twenty-four hours before both sides pulled back
to count noses, lick their wounds, and claim victory. Walt neither
knew, nor cared, about this as he slowly opened his eyes and
turned his head to gaze around the hospital tent. The doctor
bent over him, felt his pulse, glanced briefly at his wound.

"Give him," the doctor said, "a half pint of whiskey, but go
slow on the morphia; it's getting low. Then get my instruments
ready, and if that God-damn saw ain't sharp this time, I'll break

somebody's God-damn neck. Where's that damn belt we've been using for them to chaw on? Expect me to think of everything? If you damn slowpokes don't get the lead out of your britches, I'll try to see that you get other duties—fightin' 'stead of workin'. Yes, dammit, I said put him right there." Then, his tone changing, the doctor leaned over Walt while he rolled up his sleeves. "Won't be but a few minutes, son. Just chaw hard on that belt."

Walt swallowed the whiskey. His jaws worked clumsily. Sleepily he tried to say something. The doctor leaned closer, "What is it, son?" he asked.

"I was trying to sa—to say, good-bye to my foot," Walt murmured drunkenly. The straps went around him, fastening his body and the uninjured leg to the table.

A giant Negro loomed beside the table, leaned forward, and clamped Walt's injured leg in his two hands, lifting it slightly off the table. The doctor ran a thumb professionally along the edge of the knife, dipped its blade in spirits of turpentine, spoke affably to Walt: "Sease is the best God-damn surgical helper with the whole damn army. Brought him from home myself." The big Negro grinned appreciatively as the first strokes of the knife sank through the skin. Walt clamped down on the belt and chewed leather.

Walt, squirming helplessly against the straps and the ironlike grasp of the Negro, chewed on the belt. The soldier holding the tourniquet loosened and tightened on signals from the doctor's eyes. Then came the saw. At its first rasp against the bone, Walt's muscles surged, tensed, and surged again; then he lost the belt, screamed, fainted.

On both sides, and across an aisle, wounded lay on bunks in the hospital tent. The tent occupants were quiet as though sleeping, except for one man, off in a corner, who was softly singing a camp meeting hymn. As Walt told it later, he tried to raise his head, but it was too much effort. He looked at his hands. They were all right. He ran them down his body. It seemed all right, too. Then he remembered the doctor had been taking off his left foot the last he could recall. He thought there couldn't be a pain in the toes if the foot were gone. Yet he'd heard of such. He wished he could lift himself enough to see if he still had two feet.

An orderly brought some water and a cup of warm soup, supported his head while he swallowed. "Feel better?" the orderly asked. Walt sighed weakly. The orderly moved on.

"Buried your foot m'self an hour ago," he flung back, "off halfway to the knee. Reckon you'll be goin' home in no time, unless you're a big enough damn fool to volunteer for light duty, like hospital work, guardin' warehouses, or some-sich." The orderly's tone was frankly envious.

A big green fly buzzed around, came to rest on his cheek. He brushed at the fly as he felt his guts heave. He lost the soup he'd just swallowed. The orderly brought another cup.

They brought him more soup for breakfast. The doctor came, removed the bandage, told Walt, "Clean as I ever saw. I cut the bone back far enough for you to have a nice cushion for a wooden leg as soon as it toughens up enough so you can wear one. We'll give you some crutches and let you go home, soon's you're able to travel, if that's what you want." He went on to the next man.

Six weeks later they gave Walt a new uniform, a pair of crutches, and put him on the train for Chafferton, Modesty's nearest railroad station.

No, they told him in Chafferton, the stage for Anserville wasn't running any more. Stick around for a few days and he would be able to catch a freight wagon going through, maybe. There were no horses to rent, but he might be able to find some kind of a nag to buy, if he had the money. Walt didn't. He rolled his few belongings into the thin blanket they'd issued him, looped it over his shoulder, slipped his crutches under his arms, and turned his face toward Modesty.

Walt, who had had almost no practice in the use of crutches, didn't know one was supposed to carry most of his weight on his hands, instead of swinging at the armpits. He didn't know that the way he was using them would tend to create a sort of paralysis in the arms due to retarded circulation and nerve-pinching. He was almost a mile out of town when he had to stop and rest, after about an hour. At the rate he was going, it would take a week or ten days to reach Modesty. Finding a campsite for the nights wouldn't be so bad, but finding something to eat would be another matter. As Walt told it, it was then he realized he was going to miss Robin in Modesty. He said he knew Robin would have a horse if he had to steal one. He took a deep breath and started again.

Another hour and he was finished. At the end of the road as far as crutch navigation went. His muscles were still weak from his wound, and hospital idleness; besides, he realized he was too inept with the crutches to try to make it any further. He sat down on the roadside embankment to think it over. He was hungry, and there wasn't a crumb of victuals within sight or reach. Black despair took Walt Cedric to her bosom. He leaned his head into his hands and wept great shaking sobs for a few minutes. Cursing the crutches, he stood on his good leg and hurled them as far as he could into the roadside brush, then sat back down. He was white and trembly, but he wasn't crying any more.

There was the sharp explosion of a whip cracking back along the road to Chafferton. Then, the unmistakable creaking groans of a heavy wagon, the clanking of a toggle chain. Pow! popped the whip, followed by a string of loud, but casual oaths, then a voice more strong than musical, shouting the words to "My True, True Love Lies in the Cold, Cold Ground." Walt wiped his eyes on his sleeve, waited. A covered freight wagon drawn by a four-ox hitch came around the bend, the lead oxen, without guiding line, picking the smoother part of the road, the toggle between their yoke and the wheel hitch sagging on the down grade. An undersized man, with a heavily gray-streaked brown beard, was on the seat, holding the brake lever with his right foot. A wooden peg on his left leg was thrust over the footboard.

The driver whoaed his oxen, set the brake. "I'm damned," he said admiringly, "you got fudder'n I thunk you could. Wa'n't aimin' to start out myself afore mawnin', but I heeard you done

hit it out f'r Anserville on crutches. Hey, where's them crutches?
You wa'n't a-hoppin' along like a jay bird on one foot, was you?
Ain't you been a-cryin', sonny?"

All Walt said in reply to the barrage of questions was, "Yes,
Sir."

"Hell's delight!" said the man on the wagon, cheerfully. "I'd
a-cried, too, was it me. Now scramble them crutches together,
fr'm whichever way you throwed 'em, an' climb on. We got two-
three hours afore we camp."

"Hungry?" the driver asked, as Walt settled on the seat beside him. "Reach down an' git that basket. Pone and jowl. An'
they's a jug o' cider f'r washin' it down. My name's Ailanthus
Cedric. Ain't no kin, that I know of, to them Cedrics in Modesty
Valley. Call me Lanthus. Everybody does."

Walt told Lanthus he was one of the Cedrics of Modesty. "I'm
damned," Lanthus breathed slowly. "Here we is, two Cedrics not
no kin a-tall, an' we meet up like this, an' we both got legs off
jist alike. Mine was a minnie ball in the fust minute of th' fust
fight I was in. Been haulin' freight fr'm Chafferton to Tennessee
more'n twenty years, so I jist fixed me up a peg, took my team
back, an' went to work. Feller I'd sold to wa'n't goin' to pay me
f'r 'em nowise. I allus pass through Modesty but ain't never had
no call to stop there."

"You'll have it now. You'll have to stop for the night with us
every time you pass through from now on," Walt said, warmly.

"Thankee," Lanthus said, "but I allus make it a p'int to stop
at Mollie Regnar's about four miles over the ridge fr'm Modesty.
Finest place to spend th' night this side o' the pearly gates. I
reckon, though, you done been a-visitin' Mollie's house more times
as I have, bein's you live sort o' neighbor-like to her. Fine, upstandin' woman, Mollie is. Must be over forty, but she's as lively
in th' bed as ary one o' them red-headed gals o' her'n. Them gals
is powerful pretty to me, but me, I ain't one as goes back on a
old friend. So, if she ain't already engaged, I allus take Mollie."

Walt told Lanthus about his and Robin's experience at Mollie's the only time he had been there.

"That's her," Lanthus chuckled. "Fine, upstandin' woman. Since you done growed up, been to th' war an' sich, she'd be glad to see you. What with so many of her regular customers off a-fightin', her business ain't what it used to be, by a long shot. Not that she ever depended on her business to make a livin'. Her an' them gals plow, an' hoe, an' chop like men. Ain't beholdin' to nobody. A place like Mollie's is a big credit to Crinshaw County, an' don't never let nobody tell you different." He picked up his whip, swung it around his head, and popped it deafeningly over the backs of the oxen, accompanying the lash's crack with a beautiful string of ox-driver oaths. The oxen, in that rare understanding existing between them and a good driver, quickened their pace.

As the wagon crept forward toward Modesty, Walt's spirits lifted. By the time they got to Anserville, he and Lanthus were firm friends for life. Lanthus had to unload a few boxes of freight for the Peoples Dry Goods Company in Anserville. The remainder of the load, mostly a sawmill, was bound for Tennessee.

"The boxes f'r Peoples Store," Lanthus said, "is all full of fine cloth blockaded fr'm England, or France, or sum'ers, into Charleston. Son-of-a-bitch Pettyman'll hide 'em under th' counter an' pass 'em out, easy-like, to them as can pay ten times what they cost him. Well, an' hell, it ain't no skin offen my tail does he want money that-away. My business is haulin' freight, not sellin' it. But I bet, was the war over, I could tip off the Federals about him a-havin' that cloth an' they'd make 'im pay duty, or somethin', on it. Leastwise," wistfully, "I hope they would."

As the wagon was leaving Anserville, headed for Modesty, Lanthus took off his peg, handed it to Walt. "Jist set an' study her to you git to Modesty; then you c'n git a good piece o' seasoned white oak an' make y'self one jist like it. It's a good 'un. Whittled it out myself. When you git your'n made, don't try to wear it ever' day for a while. Let yo'r stump git tough gradual-like. No time at all an' you'll be gittin' 'round good as me." He flicked a fly off a lead ox with his whip-cracker.

Walt did better than study Lanthus' peg. He got a small stick and whittled a model to go by for himself. "I swear," Lanthus cried when he examined the model, "you c'n actually beat me at shapin' things, an' that's a-sayin' a heap. You make a peg like this here thing an' you an' me'll have the two best wooden damn legs in th' entire whole kentry."

Lanthus drove down the valley road, out of his way to drop Walt off at his house. "Ain't got no time to go in an' meet yo'r folks. Have to git to Mollie's afore dark. Whoa, Buck. Haw, Blue!" The whip cracked as the wagon circled and headed back up the lane.

Walt opened the gate, planted his crutches firmly under his arms, and went swinging his body toward the front steps.

The house was empty. He figured his family was at work in the fields. The hollow clump of the crutches echoed as he made his way from room to room. He went to the room he had shared with Martin, lay down on the bed, caught the pillow to his face, and burst into wild sobs, interspersed with a high giggling laugh.

Thus, Walt Cedric returned to Modesty Valley.

The day after Walt got home he started shaping a peg leg. Beamish told him to take it easy until he got some flesh on his bones.

For the next few days the family asked and Walt answered. They were only interested in his own personal experiences, since he was not the first, by a long shot, of the men from Modesty who had been invalided home from the war. The Cedrics were honest, intelligent people, and they felt, even then, that the South would ultimately have to lose. And because they were loyal to the South, along with being intelligent, they skirted away from any discussion of the grand over-all conduct of the conflict. Beamish reckoned some more Cedrics would be going before it was over. Further than that, he had no comments.

No, Walt told them, he hadn't written to Robin. Didn't want to write, either, because it might make Robin feel bad knowing he was back in Modesty, enjoying life, while Robin had to stay in Virginia until he was either killed or wounded bad enough to come home. Yes, he would like to write his grandpa. He and Robin had heard from the old gentleman a few times. Since Grandpa had recently been promoted to colonel, he would write a letter of congratulations, tell him about himself, and how Robin was when he saw him last. One thing, for sure, he could tell his grandpa: Robin knew how to take care of himself in any circumstance. He had often wondered why they never gave Robin a commission, and if he had anything to do with it, Robin would be, at least, a colonel, with his courage and initiative and knowledge of tactics.

"I reckon," his pa said, "you'll be goin' to see our cousin, the widow Malvina, she bein' an Arvane, and you already havin' seen the rest of the folks."

"No," Walt told his pa, "I wasn't counting on seeing Malvina right away. In the true sense of the word she's not an Arvane any more. I'll see her first time I happen to be in Anserville."

"The hell she ain't an Arvane. She'll be an Arvane until she marries again, and what with so many of our young men killed off, I'm thinkin' that'll be a long, long time. You ain't mad at Malvina about somethin', are you?"

"No, I just don't care anything about seeing her."

"Then," Beamish rejoined, "you must be mad about somethin'. I know we taught you better manners than to refuse to see your kin after all the time you've been away."

"I said I'm not mad at her," Walt told his pa, "but, on the other hand, I don't want to be an object of pity."

"So, you don't want to be an object of pity because you lost a leg? Hell, I think I know what's eating on you, an' I admire you for it. But I'm powerful sorry you ain't got what it takes to let folks know you won't be no object of pity. It's my studied opinion that you owe Malvina an apology for not callin' on her before. That's it. You do owe her an apology."

"Maybe I do owe her an apology, and suppose I don't make it!" Walt answered hotly, and got up and clumped out of the room. He was learning to use the peg faster than he had expected.

CHAPTER SEVENTEEN

WALT WENT UP WITH HIS PA AND TWO BROTHERS TO THE FIELDS, found that a mule walked too fast for him with a plow but that an ox was the right speed for a man with a peg halfway to his knee. He did not shirk his work, nor dodge any responsibility, but he went about his tasks, when it was necessary to work by himself, with his lips drawn in a thin line of worriment, his eyes publishing a stifling feeling of aloneness. Like millions of veterans of all wars, he was plainly lonesome. He confessed years later he disliked his own company. He said he was beginning to be afraid he would come to despise Walt Cedric, and the thought made him more unhappy.

There are times in the darkness of the night when a man's thoughts can be so sharply lucid, when explanations and solutions seem so simple, that he gives way and admits to himself that nothing has been wrong that isn't of his own doing and that cannot be corrected by his own doing. It was thus with Walt. At night he could work out his problems so that he knew he had only to wait for the coming of another day to go to certain people and say the correct words and everything would be right again.

It was then he discovered he was so wholeheartedly in love with Malvina that the very thought of her name made him catch his breath.

In the meantime, Walt's family kept after him, in a nice family-like way, to go and call on Malvina. It went something like this: "I saw Malvina the other day. She asked when you were coming to see her," or, "Pless took Malvina some fresh salads yesterday. She asked about you." It went on, and on, this exertion of family pressure, done in such a way that Walt's gentle soul allowed no fighting back. He surrendered, announced he was taking the cart and driving to Anserville to see Malvina.

He came into sight of her house, stopped the mule, hesitated for a few moments, turned around and went back toward Modesty.

The next day Malvina came to see him. She walked in, accompanied by Pless Arvane, who was shouldering little Minter. She walked straight up to Walt and kissed him affectionately. "I heard you were home," she told him brightly. "I also heard you went to Anserville yesterday to see me, but I was out here visiting Daddy Pless, so I thought I should come to see you. My, you look handsome! Come to see me in your uniform sometime. Every time you come in uniform, I'll give you a big kiss."

Malvina chattered on, but Walt hemmed and hawed embarrassedly. Suddenly Walt stood in front of Malvina and shouted in frenzied desperation, "You seem to think I'm still a child who happened to lose a foot playing soldier." Then, as though he were realizing the childish silliness of the outburst, his face reddened and he clumped noisily out of the room.

Though he looked pained at Walt's behavior, Beamish said nothing about it then or later.

A few days afterwards Beamish came into Walt's room before he rose, sat on the side of the bed. "Son," he observed, "the war ain't goin' so good for us, is it?"

"I haven't paid much attention lately," Walt confessed ashamedly, "I've been so busy and all."

"Well," Beamish said, "me and Martin've talked it over, and we decided what with you plumb knocked out of it, but still able to look after things around here, we ought to go."

"You don't mean right away?" Walt said.

"Yeah," his pa said, "way it looks, this war won't wait for us to ass around making up our minds. I couldn't feel right if we win it and I ain't there. But if we should lose, and I stayed at home right through the whole thing, I don' think I could stand myself. 'Course I tried to talk Martin out of goin'. Told him to wait until he's a little older, or 'til the conscriptors send him a notice. He said he's goin' whether or not I go. Said he'd run away. So, if that's the way he wants it, I'm goin' with him, Maybe I can bring him back in better shape than they sent me back my other boy." There was a break in Beamish's voice, a wetness in his eyes.

Father's and son's hands went out, caught, clung for a moment; then Beamish heaved to his feet and left the room.

Beamish agreed to stay around for a couple of weeks so he could get things as well organized for Walt as possible before he and Martin took off for the war. That day Walt sat down and wrote Doctor Arvane, using the knowledge of his grandpa's promotion as a hook on which to hang an excuse for his writing and taking up the old gentleman's time. When it was finished, it was probably the longest letter Walt Cedric ever wrote to anyone, or would ever write again.

The knowledge that running the place would soon devolve on him seemed to give him new courage. He was getting more and more proficient in the use of his peg. He found he could do the work around the farm with far more dispatch than he had at first thought he would ever be able to achieve.

Just one week to a day before the time set by Beamish for his and Martin's departure, Walt suddenly decided he had to see Malvina. He had to see and talk to her. Touch her with his hands. He argued, to himself, that he was being a damn fool as he climbed out of the road cart in front of the Crewes house and hitched the mule at the gate. His hand was trembling when he lifted the door knocker.

After a quick and cousinly kiss, Malvina stood in front of Walt holding both his hands, swinging them from side to side. "Oh, Walt," she cried, "I'm so glad you came. Daddy's away on some law business and Minter's taking a nap, so we can have a nice visit together." Her smile was bright, gay.

If she was wasting away from grief in her widowhood, it was not discernible. She chatted gaily of this and that. "I was terribly

despondent for a long time after they let me know about Minter,"
she explained. "Then I realized I was only one of thousands of
women who have made the same sacrifice for the Cause. I know
it's a terrible thing to say, but the knowledge that I wasn't alone
in my loss was comforting. Now I'm looking to the future." ·

"You mean," Walt asked softly, embarrassedly, "you're thinking of getting married again?"

Her laugh tinkled musically. "Sure, why not? But not to just
anyone. Isn't marriage what all women are meant for? Besides,
I have to think of little Minter."

"Who," Walt asked in a slow voice, "is the lucky man?"

"Oh," she answered softly, "I haven't got that far with it. As
I said, I've got to think of Minter. When he gets older he'll need
a good man's companionship. So, I wouldn't marry just anyone
who might come along. A widow, you know, can afford to be
practical in choosing a man. She doesn't have to use up much
time thinking about love. She knows she can take any good man,
live with him in the fullest way, and love will come naturally. I
don't care if the man I get is rich, or poor, but he must be de-
pendable—and kind. Or he must be someone I think I can teach
to be that way. Walt, honey, it's a lonely way of existence to be a
widow, with a man-child, and no man of your own in your life!"

Walt breathed in deeply. "Would I do?" he blurted.

She studied his face closely for a moment, then rose, went to
him, took his face between her hands and kissed him lightly on
the mouth. "No, Walt, you wouldn't do. I won't be taken out of
sympathy, and that's what you are trying to do."

"It isn't sympathy on my part," Walt stammered, as he came
back. "I know it doesn't sound right for me to say this, what
with Minter being my own blood kin and all, but I've plumb
worshiped you since the first time I laid eyes on you, back when
Minter brought you to the valley. You believe that, don't you?"

"No, I don't, Walt. I know you too well to believe it. You'd
marry me in a minute because you might be sorry for me. And
maybe I was silly and cruel to play up to your sympathetic nature
telling you my troubles. Besides, I'm five years older than you."

"What the hell difference does that make?" Walt asked excitedly. "If you don't want me because of my lameness, say so; it won't hurt me. Fact is, I expected that."

"No, you sensitive fool," she told him tenderly, "your lameness doesn't make the least difference in the world. If we were married I would be proud of it. I'd show it off. I know it just wouldn't work out. Now, give me a nice cousinly kiss and we'll change the subject." She walked against him, slipped her arms around his neck.

The kiss she asked for and the one she gave in return wasn't cousinly. When they stood apart they were both trembling. She dropped her eyes, as if in shame, and rushed from the room. A moment later he heard her rattling cooking utensils in the kitchen. Then, slowly, he found his handkerchief, wiped his eyes, and turned to leave the house. Although Malvina wouldn't marry him, it looked as though, if he stayed around, she would surrender otherwise. He didn't want that, especially when he knew it would be just out of sympathy. He told himself he would try not to see Malvina again.

Back at home, Walt fed the mule, picked morosely at the snack his ma set out for him. Rising from the table as his pa came into the room, he remarked casually, "I'll be gone for a few days, I reckon, if you don't need me right now. Want to see a fellow over in Tennessee."

Beamish nodded. "Be careful," he said.

Pushing the shucks from over the keg in the barn wasn't much of a task, and drawing off a gallon in a stone jug wasn't much harder. A few minutes later, with the jug in his lap, he urged the mule up the steep slope of West Ridge. "Mollie Regnar, here I come," he shouted as the mule topped West Ridge.

Mollie and both her girls were at home when Walt arrived, turned his mule into her lot, hooked a finger into his jug handle, and clumped up onto her front porch. "I'm Walt Cedric," he told Mollie. "I've got sixty dollars in my pocket and a gallon jug almost full. I've come to spend a week."

Mollie had flame-colored hair and a sprinkling of stray freckles.

She was past forty but still a very handsome woman, despite a slight plumpness. She smiled a bright welcome, opened the door further. "I know you, Walt," she said, "knowed you since you was a child. But of course I ain't seed you since you growed to a man and kilt so many Yankees. Heard you was back an' I was a-wishin' you'd come to see us. Come right in, Soljer Boy. This is the hall of Freedom, and we-uns is Freedom's slaves."

They ate of Mollie's victuals and drank of Walt's whiskey. Mollie told stories about the good old days. Her two red-headed daughters, Queenie and Duchess, sang mournful ballads to the twang of a homemade dulcimer. Walt's tongue loosened up and he told one war story after another. They had a nice sociable time for two or three hours, after which Walt, in the utter happiness that comes of a plentitude of substantial food and soul-tingling whiskey, went to bed with Queenie, Mollie's older red-headed girl.

"We-uns," Mollie explained at breakfast next morning, "is a-workin' in the fur field, so fur fr'm the house we allus tote our rations with us. But you'll find a-plenty of victuals in the cupboard, all cooked and ready to eat. Don't leave the house today, but jist sit around and eat, drink, and rest up, 'cause you're gonna need your strength tonight, bein' as Duchess is a-aimin' to be your bed partner." Her firm oversize breasts jiggled merrily in bold outline against her thin dress, as she chuckled deeply, pinched Walt's cheek, and left the room, followed by the girls, who told him good-bye as politely as you please.

Walt ate heartily at noontime. Roaring drunk by two o'clock, he sang to himself for a while, then got sleepy. He unstrapped his leg and got into bed. He had practically slept it off when the Regnars came in from work.

He liked Duchess, the younger red-headed girl, better than he did her sister. She was, he figured, about sixteen or seventeen, quiet, but intense in whatever she did. In appearance she was a perfect, sized-down replica of Mollie, or what Mollie must have been at her age, Walt decided. He resolved it would be Duchess for him from there on out.

The next day, after the Regnars had gone to the field, Walt went outside and looked around. He found some mending chores about the barn that needed looking after and went to work. As a result of the chores, it was almost sundown before he got to his whiskey, so he was as tipsy as a fiddler's bitch, laughing and singing, when the women came in. After washing down supper with more of the same, he clumped off to the shed bedroom which they had assigned him, where after a while he managed to get loose from his peg and lie down. The straw mattress was making long, slow dives, whirls, and quick stops. The whiskey and food were quarreling violently in his stomach. He looked like he was going to puke. He was, unless Duchess would come and help him hold the bed still.

The bed was still cavorting when Mollie came into the room. "Move over, Soljer Boy," she whispered. "It's old Mollie's night. I aim to show you what you been a-missin'." She slid down beside him, snuggled her body against his.

A great anger beset Walt. He put the bottom of his right foot and the end of his leg stump against her and pushed, hard. A house-shaking thump told him she was no longer in his bed. "Go 'way, you fat ol' sow," he mumbled thickly. "Can't have Duchess, rather sleep by myself. Wouldn't touch you with the thing of the sorriest dog Pa's got." He heard the door close behind her. A few moments later and he was sleeping the dead stupor of alcoholic forgetfulness.

Dawn's first feeble light was creeping into the room when Walt woke up. He was miserable in body, mind, and spirit. It didn't add to his happiness when Mollie came in and stood, with arms set belligerently on her hips, looking down at him.

"Morning, Mollie," he said weakly.

"Remember last night, Soljer Boy?" she asked.

"I remember," Walt admitted.

"I'm sorry you do," she said. "I c'n forgive a man as don't remember what he done when he was drunk. Figger if he don't remember what he done, he wa'n't responsible when he done it. But a man as remembers, knowed it was wrong what he done, when he done it. I can't forgive that. Me, I was never so insulted in all my life," she went on fiercely. "Me, that's give my life to pleasin' men, an' doin' f'r 'em when they needed it, an' allus bein' fair an' square an' honest. Me, that got kicked outen bed by a damn young sprout with a wooden leg. Now, git up, git your peg leg on, an' git fr'm my house. You c'n keep your God-damn money. We wouldn't tetch it with a manure fork. Don't you come back here, never!" She practically screamed the last and marched out, slamming the door behind her.

Walt got up, found his peg and his britches. Duchess was waiting in the front room with his coat. She held it out, her face averted. "Hey," Walt wanted to know, "you're not mad at me, too, are you?"

"Of course," she blazed at him. "You was the most insultin' thing to my ma I ever heard of. I'll have you know my ma is the, by God, decentest woman in Crinshaw County, and we don't let nobody treat her no other way." She dropped his coat on the floor and walked away.

Walt went out, fed his mule, and waited for him to finish eating before he left. As he drove away from the house, he saw Duchess coming into the road from the spring with a pail of water. She was carrying a stout stick about four feet long, held menacingly in her right hand. The thought occurred to him that she was going to wait until he drove abreast of her, then strike the mule with the stick in an affort to make it break and run away, thus wrecking the cart and possibly hurting him. He stopped before he reached her.

"Put down that stick, Duchess," he commanded.

"I'm a-goin' to break your damn neck with it," she screamed.

Walt guided the mule against the bank on the upper side of the road, swung out of the cart, started toward her. "Put down that stick, I said." His tone was firm, emphatic.

She bounded at him, swearing, the stick drawn back. As she swung at his head, he shifted to one side, grabbed the stick, twisted it out of her hand, and threw it into the roadside bushes.

She paused. She turned completely around, stamped her foot.

Then in quiet, simulated dignity, she walked to the front of him, stuck her face up close, and said, tensely, "Now, run along home, little Soljer Boy, and I hope the next time you sleep with yo'r granny she gives you the clapp."

It was then Walt's temper snapped. He caught her by the shoulders, shook her back and forth until she was practically ready to drop with dizziness; then he pushed her away and swung his open palm. He saw the blood running from her cut lips. He saw her sitting abjectly on the ground, crying quietly. She looked up at him and he saw a pitiful smile hovering around her already swelling lips. "Walt, honey, you hurt me," she sobbed convulsively.

He walked down to the spring, bathed his face, wet his hair, and drank deeply. He felt better, and a little ashamed, at the same time. She was still waiting when he got back to the cart. As he climbed from the axle-step to the seat she came close, reached a hand toward him. "Walt, please, take me with you, please." The plea was the urgency of women, since the beginning of time, who have found a master to their liking.

Walt looked straight ahead. "No," he said firmly, and clucked to the mule.

CHAPTER EIGHTEEN

As walt was riding ailanthus's freight wagon toward Modesty, Robin was walking toward Chancellorsville. Enlisted campfire strategists, as usual, had all the answers. They said Marse Robert had an immense Yankee army trapped; that is, he would have as soon as they could reach the scene. Lee, they said, was facing the Yankees' main force while three other columns were advancing from as many different directions. One was coming in from the left, another from the right, and the third being wheeled into support. Everybody knew Lincoln had been given just six weeks to finish off the war and had been told that if he couldn't, in that time, the Northern armies would be withdrawn from the field and peace envoys sent in their place. It was a beautiful dream, concocted, as most dreams are, from a whole cloth of wishful nothingness.

But in the army dreams have a way of starting rumors, like a tumblebug with his piece of spherical art which picks up growth as it rolls. Unfounded rumor, Robin reasoned, was without substance or dimension, while the tumblebug, at least, messes around with something possessing a definite amount of solidity. To hell with it; he wished he had old Walt around to make a joke with.

Robin now shared his blankets and oilcloth with Private Ludlow. Ludlow had asked if he could partner up with him, since Walt was gone, and Robin couldn't find a way of saying no. The man was strictly a clod, deeply sunk in his superstitions and prejudices, but not quarrelsome or talkative. Too, Ludlow either had nerves of iron, or he was completely without fear. Robin believed it was a little of both. Since the time in the Shenandoah when Robin had saved his life, Ludlow had been deeply appreciative, embarrassingly so, at times, until Robin told him to shut up.

"You saved my life onct," Ludlow persisted to Robin.

"Don't mention it. It isn't worth mentioning," Robin told him.

"What ain't worth mentioning? I'll have you know, Mister, my life's wuth plenty to me."

"It was worth a third of a chicken to me once, but I've eaten that. Find me another chicken and I'll save it again."

Ludlow, who was husky and strong, with the stamina of an ox, made it easy for Robin when he could, or when Robin would let him. Seeing that was the the way Ludlow wanted it, Robin accepted the man's ministrations as his due, and accepted them as a part of the natural course of events. On the other hand, Robin resolved to watch out for Ludlow in battle and try to keep him alive. It was, he had noticed, the dumb, brave ones who usually got themselves killed, uselessly, first.

Historians and students of great battles have analyzed and re-analyzed the maneuvers of troops, on both sides, before and during the battle of Chancellorsville; therefore, no effort is here being made to pose the grand strategy, nor the whys and wherefores of Lee's success.

It was not the last victory, but it was the last jarring defeat the North suffered, the last defeat after which, if Lee had owned the man power to follow up his punches, he might have, with a lot of luck, knocked the North out of the fight. The truth is, whatever was gained at Chancellorsville was more than lost at Vicksburg. Anyway, after the battle no envoys from Washington came south to sue for peace, but the Army of Northern Virginia did start rolling toward Pennsylvania and Gettysburg.

The Carolinians continued praying, and singing, and dancing to whining fiddles, and holding revival meetings, and cussing out John B. Gordon's wild Georgians, who were as apt as not to turn out yelling and whooping it up in their camp on a peaceful Sabbath while one of their bands, with fluttering flags, slogged along the regimental street blaring "Bonnie Blue Flag" or "Pop Goes the Weasel." Robin's regiment didn't like their comrades from the Cracker State, but Colonel Hedgewick said if the Georgians wanted to go to hell on a hoe-handle, that was their business, and he didn't want his men to interfere with the way the Crackers ran their part of the war. However, Hedgewick's men had it all planned out: as soon as the war was over, which couldn't be much longer, they were going over en masse and break every damn horn in those damn Georgia bands. That, they figured, would learn the pender-pea-eating bastards how to disrespect the Sabbath with wild music when honest men were trying to talk to the Good Lord.

It was between Chancellorsville and Gettysburg that Robin received two letters at the same time. One was from Pamela, whom he heard from almost every week, if the mail came through, and the other was from his grandpa Arvane. Out of a sense of filial duty, Robin opened the letter from his ma first. She wrote:

Dear Son:

I take my pen in hand to tell you how sorry we are about the bad news of your grandpa Arvane's death. Your pa got the notice yesterday that he was killed in Northern Mississippi, charging into heavy woods, leading his regiment of cavalry. We are all well and doing fine and it does look like we'll make a good crop this year. But of course everybody's very grief-stricken to know about your grandpa. I tried to get Cessie to write you about her new dress, but she just wouldn't do it. She said give you her love, and watch out for a letter from her one of these days. Right now she's awful busy, but I think she will catch up soon. Your pa is taking your grandpa's death powerful hard. We have three litters of young pigs and the apple crop looks mighty good for this fall. I always thought your grandpa was a mite too old to try this soldiering business, but now that he's dead, I can't bring myself to say "I told you so," but I know it must be mighty hard for a man his age to try to fight it out with nothing but a saber against young and supple fellows. Everybody sends love and write us soon.

Your loving mother,
Pamela Arvane

P. S. It seems old Jughead was killed too and they buried him and your grandpa in the same grave. The man that wrote your pa said that was what Colonel Arvane wanted.

Sitting with his back against a chestnut stump, Robin was still for a few minutes thinking about the contents of his ma's letter. He bowed his head and breathed a wordless prayer for the eternal soul of his Grandpa Arvane.

After a moment, Robin slowly opened his grandpa's bulky letter. It started by giving a sketchy outline of the doctor's army career for the past several months. It begged Robin's pardon for not writing for so long a time and explained that by tradition the Arvanes were notoriously poor letter writers. After his brothers left the valley, Doctor Rob said, one went to Ohio, one to Illinois, one to Tennessee, later to Texas, and one to Mississippi. They had agreed to write each other in the event of births, deaths, and marriages. Lacking either of these, they were to write anyway every five years. In addition, they had agreed to have a reunion every ten years. First had been in Modesty, and then, through a system of alternation, they were passed around. One was due for that year, and it was supposed to have been held in Modesty, with Ab and the doctor the only two survivors in attendance. It could now never be held.

The doctor commented on the fact that the Mississipi Arvane, Fielding, had never been able to get any boy children but had succeeded in fathering some very fine girls; in fact, eight of them. The girls had married well and produced some fine soldiers for the South, the doctor understood. He wanted Robin to write—in fact, he insisted that he wanted to hear from him.

The letter said in part:

You remember the promise I so foolishly extracted from you about refusing promotions. That was a bad mistake. I see it now, and a recent letter from Walt makes me all the more sure I was mistaken. Walt will be the first to pat his foot and yell you on up the ladder of promotion. I had a note from your colonel. I've known Dick Hedgewick since he was a little boy, and he told me you had turned down a commission. That was something over a year ago, as I recall. I am, today, answering that note and telling him about my letter to you and advising him to try again. I hope he takes my suggestion and that you'll have sense enough to accept any promotion offered and do the best you can with it. It's a matter of duty, as I see it now.

Of course I am not urging you to take on any responsibilities that you may think are beyond your capabilities. But if you believe, in your heart, you are capable of handling the responsibilities of command, I think you owe it to your country, your folks, and yourself to accept them.

The letter before closing said his grandpa was pretty sure he would lead an attack against some Yankee strong points in a dense woods the next morning. He thought the idea was foolhardy and the job should be given to infantry, but the general thought by attacking at dawn, with the regiment divided into four columns instead of the usual cavalry charge formation, they could ride through and be behind the Yankees before they knew what was happening. It might work, Colonel Arvane conceded, but if the Yanks should get wise to what was coming and pull back their men so they could concentrate artillery on the woods, once the Confeds had ridden into them, flying splinters could play havoc with mounted men.

In closing the Colonel wrote: "May God be with you and bring us all back to our valley together when this cruel fight is over. Your affct. Gr'father."

Robin sat for a long moment studying his grandpa's letter. Then he rose slowly, threw his head back, straightened his frame, and started down the regimental street toward Colonel Hedge-wick's tent. A sergeant sat on a stool in front of the tent reading a Richmond newspaper. He looked up quizzically as Robin came up. Robin could hear water splashing inside the tent. "I want to see the colonel," Robin said.

"He's busy cleaning his-self up," the sergeant answered. "Permission your company commander?"

"No. Please tell him Private Arvane wishes to see his colonel. If he's too busy it will be all right. More or less personal matter."

The splashing ceased for a moment, and they heard the colonel's voice call, "Come in, Arvane. Been expecting you."

Robin went in. The colonel was standing up in a small wooden tub splashing water on his little skinny frame with a sponge. He said, "Have a seat while I finish this washup. God, I was filthy. Toss me that piece of blanket over there. Got no towel for drying." He stepped out of the tub.

The colonel slipped his underwear and britches on and sat wiggling his naked toes against the soft earth. "Well?" he asked.

Robin extracted his grandpa's letter, handed it to the colonel without speaking.

The colonel read it through. When he had finished, Robin said, "He was killed the next day after he wrote that."

The colonel raised his eyes, shook his head sadly. "Sorry," he said. "He was a fine man and I know a fine soldier. Believe me, Arvane, I grieve with you in your loss. I had a letter from him this morning that cleared up some things for me. I have always made it part of my military policy never to offer promotion to a man the second time. I don't think I'm compromising my convictions on that score when I say I'm still not making you an offer of a promotion the second time, inasmuch as you are requesting it. In other words, I'm not making any concession. Is that right, Private Arvane?"

"I reckon," Robin said, "that's about the size of it, Sir."

A smile slowly gathered around the colonel's mouth and spread to cover his face. "Congratulations, Lieutenant Arvane, on making a wise and patriotic decision. I shall brevet you now and your commission will be coming through regular channels right away. How are you fixed for money to buy your uniform and other regimentals?"

"I have enough, I think," Robin said.

"If not, let me know and we'll arrange it. I'm afraid I can't do anything about a horse for you, unless you can arrange to buy one yourself. A recent regulation says that newly appointed officers, under the grade of major, will furnish their own mounts or march with their men."

"I wouldn't want a mount if they were issued. I prefer to march with the men I will be asked to lead into battle," Robin said, thinking sorrowfully of the luxury of riding, of feet that wouldn't be aching at nightfall.

"Go on now," the colonel commanded, "and assemble your regimentals while I have notices posted about your promotion."

That night Robin wrote to his mother and signed the letter, "Your affct. son, Lt. Robin Arvane."

From the very first Robin's promotion was popular with the men in his platoon, and the company. He had never made any enemies of note. Even the men who were still with the company, and who had eaten the cat meat Robin had played off on them, could and did laugh about it now.

When Robin reported to Captain Lanco and showed his newly-won brevet orders, Lanco smiled broadly and said, "I'm glad the colonel took my suggestion. Went to see him yesterday and suggested you to replace Lieutenant Walson, who, I understand, won't be coming back after his last attack of jaundice. That means you'll be leading your old platoon, where I understand the men like you very well. I've always wanted officer replacements to come by promotion from the men in the ranks of their own outfits, rather than take replacements in officers we don't know."

"Thank you, Sir, for what you did," said Robin, not knowing how much to believe of what Lanco told him.

"Pshaw," Lanco answered, "it wasn't anything but what you had coming; besides, there was my duty to my oath as a soldier. I'll send out and round up our brother officers and see if we can find something with an alcoholic content in my quarters to use in toasting another lieutenant."

After Chancellorsville, Robin followed Lee on the ill-fated jaunt into Pennsylvania, which ended after the bitter withdrawal from Gettysburg.

His platoon fought through most of the long siege of Petersburg, where Lanco was so severely wounded he was discharged from the service and Lieutenant Farrar was killed. It was then that Colonel Hedgewick called Robin to his quarters and informed him, in the tone of a man imposing a stern and difficult task, that he would, as of that moment, be Captain Robin Arvane, with full responsibility for his company. Robin thanked Hedgewick briefly for his confidence and left the tent to return to his men. It was early dark, and raining. The paths were slippery. The sword which the colonel insisted his officers carry flapped against his leg. Robin knew if he had to wear it a thousand years he would never become accustomed to it. He wished they had the sword up the backend of some general and he had one of those new Colt pistols he'd seen taken off dead, or wounded, Yankee officers. He had been trying to get his hands on one for months, but as yet he had been unsuccessful. Handled just right, the cap-and-ball six-shooter was a good gun, except for the time and trouble it took to load it.

Early in March Robin's brigade was sneaked out of the lines at night and shunted along Confederate trenches until, by making a swinging circle to the south, they were able to clear both lines and start a fast march north. It was said that nobody with the brigade knew exactly where they were headed except the general. It was believed they were out to try to pick up some Confederate wagon trains to guard and guide into the lines before the Yankees learned where they were and seized them. Lord knows, Robin thought, supplies of all kinds are sorely needed. His own half-naked tatterdemalions were fighting with extremely slender waistlines. The item the Northern experts had first predicted would be the South's downfall through its exhaustion, ordnance, was still in fair supply. Not any to throw away carelessly, but plenty to make the blue-bellies wish they had stayed at home. Food, manpower, and clothing were Lee's most pressing needs.

They marched all night, and all day the next day, so when the time came for evening bivouac, Robin was almost reeling on his feet. He resolved that there would be no courts-martial of men caught napping on post that night—only a severe and blistering reprimand. After the men had slept for an hour, he had them roused and ordered everybody to dig in. This order the men understood, and it was carried out with a minimum of gripes.

He sat down at the root of a tree and opened his knapsack, extracted one thin rasher of salt bacon and a piece of corn pone. They had left Petersburg with a three-day ration, already cooked, for each man. This told Robin they either expected them to be back within three days or to encounter the wagon train and live off its supplies. He knew any healthy and hungry man could eat at one sitting every bite of what the army had called a three-day ration. He could hear a small, waspish, and aging private from the sandhills griping as he loosed dirt with his bayonet and threw it out of his entrenchment with his mess plate.

"Yeah," griped old man Smallwood, "we're shore on th' right track now. This is the way to get the Yankees outen th' South. We head no'th, an' whilst they chase us we toll 'em out. The South's plumb ruint, and I'm ruinter. I fit this war for three year now, an' each year I been a-gittin' poorer an' poorer. Shore, I got niggers at home, but I ain't got nobody to make 'em work, so they's just hangin' aroun' eatin' my wife an' gal chillun outen house an' home. I writ my wife to free them damn blacks an' run 'em off. So, she give 'em their freedom papers an' told 'em to git; they was free as she was. They left, but they was back two days atter that sayin' they was hungry. Whatta you think she done? She done jist what I'd've done. She fed 'em, God-damn they triflin' souls.

"It's damn tough titty to fight on a empty stomach, 'specially when you know yo'r wife an' chillun ain't doin' no better. I reckon I'll go right on fightin' long's the next one. But I ain't gonna do it a-feelin' I'm a-winnin'. Not any more I ain't." Smallwood threw his tools down and sat on the edge of the hole he had dug.

The next morning the waspish man was gone, along with two others from the platoon. Deserted. Robin rubbed his cold-blued fingers under his arms and remarked to one of his sergeants, "Never thought Albert Smallwood would do a thing like this. He never showed the smallest streak of yellow in a fight. I'll bet he's headed for home. He wouldn't surrender to the Yanks. If our folks pick him up, I hope they don't send him back for us to shoot."

Next morning they resumed the fast marching, and by noon the weakened troops were moving more by instinct than by mental volition. They raised their weary feet barely off the ground and marched in a shuffling drag-step, but nevertheless they kept going on guts and force of habit. After a scanty midday swallow of food and water, Robin's company was pulled out of the main column, which was following the road, and dropped back to the rear a half-mile and off to the right flank. Outriding scouts had reported a large body, probably a brigade, of Yankee cavalry raiding in their vicinity. The company, thus as a mobile outpost, was to come forward in a loose skirmish formation. A thousand yards ahead of Robin another company was doing the same as his. Since no single company could maintain a skirmish formation and keep up with the main body of troops marching in the road for any great length of time, it was understood relief would be made on the hour. Three or four hours passed. No relief. Robin knew something was about to pop or Hedgewick would have had his company shifted long since. They moved forward through rough patches of undergrowth, over marshy ground, across small streams. The men now had wet, as well as weary, feet. The sergeants in the file closes swore at their men, and Robin did his best to march jauntily ahead to encourage them forward, make them try to keep up with him. Yet, all through the afternoon they continued to lose ground. They were lagging behind, an unforgivable sin in the Confederate Army. Four men fell while staggering up a long hill. The four were lying still, as if in death. The Yanks would almost certainly get them, but that was better than desertion.

The sun was fingering the treetops when Robin heard, faintly, the popping of musketry, far in front. They had been outmarched by two miles or more. The firing was running in waves up and down the line to the fore, and Robin knew it was sporadic because both forces were maneuvering into position. The attack would come later, probably the next morning, unless the Confederates decided to stage a night attack, a kill-and-be-damned charge, dreaded by the Yankees and anticipated with no pleasure by the rebels.

As the firing in front continued, the men in Robin's command quickened pace perceptibly. An air of purpose seemed to show in their steps as they now moved downhill in a field of bare-stripped, last year's corn stalks. Robin saw a forlorn, straggly nubbin that had, somehow, managed to hang through the winter on a stunted stalk. He broke it off, shucked it, shelled off its few grains; put some in his mouth, the remainder in his pocket.

It was then it happened, like quick sequences in a dream. Up front, and off to the right, Robin heard sharp, brassy, bugle blasts; then he saw a squadron of Union cavalry riding in a fast trot, rapidly getting in front of his company. The horsemen wheeled into charge formation barely out of musket range. A union major trotted his horse a few paces in front, lifted his saber, and slashed out the signal for a charge. The bugles blared again. At that moment Robin thought the fastest he ever had in his life and probably ever would again. He could order his men to fire. They would kill a few cavalrymen. Then, in their weakened condition, outnumbered at least five to one, they would be ridden down. No chance at all. Glancing back, he saw his Tar Heels preparing to fire.

Robin yelled, "Ground your arms. Hold your fire." He then turned to face the oncoming horseman calmly waving a handkerchief above his head. The charge slowed, halted a few yards from Robin.

"I take it, you want to surrender, Captain?" The Yankee major's voice was crisp, clear, disdainful.

"No other alternative," Robin said, matter-of-factly. "You have us cut off, far outnumbered. I see nothing to be gained by having my men killed to add to the glory-brags of bravery you might wish to tell to the homefolks. My men are in bad shape, and I ask you, as one soldier to another, to be as easy with them as possible. Right now the thing they need most is food. I ask nothing for myself." With that he reversed his sword and extended it toward the major. Then to his men: "Lay down your arms and consider yourselves prisoners of war."

The major reached for Robin's sword. "The etiquette of a gentlemanly surrender, I believe," he said, "calls for my returning your sword as a compliment to your gallantry." He took the blade, placed it over his knee, and broke it off about three inches from the hilt; then he extended the bladeless hilt toward Robin. "Please allow me to return your sword, Captain," he said.

Robin slowly took the broken sword, looked at it for a minute, then bent over and stuck the short piece of blade into the red Virginia clay and pushed it down tight with his heel. He then looked at the major. "My compliments, Major. May I make a private and personal observation, Sir?"

"You may."

"You are," Robin breathed slowly, "a pure and unadulterated, complete son-of-a-bitch."

CHAPTER NINETEEN

T HE PRISON CAMP WAS NOT TOO FAR OVER THE LINE IN PENNSYL-
vania. It was a small camp with the appearance of being new
and temporary, which indeed it was, since the Union officials
who ordered its construction knew the war was grinding itself
out to its inevitable conclusion. They knew the camp would not
be used for long. The guards, who looked husky and well fed,
made it a point to impress on their wards that they were prison
camp guards because they had all been rejected for various physical handicaps.

The prisoners were given two meals a day of sloppy quality,
sloppily prepared, but so much better, so much more in quantity,
than the Confederates had tasted for months, that they seemed
ambrosia-like. Robin's men, except for the small detail of camp
policing, lolled around, fraternized some with their guards, ate,
slept, and gained strength by the minute. Robin and the other
officers were given better quarters than the enlisted men, but they
were fed the same two meals a day. He cleaned up and mended
his uniform as best he could and felt strength flowing back into
his body like fresh spring sap enlivens a young and healthy sapling. He felt physically better and eyed the marked-off line,
guarded by sentries, beyond which he could not step.

The late March weather was unduly warm, even for Pennsylvania. The conflict was rushing headlong toward a close. They
said Grant was rapidly cutting off Lee's supply lines, preparing to
force surrender through starvation instead of bullets. The wolves
of retaliation were howling in both houses of Congress. One

noisy, but influential, senator made a speech in which he advocated, in no uncertain terms, the seizure of all property belonging to any man who voluntarily served in the Confederate Army, such assets to be divided among the black people as compensation for their generations of years of servitude. The ownership, or non-ownership, of slaves should, the senator said, make no difference for those who had volunteered to defend an iniquitous condition. They, he said, would have to pay for such treason. As to officers in the Confederate Army, the senator averred, there could be but one course. They must be court-martialed and sentenced to such terms in prison as their services to the Confederacy warranted. Some would have to be sentenced to death, particularly those who had been leaders in bringing about secession.

As Robin read these news stories and began to understand the utter hopelessness of the cause for which he had given four years of his life, the vindictiveness with which the South would have to cope when finally it was forced to lay down its arms, he felt desperation welling up within him. He thought of a thousand plans to escape and rejected all of them as pipe dreams. He found himself back in his boyhood when he had made nighttime plans to cook the goose of his professor, only to see how utterly unworkable they were when viewed in broad daylight. He'd had no mail since around Christmas, and he spent hours wondering how things were going in Modesty. How it would be there when the war was finally over.

He was lying on his cot, gazing at the tent's ceiling, when he heard a booming voice outside, and a moment later Joshua Todd walked in. Josh had late news from Modesty. It seemed he had heard regularly from Ellen Cogle. "You didn't know, you say," Josh asked, "that I am commandant of this camp? I escaped from prison, but since I have been here I have had to be in the hospital. Can't seem to get that old wound to heal just right. Got out this morning and saw your name on the prisoner list. Came around to see if it was the Robin Arvane I knew. I am truly sorry, Robin, to see you here, but believe me, I'll try to make it as easy for you as the Articles of War will allow. I don't think it will be for long. You'll be released almost as soon as the shooting stops."

"No," Robin answered, "I can't swallow that one, Josh; I've been reading the Washington papers lately, you know."

"Pay no attention to what those big mouths in either house of Congress say," Josh reassured him. "When the time comes, Lincoln and Grant will boss the terms of surrender."

"Hell," Robin said, "I don't have any faith in their good intentions, either."

"I don't see any point in our arguing the subject at this time," Josh said. "How have they been treating you here?"

"No particular kick for myself," Robin said, "but this Captain Stravo, who I thought until now was the camp commandant, has been, I believe, extremely abusive to some of my men. He tried several times to get an argument out of me. I refused to talk to the officious son-of-a-bitch."

"I know," Josh said; "he was my second in command. He was acting commandant while I was in the hospital. When I heard how he was running things, I had him transferred, and they sent me a Captain Arvane." Josh's eyes twinkled above a low chuckle. "In fact," Josh said, "I'm planning for the Arvanes to have a sort of family reunion in my quarters this evening, if they will come. I have some cousins of yours here I want you to meet."

Josh wrote Robin a parole-pass allowing him to leave the compound without a guard between seven and eleven that night. Josh's quarters were in a small shack a half-mile from the main gate. He told Robin how to get there and left with the admonition, "Remember you're on your honor to show up at my quarters at seven. You understand that, of course?"

Robin assured him he did.

When Robin found Josh's quarters and entered, he found another Confederate officer already there, along with a young Union captain. Josh made the introductions. The Union captain was Tom Arvane, from Illinois, the grandson of Robin's grandpa's brother. The Confederate officer was Major Fielding Jenkins, of Mississippi, grandson of another Arvane. Jenkins was a slender sun-bitten man of perhaps twenty-three, with Arvane physiognomy spelled out all over his face. The Illinois captain was a bit bulky for an Arvane, but the family resemblance, otherwise, was pronounced enough.

A bottle was passed around. Robin learned that his cousins knew the Ajax legends as well as he did. Josh sat back and listened to them interestedly. He learned that William Fielding Jenkins grew cotton in the Delta country—lots of cotton. Or, at least his folks had, in their day, grown lots of cotton. He didn't know what he would do when he got home, if the Yankees let him go home at all, but he thought if he could find enough money to finance one crop, he could get back into cotton growing again. He was not too much perturbed by the emancipation. Shucks, he could get enough more work out of free labor, working for money or shares, than he ever got out of slaves, to make up the difference. He said it was his firm belief his blacks would stick with him.

Tom Arvane said he was studying medicine when he gave it up temporarily to join up for the war. He would go back to it.

Robin admitted frankly he had no plans for the future except to get back to Modesty. He would, he said, feel his way on from there. Like cousin Fielding, Robin wasn't sure many commissioned officers would get home before serving long prison terms. "If I could break out from here and get back to Modesty before the surrender, which I can now see coming, I'd lay low until I saw which way things are going. If they were against me, I'd try to get to Mexico. I don't hanker to be in jail," he said.

"I think," said Tom Arvane, "that makes sense. I fully believe in the good intentions of Mr. Lincoln in dealing with the South, if he can handle that gang of vindictive hotheads around him. I say, Major, if Cousin Robin and Cousin Fielding should walk away from here tonight, how could we handle it to keep our records clean?"

"We couldn't," Josh answered; "it would be treason."

"Treason to what? We'd only be releasing a couple of Confederate officers who would, in turn, give us their solemn oaths that they would not again take up arms against the United States."

"The war department might object," Josh told Tom.

"I suppose they might, at that," Tom Arvane said, meditatively. "I sure would like to do something to see that my cousins don't wind up in prison."

Robin looked at Fielding and saw Fielding looking at him. Their glances crossed for a second, and each understood the other. Both sat back, simulated relaxation, waiting to see what Josh would say.

"There is," Josh said, ponderously, "a way we might be able to work this out. I said we *might* be able to work it. I could take their names off all records that have been furnished me. That is, have new ones copied, with their names not on them. Washington has copies of the original prisoner list, but I doubt it will ever come to a check-up. Meatime, I could let the word get out they have been transferred to another camp—and—no, that wouldn't work. Blast it, we'll just have to forget it. Gentlemen, this is a fine steak—shipped in from Iowa, I understand."

They ate in silence for a few moments, but it was evident that Tom Arvane, like a terrier, was still gnawing at the idea. "They could escape," he said.

"Not honorably," Josh reminded Tom. "After all, they are here as my guests, and on parole to return to their quarters at eleven o'clock. Knowing Robin as I do, I know he wouldn't violate his parole."

"Well," said Tom Arvane, vehemently, "knowing me as I do, if I were in their place, tomorrow morning would find me far and away from here." He folded his doily, crossed his knife and fork on his plate, muttered, "Excuse me," and left the table and paced back and forth across the floor.

Robin winked at Fielding. Fielding winked back. Robin got up, walked around the table to where he could see Joshua Todd's Colt six-shooters and holsters hanging on the wall. "Josh," he said, "I've always wanted one of these guns. May I examine it?" He broke the gun open, and as he suspected, it wasn't loaded. The gun belt was studded all the way around with cartridges, and he began loading the pistol's chambers. "Some gun," he breathed admiringly.

"Some gun, is right," Josh answered, "but unload it." He went on, "I don't like to have loaded guns around."

Robin loaded the pistol, walked back to the table, sat down. He cocked the gun, with the muzzle pointed in the general direction of Josh and Tom. "See that pistol, Josh, and you, too, Cousin Tom. I'm not making any threats, but I do want you to know I'm leaving your God-damn camp tonight. I hope Cousin Fielding decides to go with me."

Josh looked slightly flustered, but unafraid. "Suppose I say you can't. Suppose I remind you of your parole."

"I gave you my word to be here at seven, or a little after. Nothing was said about returning to my prison quarters," Robin said. "However, if I had promised, this is one time I believe I would break my word. This chance is too good to miss. As for you stopping me, Josh, you know me too well to try, as long as I have this gun at hand. I don't need to make any threats for you to know what would happen."

"Yes," Josh said, "I know you'd shoot me if I were foolish enough to tempt you. Give me your terms."

"We'll need a three-day ration of oats for two horses you're going to let us have, some blankets, all the food we can find around here wrapped in oilcloth, and of course we'll take your pistols. Is that about all, Fielding?"

"All I can think of," Fielding said.

"I'll go get the horses," Tom Arvane volunteered. "We can say you held me up and took them."

"You can't take that chance for me." Fielding spoke up. "Tell me how to find the picket line and I'll bring a couple of good nags in a few minutes." He was at the door almost before he got through speaking.

"Bring only one horse," Josh called gently, to Fielding. "I've got one of the army's finest staked out in the back yard here. Robin can ride him."

"Back in a minute," Robin heard Tom say, as he slipped easily out the door.

Josh was talking again, his voice rumbling. "I would head south through the edge of West Virginia and Kentucky. Keep to the back roads as much as possible. Since you'll have bright moonlight, try to do most of your traveling at night. Forge yourself a safe conduct pass from the Confederate Army and wear your uniforms. That way, if you meet up with Rebels you can get information and help, maybe. If you get captured by our men, you'll be uniformed soldiers, not spies."

Josh went on telling Robin about how he came back from a Georgia prison camp, after his escape, up through the mountains, hiding out by day with Union sympathizers and traveling at night. "When you find one family sympathetic to the South, they'll pass you on to others all the way from here to Modesty. At least, I think so."

Tom Arvane reappeared first. He had two neatly packaged bundles wrapped in oilcloth. "I remembered I had a small head of cheese and a loaf of bread the folks sent me. Made up two packs of rations with them. Cheese won't taste so good after a steady diet of two or three days, but it'll keep your strength up mighty well."

"Got a good horse. Didn't pick him for speed. He looks like a horse that could go from here to Mississippi without a single stop," Fielding said.

"Tell Ellen for me," Todd said, as Robin and Fielding were preparing to mount, "that I'll see her as soon as I can. Tell her that I still hope to come back to the valley to live, but if the people don't want me, we can always go to another section of the country. If you get caught, stick to your story. Don't ever let them know you're escaped prisoners."

The moonlight was a shimmery golden veil, draping itself over trees, bushes, and fence posts or pouring in a steady stream against the road in front as the riders eased their mounts southward, walking the horses in the softest part of the road until they were sure the prison camp was well to the rear. At a crossroad, two miles south of the camp, they were challenged by a lone sentry with a nervous quaver in his voice. Rising as high as possible in his saddle, Robin pulled his horse up, looked off to the right and called out, "All right, boys, let him have it." As the sentry looked hastily off the road, Robin dug his heels into the tall black he was riding, reining him straight for the sentry. The sentry dodged, but not in time to prevent the shoulder of the plunging horse from sending him back somersaulting into the ditch at the side of the road. The black wanted to run, and Robin let him have his head until he pulled up to a fast walk of his own volition. As Robin felt the tremendous power in the mount under him, his blood went singing through his body. He wanted to shout, "Modesty, here I come." He could hear Fielding pounding along behind but losing ground with every second. Robin decided to keep the black horse, whether he stayed in Modesty or decided Modesty was too hot for him.

The first streaks of dawn found them forty miles south of the camp. In the first hint of daylight they guided their mounts off the road and took to the woods. Fielding said as soon as they reached Kentucky he would turn right, try to cross the state to the western slopes of the Cumberlands, and slip through the Yankee lines that way. They both agreed that one man had less chance of capture than two traveling together. At noon they stopped, slept, and rested until almost dark, then picked their way back to the road and headed south.

As they penetrated further into the South they grew bolder. They still kept to side roads as much as possible but rode forward in broad daylight, keeping wary eyes in every direction, remaining on the alert. That afternoon they came to a large log farmhouse set well back from the road. Its roof was invisible from around a bend. Fielding said, "We don't know yet exactly where we are and we have to know. Keep out of sight, cover me, and I'll go up and ask at this house." Robin guided his mount into a thicket and dismounted, followed on foot.

He found a sassafras clump from which he could get a good view of the front door. Fielding knocked, was let in. After ten minutes he was still inside, and Robin grew restless. It might, he thought, be necessary for him to find out if Fielding was being held captive. Fielding came to the door and motioned. A white-haired woman wearing a lace cap let him in. She sent a black boy to stable their horses, explained that they were now in Kentucky, and invited them to spend the night, rest up a bit. She was sure if a Yankee patrol showed up she could keep them hidden. Robin knew he had to take what she said on faith, and he would have staked his life on that faith, but he didn't want her to run any risk because of them. She dismissed his suggestions with a grunt of disgust. "I have," she said, "a brother who is one of Lee's generals and an uncle who is a United States senator in Washington, so, pray tell me how I can get into any lasting trouble?"

That night she sketched out two rough maps for them. One for Fielding, crossing the state as he had planned. One for Robin, heading south through Kentucky toward Cumberland Gap, but not going all the way. He was to stay in the mountains but keep bearing left enough to take him diagonally across southwest Virginia. "You'll find," she said, "some of the people are ardent secessionists, some for the North, and some who don't care either way, but your greatest enemies are a few small bands of outlaws operating as so-called guerillas. Their missions are robbery, arson, and murder of anyone as long as they can make it pay. Of course they operate mostly in the mountains, though you can't rightfully say they are mountain men. More like a conglomeration of cutthroats assembled from the outlying portions of Hades. There's a ten-thousand-dollar reward from the State of Kentucky out for the Belton gang."

Robin and Fielding slept late the next morning, luxuriating in real beds. Next morning their hostess burst excitedly into their room. "Lee surrendered yesterday," she sang out with no trace of regret in her voice. "I'm so glad it's over. It was so useless to begin with, and so much more so as time went on. Gentlemen, can you come down to the drawing room right away? We are meeting there for prayer, and I would appreciate your presence."

Robin got out of bed and stood thoughtfully for a moment,

studying his cousin, but the expression on Fielding's face told him nothing. Then, after a moment, he saw tears gathering slowly in Fielding's eyes, his lips setting in hard lines. Robin turned away, wiped his own wet cheeks with the back of his hand. "God dammit. God dammit to Hell!" he said slowly, emphatically, as he pushed his right foot through his britches leg.

"Amen," he heard Fielding say, as he reached for his own outer clothing.

Shortly after the noon hour, a black boy came back from the nearest railway station with a late Washington newspaper. The terms of surrender were on the front page, and they were far more liberal than Robin had dared hope. In fact, their very liberality wiped his soul clean of most of the bitterness that had slowly accumulated and cankered through the past four years. That Reconstruction would later gall and fret him almost to the point of violence did not mean he would ever again feel an all-consuming hatred for any group who might honestly disagree with him. He felt planted within him, at that moment, a spark of tolerance that would stand him in good stead in many crises during the remainder of his life.

On the vehement insistence of their hostess they remained at the house until early next morning when, equipped with the rough maps she had helped prepare, but refusing to take more than token supplies from her meager stores, they rode away, never to see or hear from the lady again. At a later date Robin wrote her a note of thanks for her generosity, but his letter was returned, with the notation, "Mrs. Danvard is deceased."

At the first crossroads Fielding turned right, while Robin rode straight ahead after a brief hand-shake and the usual wishes for good luck. They had met as cousins. They parted as friends.

CHAPTER-TWENTY

T HERE WAS LITTLE TRAFFIC ON THE ROADS, BUT JUST THE SAME Robin kept his eye peeled at all times. Once, hearing horses to the rear, coming on fast, Robin rode off the road, sought concealment. They were Union troops. Just after passing his hiding place, they met a squadron of Confederate cavalry heading north. Both units stopped when they met. After a moment of conversation the Confederates surrendered their arms, the two commanders sat down by the roadside, and Robin saw the Yankee officer writing on a large sheet of white paper. The writing finished, the two officers affixed their signatures. In the meantime, the Union non-coms were handing out slips of paper to the members of the Confederate unit. Robin knew they were receiving safe conduct passes. Then the Union commander remounted, faced the men in gray and told them, "Now that your surrender has been completed, you will be asked to disband immediately. You are to be allowed to keep your horses, by order of General Grant, so that you may use them in making a crop this year. In my personal opinion, you have been granted the most liberal peace terms ever offered to a beaten people. It is not my doing, God knows, but luck to you. Consider yourselves disbanded and dismissed."

Robin contemplated going down to the Yankee officer and surrendering, getting it over. Then he thought about his horse having a U.S. Army saddle, and his having just escaped from prison, and dropped the idea. Even if they let him go with the others, they'd most certainly take his mount, and he figured he'd need the horse when he got back to Modesty. So, he sat still and waited until both sides disappeared and were well out of earshot before he made any move.

On the second day after that, at three hours past sunrise, Robin found the road he was following had petered down to a trail, barely passable for wheeled vehicles. He was resting on a rock in a gap through a high crooked ridge. He had climbed steadily since daybreak. Somewhere along the way he had wandered off from the course set by his map, but he knew he was somewhere in southeast Kentucky. Man and horse had eaten the last of their rations and both were still hungry.

From his perch on the rock, Robin studied the valley below through a thin smoky mist that swirled in the coves and spiraled over the peaks. Through it he could see a trail far below, and as his eyes followed the trail up the valley he spotted a rock chimney standing starkly naked and alone. Further, he spotted another and another. There was no smoke, so the burnings were not of recent hours. Guerillas had probably looted the valley. Robin wanted to use the trail below, for he saw where it led on to a gap in the next ridge. Softly whistling a nameless tune, he started down the trail leading the black horse.

The chimney at the first clearing stood woefully alone, with ashes from the house and outbuildings cold. The same was true in the next, and the next, place. The only signs of life were two scrawny chickens scratching around the ashes of the third house. He found some well-shaped throwing rocks, knocked both chickens over, picked, dressed, and put them away in his oilskin. Since he was without salt, he would have to cook them soon. He rode cautiously up the trail, his eyes searching in every direction. He didn't want to meet any guerilla band on the road, nor did he want to be bushwhacked from concealment along the roadside.

Robin saw the top of the chimney first, through the treetops; then he saw the roof. A house left standing. Could mean anything. Probably meant the occupants were friends of the guerillas who had burned the other homes in the narrow valley. He slipped to the ground, led his horse to a thicket, tied, then muzzled him with the crown of his hat in hopes that would keep him from nickering. He circled until he could approach the clearing from behind the corn crib. As he neared the back of the crib he could hear the voices of men arguing, cursing back and forth. He peeked around the crib's side and saw two large and burly men. One had a grey-tinged beard, the other black sideburns and a heavy mustache. "Iffen yuh hadn't of hit 'im so hard that last time, we could've made him talk. No, damn it, yuh had to come down too hard an' kill 'im. Now th' only chanct we got at that gold is to wait and ketch th' gal." The full beard ended up with a string of oaths.

"Do we git our hands on her, we c'n make her talk fast," observed the heavy mustache.

"Do we git our hands on her, I'll handle it. I'll make her tell where it is an' I won't have to beat her to do it, neither," the bearded man said. "We better start lookin'. 'Tothers'll be along in two-three hours. I want her caught 'fore they git here."

Both men were seated, hunkered down, with their backs to Robin. He squeezed the trigger on the Colt and saw, before the smoke could form a cloud, that the man nearest him was hit just under his left shoulder blade. Even as he pulled the trigger, Robin was on the move to the right, running fast. As he cleared the smoke he glimpsed the other man hastily grabbing a rifle that was leaning against a near-by tree. The Colt roared again, bucked hard against his hand. The man's knees sagged. He pitched forward slowly, lay still. Robin broke the Colt, slipped in two fresh cartridges; then, with his gun cocked, swinging in his right hand, he moved toward the men on the ground. The first was shot through the heart. The second had taken a bullet in his mouth, which had come out through the back of his head. Robin confessed later that his first thought was one of reverent admiration for Mr. Samuel Colt. Robin turned the two bodies on their backs, started searching pockets. He whistled low, but keenly, when he pulled a heavy buckskin bag of gold coins from an inner pocket of the first. Probably called themselves guerillas, but these are just plain, ordinary cutthroats, Robin thought.

Robin dropped the two bags of money in the side pockets of his own coat, then stood looking down at the dead bandits, wondering what should be his next move. The sensible thing to do, he knew, would be to get further, fast. On the other hand, he had heard them say something about a girl, and there would be others along in a short time looking for her. He decided to hide out and wait to see what happened when the others arrived.

At that moment he heard a voice from the direction of the corn crib: "Stand still, don't move, if you want to live." The voice was low-pitched, half-hysterical, and feminine.

Robin turned slowly toward the voice. He saw a girl with dark wavy brown hair, eyes as blue as the bluest pools in Modesty Creek. Her skin was fair, her features in smoothly chiseled lines. She was neither large nor small. She was beautiful. At the moment, she stood with a rifle pointed waveringly at Robin. There was near panic in her eyes, in her every movement. Then, as Robin turned and she caught a full sight of his uniform, she sighed breathlessly. "Oh, thank God, a real army officer!"

She dropped the gun and started toward him, reeling on rubbery legs. Robin met, caught her as she fell forward. She clung to him, her head against his chest, weeping. Robin stroked her hair, wiped the tears off her cheeks lightly with the tips of his fingers, patted her lightly on the side of her face. He led her to the back steps of the house, sat down, kept talking in an effort to calm her. She would stop momentarily, start to speak, then go back into a fit of weeping. Robin loosed her, then stepped back, shouted sternly, "Now shut up, tell me about it, if you want me to help you." He was trying to shock her into coherence.

She stopped for a moment and looked straight at him; her lips parted, her eyes widened, she leaned back and screamed piercingly. Drastic conditions call for drastic measures, Robin thought. He bent toward her, swung his hand, palm open, against her cheek. Her mouth snapped shut in midscream; the wild look left her eyes. She looked at him, panting rapidly. "You—you—hit me," she said sorrowfully, in bepuzzled wonderment.

At that moment Robin Arvane fell in love deeply, unequivocally, and forever. In the next moment he was groveling before her. "I'm sorry. I wouldn't hurt you for anything in the world, or out of it. I thought it would make you stop crying. Here, take my gun and shoot me for the low-down thing I am." He held his gun toward her. Then, not knowing what else to say, he said, "I don't know your name, but I know you are the loveliest creature on God's green earth."

He realized she was no longer crying. Her face was settling into calmer lines. "Did you hear me?" Robin pleaded. "I'm trying to tell you how lovely you are."

She was calm now. "I heard," she said, "and I thank you. And this is for saving my life." She pulled his face down, then turned his mouth up to hers.

She told him her name was Sarah Susan Bassett, but she had always been called Sallie. He told her his name was Robin Arvane and he had always been called Robin, and he didn't want her to make the mistake of addressing him as Captain or Mister. They agreed on that; then she told her story, quickly, succinctly.

She was, she explained, an orphan. Her father had operated a private school for boys in Louisville until a year before, when he had closed it and gone away to join the Union army. Being without other kin, he had sent her to his brother here in eastern Kentucky to wait out the war. Since her father's death a few months after he joined up, she had remained with her uncle, keeping house for him. Her uncle, who was several years older than her father, was a bachelor, and not too strong. He had been in business in Washington before his health failed and he came to the mountains to live. Here he had kept one horse for a little patch farming of things to eat, a few good books for pleasure and contentment.

The two men Robin had killed were two of four Belton brothers, leaders of a notorious outlaw guerilla gang. How they had learned her uncle had a cache of gold around the place she never knew, but they had either learned about it, or surmised as much.

Anyway, there was a cache of gold, between five and six thousand dollars, somewhere around the place. Her uncle had never told her where he had hidden it, but had, more than once, told her it would be hers when he passed on. He had figured he would never use more than a thousand dollars, or a little more, during his lifetime. Her uncle, she explained, feared the Beltons, so much so that he had built a cleverly concealed false wall in the corn crib and put a cot in back of it, for her to hide in. One day the Beltons did come, as her uncle had expected. They came up the valley, burning and pillaging as they came. They had seen the smoke from the burning buildings, and her uncle had made her go to her hide-out while he waited in the front yard with loaded rifle. He had pulled down on them as they rode up to the house and ordered them off his property. They had sat their horses and told the old man he didn't have a chance, but if he would give them the money they knew he had hidden on the place, they would go away and not burn him out. It was then that someone had shot the rifle out of her uncle's hands, from ambush, and the gang rushed him.

Her uncle had warned her time and time again, even to the point of extracting a solemn promise, that no matter what might happen, she was not to show her face to the Beltons at any time. So she had lain in the hide-out and heard them abusing her uncle; then she had heard them leave. When she ventured out she found her uncle dead and the bandits gone. She presumed they had made him tell where his gold was. She had stayed on because she had nowhere else to go, and since they had taken the horse, no way to leave except walk, if she had a place to go. Mostly, in daytime, she had hidden in the woods and crept back to her hiding place to sleep when night came.

She had been in her hide-out when they came this time, and she had learned then that they hadn't found her uncle's money after all. She had her rifle, she said, aimed through a crack and was trying to catch them lined up in such a way that she could get both with one shot from the heavy bear gun when Robin came up.

"Oh, damn, damn, damn such people," Robin swore. "Get your things together quick. I'm taking you away from here. You can ride one of the horses tied out front. We'll have to hurry, before the remainder of the gang gets here. I took about twenty pounds of gold off those two over there. It belongs to you for part of what they made you lose. When I know you're safe, I'll get some men from Modesty and we'll come up here and clean out the remainder of the gang. I promise that."

"I'll soon be ready," she said, "in about ten minutes. I know we have to hurry. You can't give me any part of the money you got off them. I won't take it. Not any part. I do wish, however, I knew where Uncle hid his gold."

"I know," said Robin slowly, "where he hid it. It has to be there. See those martin jugs?" He pointed to four jugs hanging from crossarms on a pole. The jugs had small punctures in their bottoms to let water through, and holes half the size of a man's fist knocked through at their shoulders. Such jugs were a common sight along the countryside, serving as nesting places for those fierce little hawk-fighting birds.

"Notice," Robin went on, "that the jug on this end doesn't sway the least in the breeze, while the others swing gently back and forth. That means it's weighted heavily." Robin walked nearer, took a careful bead, and shot the rawhide thong supporting the jug for a clean break. The jug fell, broke open; gold coins streamed out on the ground. "Hand me a poke to put it in," Robin called, "and hurry and get ready to leave."

CHAPTER TWENTY-ONE

In a few minutes she was out dressed in worn, but city-style clothes, carrying a small carpet bag in her hand. "This is all I'll need to take," she said.

"You won't need any more," Robin told her; "you're a rich girl now. Throw your money into your bag while I get you a horse from out front. Unless you have your own saddle, you'll have to ride straddle."

"I thought of something else," Robin said, as he came back with the horse. "How much powder and lead do you have around?"

"About two hundred loads, with lots of caps, up in my hideout. Why?" she wanted to know.

"Little experiment in disaster. Hurry while I get down a jug."

Robin found, on inspection, that the martin jugs were fastened with a slip string so that they could be lowered, or raised, from the ground without climbing the pole or using a ladder. By the time she came with the powder and hand-moulded bullets he had lowered one of the jugs to the ground. Quickly he scattered caps over its bottom; then he put in a mixture of powder and bullets for three inches, then another layer of caps. He went on with the procedure until the jug was filled. Handling it carefully, he then pulled the rawhide string until the jug was raised to a height of eight feet, or so, from the ground, before he refastened the string. Next, he dragged the bodies of the two outlaws and placed them prone directly under the trap. "Let's go," he said, dusting his hands. He pointed to the woods in the rear. "Head that way, leading your horse. I'll get mine and meet you."

A few minutes later he came to where she waited, two hundred feet from the house, behind a dense growth of laurel and rhododendron. As he came to where she was, he constantly jerked the rein lightly on the black horse to keep him from whinnying. He noted with gratitude that she was doing the same with the neat little bay mare he had taken from the hitching post in front of the house. Handing her the horse's rein, he cocked an ear. "U-m-m-m," he muttered, "there they are." Without saying more he slipped silently away, back toward the house.

"I'll be waiting here," she called softly.

Before he got where he could part the bushes and peer through the yard, Robin could spot several horses tied to the front fence by their nervous stamping. He saw six piratical looking men, ranging in age from twenty to sixty, he judged, standing looking down at their two dead comrades.

"They're dead," someone in the crowd said. "Let's get out of here." He turned to leave.

"Wait," a tall man wearing two pistols called out. "I see they're dead, but I can also see that Will's hoss is gone. So whoever done it, got away on his hoss. Let's see if they was robbed by th' bastard as shot 'em."

All six crowded forward, bent around the dead bandits. "I hope it works," Robin said to himself as he crouched behind a tree and aimed at the loaded jug hanging over the heads of the desperados. It worked. The jug exploded with a roar, blowing the martin pole into smithereens and scattering broken, bleeding bandits all around for twenty feet. From behind the tree, Robin felt onrushing air from the blast and heard whistling bullets clipping leaves and small limbs.

It was a little while before the smoke cleared sufficiently for him to inspect the results. Methodically Robin started going through the pockets of the dead bandits, taking what money he could find on them. He found it in amounts from a few hundred dollars up to more than two thousand, all in gold coins. He was looking around for a container to put the haul in, when Sallie appeared at his elbow. "I realize," she told him seriously, "it's sinful to be glad anyone is dead, but right now I'm one of the happiest people in the world."

"I know," Robin said, "how you feel, and I should feel that way too, but somehow I don't. For some reason, I feel like a civilian again, and killing isn't rightfully a civilian's business."

"Will the thoughts of killing this many people, all in one day, haunt you in your dreams, Robin?" she asked, her voice serious.

"No," Robin told her, "at least I hope not. Rightfully, I shouldn't consider putting that kind away as killing, in the true sense of the word."

Robin went to see about the horses tied at the front fence. He found each horse carrying a half-bushel bag of shelled corn, while the saddle bags were stocked with food. "They were on their way, pulling out of the country," he explained to the girl. "This was probably meant to be their last haul in this part of Kentucky."

She walked toward him, reached her arms up around his neck, kissed him soundly.

"Don't do that any more," Robin pleaded banteringly, "unless you aim to marry me. Look around, now that we can afford to take more time, and see if there's anything else you want to take. We have plenty of time, and plenty of pack horses. I turned them loose, but I can easily round up some of them."

"Outside of Uncle's books there's nothing here I want," she said.

"I'll catch a horse to take them."

When Robin came back she had arranged two packs with bed sheets, tying the books into them in such a way as to balance their load when they were put on the horse. "I put a pair of Uncle's pants on under my dress so I can ride straddle with due modesty," she giggled.

The Hembree family, she said, were friends of her uncle, though she had never met them. They could make it there that day, if they started right away. It was some fifteen miles beyond the gap. Robin noticed as they rode along that her dress rode high up on her thighs and that the trousers had been cut off at her shoe tops, so they constantly climbed to her knees. Sallie noticed him covertly watching her limbs. She lifted one foot from the stirrups and held it out. "Anything wrong with my calf?" she asked, laughing.

"Not that I noticed. Excuse me for looking," Robin said. "I won't be guilty again."

"Why not? I think I have pretty calves, and I can assure you this is a private showing, meant for you exclusively."

"I see," Robin told her, "that I'm going to have to marry you to keep you from being a hussy, and that I'll have to beat you often."

After they passed through the gap, Robin guided them off the road and found a likely hiding place in the forest a half-mile back. There he counted her gold and found it was an even five thousand and ten dollars. The amount he had taken from the bandits he estimated at approximately fifteen thousand. Pouring it all together, he then divided it into four parts, holding out a thousand dollars, which he put back in one of the buckskin bags and placed in his pocket. The four divisions were then placed in the bottom of their saddlebags. "This way," he explained, "if we're stopped and searched, they may think this is all we have when they find the bag in my pocket, and we may be able to talk our way clear by surrendering it. We really ought to hide it all and come back later for it, but on the other hand, it probably will be just as dangerous to travel with it a year from now as it is at present. Too, we may be on the move for several months and not have a chance to come back for it. If we're caught, we have as good a chance of living as we'd have if we didn't have it. In fact, probably better, because we could always tell them we have more where that came from, and maybe talk our way out."

"You're in command," she said.

That night they stopped with the Hembree family, whom they found living in the wasteland of precarious day-to-day existence on corn pone, wild salads gathered from fence corners, and whatever game the head of the house could knock down. There was

a stunted cow which gave a trickle of milk for the smaller ones
of the numerous Hembree brood. Dimler Hembree explained
that the Lord had been extremely good to them, in that they had
not gone hungry one whole day throughout the winter, despite
the fact that his sawmill had long since ceased operations. Sallie
told the Hembrees about their experiences with the Belton gang,
omitting, of course, reference to the gold. When she finished telling how she had sneaked into the yard in the night and manhan-
dled her uncle's body to a grave she had prepared in the woods,
she sobbed uncontrollably for a minute in the arms of Mrs. Hembree.

When the girl had herself under control again, Hembree asked,
"Air yuh shore the Belton gang is all kilt, plumb dead, all eight
o' them?"

When Robin assured him that he was positive there were eight
members of the gang dead, and told the manner of their going,
Hembree said, "Let us pray!" He knelt on the uneven floor by a
rough homemade table. First, Hembree thanked the Lord for
sending Robin to rid the world of such men as the Beltons. He
told the Lord how Robin had acted as the Sword of Gideon, cutting down the weeds of wickedness so that His children might
bloom and prosper in the good things of God. He wound up by
again thanking his Maker, and admonishing him to make the
Belton gang's punishment fit their crimes, so that they might
look out from the gates of Hell a thousands years hence and gnash
their teeth in agony and repentance for their misdoings. Crimes
that had doomed them to a million, million years of torture in
the flames of Hell's furnaces.

Robin couldn't quite understand some of the parallels his host
drew from the Holy Writ, but he agreed with the general princi-
ples of the prayer.

They shared, with the Hembrees, from the provisions they had,
which provided for that family, in all probability, the best meals
they had enjoyed for months. The Hembrees made no comment
about Robin and Sallie traveling together, though they were un-

married, except in a roundabout way. Hembree said, "These be funny times, an' folks've got to do th' best th'y kin."

As they were saddling up to leave, he told them, "Fr'm what I kin hear, y'u don't need to duck an' dodge no more. The Confeds is a-fillin' the road, goin' home, an' th' Yankees y'u mought meet won't bother y'u a-tall. An' th'y say them bridges and ferries is still a-workin' down Abingdon an' Bristol way."

"How fur be'n't y'u goin'?" he asked Sallie.

"She's going to Crinshaw County in North Carolina to marry me," Robin put in. Sallie blushed prettily but held her tongue.

They presented the pack horse carrying the books to the Hembrees, asked them to save the books until they were sent for, and advised them to look for the horses they had left behind.

As they rode, Robin could tell Sallie was sore in every muscle from riding the day before, so he took it easy until he knew she had had plenty of time to limber up. Several times, as they talked, Robin mentioned Modesty Valley and Crinshaw County. "In some vague way, Modesty sounds familiar," she told him, "but, for the life of me, I don't know why. Crinshaw County doesn't mean a thing, yet Modesty has a familiar sound."

"Probably heard it so much from me it sounds familiar," he answered.

In midafternoon they were stopped by a patrol of Union troops. Robin had his pistol out of sight, hoped they wouldn't search him.

"You got a safe conduct paper, Captain Johnny Reb?" the sergeant patrol leader asked. "Two fine horses you got there. Got papers for them?"

"I'll surrender," Robin bluffed, "but please let my wife go. To tell the truth, I deserted. Stole this horse from our picket line. Knew the war was about over and decided I didn't want to stick around any longer. Came over by Kentucky to get my wife, then headed for home in Carolina. If we hadn't learned this morning the war's over, we'd be sneaking through your lines."

"The news is," the patrol leader explained, "they're lettin' the rebs keep their horses to make a crop with, in most instances, and givin' safe conducts to get home on. Orders don't say nothin'

about how to handle deserters an' stragglers. We met up with
several today, said they was stragglers, an' we let 'em go. Cheaper, an' easier to let 'em go, I figure. Me, I can't see no difference
between a man as deserted the rebs an' one that surrendered.
Now, if you happen to have a little chawing tobacco, we can
really talk business."

"Don't have any chawing. Don't have any money. Don't
have anything but enough rations for about one more meal.
You're welcome to that," Robin answered earnestly.

"Looks like to me you ain't got nothin' but the purtiest gal in
the South for a wife, an' two good hosses. We can't take your
wife, an' we don't need your hosses. If you're goin' this way don't
spend the night at no houses along the road. They's all kinds o'
people on this road, and while you ain't got nothing but them
hosses, well, a man on foot-back'd do most anything for a hoss,
especially when his shoes is wore out an' he's a long way from
home. My advice is get off the roads an' hide out to camp when
night comes. You could make it easy by yourself, but with that
purty girl. . . ."

He waved the patrol forward and rode away.

CHAPTER TWENTY-TWO

THEY RODE ON UNTIL THEY CAME TO A TURNOFF LEADING EAST-ward from the Abingdon road. It was a dim and crooked trail, pointing haphazardly toward the mountain ridges rising in the east, and southeast. As the sun dropped lower, the road became rougher, until it was little more than a fair trace among rock-choked weeds. The homesteads and cabins along its side became smaller and smaller, and further apart. There were signs of oc-cupancy, but no sign of occupants. The people, Robin reasoned, were away in their fields at work, trying to coax another crop out of soil badly leached during four years of wartime scarcities.

These people, here in the foothills, who had stuck to their homesteads, regardless of size or worth, through four years of sending their best manhood to the war, with the remainder stay-ing at home trying to do their part financially for the Cause, had courage of a high order. Theirs was a courage they didn't know they had. A determination which they believed was prompted only by a desire to keep on living. Yet, Robin thought, had they been motivated only by a desire for existence, it would have been easier for them to pick up and move. Go into an adjoining town, where they would have been sure of less hard work and easier living. They felt, Robin knew, without realization, that by sticking to their acres, keeping them in some kind of production, they were fighting along with their men. A man off fighting a war likes to feel that the folks at home are keeping things as much as pos-sible the way they were before he left.

When the road was smooth enough, Robin rode by Sallie's

side and they talked seriously, told stories about their childhoods, laughed, and a few times sang together. While Robin had been raised to hold nothing but the greatest respect toward the pristine purity of good women, he was, nevertheless, not the least monkish in his imaginings about beautiful girls. Too, he would have been one of the first to confess that any human female over fifteen and under fifty is a beautiful girl to a soldier after several months in the field. It was thus he got a small shock of wonderment in the fact that Sallie aroused in him first a greater desire to protect than to cohabit. He knew in some vague way he was in love, and he was glad of it, even if it ended right there. After all, she hadn't even promised to marry him, yet. She must trust him completely, else she would not be here. He would like to settle the question, once and for all, of whether she would marry him when they reached Modesty; yet, to ask her while they were this far from civilization, he thought, would be taking an unfair advantage. He resolved to have a showdown the minute he got her where she was completely safe.

"What are you thinking about so seriously?" she asked Robin.

"I'm thinking," he told her, "nice thoughts, but I can't tell you what they are until you are safe in my Ma's house in Modesty Valley."

"They can't be very nice thoughts to make you frown like that," she said teasingly, and he heard her silvery, tinkling laugh spill into the Virginia sunshine.

They still had an hour of sunlight when Robin left the trail and guided them along the edge of an abandoned clearing that skirted a cut-over hillside. Their horses' heads were pointed southeast toward the misty peaks of Carolina's southern Appalachians, which were dimly silhouetted in the distance. The girl rode behind Robin now, silent, uncomplaining, even though the pace he set was hard over the rough ground and the little bay had to stretch her legs to keep up with the fast-walking black horse. Robin was alert, an eye out for other travelers, while at the same time he looked for a likely place to camp where they would have small chance of discovery by others.

He led until the trail became a footpath meandering through the woods, dipping and twisting around thickets. In some places limbs intertwined over the path so heavily they had to dismount while their horses bent legs to allow saddles to scoot under the archway. "Sorry to make you walk, honey," Robin said, "but this little old trail points where we're going. When it runs out, we'll have to take to the brush. We won't be able to make as good time through the brush, but we'll be able to ride most of the time, maybe."

"You're the cap'n," she said, and tossed him a rare, trusting smile. "We can play Indian. You can be the heap big brave chief and I'll be the lovelorn princess chasing you through the forest with evil designs on your virtue." Robin heard her giggling quietly to herself, and again that achy feeling of exaltation welled up in him, went tingling through his being. Though they hadn't stopped to eat a bite since early that morning, Robin did not feel the least pang of hunger. He felt like he was being pushed onward toward something, some distant reward, or destiny, that seemed to be pulling him like a lodestar, hurriedly forward, to meet and have done with the next few hours as soon as possible.

The path ran out, and Robin took a peak in the distance for his guidepost and headed toward it. They stopped to camp as the sun went down. Robin slipped off his horse and Sallie started to climb off hers stiffly, then tumbled into his arms. He held her against him for a minute, then walked her around until the stiffness had gone from her limbs. He knew she was tired, hungry, and probably vastly discouraged. There was a small spring bubbling up by a large grove of willows. The spring's run tumbled into a little stream, which sang a gurgling melody as it disappeared in the stillness of the woods. The willows were thick and they grew around a sandy cleared spot in the center of the grove. The rain-spattered remains of a cooking fire, plus a cooking pot hanging on a convenient limb, told Robin the place had been used for a camp before, but not for the past few days. He looked around for tracks and decided not more than one person had used the camp. He saw Sallie looking at the dead ashes of the old fire, quizzically eying the cook pot, before her face turned toward his. "Yeah," he said, "this camp's been used by somebody lately, but it's too nice to leave; besides, you're much too tired to go on. We'll spend the night here. You can bed down in here and I'll keep watch outside." He was arranging her blankets.

"You," she sighed contentedly, "are the cap'n." She dropped on the blanket, tucked her head down on one arm for a pillow, and was sound asleep when Robin came back from fixing the horses for the night. Robin sat on his heels for a few minutes resting, looking at the face of the sleeping girl. Finally, her face twitched slightly, she groaned, turned over facing away from him, while the cadence of her breathing told him she was, for the time being, dead to the doings of this world. His heart ached in the presence of her loveliness. After a while he reluctantly pushed himself up, found some dry wood, got a blaze going, and opened the ration package.

The pone and side meat were laid out neatly on the oilskin when Robin dropped to his knees by the sleeping girl and called her gently. She stirred, turned her face upward, but slept on. She didn't wake when he cradled her head in his arms and rocked gently back and forth. Then he leaned over, kissed her softly, almost reverently. Her lids fluttered, wide at first, then, as realization came, she lifted her arms and pulled him fiercely toward her, lifted her mouth to his. For several moments they were still, locked together in their first kiss that fully acknowledged lovers' passion. Then Robin stood up, shakily, lifted her to her feet.

"I love you!" he chanted, in a half-singsong. "I love you, I love you!"

"You told me that, without saying it, when you kissed me, but I like to hear it in words. The more times, the better. Don't ever quit saying it. Not ever."

"I'll shout it from the top of Mount Acacia, if you want me to," he told her. "I'll tell every soul in Modesty how much I love my wife. That's the way I want us to arrive in Modesty, as Robin Arvane and his new wife."

She pondered for a moment, her brow slightly puckered in

puzzlement. "Robin, that name, Modesty. It's strangely familiar, half-remembered, from some story connected with my early childhood. How large a town is Modesty?"

"Well," he explained, "Modesty can't rightfully be called a town. It's a settlement in Modesty Valley. It was settled by my grandpa Ajax Arvane and his partner, Zebulon Cedric. Wait until I tell you about them."

"What town is Modesty nearest?" she wanted to know.

"Bless your sweet soul," Robin told her, laughing, "Modesty isn't near any town. The town of Anserville, though, is near Modesty."

Her face lit up. "I have it now. Modesty Valley is the place mother and grandfather lived when she was small. She told me all about it but said it would be better not to tell others. She said Grandfather had to leave there because some woman told lies on him. She didn't say what kind of lies, but I think she wanted to marry him. Anyway, Mother said they left there one night, and she never saw the place again. It's a beautiful and rich valley, she said."

"Your mother said they left there and never went back? I believe I know the name of everyone who ever lived in the valley. What was your grandpa's name, honey?" Robin asked.

"Gherkim. Peter Gherkim. Ever hear of him?"

"Seems like I have," Robin answered, slowly. "Would it make any difference to you about going to live in Modesty if you should find your mother was—well, slightly mistaken about your grandpa?"

"She wasn't," Sallie said, flatly. "He died about two years after they left Modesty, of typhoid, in Salem, and he's buried there."

"Did you ever see his grave?" Robin asked slowly.

"No, of course not." Anger flashed in her eyes. "What is this? What are you trying to say, Robin? That I don't know where my grandfather is buried, or that I didn't have one?"

Robin stepped in close, caught her to him, held her tight against his chest. At first she held herself back, then she stood still, rested her head against his shoulder. "Sweetheart," Robin said, "please listen closely until I'm through, and remember, I'd rather cut my throat than have to be the one to tell you what you're going to hear."

"Go on, Robin," she said, her voice muffled against him.

So Robin told her the story of the execution and burial of Peter Gherkim. Told it just as she would hear it in the valley. Told it flatly, without embellishments. Told her, "When we reach the valley and anyone starts to tell you the story of Peter Gherkim, tell them you don't want to hear it any more, that you heard it from me, and you consider the story unpleasant. The people of the valley are kind. They'll respect your wishes. They'd better," he added, as an afterthought.

He could feel her body trembling as he told the story. Finished, he stood stroking her hair, while she seemed to burrow her face deeper into the front of his coat. Suddenly she was shaking with fierce sobs. "I'm ashamed," she cried thinly. "Oh, Robin, I'm so ashamed."

"You have nothing to be ashamed of, except me. I can see how you might be ashamed to be hooked up with me, but I don't see how I can let you go now, even if you are ashamed of me."

"I don't mean it that way, you fool," she cried. "I'm ashamed for myself. And unhappy. Oh, Robin, I can't go home with you now. I can't face your people. What would they think of you? What would they think of me? Or both of us? Don't you see, I would be pointed out and laughed at behind my back. You'd be laughed at. I couldn't stand that. I would know it. You would know it. After a while I wouldn't be able to face you. As soon as we get back on a decent road I'll go and leave you to return to Modesty Valley and your own people without me."

"You," Robin said flatly, "will do nothing of the kind. If you won't go to Modesty with me, then I'll go with you, wherever that may be. We can head for the West, if you want to, or any place. We have the money, you know. Wherever you go, I'm taking you. The only place I'd live without you would be in Hell."

"No, my dearest," she said, "I love you for what you're saying, but it couldn't work out. You might some day remember. And

remembering might hurt. I know I might remember, and feel
shamed. Especially if things shouldn't go so well with us. I might
start blaming myself. Try to see it my way."

"I can't," Robin said in a hurt voice, "understand your way of
reasoning. Let's drop the subject now and discuss it later. I can't
help feeling that if you loved me, as I do you, you'd be as willing
to go with me to the ends of the earth as I'm willing to go with
you."

"Darling," Sallie said, "I believe you're telling the Gospel
truth; truth as you see it. But what is true today is not always
true tomorrow. I love you so much it hurts. I mean," she was
groping for words, "my love is exalting to—to my soul; and my
body's desire is so intense it hurts. I pray you to understand what
I mean, without thinking I'm a bad woman. If I married you, I
would, I'm afraid, live in dread that the ghost of Peter Gherkim
would one day walk between us, twisting at our pride, pushing
us apart. I try to think it would make no difference with you, but
I fear for my silly pride, the pride of a jealous woman, which is
not always based on reason, or so my father always said. If I gave
myself to you, without marriage, which I would do if I did only
what my body craves, I would want to know even then that I
was for you and you alone, and forever; still I would always have
the thought, gnawing at my soul, that if you would take me that
way, you might take another. Oh, Robin, say you wouldn't want
me except as a wife; say it, please!"

"I can't say that," Robin told her. "I do want you, and always
shall, but I can say I'd rather have you as a wife. You have planted something inside me, some inner strength, call it love of God
if you want—that I didn't have before. I'm not being disrespect-
ful when I say I want you in my bed, now and forever, and if you
have no better reasons than the ones you mentioned, the subject
isn't closed, not by a damn sight."

Sallie's face flushed, but her tone was still quiet, intense. "Robin, it couldn't work out. Peter Gherkim's granddaughter couldn't
live in Modesty Valley with you, or anyone else for that matter.
And she wouldn't allow you to leave the valley, the way you love

it, because of her. Don't you see?"

"No," he answered forcefully. "I don't see. I think you're
trying to be honest with yourself, with me; but it doesn't make
sense. It sounds silly. Of course," he added quickly, "if you
couldn't be silly once in a while, I would be afraid to get within
ten feet of you."

"If that's the way you feel I wish I could be so silly you
wouldn't get a thousandth of an inch away from me, ever." She
laughed, but there was a slight catch in her throat, undertoning
her laughter.

"We are supposed to be two grown-up folks, yet here we are
carrying on an argument that would sound foolish to a seven-
year-old. I'm not going to talk about it any more, at least, not tonight. Go on to bed. I'll bed down out by the spring and keep
my eye out for things." Thus Robin told her good night.

CHAPTER TWENTY-THREE

H E SAW ABOUT THE HORSES AGAIN, PICKED UP HIS OWN BLANKET roll, kicked dirt over the fire, and slipped through the willows to the side of the spring. He found dry ground at the root of a giant poplar, where he prepared to doze watchfully through the night.

With his haunches drawn up so his head rested on his knees, with the pistol across his lap, he slept; dozed fitfully, ready to come awake at the slightest untoward sound. Another trick four years of war had taught him. The noise that woke Robin was no slight, cracking twig. Someone was blundering toward them, following the course of the stream, grunting and swearing to himself as he came. His clumping feet told Robin their visitor was toting a heavy load, something that was probably unhandy to carry. Because the intruder was carrying a small candle-burning lantern, Robin could see, when he came within a hundred feet, that he was alone and that he had a bulky object on his shoulder. In the dim light Robin could see a rifle barrel sticking up over the man's back and knew it was supported by a strap across his chest and over one shoulder. He stood up with his pistol hanging loosely, cocked, in his right hand. The intruder dropped his load to the ground by the spring, let out a sigh of fatigue; then by his lantern's light he saw the fresh tracks of Robin, Sallie, and the horses. He carefully set the lantern down, started to unsling his rifle. "What the hell?" he growled.

"Hold it," Robin called, sharply. "Leave the gun where it is, pick up your lantern, and light a shuck back down the hill. Don't stop going before morning, if you want to keep living."

"Who is it?" the intruder asked, shakily.

"You mean who are we, don't you?" Robin answered. "We're Confederate stragglers who haven't surrendered yet. We've taken over these woods. So, move on, but keep your light going. Our men are listening to what I say, and they'll be on top of you the minute you put out that light. You look to me like a Yankee deserter. If you are, we don't like you. But if you can prove you really are a Yankee deserter, we'll let you spend the night and talk it over with you in the morning. Take your choice."

"Can I take my venison?"

"Cut us half and take the rest. Leave us half your salt, too. But work fast."

"I don't have but a pound of salt, and a few other things, all hid in the hollow of that poplar. I don't think I can spare the salt."

"Nobody asked you what you can spare. Leave half the salt, and venison, and you can take the rest, if you hurry, and leave off the back talk."

A few minutes later Robin could see reflections from the lantern flashing in and out among the trees as his late visitor made rapid time going down the slope, following the stream. "Poor fellow is a Yankee deserter, sure as hell," Robin told himself, soberly.

Then Sallie was standing beside him. "I woke up and heard it all. Will he be back?" imploringly.

"No," Robin reassured her. "He was a lone polecat in this den and he won't be back. We can sleep without posting a guard now," he laughed shortly.

Her hand found his. Gently she led him through the willows, and to her bed on the soft sand. "Please, Robin, listen and don't interrupt till I'm through. Promise?"

"I promise," he told her.

"I told you," she said, "I woke up. That wasn't true. I haven't been asleep. I was thinking. I know I can't leave you, ever; that is, never as long as you want me. I want to marry you, now, tonight, right this minute. I want to feel as sure of you as only marriage can make me. Come what may, I want this to be our wedding night, Robin. We can get married here, right now, and later if you want a ceremony performed, I will go through with it, but it won't make me feel any more married to you than I shall feel tomorrow morning. Do you understand, darling?"

"I understand the words," said Robin, "but how am I to know you mean them?"

"Darling," she implored, "you can have me either way. It's your choice. For as long as I live I'm yours, and I will cling to you no matter what may come, good or bad." She walked into his arms, her silhouette enveloped in the eerie darkness of the willow thicket.

Clinging to him, her voice husky with emotion, she spoke softly, but clearly, "I, Sallie Bassett, do here in the presence of God, take Robin Arvane to be my husband. Now, darling, you say the same."

"I can't remember all the fine words you used," he told her, "but I promise God to live up to all you said."

"Then we're married and I thank the Good Lord for you, Robin Arvane."

"And I thank the Good Lord for you, Sallie—Arvane." They clung together, and never was a bridal kiss more impassioned.

Sallie turned away, sank into her bed. "It's getting late, husband," she said gayly. "Come on to bed." Robin started unbuttoning his coat.

The next morning they decided that since they had a haunch of venison on hand, salt, and a cooking pot, they would delay going back to Modesty until they had a honeymoon of their own making. Although Robin ached to see his folks and hungered for a sight of the valley, he was also fierce in his desire to keep Sallie to himself for at least a time. Thus it was, after crossing the river and making a turn to the south, they found a honeymoon site. There was a ten-by-ten dry rock cavern overlooking a large rock-studded pool in a creek that came tumblingly roaring and sighing, by turns, down the mountainside. Robin cut boughs and made a comfortable bed inside the cavern. Outside he arranged rocks for a cooking fireplace, and one to keep warm by in the chilly evenings and early mornings. Before they broke camp that morning he had slit the venison to the bone in a dozen places and rubbed salt into the cuts. He took it now and sliced it into thin strips and laid them out on the rocks to dry in the sun. "You have to boil hell out of jerked venison to get it tender enough to eat," he said, "but it's good if it's cooked enough."

They lived in the cavern for a week. Each day they took long walks, rambling slowly and aimlessly through the woods, their arms around each other. They lay for hours on their bed of boughs and talked, or in silent, happy companionship. They heated water in the pot and took baths, scrubbing each other's backs, using the strong home-made soap Mrs. Hembree had given Sallie. One day the sun warmed up and there was a hint of summer's coming. Robin removed his clothes and dived into the pool to handfish under the rocks and crevices for brook trout. A minute later there was a flash of white as Sallie dived in with him, swam strongly across the pool, upended and went down to feel under a convenient rock for fish. In a moment she was up, pushed her hair back, took a deep breath, and tossed a nice-sized trout to the bank, where Robin could hear it flapping around on the leaves and pine needles.

In a few minutes the frigidness of the water forced them out. They lay on the smooth rock ledge and let the sun bring back the warmth to their bodies. "You," Robin told her, "are the only girl I ever heard of who could swim, except Cessie, and she only dog paddles." There was a touch of awe in his voice.

"Don't be astonished, my dear," she answered. "Lots of city girls can swim, and I used to be a city girl, long ago, before I found you."

"You didn't find me. I found you, and I claim 'Finders Keepers' privileges."

"Robin," she said, turning serious, "I hope we start us a baby now, while we're both so happy."

"I'm doing my best," he laughed, "but why now? Hadn't you rather wait awhile?"

"No, I'm superstitious. If we started a boy now, perhaps he would always be as happy as we are at this moment."

Robin laughed. "I'm working for a girl that'll look like you, and I never try but one thing at the time. When I get my girl I'll start on a boy." They both laughed gleefully and rolled into each other's arms.

It was an easy six hours' ride from the honeymoon cavern to the gap on East Ridge overlooking Modesty Valley. They had decided that in order to avoid any embarrassment for Sallie they wouldn't mention her relationship to Peter Gherkim. "The people in Modesty are always kind at heart and not one of them would ever say anything to hurt you, knowingly," Robin assured his bride.

They sat their horses in the gap and gazed down at the valley below. "Modesty was, at one time, probably the richest valley of its size in Carolina," Robin said. "It is now, in all likelihood, like the rest of the South, poor as poor can be. What with the Belton money and the money your uncle left you, we're likely far and away the richest people in the valley. We must, of course, help our own people the best we can, but we can't afford to ever tell too many folks how much we have, nor where it came from. It could cause trouble for me if someone talked. You understand, of course."

"Trust me, darling," she laughed. "I shall take all my cues from you. If you say black is white, I'll take oath that it is."

Robin turned his eyes to hers; the corners of his mouth curved upward in a grin. "How," he asked her, "does it feel to be a rich heiress, married to the wealthiest farm hand in Modesty Valley?"

CHAPTER TWENTY-FOUR

As THEY CAME THROUGH THE GAP AND HEADED DOWN EAST RIDGE, the unkept, rock-studded path, with its deep muddy ruts, brought the fact forcibly home to Robin that the war had been to his beloved Modesty, despite the fact that no soldiers' marching feet had been heard in the valley.

The depredation of war showed on every side. It shouted from the unpruned and weed-grown apple orchard near the gap. It screamed from the jambs of the broken-down fence. There could be no doubt that Modesty was beset with the same war-made miasmic inertia, though in a lesser degree, that he had seen in the battle-wasted lands of Virginia. It seemed to him he had just had the news of Minter's and his grandpa's passing; that his homecoming would serve as a fresh reminder to his folks of the loss of his brother and his grandpa.

It came to him that at the time he had heard from his folks that Sergeant Minter Arvane had been cut down by grapeshot, he was resting from three days' hard fighting, and the news had not been unduly shocking. At the time of his grandpa's death, Robin had been older, and the hardening processes of the war had toughened his fibers until he could digest any situation philosophically when it was one he could do nothing about. He did remember keenly how he had marveled at the thought of his grandpa obeying orders that he knew would take him and hundreds of his beloved men to certain destruction, because a muttonheaded general had a pipe dream. Grandpa had always been an outspoken individualist.

Sallie said, "Would it be easier and better if I waited for you to see them alone? You could come for me when you need me."

"I need you now," Robin said. "It's just that I'm afraid the sight of me will bring back the loss of Minter to Ma. I reckon I'm just being a damn fool as usual."

"I always dreamed of having a lovable damn fool for a husband. That's why I shall cling to you always, Robin Arvane," she said.

As they came upon the bridge, the brassy notes of a large bell rose, fell, and bounced against the rock ledges high up on West Ridge.

"Church?" Sallie asked.

"No," he told her, "that's our farm bell summoning the Arvane clan to greet us. Ma saw us coming. Nobody but her would know me at this distance; with you along, nobody but Ma."

The clan was in the process of gathering. Pless, Pamela, and Cessie were on the lawn. In the distance, Robin and Sallie could see Zack, his wife and brood, on the way.

The women's kissing, the men's quiet hand-shaking, the introduction of Robin's bride, were over. As they gathered in Pamela's kitchen, Robin noted that Zack looked pale and emaciated, an appearance that was heightened by his black hair plastered tightly against a bony skull. The children, in threadbare clothes, were clean, but they looked undernourished.

Everybody talked at once. Everybody asked questions at the same time. Then came one of those breaks of silence when everybody stopped talking for a moment to listen. Robin looked quizzically at his sister Cessie, now a tall, willowy blonde with level blue eyes, who returned his look for a moment, then with a squeal of delight threw her arms around his neck and held him chokingly until he gasped.

"That," she said, "is to pay you back, Mr. Smarty, for what you did to me."

"Me, to you?"

"Yes, you fool. You brought home a pretty wife, far too good for you, when I was looking forward to lording it over you for a while." She released him, put her arms gently around Sallie, and kissed her. "I love you already," she said simply.

Pless, Zack, and Robin were talking things over. Robin learned Pless had let the Confederacy have most of the work stock. The horses had been first, then the last pair of mules had broken out, run up the ridge, and fallen to their deaths over a cliff.

He was starting a crop with a pair of undersized steers which he had broken to work the fall before. "They walk mighty slow with a plow, but I can't stand too much fast walking, and Cessie shouldn't have to keep up with a horse or mule anyway. Since they cost less to feed than horses, I figure we're about as well off with 'em."

"You mean Cessie's been working in the fields like a man?" Robin sounded incredulous.

Cessie, who had walked in and heard the last, answered for Pless. "Sure, and I'm only one of hundreds of thousands in the South who've learned we can be useful as well as ornamental. Pa didn't want me to; Ma didn't like the idea; but if I hadn't helped Pa last year we'd be short of a small item known as food in these diggin's. We grew it ourselves and it doesn't offer much variety, but it will keep your belly skin from growing to your backbone."

"After I was commissioned," Robin said, "I could have helped some, perhaps enough to hire a man to help keep you out of the fields."

The laughter of Pless had an undertone of bitterness. "I've a trunkful of Confederate money, but you can't hire men where there is no man to hire. Those who were tall enough to reach up to plow handles grabbed guns and went off to shoot Yankees, or to join them and shoot Confederates. Those too old to fight were too puny to work. With us, it was 'root hog or die'; we chose to root."

"God damn Jefferson Davis and Abe Lincoln," Robin snorted.

"Damning by me or you won't do any good, but that's about the way I feel," Pless said.

Pamela moved into the discussion. "Such language harms nobody but you, Robin."

"Yes, Ma'am, I know," Robin said, "and I beg your pardon. Time was when you would have won your point with a willow switch. Be good for me to have you wear one out now on the seat of my britches."

His ma laughed easily. "Britches are too hard to come by, and I'd be mortally ashamed to make you let them down for me to switch you."

Cessie curtsied to Robin, then did a fast pirouette, revealing in outline a rich, ripe figure under her thin and faded dress.

"I'm sweet sixteen, and a mite over, full grown, mellow ripe, and I've never been kissed by any man but kinfolks and never even had a beau. Are you going to get busy and find me a man, or are you going to allow your own flesh and blood to languish on the vine until I fall, kerplunk, into the middle of a pack of hungry old maids?" Her eyes danced mockingly.

"My duty," Robin said, "is to warn male mankind against you."

Pless brought in a jug. "I'm going to fix each of us, ladies included, one of my famous honey-sweetened mint juleps. We're celebrating having you and your beautiful bride with us and I, for one, hope the neighbors leave us to ourselves tonight."

The glasses filled, Pless started to lift his to his lips when Pamela's voice cut through sternly. "Pless Arvane, give credit where it is due."

Pless's shoulders went straight. *"Our Father, bless these cups taken in rejoicing that thou hast delivered our beloved son back to us. Bless the lovely bride of his bosom, his brother and grandpa, who suffered and surrendered all for their ideals, and when our time on this earth is done, join us all together in Thy presence. All this we humbly beseech in Christ's name, Amen."*

He drained his glass, then turned to Robin. "Now, tell me how come we lost the war."

"I don't know," Robin said. "I expect you know more than I

do, actually. You had a chance to view it from more angles than I did."

"You may be right, at that," Zack nodded. "You were standing too close. While you were fighting, after that minnie ball clipped a corner of my lung, I was watching and studying. We could have won nine out of ten battles and still we'd have lost. They had too many marbles for us. With twenty-two millions against our five, and practically all the nation's industries, they couldn't help but swap us down."

"Then what comes now?" Pless asked.

"We'll have to do the best we can and hope they'll go light on us," Zack said.

"I can't see any answer but to settle down to work and try to forget the bitterness without forgetting our dead." Robin's voice was serious. "Sallie and I have a little money; in fact, by local standards we have quite a lot. I aim to find somebody to take a load of work off you and get Cessie out of the fields, and to have somebody do Zack's heavy work so he can rest enough, like the doctor said, for that corner of lung the Yankees shot off to have a chance to grow back."

Pless was skeptical. "Where do you expect to find these workmen when they don't exist?"

Robin laughed easily. "Right now they don't, but remember, demobilization is still going on. In a few days there'll be plenty, able and willing to work for anything they can get that will put clothes on their backs and food in their bellies."

"That last part makes sense, but if I was a young man with a wife, a little money, and two good hosses, I'd start riding west and go so far they never heard about the war—that is, if your money ain't Confederate issue. If that's what it is, you can dump it out in the backhouse where I'm taking a load tomorrow. That's about the only use we'll ever find for it."

"Not me," Robin laughed. "The Arvanes hurt the valley enough when the sons of Ajax let him talk them into leaving Modesty."

"But you will admit the ones who left did pretty well for themselves," Pless said.

"If they had remained in the valley and worked together, the Lord only knows what we might have accomplished, if not for ourselves, for the valley." Robin was deadly serious.

"I'll admit," Pless said, "every dog has a right to his own fleas. Cessie has your bride locked up somewhere, talking her to death. Your ma'll soon be through in the kitchen. Let's take another round, then we'll chase Zack home to his wife and family where he belongs. They left some time ago when the children got sleepy. Then we'll whistle up our folks and run jump in the bed for a good night's rest."

Thus Robin Arvane came home to Modesty Valley.

CHAPTER TWENTY-FIVE

NEXT DAY ROBIN TOLD HIS PA AND ZACK HOW HE CAME INTO possession of the gold coins which he had temporarily cached in the attic. He omitted some of the details which he considered personal or irrelevant. He did not mention Sallie's heritage, though he did mention that he rescued her in Kentucky, and that they were married in Virginia. He pledged both to secrecy regarding the entire matter. "That's why," he told them, "I think I will be able to partially pay my folks and the valley back for some of the things they did for me."

When he had finished, Zack spoke up, strongly. "All I have to say is you have a hell of a strong sense of responsibility."

"I reckon," Robin said, "the more you love a thing the more you feel you owe it."

Just then Lissie, Zack's wife, came from the cook room where she had been helping Pamela, announced the meal was ready, went to the verandah to call her children in, then went in search of Sallie and Cessie, whom she could faintly hear in the company room talking and giggling in low tones, confidentially, delightedly.

The meal was bread from wheat meal ground in Weldon's water-powered grist mill, the meat was streaked pork middling from the smokehouse, the vegetables, dried black-eyed peas. There was honey, but no sugar, and buttermilk, but no coffee or tea. Even while Robin eyed the table hungrily, he could not help remembering the loaded spreads his ma had so prided herself on before the war.

"This," Pless told Robin and Sallie by way of explanation, with no hint of apology, "is the best we got, but we got plenty of it to last until we can grow some more. That, I hear, is lots better than they are faring in the flat country."

To Robin the meal was a feast, and he ate like he had never tasted such delicacies. His ma smiled briefly when he complimented her on the food. He noticed she wasn't eating much—that she was toying with her food, trying to cover up the fact that she wasn't eating.

Pless spoke out. "I wish Pamela would eat better. I think she will, soon's she gets used to Robin being home. She hasn't felt right for almost a year now. I took her to Chafferton a while back to see a doctor, nearest one here, and he said she had something wrong with her blood, he thought. He gave her some kind of an iron tonic and said it would fix her right up. I can't tell's it's done any good at all."

"I think I must have been worrying too much about Robin, and tired, too," Pamela said.

"After Cessie had to start working in the fields with me, we had Angie Sassnet from across the creek—you know old Abe's girl—helping your ma. Then Abe broke both legs and Angie had to stay home and do his plowing and chopping. The way he's not getting his legs well, it looks like Angie'll be plowing from now on," Pless explained.

Pamela gave a short laugh. "Please," she pleaded, "don't you all start worrying over me. I have enough to bother me without being bothered by you worrying over me."

Despite themselves they all laughed. "I think she means it just that way," Lissie told them quietly.

After the meal, Cessie and Sallie appeared briefly in the parlor, then slipped away.

"Those two," Pless said, "are already thick as thieves. I can read Cessie like an open book. She thinks Sallie's something extra special out of the Bible."

"She is," Robin put in quickly. "I'll swear to that."

"I know, Son," Pless told Robin. "We all think so too." Then he continued, "Let's go for a little walk around the place and see what needs to be done."

Hours later, Zack fumblingly found the latch to the pasture gate, reeled erectly down the path, heading blithely home to the bosom of his family. Pless said to Robin, "I swear, since the minnie ball nicked the corner of Zack's lung, he hasn't been able to hold his licker, nor do any work, worth a dang!"

"All of my small aches and pains are completely gone," Robin told his pa.

"Well, Son," Pless said, "let me tell you, if you feel dog-bit of a morning, remember the same dog's hair that bit you's the only remedy, when it isn't carried too far."

Later that night, Sallie was either asleep or pretending when he crawled in beside her on the feather bed. Her even breathing told him she was really sleeping, and he didn't have the heart to wake her up. He lay there, half-drunk, trying to marshal his thoughts into sober channels. Suddenly he was smothered with a sensation of strangeness. The soft bed he had dreamed of so much didn't seem real. The whiskey, to which he was unaccustomed, was at work arousing an ancient tiredness in his body, while infinitesimal bolts of lightning leaped from muscle to nerve, and back again, pounding on one, yanking at the other, as his rum-roused, but blunted, imagination sagged and soared, trying to review in retrospect what he had learned about conditions in the valley since his return. Without reason, he recalled a phrase from one of Arch Barnes' sermons, something about a man being a stranger in his own house. He remembered how Arch used to speak of smiting the devil hip and thigh. He would, he thought, hate to be a Yankee in front of Captain Barnes's company when Arch was having a Yankee-smiting spell.

The night song of a bullfrog on the creek's bank, the eerie laugh of a screech owl, the distant bell-tone baying of a hound, all came to him as disturbing echoes instead of beloved sounds for which he had spent countless hours of longing. He felt the movement of the bed under him and knew he would be sick if he lay where he was. He pushed his feet out of bed and sat with elbows on knees, resting his head in his hands. He shook his head, tried to swim back into reality. Wondered where he was. It was the quiet easy breathing of the girl on the bed that showed him the way out of the maze of disjointed dreams. She was real enough. And he thought he ought to cry about it, only he wasn't sure he would know how.

The alcoholic cobwebs began to clear and substance began taking shape in his thoughts. It was a nameless dread of things to come, a fear for his ability to meet the demands that might be made on him. As his mind became clearer, it came to him that perhaps his pa was right. Maybe he should pull out of the valley and head west. The valley would be as well off without him, and perhaps he would be better off without the valley.

Robin needed to get out of the house to think it over. He eased quietly out of bed, slipped into his britches, and took his shoes in his hand. He would like to take Sallie with him, but she seemed to be sleeping so peacefully he didn't have the heart to reach out a hand to rouse her. He slowly picked his way up the moonlight-splotched path through the apple orchard to the spring-house, where the split log seat under the big poplar near the spring was so alarmingly familiar. It seemed like only a few hours since he and Cessie had been there for a last confab before he went away to war. As confabs go, it had been a complete failure. There wasn't, after all, much to say. Cessie had made him promise to take care of himself, be brave, smite the Yanks, and not get killed. After that she had kissed him fiercely, then run off down the hill, her blonde hair glinting among the apple trees as she fled toward the house.

Thinking about his sister made Robin warm and mushy inside. That wasn't what he wanted. He'd come to the spring to do some heavy thinking about the future. He remembered hearing Arch Barnes say that the devil always promised some reward for a man's services. It might be small, and might not be paid at all if the devil could get out of it, but one thing was sure, the old fellow was a powerfully good promiser. Robin got up, walked around until he found a good throwing rock, then leaning back on one leg, and throwing his body forward as his arm came over, he hurled the rock far up the hillside. He sat back down.

"Oh, hell," he thought, "being here doesn't help my thinking any." His mind was still jumbled. He heard feet padding lightly up the path, coming nearer. Cessie, a quilt thrown cape-wise over her night dress, sat down beside him.

"I couldn't sleep, either," she said. "I heard you leave the house, and when you stayed so long I thought you'd come up here. I can go back if you want me to. If you have bothers, I wish you'd tell me about them. Are they good or bad?"

"What do you mean, good or bad?"

"Oh, the war, being away from the valley. Not being able to see your friends in the valley. Having to kill folks you didn't know from Adam's house cat. Being cold and hungry. Walt tells everybody how brave you were, but I know better. I know you were scared, just as I would be, deep down. Tell me about some of the scrapes you got into with women, that you wouldn't dare tell anybody else. Something we can laugh about."

Robin knew, with more sadness than he dared show, that she was trying desperately to recapture something for them which was dead and gone forever. And suddenly he realized he had come up to the outdoor house with the same idea in mind. He knew they would both try to carry off the old camaraderie of their childhood.

"Tell me something that will make me laugh, like the time you swiped Pa's licker, and you and Walt poured it into the church wine. I remember nobody knew how it got into the wine, but everybody said Mr. Barnes gave the best sermon in the history of Modesty Church." She giggled.

"If you ever tell Pa about my part in that, he'll still warm my britches." Robin threw his head back, laughed heartily.

"I am," Robin said seriously, "thinking of leaving Modesty and going west. Zack thinks there's no future for anyone here in Modesty. I'm almost ready to agree with him."

"No, Robin," Cessie said, "you won't be leaving Modesty. The only person could take you away from here would be Sallie. I think you'd go for her sake anywhere."

"Maybe it's Sallie I'm thinking about when I say I may be leaving. Suppose I said I would leave it up to her?"

"Then it's settled. You'll stay in Modesty if you're waiting for Sallie to drag you out. She's not the kind, I would have you know, who jumps and runs every time she hears a horn on the other side of the hill. Your roots are so deeply planted in Modesty that you are a part of every rock, tree, and blade of grass in the valley. Sallie has no roots put down, she told me, except in you. She'll go wherever you want her to go, and like it. That's all she asks. She's too fine to drag all over the country. She needs to settle down, here in Modesty, and have her home and family here. Besides, Ma'll need a daughter to love when I'm married and gone from the valley."

"Who are you marrying outside the valley?" Robin asked quickly.

"I don't know," she told him. "I've never had a beau yet. Ma cut up her wedding dress and made me a beautiful frock, but so far I haven't seen anybody I want to wear it for, and I can't think of anyone in the valley now, or who'll be coming back from the war, I would want to wear it for. So I guess I'll have to look outside for a husband. Now that the war's over, and I won't have so much to do, I'll have more time to look around. What with knitting, making bandages, and working in the fields, your little sister's been a busy woman."

"Busy saving chamber water," Robin teased.

"Yes," she said, "saving chamber water." She laughed shortly. "Pa was afraid some fool would start a joke about that and cause the women to quit. He was wrong, as he learned when that big fat man, from Anserville, came out with a wagon collecting the water and tried to tease Mrs. Elco Wallace. He teased that with her size she should produce twice as much. She let him have a pot full in his fat face. The women snickered behind their hands for a month, but they went right on saving. It caused the only real laugh we had during the war."

"I'll promise you this," Robin told her, "if you're all-fired certain you want to look outside the valley for a beau, you can count on me to help all I can."

"I know it," she said simply. "Robin, I wouldn't have the first idea of how to make him come my way. Ma doesn't believe in discussing such things, and I've never had anyone else but you really to talk with. You'll have to teach me a lot of fine points about courting."

"Pshaw," Robin sputtered, "I can't teach you anything that way. To tell the truth, I never courted any girl except Sallie, not anywhere, not any time."

"But you did court Sallie?"

"There wasn't much courting done. It sort of came natural with us. Tell you what, honey, be your own sweet self, just as Sallie did, and when the time comes, the Good Lord will look after the rest."

"I hope so," she said softly, stroking his cheek with the palm of her hand, "in a willow thicket. Sallie told me. She said she thought I ought to know." She laughed affectionately. "She'll probably tell Ma, too. She's so sweet it won't make a bit of difference to Ma. A willow thicket would be fine with me if I could be as honest and real about it as Sallie is."

Robin wanted to change the subject quickly. "There'll probably be some Union soldiers sent into the valley, checking on things and such."

"Uhmmm," Cessie mused. "I might fall in love with a bluebelly. I wouldn't try to, but I might anyway. If I did, you can bet your last dollar I'd be whooping and hollering like hell for Abe Lincoln if that was the way my man was hollering. Bend over and I'll tell you a secret. One thing's for sure. I wouldn't, in a thousand years, marry a man like the Arvane men I've known all my life."

"Can't say that I blame you," Robin said teasingly, "but I'd like to know why."

"It's like this," she said. "You can feed an idea into an Arvane man, turn the crank, and you know, not only just where it will come out, but exactly what it will look like when it does. They are, my dear brother, the Lord's finest, but for me, they're too damn predictable. I want a man so unpredictable that when an idea is put in and the crank is turned, it might come out here, it might come out there; then again, it might blow up in my face."

She patted his cheek again, like he was a little boy, then trotted down the path toward the house, leaving his lean frame a dim silhouette standing in the moonlight.

CHAPTER TWENTY-SIX

Robin woke slowly next morning and lay peacefully, half-dreaming over the events of the day before. Sunlight seeping through the shutters told him they had slept late. He stretched in contentment, wondering how he had ever become confused or despondent over his future in Modesty. He made a resolution that thereafter he would never indulge in enough of the cup to get his thinking crossed again, not ever, as long as he lived. Long hours of sleep had washed out most of his physical hangover, but it could not wash out the memory that he had allowed himself to think of fleeing the valley in a moment of weakness.

He turned his head on the pillow and found Sallie looking quietly into his eyes, while a ghost of a smile hovered around her ripe lips. "Did you get it settled with yourself; last night, I mean?" she asked.

"Yes, definitely. But how did you know?"

"I heard you twisting around; then I heard you slip out. I pretended sleep because I knew it must be something you wanted to think out for yourself. I was still pretending when you came back. When you went to sleep, right off, I knew you had worked out your trouble to your own satisfaction. I wanted to let you know I was awake, but I also wanted you to make your own decision as to whether we stay here in the valley or try it somewhere else."

Robin laughed softly, deep in his throat. "What a wife! A few days ago she didn't know I even existed. Now she knows what I'm thinking about as well as I do myself."

"It's easy, darling. You know the Arvane men are all so damn predictable—and trustworthy." She whispered the last two words.

"Where did you get such an idea?" He sat up in the bed to ask.

"Cessie explained it. She says once you get to know an Arvane you can predict exactly how he'll act in any given case. Cessie says I'm the type to fall in love with all the Arvanes."

"Cessie," he whispered fondly, "is a smarty-britches, and I ought to spank her for the hussy she is. She doesn't even like the ways of the Arvane men."

"Oh yes, she does," teasingly. "She's so much of an Arvane herself she couldn't bear to live with a man cut from the same pattern. I think she's right about that."

"Say," he wanted to know, "what kind of talks did you and Cessie have yesterday and last night?"

"None of your business." She giggled lightly, snuggled against him. "It was strictly sister talk, and very, very confidential. There'll be others like it. Somebody's got to tell Cessie a lot of things she hasn't had a chance to learn for herself."

Robin kissed her, hard. "Next time you have a sister talk, please let her know that a feather bed's almost as nice as a willow thicket," he whispered. She sighed happily and returned his kiss.

Before breakfast was over, Walt, his ma, and smallest brother came in, along with Zack and his brood. Walt said they were expecting his pa and Martin back any day. Should have already been in the valley, but he reckoned they were having to walk all the way from Virginia, and that would take more time. Once experiences had been exchanged, they discussed the future of the valley. Walt agreed with Robin, there was nothing wrong with the valley hard work wouldn't cure. On a sudden impulse, Robin said he was going to build a large general store at Modesty crossroads. Robin said he would stock it with everything they could find in Pettyman's store in Anserville. He said he was looking for a store manager, and the best man he could think of was a young fellow named Walter Cedric.

Pless, who had sat listening, spoke up: "Pettyman won't like competition. He's said right along that he won't allow anyone to operate against him in this county as long as he's got any money to fight with. He says he'll cut prices, and keep on cutting them, until the man quits. He's been able to do that right along. About the best bet I can see from here is to open a sales stable in Anserville. Folks've got to have work stock, and you could buy cattle and hogs on the side. Make a good living at it, too."

Robin laughed. "Not me. If I got a good horse in I wouldn't have the heart to sell him, and I couldn't bring myself to do the necessary lying to sell a bad one. Ours will be a one-price store. Once people get used to it, they'll like it better. Besides, in a store I'll have lots of time to study law during slack business. I just decided on the law, as of this minute."

"I'm not so sure the valley needs the kind of store you're talking about, and I'm danged sure we don't need any lawyers—at least, I hope we don't," Pless spoke out.

"That's what I'm hoping too," Robin said. "A conscientious lawyer can keep a lot of people away from the courthouse by doing the right things at the right time."

"I'm not telling you how to run your business," Pless put in hastily. "I put your money in the bank like you asked me."

"Good," Robin said. "Thanks. It will be where we can check it out when we need it."

"That it will."

"I would," interrupted Walt, "never put one dollar in a bank now. Nobody knows what will happen."

"This one's safe as the Bank of England," Robin told Walt.

Neither Robin nor his pa thought it was necessary to let anyone know that the bank they were speaking of was a recess ten feet above ground in the big hollow poplar at the springhouse. It was so cleverly concealed that a man could climb all around inside the hollow and never see it. It had been laboriously prepared by Pless during the war to hide Pamela's silver in the event of raiders, or hostile Union troops, invading the valley. Pless still wasn't satisfied about losing the war, so he brought up the subject again.

"Well, it was like this," Robin explained. "If Walt hadn't bolixed up things by getting his foot shot off, I honestly believe we could have won. It was more than I could do by myself. I needed Walt. He left me fighting practically the entire Yankee army alone, and powerfully discouraged, too, because I knew all the time Walt was back here in Modesty Valley, stomping around like a deacon at a baptizing, having the time of his life gathering chamber water!" He dropped an arm over Walt's shoulder. "How come you didn't send me some of that special Modesty Valley ammunition we'd been talking about just before your foot ran off and left you?"

Walt grinned. "You mean the extra special?"

"Any from the valley would have been extra special, but there was a special extra special we talked about."

"Ellen was donating, but I was always afraid it was probably just branch water, because she would have been afraid it might be used to shoot Josh Todd," Walt joked.

"Shucks, I forgot to tell you, I sent Josh to our hospital a few minutes after you got hit. Way he talked, he'd have been glad to die if he knew the bullet was being pushed along by Ellen's ammunition," Robin said.

Robin insisted to Zack that he would lend, or give, him the money to hire someone to take his place at heavy work, so that he might have a chance to rest up as the doctors advised. He said he thought his pa should turn his steers loose to grow fat and tender up before fall, so they could have them for beef. After all, he and Sallie had brought home a couple of horses who couldn't begin to earn their keep with the small amount of riding they would be doing. When he had to ride, he could borrow one, he said.

Pless asked Robin if the horses would do farm work. Robin didn't know, but he was pretty sure the big black would, and he thought they could break the frisky little bay to the plow.

There was a zip to the air the next morning when Pless and Robin took the two horses to the field to see how they would work.

Pless had named the large horse Blackie, and Sallie said she would like to call the little bay Red Bud. They started with the black horse, and after being led by Robin for a short distance the big gelding arched his neck and settled down to the prosaic labor of pulling a plow with as much pride as if it had been a golden chariot.

It was a different story with Red Bud, the little bay mare. When she felt the collar tighten against her shoulders, she promptly stood on her hind feet and pawed the air wildly. They worked patiently with her for an hour until Red Bud was snorting, trembling with fright and indignation. The furrow they had made was less than ten feet long.

"I'll take her back to the barn and bring a steer. We'll never make a work horse out of that proud little devil, and I can't say that I blame her," Pless observed. "She was bred to the saddle." He stroked the mare's neck, soothed her.

It was then that Sallie and Cessie came into the field. Cessie unhitched Blackie from a fence post, where he was tethered while they struggled with Red Bud, and started him across the field. Sallie patted Red Bud on the nose and jaw, then leaned her weight against the mare's shoulder. Red Bud stood quietly, momentarily bending her neck around, nuzzling at Sallie's sleeve. After cooing baby-talk to the mare for a minute, Sallie said, "Give me a hand up, Robin. She'll go if she thinks I want her to work."

Robin made a hand and Sallie swung easily astride the mare. Her skirts wrinkled and rode up to the middle of her thighs. She was wearing short pantalettes and Robin was sure her legs were the prettiest this side of Heaven, and maybe within the Gates themselves. She sat still, stroking the mare's neck and withers, sweet-talking her for a minute. Then she saw Pless covertly glance at her thigh, then, embarrassed, look intently across the field as though studying some distant, but fascinating, object. "Pop-Pless," she called out to him. "You don't need to bother to look away. Robin thinks my legs are so pretty he's dying for you to see them. He wants your opinion on his judgment of feminine beauty." Her laugh tinkled like a silver bell.

"Well, in that case, I'll say they ain't hard to look at; it's just that I ain't seen any women's legs, except Pamela's, since I was a young shaver. I haven't seen too much of hers, either. Pamela thinks a woman's legs are something like a defect in her character, to be kept out of sight as much as possible." His tone was rueful.

"Pa means that," Robin said. "Ma always dresses as she undresses. As one layer is peeled, she drops it and another falls into place where it came from. I remember so many times hearing her lecture Cessie on the fine points of a lady's behavior. She says a lady never removes all of her clothes at once."

"Isn't she an angel? I already love her too much to ever show her anything but my very best side." Sallie laughed happily. "Now, Robin, take the plow handles and let's get on with teaching this little baby that she's a grown-up horse now."

Robin took the plow handles, while Pless moved in close to take Sallie off if Red Bud decided to start pitching. Sallie clucked softly to the mare. Red Bud tightened against the collar, stopped, danced a little jig. Sallie reached forward and scratched her ears, then clucked again. The mare tightened, hesitated, then pranced forward a few steps before she settled down to a steady walk. Sallie rode her for a while, then dismounted, took the rein, and led her a few minutes. Soon the little mare was contentedly plowing row for row with the big black.

"I think we should rest our horses for a while," Pless said. "Have to start working 'em gradual-like. After all, they're not plow horses by nature. Me, I'll dig into the nubbins and pick out some seed corn, while I'm resting. Thought you might like to do a little visiting around with the neighbors." Then, wistfully, "It's been a long time since we had a nice mess of fish on our table."

The red wigglers, in the worm bed back of the barn, seemed smaller to Robin than he remembered them. "The damn war even stunted the worms," he joked to Sallie and Cessie, who had found fishing poles for themselves. Cessie was enthusiastically explaining the fine points of trout fishing to Sallie, as they waited to follow Robin to the creek. They climbed the road to the long pool and fished downstream. Robin had never seen so many fish biting so hungrily; big ones, too.

Cessie explained there had been little fishing in Modesty Creek during the war. "Valley folks had little heart, and less time, for it."

As they approached the house, Robin saw two back-sharpened, lice-bitten mules and an equally scrawny horse tied in front of the hitching rail. The mules waved their huge ears back and forth at the spring flies, while the horse stood hip-shot, forlorn, as though he would like to lean against the fence to hold himself up. Robin looked the stock over. "Good mules and a good horse, if they had enough feed into them to put a little fat on their bones and a mite of spring back into their muscles," he said. The horse carried a worn military saddle, but the mules had only bags of shucks over their backs to ease their riders' rear-ends from the effects of their saw-toothed spinal joints.

Seated on the front steps, in ragamuffin Confederate gray, with weeks of scraggly beard covering hard-pinched faces, were three of Robin's late comrades-in-arms. As Robin opened the gate and came into the yard, the men rose from the steps, stood in line together, brought their hands up in a smart salute. "Private Axiom Ludlow reportin' for duty, suh, Cap'n Arvane," pronounced the first.

"Corp'l Joe Ben Johnson reportin', suh, to his cap'n, Robin Arvane," said the second.

"An' Private Penderlow Sneed, at y'r service, suh, Cap'n Arvane," rumbled the third.

"Cut out the salutes, you old buzzards," Robin yelled, and a minute later he was shaking hands and back-slapping the three ex-members of his company, all of whom he thought were still in the Pennsylvania prison.

Joe Ben Johnson, who was the most articulate of the three, explained. "'Twon't no time atter yuh got away fr'm them Yanks afore their major come around an' told us th' war was done over, an' we'd be turned loose in no time. He said as how them as didn't try to 'scape might be sent home on th' railroad cyars, but them as didn't have no better sense as to walk off if they wasn't gyarded too close, would have to make it theyselves, th' best way they could. After that, it plumb looked like he was a-tryin' to make it easy for us to 'scape. They wasn't hardly no gyards a-walkin' past, an' them as was, wasn't payin' no 'tention to nothin'.

"Well, suh, Cap'n, me an' Axiom an' Penderlow, we couldn't b'lieve nothin' as was told to us by no Yank, so the fust chanct we got we lit a shuck outen that there prison camp. Well, suh, as we was a-goin' down the road, we come to this here Yankee re-mount station with a whole slew o' the sorriest lookin' passel o' mules and hosses it was ever f'r me to see in this world, they was so half-perished. We stopped an' axed this gyard if he c'd sell us a few of 'em to get home on, an' he said he could, iffen we had any money, but our credit wasn't no good. So we went down th' road a piece an' rested 'til 'twas dark, on account of we was so tired o' walkin'. When it come down good an' dark, we snuck back to that there picket line to git us some ropes to kinda tie up any bundles we mought find on th' way down here. I swear, Cap'n, 'twon't our fault if, come mornin', these three buzzard-bait critters was a-hangin' onto them ropes we was a-draggin' behind us. We was afeard to take 'em back, so we jist clumb up on their backs an' rid on down here."

"Your story isn't exactly original," Robin laughed, "but it isn't as old as the idea of horse-stealing, so I reckon it's new enough to serve the purpose. I reckon you mean to take those critters down state and make yourselves a cotton crop."

"No, Cap'n," Axiom spoke up, "'tain't nothin' like that. You see, we was jist sorta workin' around, when an' where we could find anything to do, 'fore the war. Me an' Pa, we kinda worked together, an' Joe Ben and Penderlow they sorta teamed up. Pa, he hauled off an' died while I was in th' war, an' Joe Ben an' Penderlow they jist don't give a damn no-how. So we-uns decided to come right on down here an' give you our mules an' hoss an' let yuh kinda give us a job o' workin' f'r yuh. We ain't none hifalutin' an' educated, but we all knows how to give a body a whole day's work. Course, if it's so you can't do nothin' f'r us, an' 'll let us sleep in your corn crib tonight, we'll start proguin' along come mornin'."

"Why, bless your little black hearts," Robin cried, "you fellows are the answer to a maiden's prayer, in a manner of speaking. We'll give you a house to live in, food to cook in it, such as we have, plenty of work to be paid in gold, and I'll buy your stock from you. We'll all have a good fish supper; then I'll take you down to your new house. It belongs to my sister-in-law, but you go ahead and stay there tonight, and I'll see her tomorrow about renting it for you. Axiom, you'll work with my brother, Zack; Joe Ben and Penderlow can work for my pa."

"But," remonstrated Axiom, "we want to work f'r yuh. That's what we decided on 'fore we got here."

"I'm not working, right now," Robin explained, "and I don't especially need anybody to help me loaf. At least, I don't need a man to help me enough to pay for it."

"Well," observed Penderlow, "that's all right with me. Main thing I want is to git to work. I c'n do anything long's it don't want nothin' but a strong back an' tough muscles. If you got any hard stuff like writin' letters, an' sich, I ain't yo'r man."

"All right," Robin said, "here are your duties. You start in tomorrow getting paid, but for the first three days you're working for me, and here's what I want you to do. Feed your stock well, but don't give them enough to founder, and don't work them one minute. Stuff all the rations you can into yourselves, and go fishing every day. That will finish out this week. Then, beginning Monday, you'll be seeing my pa, and my brother, about what you're to do. All I'm doing after that is guaranteeing your pay as long as you satisfy them. Is that fair?"

They turned toward him, stood at attention. Three ragged sleeves rose in salute. "Cap'n Arvane, suh, we got yo'r o'dahs. They'll be obeyed jist like we done when you was ouoh commandin' officer. Is that what you want, suh?"

"Hell no," Robin laughed. "You'll have to carry out orders a damn sight better than you did in the army. None of you ever carried out orders, except in battle, any longer than an officer was watching you. This time you'll be working for my money, not the Confederate Army."

CHAPTER TWENTY-SEVEN

W HEN ROBIN TOOK AXIOM AND THE OTHER TWO NEW FARM workers down to Malvina's house that night, after giving them supper, he took some of his ma's old quilts with him for them to bed down on. To his surprise, he found most of Malvina's things still in the house, dusty and covered with cobwebs. All she had taken to Anserville were little Minter's and her own personal belongings. Pless had issued the men meal, dried peas and beans, some sweet potatoes, sorghum molasses, and a sizable cut of smoked meat. Robin pointed out everything to them, and just before he left, said, "You-all will find it lots easier to get along with each other in civilian life than it was in the army. But, I want you to promise me one thing: if you ever get to yipping and yapping at each other, don't do any actual fighting until I have a chance to talk it over with you. If you do, without letting me know first, the man that starts it had as well start packing. We're powerful peaceful folks here in Modesty Valley. We don't want our folks fighting each other, and we want to consider you our people."

"Cap'n, I'm plumb right with you on that stuff, Sir." It was Axiom speaking up, but the other two echoed him quickly.

"All right," Robin said, "be sure and make it that way. And don't call me cap'n any more. My name's Robin to my friends. When we get to where we're not friends any more, then I'll be Mr. Arvane. Is that clear? Another thing, and this is something I hate to bring up with a bunch of friends, but you know when we were in the army we didn't care where we slept, nor how dirty and filthy the hole we slept in. That is, we cared, but there

wasn't much we could do about it, so we slept where we could."
He was evidently embarrassed.

"Shucks, Cap'n, I mean Robin, suh," Joe Ben spoke up, "I
know exactly what you're tryin' to say. What you mean is we all
jist druv up fr'm a lousy prison camp, an' we're awf'lly filthy an'
dirty, an' we should ought to clean up a little bit afore we gits
on your sister's nice clean beds. That's e-zactly what we aims to
do. We're gonna bile all o' our clothes, then git us some hot water, an' some o' that air soap yo're ma give us, an' clean ourselfs
up like we ain't been washed since we was babies. Don't you worry 'bout that none. We done talked about it, an' we aims to start
gittin' clean right atter you leave."

"In that case," Robin laughed, "let me apologize for what I
was about to say. I should have known that nobody from our
company would ever allow himself to even need a bath unless he
was situated so he couldn't get it."

"Damn know it, we aim to be clean, all th' time," Penderlow
put in. "We done decided we'd all wash ourselfs all over ev'ry
week, or two, 'til warm weather gits here. Then we aims to git
in th' creek an' cool off jist about ev'ry night. Man don't do it,
gonna git a pole took to 'im by me an' th' other'n."

"I fully appreciate your wonderful cooperation in this most
vital matter," Robin told them gravely. "It behooves us all to remember that 'cleanliness is next to Godliness.' See you later."

As Robin was going out of the door he heard Axiom asking
the other two, "Now I ax yuh. What in the hell caused Cap'n to
start in cussin' that way, jist afore he left, he'd been so oncommon
friendly? And all of a suddent-like, too."

"I ain't so shore what he was a-cussin' about," Penderlow
grinned, "but it shore sounded powerful good. Jist like it was in
the army."

"I didn't understand it neither," Joe Ben told them. "But that
'Godliness' shore sounds like a powerful cuss word. Takes
an educated man to use hifalutin' cuss words like that. We all
know if they ever was a man as was tall in th' sight o' God, it's

Cap'n Robin Arvane. Ain't nobody ever goin' to tell me nothin' different. If any man do, I'll make 'im wish he hadn't!"

That night in the darkness of their bedroom, Robin remembered something that gave him a slight jar. He told Sallie. "It just came to me this minute that Axiom, Joe Ben, and Penderlow were the three most famous foragers in my company. They could smell out a chicken roost a mile away, or a patch of roasting ears in the next county. They could find food where there just wasn't any food. The only way they did better than country dogs in town was they didn't pee on what they couldn't use."

"Don't you think," Sallie said, perturbed, "that you had better get your pa's hogs in the barn and lock them up? And lock the corn crib, as well as your ma's chicken house? Do you think they might come into this house while they're prowling around?"

Robin laughed easily. "Shucks, no. They'll be all night cleaning up, getting an accumulation of four years of Virginia mud off their hides, and boiling and washing their clothes, By the time they get through with all that, they'll be too tired to do anything but sleep. Besides, every last one of them would cut his right hand off before he'd harm anything that he thinks belongs to me, or mine. It's the other folks in the valley, and out of it, they would consider fair game. I'm going to ride into Anserville in the morning to see Malvina and get her permission for them to live in her house. Pay her some rent for it, if she'll take it. Before I go, I'll explain to them how we live here in Modesty Valley. I think I can keep them honest in actions, if not in heart."

"I think, Son, you ought to ride into Anserville and ask Malvina about using her house for the men you hired yesterday. Know it'll be all right with her, but we owe her the courtesy. Besides, she'll be wanting to see you, anyway," Pless said to Robin next morning at breakfast.

"I was going to ask you if I could borrow your black horse for that very thing, this morning," Robin rejoined.

"Now listen," Pless told Robin levelly, "I appreciate you telling us we can use yours and Sallie's hosses to work the farm. Appreciate it a lot. But damned if I'm going to have you asking me when you can use one of them. If you won't take first call, and use them any time you want, then dammit, I won't use them at all."

Robin laughed. "Same old independent Pless Arvane, the one I knew when I was a young man. An uneducated, uncouth, indignant, and independent mountain man, despite the fact that grandpa sent you to Oak Ridge Military as a boy. Pa, if you had just shaved this morning, or even yesterday, I'd kiss you."

Pless's eyes misted over. He dropped his shoulder as though shrugging something off. Then, in a voice that he meant to be gruff, but that came up in a throaty croak, said, "Dang it, Robin, won't you ever learn to act like a grown-up man? Pamela, pass me the honey and butter for my grits."

Robin took his place back by the side of Sallie, sat down, and helped his plate. Sallie was looking into her plate, but after a minute he felt her hand resting lightly on his leg. She gave it two or three understanding squeezes, until he dropped his down and locked hers in it. Understandingly their fingers tightened for a moment. Then Robin resumed his breakfast. He could see Sallie was only toying with her food. He could also feel her glances, knew they were lingeringly searching his face. He knew she was openly making love to him with her eyes, a warm glow suffused him from head to foot, and he began handling his food as absent-mindedly as she was hers. Cessie woke them up. She shook a fork at each of them and laughed mockingly. "Don't you wish it would just stay night all the time?"

"Cessie!" Pamela cried, shocked.

"Well," Cessie said casually, "I'll bet they do. I would if I were Sallie."

"Cessie," Pless barked, "you heard your ma. Either keep a civil tongue, or leave the table, right this minute."

"All right," Cessie said, dimpling at Pless. "I'll apologize. But you don't want me to tell a lie and say I'm sorry, do you, Pa?"

"No," Pless told her, thoughtfully, "I want you to eat your breakfast and keep your dang mouth shut for a few minutes, for a change."

"Pa," she answered him, "you don't know how much you just hurt me—deep down, that is."

"You don't have any deep down, nor high up, either," Pless told his daughter. "You're the homeliest girl in the valley, which is the same as saying the State, the sassiest in the county, the laziest in the world, and the big stumbling block in the lives of your ma and pa."

"See what I mean?" Cessie said to Sallie. "I told you, come what may, Pa's always on my side." Her laugh was infectious.

"I can never tell when Cessie's teasing," Pamela spoke up resignedly.

"I wouldn't tease folks I don't love," Cessie said.

"We all know that, honey. Let's get through our breakfast, now," Pamela said.

A few minutes later Robin told Sallie, "I've got to ride into Anserville to see Malvina about using her house for our new hands. You can take Red Bud and ride in with me, if you wish, but this is something I'd rather handle alone."

"Cessie wants me to go with her to your Picnic Ledge this morning," she said, "and I think I should. You've never talked much to me about Malvina, but I can tell she is your favorite sister-in-law. I think, as you do, you should see her alone the first time. I want things washed out clean as soon as possible."

"I won't be long, but I've got to drop by and see our new field hands," Robin said. He was afraid to ask Sallie what she meant in her last statement.

Robin found the new hands lounging on the porch. Their ancient, makeshift Confederate uniforms, which were the only clothes they owned, just as Robin's uniform was his entire wardrobe, were wrinkled by the previous night's boiling. They didn't look, or smell, like the same men. As he came up to the hitching post, he saw all three make the first motion of getting up to attention. With a downward wave of his hand he stopped them, climbed down off the black horse, went in, and sat on the steps.

Axiom grinned affably at Robin. "We was jist a-settin' here a-talkin' when you rid up. Right fr'm this piazzer yuh c'n see at least ten houses, an' I bet they ain't one of 'em got a lock on they chicken houses. It's a fact; we was a-talkin' about how good we c'n work f'r yuh f'r almost nothin' an' still live like them Babylon kings. We done had honey an' butter an' slices o' mighty good smoked meat f'r breakfast, but dammit, Robin, it's hard to set on our tails up here when we know they's chickens in ev'ry direction wantin' to be took an' fried f'r breakfast. It jist ain't right. If all them chickens is a-runnin' around loose, an' the people what's supposed to be lookin' atter 'em ain't got sense enough to eat 'em up, or put good locks on they chicken house doors, then 'tain't nothin' but right as we should have a teeny-bitsy fryer for breakfast now an' then. We done decided to do th' right thing by these here folks in this here valley. We forage a chicken one place tonight, we won't go back there no more until we done foraged ev'rybody else. That way they won't be no chickens missed. Same as we aim to handle all o' our foragin'.' "

Robin got up and clapped his hands together in applause. "That," he told them, "was one of the finest speeches I ever heard. But let me ask you one thing. Would you forage around our place?"

Joe Ben answered indignantly, "Cap'n Arvane, suh; I mean Robin, that was almost a insultin' question. You know we ain't that kind o' folks."

"Sure I do," Robin told him; "that's why I brought it out. Here in Modesty Valley everybody is everybody else's friend. We live that way. At least, before the war we did, and I don't see why we can't again. I'm going to do my best to keep peace in this valley. If some man wants to wear a chip on his shoulder because he fought on one side, or the other, we are going to try and ignore him so much that he'll finally catch on and knock it off himself. I've decided to devote all I've got into trying to build Modesty Valley back and not let a few damn fools tear it down. I know you fellows haven't got a dime in the world of your own. You are poor folks. But that won't mean a damn thing in this valley. You do an honest day's work, treat folks right, tell the truth, and you'll always be just as good as the next one. This is not the cotton country. Another thing, the valley is quick to act when any-body doesn't want to be a good citizen. To show you what I mean by that, get your hats and come with me."

They all went up the road, with Robin leading his horse, walking with them. They crossed the big road and went on to the entrance to Modesty graveyard. Robin pointed up its pre-cipitous slope. "Go up to the southwest upper corner and read the inscription on the big granite stone over the grave of Peter Gher-kim. After you've done that, go back to the house and talk it over. If, after you've done that, you've made up your minds you'd like to do a little foraging in Modesty Valley instead of becoming one of us, don't bother to talk it over with me. Saddle your critters and get going. Foraging is something we don't like, and won't have, in this valley. If any of you are here when I get back from my little trip into Anserville this morning, that will be just the same as telling me that you fully agree with what I just said. I don't think we'll ever have to mention this subject again."

He mounted his horse and rode away. The three climbed the hill until they found Peter Gherkim's grave. There, between them, they laboriously spelled out his epitaph until its cogent mes-sage sank into their consciousness. Without saying a word they came off the hill, walked slowly back to the house they were liv-ing in. The three were ranged on the porch steps, slumped in the attitude of men thinking, when Axiom broke the silence. Be-fore he spoke he fished out a large-size twist of burley tobacco, home-grown on the place, which Pless had given him, broke off a jawpacker, chewed meditatively. "I'll swear to Gawd," he finally pronounced, "that Cap'n Robin Arvane knows more ways to preach a sermon than Saint Paul his-self. Me, if I ever feel like I gotta do a little foragin' to keep my hand in, as you mought say, it'll be fur, fur away fr'm this here valley."

Joe Ben nodded solemnly. "It's jist like I said. I thought I knowed all they was to know about cussin', but he can cuss in words I ain't never heeard afore. I bet th' Good Lord don't have to bend so awf'lly fur down to shake his hand. Me, I'm gonna do what I think he wants me to whilst I live here."

"I feels e'zactly like you do, Joe Ben," Axiom said. "You know I can't never forget he kept ol' Jack's officers fr'm shootin' me onct."

"You ever mention that to him ag'in an' he'll cave yo'r skull right down to yo'r shoulders," Penderlow told Axiom.

"Listen, Penderlow," Axiom answered, "I got better sense'n that. I was jist a-tellin' yuh."

"We heeard it afore," Penderlow rejoined shortly.

CHAPTER TWENTY-EIGHT

Robin rode toward Anserville, slowly, taking his time. He couldn't help remembering how the very sight of Malvina, the touch of her hand, had set him on fire the last time he had seen her. He wondered if Malvina could still disturb him as she had in the past. He hoped, with all the strength of his being, that after Sallie she couldn't reach him. If she tried, he meant to insult her so crudely that she would ever after have nothing more than contempt for him. He would do that, regardless of whether she shook his passions out of line or not. It was something he had to do for Minter. For Sallie. For the Arvanes.

He rode his horse to the front of lawyer Samuel Crewes' house and went to the door. Before he went in, he glanced around at the little town of Anserville. He noticed the mudholes in the streets, the run-down look of the yards, fences, and houses. It reminded him, he thought, of a slattern whose best dress was not only wrinkled and torn, but disgracefully unwashed, as well.

He hit the brass gong on the door, and while it was still echoing he thought he heard low conversation, then silence. He hit the gong again. Light steps came through the hall, a skirt swished. He knew Malvina's step. For a few moments she looked at him without speaking. He noticed her skirt was twisted slightly out of shape, her face flushed, her hair disarrayed.

"Oh, Lord," she cried, half-confused, "it's Robin. Come in." She kissed him lightly on the cheek.

Robin followed her through the high-ceilinged parlor, and on to the cramped family sitting room, where he found a heavy-jowled, but well-set-up, Union lieutenant of cavalry standing by the mantel, toying with a mint julep. Lieutenant Gustave Schweitzer nodded coolly when Malvina introduced them. Robin decided not to like Lieutenant Schweitzer.

Malvina chattered away excitedly, half-apologetically. "The lieutenant is here with a platoon of men to occupy Crinshaw County. He says our mountain people are so docile he doesn't expect any trouble at all in seeing that the terms of surrender are carried out. He says his first duty is to see that every ex-slave in the county gets a fair deal, and that none are still in bondage. I told him we never had any slaves in this county, but I don't think he believed it. Papa went to Chafferton, on business, right after the lieutenant came, or he could explain to him about our not having any slaves, ever, in Crinshaw. His men are quartered in our carriage house and they are using our kitchen for cooking. We are to take our meals with them in return for the loan of the kitchen." She finished lamely and, Robin thought, still apologetically.

"I'm sorry, Malvina," Robin stated flatly, "but there is one section of the country where there are, or were at one time, lots of slaves, so I've been told. It's pretty far back in the hills, and I don't reckon the Union Army would want to fool with it, for it's away out in Jumping Cat Cove. Only one road in, and the same one out. Next to impossible to get over it except by horseback. Not over fifteen or twenty families in the cove, all of them kinfolks."

"But Robin," Malvina interrupted, "I heard every man that was big enough to carry a gun in Jumping Cat fought with the North."

"I heard that, too," Robin answered, "and maybe they did, maybe they didn't. It may be they didn't fight for either side. I wouldn't want to be the one to go out there telling them how to conduct their business." He looked meaningfully at the lieutenant.

"I don't care," the lieutenant said, "on which side they fought. They still live in the South, and certain rules and restrictions have been imposed to teach all you people not to try the same thing again." He extracted a notebook and pencil. "I'll see to the Jumping Cat situation as soon as possible. In the meantime, please say nothing to anyone. I want to arrive in that little cove completely unexpected."

Malvina still wanted to change the subject. "Papa's away working with some kind of committee. You know he wasn't very active either way, but he was always opposed to the rebellion. He says we have to work with the North in every way possible, so it will be easier on us in the long run. I'm sorry I asked him to take little Minter with him for company. I wouldn't, if I had known you were coming. I didn't know you were back. I suppose you came back with a whole flock of Virginia girls' names clustered in your heart?"

"Nope," laconically, "just one Kentuckian. She's my wife. The most beautiful woman, in body and soul, the Good Lord ever made."

"Oh, I'm so glad for you, Robin." She smiled, but her eyes darkened and narrowed perceptibly.

"Getting back to what we were talking about," Lieutenant Schweitzer butted in, "I would like to tell you more about what we expect of the South, and I would like to learn a little more about this Jumping Cat Cove business."

"Lieutenant," Robin told the Union officer, "we lost the war. As far as I'm concerned, we lost it fair and square. Your side is in the position to enforce just about any peace terms you want. But I do hope you have some folks in Washington with enough sense to realize that the harder you make it for us, the harder it will be for the whole country in the long run. You are, I hope, handling your job according to your orders, which I presume come down through command. I came to Anserville today to talk business with Malvina, my sister-in-law. I didn't come to discuss religion, politics, military strategy, nor the peace-time conduct of Yankee soldiers in the South. If that's what you want, I advise you to drop by Boyle's Golden Glove barroom, up the street, pick out the smallest man you can find, and start an argument. It will surprise you how easily he'll slip a knife in between your ribs. You'll hardly feel it."

Robin didn't wait for Schweitzer's reply. He took Malvina's arm and gently guided her toward the rear of the house, and to the kitchen.

Seated at a kitchen table, Robin told Malvina about being married. He told her about hiring some hands whom he had already put in her house, but that he had thought he should see her and find out how much rent she thought was right. Learn if she would sell her furniture and cooking things.

"I would," Malvina told him, "sell them to anyone but you, Robin, for a hundred dollars, United States money. I'll give them to you. I couldn't feel right charging for them. The way I feel now, I don't ever want to see anything in that house again. They remind me too sharply of Minter—and you, Robin. You fool," her brow puckered, her eyes misted, her tone was husky, "do you think for a moment I'll ever forget the last night I spent in that house, or that it was spent with you?" She rose, stepped around the table to Robin's side, dropped her arms around his head, and pulled his face against her breast, held him hard, pressingly.

Robin squirmed loose. Stood up, caught her shoulders, pushed her down in the chair. "Listen, God dammit," he told her, "don't ever do that again as long as we live. I'm not a wooden Indian, standing here with a leaf of tobacco in my hand. I'm a man, and my boiling point can be reached just like any other man's. It was a low thing we did, and I was equally to blame with you. It worried me sick for a while, what I had done to my own brother. Now I don't worry any more about it. Since it only happened once, and we haven't let it happen again, I'm glad. I wouldn't hurt you for the world, honey, but you have to understand. You are still my sister-in-law, and will be so long as you stay single. And even when you're married again, you'll still always be a little bit extra special to me. Somebody I'd fight for, no matter who might try to go against you. Understand?"

When he finished, she looked at him speculatively. Her face

had resumed a placid expression. "Robin," she said, "you talk powerfully well, I think. You should study law."

"I aim to do just that," he answered.

Robin laid some gold coins in front of her. "Since I'm using your house, and things, for our hands, I think it's only right they should be paid for." She picked up the money, silently.

He jerked his head toward the front of the house. "You and the Yank here in the house alone while your pa's away?"

"Why not? Widows are always allowed to take boarders without benefit of chaperon. Papa says it's all right. Besides, he wants to marry me, I think. At least I did think so."

"How long has he been here?"

"Three days, and he's been in the house almost every minute since he arrived. You see, Papa and Minter left the day he arrived with his men." She went on whispering. "Yesterday he asked me to marry him, right then, as soon as we could get to the courthouse. I told him he'd have to wait and let us talk it over with Papa. He got terribly upset and started drinking juleps. He wasn't raving, or anything like that, but he seemed terribly hurt."

"Fine excuse to get drunk," Robin said, dryly.

"But, Robin," she faltered slowly. "I got sorry for him after supper, and we both got drunk. After a while we—we lay down together. I don't know what to do. I can't tell Papa. If the news didn't kill him, he'd kill Gustave, which would be almost as bad."

Robin was angry, and disgusted. "Don't," he blurted, "tell anybody anything. Go ahead and marry the son-of-a-bitch, if you want him, and if you don't, put him out of the house."

"That's what I meant to do last night," she whispered, sadly. "But he's different today. He says he doesn't see how we can afford to get married now, not until the country is more settled and the war forgotten."

"So he wants to wait about twenty thousand years, does he?" Robin asked, gruffly. "Do you actually want the bastard? Would he be the man of your first choice?"

"You know better," she answered pointedly. "Walt Cedric offered to marry me once because he was sorry for me. I'd do almost anything to get a good man, but I wouldn't take one who married me out of sympathy."

"Getting back to the question," Robin interjected, "do you want this blue-belly for a husband?"

"Yes, Robin, I do," she confessed, "if you put it that way. I think, perhaps, I could learn to love him. He is," she smiled ruefully, "a wonderful bed partner, and the woman who won't admit that's important in a husband is either lying or she's not all woman. He's been married and divorced, he admits, but actually he's good underneath his rough ways, I think. If I wait for someone who might be coming back from the war, I'll probably be a lone widow the rest of my days. That's not going to happen to me, if I can help it. I couldn't tell anyone else except you, but the truth is, I can't stand the thought of going through the rest of my life without the nearness of a man's body in my bed. I don't want any of the lefthanded honors they give to a chaste and dependent war widow."

"All right, Malvina," Robin told her. "I'll do my best. Now, let's get back to your Gustave; he's probably getting mighty anxious about his bride-to-be staying away so long."

CHAPTER TWENTY-NINE

BACK IN THE SITTING ROOM, ROBIN SAT COMFORTABLY, STRETCHING his legs, as though he didn't have a care in the world, nothing on his mind. Lieutenant Schweitzer was standing by the mantel, just as they had left him, one arm resting on its shelf. He was working rapidly down toward the bottom of another julep. His face was stormy. "I see where your uniform once had some kind of officer's insignia on it. So, I presume you were an officer; that is, if one could call the farm boys and store clerks who had commissions in both armies, officers. My personal opinion is that the only real officers, on either side, were those who were trained at West Point. Of course, you could have gotten your uniform through someone giving it to you, stolen it, or bought it. By what rank shall I address you?"

Robin was nettled, and showed it. "Just call me Mister. Mister Arvane, to you, for the time being."

The lieutenant swallowed the remainder of the contents in his glass, went to the sideboard, made another julep for himself without offering one to Robin, and stood sloshing the liquid around the glass slowly. His next words carried a ring of philosophical sarcasm. "You know, Arvane," he said, "if we could have disciplined our troops according to the standards set by the old regular army, we'd have finished the war in a few months instead of taking four years, but that big, ignorant backwoodsman they had in Washington wouldn't let it be done. The men I have here with me are a bunch of duration volunteers who think they're as good as their officers. The worst of the lot in this unit is a sergeant,

John Littlebow, who happens to have attended some little Mid-western grasshopper college. I gave him a lecture one day on the difference between an enlisted man and an officer and gentle-man. He told me, 'I'm not an officer, thank God, but I'll match you to see who is a gentleman and who's a son of a you-know-what.' I'd have court-martialed, and busted him, except for the fact that this isn't my outfit. I'm temporarily relieving Captain Clabberd while he's home on a short leave. When he gets back I'll go west to a regular army regiment. Of course, I'll report the incident to his captain to see that it's properly handled."

"Now," said Robin, meaningly, "I think that is real smart of you, Lieutenant. Do you handle all enlisted men with an iron fist?"

"No other effective way to do it," Schweitzer answered.

"Uh-huh—well, did you ever think that most of the enlisted men, on both sides, were only war-time soldiers, and that as ci-vilians they have the right to meet up with you sometime and beat the very living hell out of your frame?"

"Say," Schweitzer was angry, "I don't like the tone of your voice. Perhaps you'd like to take on the small detail of chastising me. Before you do, I'd like to give you fair warning, I was one of the best boxers at the Point."

"Why would I want to beat you up? The Arvanes don't go around picking fights with their kin, and I consider you as prac-tically a kinsman, since you and Malvina are getting married so soon," Robin answered.

"Who said anything about Mrs. Arvane and me getting mar-ried soon, or at any time?" Schweitzer spluttered at Robin, but his eyes were on Malvina, who sat with hers lowered.

"Don't get excited," Robin interposed. "Nobody said any-thing about it. I was presuming from the fond way you looked at her when she came back into this room. If that wasn't a love-look, it was one I could shoot you for."

The lieutenant drained his glass, set it carefully on the mantel. "See here," he glowered, "if you weren't Mrs. Arvane's brother-

in-law, I'd take off my officer's insignia, drag you out in the back
yard, and give you the thrashing of your young life."

Robin stood up. "That," he said, "would be dandy. You can
save your strength for fighting as far as the dragging goes." He
got up and headed for the back of the house. Schweitzer followed. Malvina made a motion to stop them, then dropped back
into a chair, sobbing.

They stopped when they were near the center of the yard.
Schweitzer started to unbutton his coat. Robin faced him, erect,
smiling. "Hold it a minute, Lieutenant. We want to have a little
talk, as one officer and gentleman to another, as you might say,
before we get into a common brawl. Let's talk things over first,
since one of us may not be able to talk when it's over."

"Of course," the lieutenant began rebuttoning his coat, "since
you want to apologize, I'll have to accept it. It's lucky for you I'm
willing to do so. Now say your say and get away from these
premises. I don't like your face, or any part of you. Is that clear?"

"Sorry you don't, Lieutenant. You may see more of it later.
I just wanted to suggest that you and Malvina rush to the courthouse and get married before the sun goes down." Robin's tone
was carefully casual.

Schweitzer's face reddened, he growled in his throat, advanced
a step. "See here, Arvane, for the last time, let me tell you, I've
seen enough of you. By God, were you, in some way, trying to
threaten me?"

"Lord, no, Lieutenant," Robin explained. "I never threaten.
I was getting ready to tell you, in a calm and peaceful way, that
General Arvane, who we understand is in command out in the
Fort Seneca section of the West, is Pa's cousin, and although we
fought against him, blood runs thick in our family. I was just
thinking how he will feel when he finds out how you came down
and seduced his kinswoman and then ran off without doing the
gentlemanly thing about it. Of course, if Cousin Cedric Arvane
should feel it was a matter he couldn't do anything about, then I
would feel it my bounden duty to trace you down and shoot you.
Please don't take that last for a threat. I don't mean it that way.

I was only stating a plain fact. Making you a promise, as one gentleman to another."

"God dammit," Schweitzer swore, "you must not know what you're saying. You're threatening the life of an officer in the United States Army. I could have you shot for what you just said. You know I can do that, don't you? I may just do it, too, to teach these damn fool rebels around here a lesson."

"You're the biggest damn fool I ever saw about getting your feathers up over nothing," Robin told the officer. "I explained I wasn't threatening. A threat is one thing and a solemn promise is another. Besides, it would be your word against mine, and you might, by using military law, get me good. I don't know much about military laws and regulations. All they ever taught me was how to fight. We knew that pretty well, I think. Even if you got me, you'd be laughed out of the army, and a big hunk of cheese like you couldn't stand that."

Schweitzer snorted, took a deep breath, controlled his voice. "No, I wouldn't for any reason fall back on the army for my personal protection. But while we're at it, I can promise you, I'm considered one of the finest shots with a pistol in the army."

"I don't doubt that in the least. I know a rattlesnake strikes mighty accurately, too. So, I've made it a practice, since I was a little boy, to never give a rattlesnake first bite. Shucks, how do you know I wasn't joking all the time? Fact is, I want to do things for you, and to prove it, I'm going to give you the pleasure you came out here for in the first place. Slip out of your coat."

Robin was as tall as the lieutenant, but about fifty pounds less well fed, which he showed, unmistakably, when he came out of his bulky military coat. Schweitzer, snorting like a mad bull, went at Robin, feinted with his left, and swung with his right for the jaw. He wanted a quick knockout. Robin ducked and side-stepped at the same time, and as Schweitzer went past, carried forward by the momentum of his mad rush, Robin reached out, caught his left arm around his opponent's neck, tightened. As he tightened, he fished a rawhide pouch of gold coins from his pocket with his right hand, swung it once to Schweitzer's temple.

Swung with a short jerking snap that looks like it wouldn't break an egg, but hits so hard. As he felt Schweitzer sagging to the ground he turned loose and stepped back, quickly replacing the bag in his pocket. "Damn," he breathed slowly to himself, "it was nothing but good luck the day I met up with the Beltons."

A tall, young, handsome sergeant, and two privates, came out of the carriage house. The sergeant looked down at Schweitzer, threw back his head, laughed. "We were peeking, Mister, but for our lives we didn't see a thing."

"I saw everything that took place," a young private spoke up. "I was looking when I saw the lieutenant come down the steps drunk, swing at this gentleman, fall down and bump his damn head. I would take oath to that anywhere." He turned to the other private. "That the way you saw it?"

"Shore was."

"If you put it that way, I'll have to back you up," the sergeant said. "That's the way it was. Do you think he'll be all right pretty soon, like in a year or so?"

"Take him in the house, put him on a couch, and leave him with Mrs. Arvane. He'll be coming around in no time," Robin advised. They picked up the unconscious Schweitzer and lugged him, not too gently, up the steps—Robin followed with the lieutenant's coat over his arm.

"Don't count on us for anything but help, if anything should come of this," the sergeant said to Robin and winked. He led his men back out of the house.

Malvina fluttered around Schweitzer, on the couch, crooning sympathy. "There he is," Robin told her, "sealed and delivered. Give him a slug of licker and he'll come out of it soon enough. If you think you still want him, he's yours."

She got the brandy bottle, poured some down Schweitzer, turned to Robin. "Did you threaten him, Robin?" she asked intensely. "You know I wouldn't take him in a million years that way."

"You heard us talking," Robin told her. "We went outside to fight. We did. He lost. That's all there is to it. However, I will say, that for his own sake you'd better marry him. I'm afraid he's reached the point where he can't live without you."

He picked up his hat. At the door he turned and said, shortly, "Good-bye and good luck, Malvina."

CHAPTER THIRTY

W HEN ROBIN GOT BACK TO THE VALLEY FROM MALVINA'S, IN-
stead of going straight home he turned down the creek road and
headed for Justus Massie's. He knew he would find what he
wanted there. He knew that come rain, come shine, come war,
come peace, Justus would have a fine stock of peeled and seasoned
logs, hand-hewn flooring, and smoothly riven puncheons on hand
against the time when someone might want to raise a house.

He explained to Justus what he wanted and told him to begin
construction of his store building as soon as possible; that the work
would be paid in spot cash, Government gold. Justus said he
couldn't get a crew together and start before six or seven next
morning. That night Robin, Pless, and Walt sat up late sketching
roughly the arrangement of counters and shelving, the dispersal
of stocks. Whiskey, they decided, would be kept back of screens
in the rear. Robin said, "We'll settle on three different brands,
at three different prices, and buy them by the full barrel. We can
sell cheaper that way."

Pless, whose early pessimism had shifted to mild enthusiasm,
said, "I don't see how you can make much money to start with,
but as the valley gets back its old-time prosperity, you'll be coming
up with it. Then, you ought to have a good law practice in a year
or so, and that'll help out a heap."

"If I can just get a very small law practice started in a year
or so, I'll think I'm doing well," Robin said.

"When you and Sallie go to Chafferton to buy your opening

stocks, don't buy too much of any one item," said Pless. "There's nothing deader than dead stock in a country store."

Next morning early, Sallie, Robin, and Walt were working over a list of what they would buy in their initial order when a flashy livery stable rig swished up the drive and stopped at the gate.

Lieutenant Schweitzer climbed dignifiedly to the ground and helped Malvina out of the buggy. Walt went to the rear of the house to tell Pamela she had company. Pless looked fixedly at the lieutenant. "What," he asked, "is Malvina doing running around with that damn blue-belly?"

"I think," Robin told his pa, quietly, "he's her new husband. Probably came out to tell us good-bye, since he expects to be transferred to the West soon."

At that moment Cessie came through the front and scooted out to meet Malvina.

"Robin," Cessie called from the yard, her arms around Malvina, "they're married, since this morning, and she's moving away from this section."

"I was afraid of that, but I'm glad, too," Robin said slowly, but only Sallie heard him say it.

Schweitzer came in, friendly but aloof. He bowed gallantly to Sallie and Pamela, shook hands with Pless and Walt, then stuck out his hand toward Robin. "Glad to see you, Arvane. Hope to see you again when time and place are more propitious for our type of fun." There was mockery in his voice. "I know it will appeal to your ungodly sense of humor to know I sent a corporal and two men out to Jumping Cat Cove to check on the report you made to me," Schweitzer went on.

"Report I made to you? As I remember, you butted in on a conversation, a little good-natured joking, I was having with my sister-in-law. Hell, I wouldn't report a dogfight to you," Robin bristled.

"Anyway," Schweitzer came back, "an old woman with a middle-sized boy and a pair of squirrel rifles met them in the road and ordered them out of the cove. She said they don't have any

Negroes, and don't mean to have any soldier around, either blue
or gray. If the information you gave me had caused one of my
men to get hurt it would have been bad for you. Of course we
can't fight women and children, so our boys left and reported
back to me."

"The woman who ran your men out of the cove was, I imagine, Minnie Gluck," Robin said. "She had four sons and her old
man off helping the Yanks. Two of the boys aren't coming back.
Minnie is convinced that both sides were aided, abetted, and led
by a passel of damn fools. Sometimes I think she's right." Robin
bowed, courteously, and turned away.

Cessie herded them into the parlor. Pless brought out his jug.
"This," he explained, "calls for a round of mint juleps, sweetened
with honey, to be drunk to a very lovely bride." He began mixing while Cessie slipped away to bring the mint.

While they were all talking, Robin noticed, from the corner of
his eye, that Malvina was gracefully tolling Walt off to one side.
Presently they were out on the porch, engaged in low conversation. Although Robin could hear nothing of what was said, he
could tell both were very intense in their words to each other. Presently he saw Malvina lean forward, kiss Walt full on the mouth,
then put both hands to the sides of his face in a most uncousinly
manner in their caressingly hovering touch. He saw Walt step
back, his face stormy and red. Suddenly Walt lifted the back of
his hand to his eyes, whirled away, and went down the steps.

Schweitzer had moved up to the side of Robin while Walt
and Malvina were visiting on the porch. She came back in the
house, made a gay, but wavering, gesture toward both of them,
and went on to the back parlor where Cessie and Sallie were.
"Did you see what I saw, Arvane?" Schweitzer asked Robin. "I
don't like to have my wife running around the country kissing
every tom-fool mountain jake she sees. After all, she's the wife of
an officer in the United States Army now, and by God, she's going to act like one."

"Listen," Robin said, "you tub of loose guts. Walt and Malvina have been kissing kin ever since she married into our family.

He has as much right to kiss his cousin as the next one. He wouldn't like the tone of your voice if he heard you mention it in that way. You can apologize to me right now for it, or I'll make you look him up and apologize personally. And, for your information, he might not accept your apology but shoot you anyway, instead." Robin leaned forward, almost whispering. "Which do you prefer?"

"If you believe I've said anything to insult my wife," Schweitzer said, "of course, I have to apologize. Actually, I suppose it meant nothing, but if you have any idea I'm doing it out of fear of a lame country bumpkin, you can think again." He turned smartly in an about-face.

When Pless had finished the drinks, he looked around, bade Cessie call Robin and Walt. "Call 'em in. This can't be done right without them," he declared.

Cessie went out the back. She returned in a few moments. "I whistled our old call three times. If Robin were in hearing distance, and wanted to come, he'd have answered back," she explained.

Pless bowed to the bride, the groom, the other ladies present. "Can't wait all day on something this important. Here's a toast to you both. Drink up."

Schweitzer sipped his drink, made a grimace. It was evident he didn't think much of mint juleps with honey. He said in a hard voice, "Sorry we have to hurry. Mrs. Schweitzer has to get back to start packing, as we're expecting to be ordered elsewhere very soon. We want to be ready when my orders arrive. We don't want to stay in this part of the country one minute longer than we have to. You'll pardon my saying it, but we are both accustomed to more of the decencies of civilization than can be had around here at this time." He was drawing on his gloves.

"In that event," Pless told him courteously, "may I wish you Godspeed."

Schweitzer turned toward the door without further ado. He ignored Pamela's hand when she thrust it forward to tell him good-bye. Malvina's face wore a look of utter puzzlement and disappointment as she kissed them all good-bye and followed her new husband out to the rig. The horse left in a fast trot, and it was only a few moments before they heard the roar of the loose planking on Modesty Creek bridge as the wheels of the rig whirled over it.

After Robin's passage of words with Schweitzer, he had left the house and gone in search of Walt. He didn't find Walt around any of the outbuildings, so he went up the path to the spring-house. Walt was there, seated on Robin's old poplar log, and Robin could tell when he was yet a good distance away, from the manner in which Walt's shoulders heaved, that he was crying. As he got nearer, he could hear both the sobbing and the cursing of a man suffering deep and abiding grief. He sat down by Walt. "Stop it," he said, sternly.

Walt raised his face, put his sleeve up to his eyes. "All right," he said, "I know I'm a baby to cry about her. But if you say she isn't worth it, I'll try to knock your teeth down your throat."

"I wouldn't say it," Robin answered. "She is worth it, and then some. But I do say grieving after her won't do you, or her, any good. You haven't any right to cry. I know about the time you asked her, and how you got the idea she didn't want a crippled man. She had the idea you were asking her because you wanted to take care of Minter's widow. If you'd had gumption enough to insist you wanted her for herself, and herself alone, you would have been her husband, right now, instead of that bastard blue-belly."

"How do you know all this?" Walt queried.

"Malvina told me," Robin said, simply. "She always tells me everything. She's married to someone else, and you have no right to interfere, but you can always know she loved you first; that you could have had her."

Robin wasn't sure he was cutting the truth anywhere near the actual pattern in what he was saying, but he believed Walt would get well of Malvina quicker if he could salve his ego. Too, Robin had a feeling that Malvina's marriage to Schweitzer wouldn't last very long, a year or so at the most; then Walt would have another chance to try his luck.

He and Walt came down the path through the apple trees, together. Walt went home and Robin went in the house. He expected his pa to be mad at him for disappearing but still wasn't sorry he had left.

His pa cocked his head and looked at Robin quizzically, but said nothing. Not so with Cessie.

"What I'd like to know, Robin, is why you were so rude to our guests. Especially to Malvina's new husband. He probably went away thinking we're the lowest of mountain trash." Accusingly, "Malvina was hurt, too."

"I met him yesterday, at Malvina's. Had to slug the bastard. I was afraid if I hung around I might have to do the same thing over. I couldn't afford to do that in Ma's house. That's the main reason I got away from him."

"But, Robin," Cessie wasn't satisfied, "he's Malvina's husband, and we owe her the courtesy of being nice to him."

"I owe him nothing, and precious little to Malvina. She wanted him. She's got him. She admitted to me she wanted him. So, now she's got him. Far as I'm concerned that makes us all even. I told you I don't like him."

"That's silly," Cessie argued, hotly. "Why don't you like him? I admit he was rude as he was leaving, and that he didn't sparkle very much at any time. He might have been rude because you said something to get him riled up. I know you wouldn't have slugged him, as you say, because he fought on the other side. You must have some other reason for your dislike. What is it?"

"I'll tell you," Robin told her, soothingly. "I don't like the way he trims his sideburns."

"But he doesn't wear sideburns," she argued.

"Then it must be that I don't like the way the bastard would trim them if he had any. Now, after what I've been through, I think I deserve a drink, so I'm going to erect one for myself, maybe two. Who'll join me?"

Robin heard Pless say quietly, as he started to the kitchen. "I don't like him, either, but I'm not suffering enough to need another drink."

Robin was mixing his drink when Sallie ranged herself at his side. "I don't mind about you slugging the lieutenant, nor about the way you treated him today, but darling, please tell me you weren't a little bit jealous of him because he married Malvina. She is truly a beautiful woman." Her eyes were pleading.

He caught her in his arms in such a way as to reassure her as to his feelings about her. "Bless your nasty, dirty little jealous heart, honey," he said laughing. "Malvina is a beautiful woman. Didn't she marry one of the handsomest of the Arvane men, my brother Minter? You know she's a few years older than I. She still thinks I'm her little brother, which is as it should be. If I had wanted her, I'd have hurried home to ask her. Instead, I took up with you, and here we are, thanks to the Good Lord."

Sallie didn't answer, but her hand on his arm told him she felt nothing was amiss.

CHAPTER THIRTY-ONE

During the noonday meal Robin said he thought he would ride into Anserville that afternoon to talk to Levi Pettyman and see if he could get some pointers.

"The further you stay away from old Pettyman," Pless said, "the better off you'll be. I would go ahead and open before he knows it. You know he won't give you any information worth anything, don't you?"

"I know he won't if he can help himself. But it can't hurt for him to know what we're planning. I believe I can winnow some few facts out of the lies he'll tell me, if I can get him to talking. I know Pettyman's a shrewd merchant, ruthless with competition, and out to cheat his customers, if he can. I think I'll talk to him anyway. That is, if you don't need the horse this afternoon," Robin said.

"Sure," Pless said, "we can get along without the black horse for a few days. Fact is, we got enough to do fixing our fences up to spare both of them for a while."

When he was ready to leave for Anserville, Robin hitched the black horse to Pless's light wagon and took Sallie and Cessie with him. The girls went to help Malvina pack, leaving Robin to himself. They found Malvina in the midst of putting things in boxes and cases for shipment. Her husband was nowhere around, but Malvina said he had ridden out to Jumping Cat Cove to look into things there. She said she tried to tell him he was wasting his time, but he still believed he had been flimflammed. He still thought there had to be something wrong in Jumping Cat that should be investigated by the army. Cessie laughed that they should all get together and kick Robin's britches off. "You wouldn't have needed to tell me Robin started the lieutenant off on a jaunt like that. I would have known it anyway. It's a typical Arvane trick. Now you know what I mean, Sallie, about knowing what an Arvane man will do in every case—if you know the Arvane men."

Robin went straight into details with Pettyman about his aim to start a store in Modesty, told him something of what he hoped to carry in stock, what he hoped to do for the valley by providing a convenient trading place for valley folks. Pettyman didn't, he told Robin, think it was advisable to start any kind of business right at the time. Especially for a man with no experience, and with things as uncertain as they were. There was, he pointed out, so little business to be had that if it were divided nobody would make any money. "Not," he added, "that I'm making anything out of this store, but if we have even one more to open in this county, there won't be enough for either. My boy," he said unctiously, "I'm glad you came and talked it over with me before you spent any money; that is, if you have any money to spend. I mean United States money. You know Confederate money ain't no good for nothing but making a fire, and it don't even burn so good at that. I'm awfully glad you came in. I'd like to explain to you how I have to scratch and dig to make ends meet. I certainly would be hurt to see a fine young man like you headed for bankruptcy."

"Hell," Robin told Pettyman, dryly, "I have a lot of confidence in Modesty Valley. I think times will get better for everyone. They can't get much worse. A little competition is good for all of us. Do you and me both good."

"I'll tell you what I'm going to do," Pettyman's voice was persuasive, "I'm going to take the goods you've bought for your opening off your hands at cost, except for just a small discount, just to help you keep, your losses down. It would hurt me too much to see a fine young feller like you, a brave soldier, just back from the war, making such a dreadful business mistake. People in this town are always saying, 'Pettyman's got a soft heart and a softer head,' but I don't care what they say, I couldn't sleep good if I didn't tell you the truth about what you're getting into. Of course, I don't know how much stock you've already bought, if any, but no matter. Big or little stock, you better take me up while I'm still soft-headed. Better you should stick to something you know instead of store-keeping. My stocks are low, but business is so bad, I'm bad overstocked, yet I'm willing to help you out. It's Pettyman's soft heart. Foolish in the head, my wife says."

"Why, Mr. Pettyman," Robin drawled slowly, "you know I wouldn't have you losing money on account of my bad business judgment. I'll just keep right on, like I planned, do the best I can, and take my losses. The experience will probably be good for me. I need something to teach me a lesson."

"Hah, hah," Pettyman forced out a squeaky laugh. "I see you are a very determined young man. To show you my heart is still soft, I will prove that I'm always willing to help out a young feller with ambition enough to go in business for himself." He winked slowly, solemnly. "It so happens I've got a tremendous overstock of the finest imported silks and satins and such. Things the elegant ladies out in Modesty Valley will mob your store to buy when they learn you've got 'em. You couldn't buy these things anywhere this side of Philadelphia, and then they'd cost you many times what I'm going to let you have 'em for. Tell you what I'm going to do: I'm going to let you have these fine goods at a lot less than they cost me; yes, a big less than cost. These goods was smuggled in through Charleston and I bought 'em months ago. I was holding 'em back to sell when people have more money. Now I just learned I got another shipment coming in, and I need the money to pay for it when it gets here. So, I'm saying to myself, 'Pettyman, don't be a hog. Divide with this young man and let him make a nice profit.' " He rubbed his hands together in a gesture of generosity, then stepped to the front, closed the door, and locked it. "Don't want anybody should come in and see me selling you these goods so cheap."

Pettyman brought three cases out from under the counter and opened them up. They were truly gorgeous fabrics, with each bolt bearing the stamp of a famous French concern. Robin knew nothing whatsoever about silks, and less about French manufacturers, but he recognized sheer beauty when he saw it. He was enthralled. He asked how much.

Pettyman made a gesture of surrender. "To you," he said, "I'll sell for fifty dollars and guarantee you can sell 'em for ten times as much, but you'll have to come and get 'em out before opening time tomorrow. Like I said, I can't afford to take no chances on my regular customers knowing I'm selling these fine goods so cheap. If you'll take 'em with you now, I'll make 'em at forty-five."

"See here, Pettyman," Robin asked bluntly, "you didn't steal that merchandise, did you, and fake up a bill of sale?"

"Ah, now, he makes a joke." There was great sorrow in Pettyman's voice. "My boy, you should never joke about goods of this quality. And you'll have to learn that businessmen must trust each other's word. I'll take forty, just to show you I want to help you out."

Robin pulled out his buckskin pouch, counted out forty dollars. "Anyway," he said, "I know I'm not stealing them. Give me a receipt."

"Ah now again, he don't trust his friend Pettyman. Wants that I should give him a receipt. Besides that, he only lays down forty dollars, when I told him plain as day I would take forty dollars a case to move these goods. Nuh, nuh, nuh. Pettyman is soft in the heart and soft in the head, but Pettyman ain't plumb crazy."

"I don't think I'm crazy, either," Robin told Pettyman. "You said forty dollars, and there it is, if you want it. If you don't, say so. I have to go, now."

Pettyman shrugged in a gesture of surrender. "If you think I said forty dollars for the lot, I'll have to take it. Pettyman never goes back on his word, even when it's said by mistake."

"A receipt," Robin insisted. "And I'll take them with me, now."

Pettyman grumbled about businessmen having to trust each other, finally gave in and wrote a receipt, but the receipt only specified that it was for merchandise. "You'll have to come around and take them out the back loading door. I can't afford to have my customers know I'm practically giving away these fine goods to a raw country boy who thinks he wants to be a merchant."

On the way home, Robin opened the cases and showed their contents to the two girls. "They're beautiful, and expensive," Sallie murmured dreamily.

Cessie caressed a bolt of richly shaded satin. "Um-m-m-m-m," she crooned over it.

"There's a nigger in the woodpile, somewhere, in this deal. Pettyman claims they're smuggled goods. If so, the most they could do to him would be to seize them for duty, unless he wanted to pay it. At least, I think it's that way. If they were stolen, we'll soon hear about it, and I have a receipt. If I learn they are stolen, I'll look up the owners and return them. But believe me, I'll jerk a big knot in Mr. Pettyman's tail. I'm going to hold them back, not let anyone know we have them, until I'm sure of how Pettyman got them. I mean to learn his side of this deal."

CHAPTER THIRTY-TWO

W HEN JUSTUS MASSIE NOISED IT UP AND DOWN THE VALLEY THAT
Robin Arvane was going to build a store at Modesty Crossroads,
and would be paying for labor in gold, men flocked to the job.
Some of them had, before the war, considered themselves men of
such means as to scorn any type of manual toil except for emer-
gencies and piddling around their barns and gardens. Now,
short of about everything they needed to clothe their families,
and with no money to buy the food they couldn't raise themselves,
they welcomed anything that gave them a chance to lay their
hands on United States money, paper or gold. They came in such
numbers as to be practically walking over each other, yet as Robin
watched them work he realized that Justus had his crew so well
organized that there was little waste motion. The building was
taking shape rapidly before his eyes.

Getting the men of the community together, working together,
talking together, laughing together, with a lot of good-natured
arguing together, was fine for the morale of the valley. It made
them think, so they mostly agreed, that their valley wasn't licked.
Here it was, with the echoes of the guns scarcely stilled, and Modesty Valley was beginning to rise from its bed of mournful despair and make a start toward rebuilding itself. Yet there had to
be some—good men and true, withal—who were of a school nur-
tured by the prophets of gloom. Among them was Jarrett Cogle,
bent and gnarled by the years. He had been on the sunny side
of middle age when he married the Widow Cedric, within a
month of the execution of Peter Gherkim, and at that time the

widow, too, had lost her pinfeathers. She had done her best by him, in the production of heirs, until the menopause caught her in the middle of a good start. Alan and Ellen closely resembled their father, but Phil, the eldest of the flock by several years, due to the loss of a couple of children in between, resembled neither a Cogle nor his mother's folks.

Robin and old man Cogle sat on a log in front of the rapidly building store. Cogle said, "Powerful fine shack for a country store. Would have been a fine thing for Modesty ten years ago, when everybody was making so much money farming the rich soil of this valley that nobody wanted to fool around with a store. But now, I'd like to know who in hell's got anything to buy with. I'm afraid you'll be in the fix of a preacher with a lot of visitors to his church, but no members."

"I mean," Robin said, "to sell on credit to anyone living in Modesty Valley I know to be honest. That way, people will have a chance to make a little money from this year's crop before they pay me. I'm betting everything I have on the valley, Mr. Cogle."

"Um-m-m-m," Cogle mused, "couple of weeks ago I might have gone for that, too, before I was called to Raleigh for a meeting with the Yankee officials, sent down here, as they said, to look after our interests. Will Holden was there, and how he got into the meeting I'll never know, being as he was one of the loudest hollerers for States' rights before the shooting started. Now he's done managed to horn his way into the good graces of them bastards as is coming in faster than our boys are getting back from the fighting.

"The South's in a hell of a fix, and it'll stay that way until it has a chance to grow enough stuff to get the wrinkles out of its belly and some clothes on its back. On top of that, we've four and a half million niggers, in the flat country, who think freedom means they are going to set down on their behinds whilst the white folks feed 'em. Some of 'em are fool enough to believe that forty acres and a mule stuff, too. I'm plumb discouraged, and nothing less." Cogle snorted.

"But," said Robin, "don't you think we can try to get along with everybody for a while until we see how it will work?"

"Ain't nothing going to work whilst they's enough whites left for the Yanks to pester and enough blacks to make a pizen proposition to." Cogle was bitter. "Me having a boy on each side is like being about half-North and half-South. Now I don't know where I stand," Cogle finished.

Alan Cogle, formerly of the Twenty-ninth Carolina, put in, "I hear the blue-bellies in Anserville have been passing out a lot of stuff about making the South pay all war costs. Hell, the big boys up North know if the South had anything left to pay for a war it would still be fighting."

"We were a mite low on rations," Robin admitted.

Said Alan, "I only hope Phil don't bring back that line of guff."

"Did he say anything about coming home?" Robin asked.

"He wrote Ma he was going to be mustered out in Ohio and that he would probably stay up there. Finest part of the country he ever saw, he said. In fact, he wrote Ma he'd be taking his life in his hands if he came back because there are people in the valley would shoot him in the back. He told her he wasn't afraid, and when he got ready he would come on, hoping his enemies would try something."

"He may be," Robin confided in Alan, "talking about me. Write him that if he thinks I want to kill him he can forget it. He can come home a-running and I won't bother him; that is, if he treats me right."

"I'll tell Ma what you said, and she can write him. We don't get along too well. We faced that Ohio cavalry he says he was a lieutenant in, twice, and I'd have shot him just as quick as I would any other Yankee. Phil's a bigger man, in size and strength, than I am. But if he starts trying to take and walk over me like he did when I was little, I'm going to shoot him. And if he starts jawing about the war, and sniggering at me for being on the losing side, I'm going to warn him once; then if he can't stop, I'll shoot him, so help me God."

"That," Robin pointed out, "would be about the most foolish thing you could do, Alan. He's your brother, and we have other men in the valley who'll be glad to take him down a notch without killing him, I hope."

"Well, probably I won't shoot him," Alan promised, "but I can't say positive what will happen if he starts his old ways with me."

The next day, with both horses trotting spiritedly pulling the light spring wagon, Robin and Sallie passed through Anserville at four in the morning on the way to Chafferton to buy the first inventory for the new store. Robin believed, if he could keep from getting cheated in his purchases, he could figure out fair retail prices at which he could make a profit. It was almost dark when they reached Chafferton, where, tucking Sallie's hand under his arm, he led her off to the nearest public inn.

A merry-faced, little dumpy woman presided at the registry of the hotel. She looked perkily at Robin, asked, "You a Arvane fr'm Modesty, ain't you?"

Robin admitted as much.

"This must be your wife, though I ain't heard of no weddings up that way lately. But that don't mean nothing no more. News don't git around like it did before the war."

"Well," Robin told the lady, "let's not come right out and say we're married—that is, not too much. You know how some fool husbands are about their wives traipsing around the country, stopping at this and that hotel with just about anybody. I think we'd better keep it kind of quiet that we're stopping here. We'll sort of slip up to our room and lay low until we're ready to leave. You being in the hotel business know how it is."

"Yes," said the lady, frowning mightily and laying the registration card back on the stack. "I know just what you mean. And it so happens, young man, I ain't in the business of operating a house of assignation. You can use the same door you came in, or if you're afraid of being seen, you can slip out at the back—right now." Her eyes snapped angrily.

"Now wait a minute," Robin argued, "we're tired and hungry.

Give us a room and I swear I won't touch the lady, except maybe to hold her hand. You're a young and handsome woman. You know how it is when you're young and full of vigor. You wouldn't throw us out, would you, just because we happened to have married people we don't like?"

"I'm not young and I'm not full of vigor. And I never spent the night in a hotel with anyone except one of my three husbands. The quicker you leave, the better for you."

"O-ho," Robin crowed, "so you're a bigamist. Married to three men, and you want to tell me I can't go to bed with just one woman." He winked at the landlady several times, trying to make her catch on. His aim was to tease Sallie, with the landlady going along with the joke. The landlady had failed to get the joke, and she was almost on the point of throwing things. In the meantime, Sallie, whom Robin had wanted to tease, was stuffing a handkerchief in her mouth to keep from laughing. Finally, she could hold it no longer. She whooped hysterically, then went off into a long series of uncontrollable giggles. After a while she stopped, with the landlady looking quizzically at her, while Robin urbanely walked to the window and gazed out into the street.

"Robin," Sallie said, "if our good hostess will kindly stick a knife in you on one side, I'll hit you on the other with one of these big spittoons. You big fool, why did you want to tell the lady we're not married? Were you trying to tease me? Ma'am, we're about as married as it's possible to be, and if you'll just give us a room I'll take him into the dining room and feed him, then take him to our room and cut his confounded throat. I may take him up and cut it now, and save the price of feeding him!"

The landlady's dumpy bulges shook happily. "I should have known he was joking all the time. I'm sorry, my dear, I should have known better. I should have noticed you are the kind of lady what don't go around stopping at hotels with every strange man that comes along."

Robin wasn't through; not yet. "Well," he said, solemnly, "you've got me. I'll have to admit she is my wife, even if it does make me look like a fool. I'll even have to admit that she doesn't go around stopping at hotels with strange men. But I want you to understand one thing: I'm no stranger to her, and she'd stop at any hotel in the world with me, married or not, thank the Good Lord."

"Robin!" Sallie cried, as he deftly ducked the reticule she threw at his head. The landlady swept regally from behind the desk with a lamp in her hand to show them to a room. Robin was still chuckling as they went up the stairs.

Their first port of call next morning was Ed Brownlow's Emporium, Chafferton's largest retail store. Brownlow's stocks were low, and he frankly admitted they had gone down badly during the war, and now, due to the generous credit he had extended his customers, he had little money with which to replenish them. "I'll hold on," Brownlow explained, "try and build my stocks back as I can. In the meantime, lots of people who owe me will begin paying off. I expect to be back in business in a big way, in two or three years, if the Yanks will let me."

Robin frankly told Brownlow what his plans were and explained that he wanted some advice before he visited a wholesaler. Brownlow studied a bit, reached for his hat. "I've known three generations of Arvanes and never found a bad apple in the lot. The kind of folks," he was addressing Sallie, "who always look straight ahead, and go that way. Come," he said, turning to Robin, "I'll go with you. We have two wholesale factors here in town. Both are almost honest, but not so much that they would turn down a little extra profit. We'll go pick out what you want from their available stocks and leave orders for the remainder to be shipped as it arrives. I suppose you got cash to pay. If you have, they'll ship you just as fast as the stuff gets here. I'll guarantee they won't try to overprice you for anything when I'm with you. They'd better not," he finished, under his breath, but Sallie heard him.

By noon, Robin was the owner of a fair stock for a country store. He left orders for the goods he wanted that were not on hand at that time. They told him Lanthus Cedric's outfit would be through Modesty with his merchandise before the week was out. Robin's pocket pouch was lighter when he finished counting out gold coins to pay for his purchases.

Ed Brownlow thought he had bought wisely and well. He said so. "It does me good," he told them, "to see a young, returned veteran buckling down and trying to get the pieces back together again." He sighed heavily. "I won't live long enough to see all the pieces back in place; that is, as they will finally be set up, but you will. Any time I can help, you let me know." He shook hands with them, bowed to Sallie, and trotted off to his own store, after waving their attempted thanks aside.

"There goes a man," Sallie mused softly to Robin, "who couldn't do anything but good. So kind and gentle. So anxious to help others. He couldn't harm a fly."

"I believe you," Robin laughed, "but they say he wasn't always that way. They tell it that about forty years back he killed two men, within a few months, for messing with his wife. The only reason he didn't kill the third one was because she ran away with him before Mr. Brownlow caught 'em."

"I don't believe it," Sallie spoke hotly.

"I don't either," Robin told her. "Probably just one of those rumors that get started and pick up mud as they roll along. Shucks," he was laughing softly, "I reckon a mild man could get pretty wild if he knew his wife was cuckolding him."

"But, Robin," Sallie argued, "if a man knows his wife is untrue, he is not a cuckold. He can only be a cuckold when he doesn't know, or suspect, a thing while the affair is going on. He has to be completely unaware of her infidelity before he can grow the invisible horn on his head. He doesn't know its there; nobody else can see it, or feel it; but it's there, just the same. At least, we know that's what they believed in the old days."

"Tell me one thing," Robin asked, facetiously. "If a man grows this invisible horn, will it interfere with his wearing an invisible hat?"

"That," she told him, fondly, "is enough of your smart talk, you fool. Let's hurry, and we'll have a whole hour in our room before supper."

CHAPTER THIRTY-THREE

THE SOUTHERN ARMIES WERE PROBABLY DEMOBILIZED THE MOST rapidly of any fighting group ever assembled in comparable numbers. Since spring comes late to the mountains, most of Modesty's men who fought with the South were at home by May, or before, working hard, putting in crops, using whatever methods they could devise for the operation, swapping seeds and work.

It must be admitted that though corn, wheat, and cotton went out of sight in price, the greater part of the agricultural South suffered agonizingly in 1865. Not so in Crinshaw County, which had always lived at home as far as the necessities of existence were concerned. So, it is putting it mildly to say that the mountain counties of the State did not feel the economic heel of Reconstruction the first year after the war as did the remainder of the South.

By the latter part of May Robin had the store open for business. It immediately became an unofficial meeting place for the folk of the valley who came to discuss politics and cuss out those of their own people who had gone over to the other side, politically, with no other idea in mind than self-aggrandizement. The pattern of things to come was dim and wavering in the late spring and early summer of 1865, but its noisome shadow was there nevertheless. The pattern could be seen by the discerning who studied the ominous rumblings coming out of Raleigh from the citadels of the carpetbaggers, the mugwumps, the Will Holdens, and others of their ilk.

Robin had been talking with ex-judge, ex-colonel Ambrose

Bower, who had returned to Anserville after a short stay in a Yankee prison. Bower, of course, was disbarred, along with all other ex-officers of the Confederacy who had held a rank above major. He had, however, reopened his office to have a place to hang out and look after his other interests. Too, there was nothing to keep him from dishing out free legal advice as long as he kept away from a court appearance. He looked forward to the day when he would return to active practice. He loaned Robin law books, told him how to go about study, promised periodical quizzes to see how he was progressing. Robin allowed Walt to do as much as he could alone, while he busied himself with his studies. They watched the total of accounts receivable mounting, and Robin wondered if he would have enough money to last until gathering time. With these thoughts came the reminder of the independence of the Carolina mountaineers. How badly they hated debt. He believed, if he could hold on until a crop was in, he would get his money, or most of it.

Thus, Robin resolved to go along with his neighbors as long as he had anything to throw in the pot. He told Sallie he was willing to risk every cent he got out of the Belton episode, but he didn't feel right using her heritage. She told him that, all right, if he felt that way, she would, by damn, take her money out and lend it to people to pay cash with in his store. He promised to use her money along with his.

Folks in the valley wanted things back on as even a keel as possible. Old man Jake Weldon, who had the most vinegary tongue in the valley, the Lineberry brothers, and old man Massie, along with Beamish Cedric, who had by now returned from the war, were vociferous. Weldon said, "We got us a store for the valley, thanks to Robin Arvane, and we got most of our men back, who'll be coming back, but we still ain't got no school, n'r a preacher for Modesty Church. I tole that dang fool, Arch Barnes, not to go off to no war and git hisself kilt when the valley would be needin' him the rest of his days, dependin' on him, jist like it done his pappy, but he wouldn't listen. Arch had to be a-leadin' an' a-hollerin' hell and damnation when that there minnie ball cut 'im down. Josh Todd, he even done worse. He run off to fight with the North, but bein' as how he was fr'm up there som'ers, we can forgive that. Now we ain't got no preacher in our church, an' no teachers in Modesty Academy. All on account o' Arch Barnes ruther be dead than not be a-leadin' somethin'."

Massie cut Weldon off. "Th' way you're talkin', Jake," he said, "don't do no good. What you said is true as Gospel, but it don't git us no teachers and preachers. We ain't got but damn little to pay 'em with if we could find 'em. The teacher we must git. We can't let our chillun raise up in ignorance of schoolin' an' ignorance o' the Good Lord. Talkin' won't git one. We got to do somethin'."

Robin hadn't meant to tell them Josh Todd was coming back to the valley, even though he had a letter in his pocket at that minute in which Todd said he would arrive very soon. That he was bringing a sawmill with him, and that he hoped to get the school for its next term. Before he could say anything, one of the Lineberrys spoke up. "We ain't got but one valley man, as I know of, who could teach Modesty, an' that's Phil Cogle, an' while I heeard he's got a lot o' college learnin', I likewise heeard tell he ain't got nothin' else. My chillun swears they just wouldn't go to school to Phil. Robin here, or Walt, fr'm what I heeard tell, could teach everything but them Latins and high up 'rithmatics, an' chillun don't really need such trash, nohow."

Robin butted in. "I have a letter here that says Josh Todd's on his way back to Modesty. He wants the school. So that problem is automatically solved. He'll be marrying Miss Ellen Cogle when he gets here, and he'll probably let her help with the primary grades. Now, I have an idea. I know we need a preacher as much as we need a teacher in Modesty. So, let's sort of get together and elect Josh Todd to both jobs."

"Josh Todd's a good teacher, but he damn shore ain't no preacher," Weldon snorted. "We want a man as feels he was called by the Good Lord to preach the Gospel. How we gonna git Josh Todd to feel that way?"

"Let's put it this way," Robin told Weldon and the others,

persuasively. "We all know Josh Todd's a good man. We know he has to love the Good Lord to be that way. Preaching His Word for one who loves him shouldn't be so hard. I happen to know Josh Todd will do most anything to stay in Modesty because he's so much in love with Ellen, and because he loves the valley. As far as Josh is concerned, the valley's the only home he ever knew. He was booted around from one boarding school to another, until he grew up, then into West Point. From the Point he was in the army for a good while, but he never had a real home, with real people to love, until he came to Modesty Valley. We all believe the Good Lord works through His children, don't we?" Weldon had to nod agreement to this premise.

"Then," said Robin, adding a clincher, "the Good Lord will be working through His children, giving Josh the call to preach when he's told he's the new preacher in Modesty Church."

Beamish Cedric spoke up. "Suppose Josh don't see it that way? Josh can be powerful stubborn, sometimes."

"He'll see it all right if you tell him we haven't got the means to support both a teacher and a preacher, so it will have to be both or nothing. Of course, you can't be bossy about the way he's told. You'll have to sort of ask him, and act powerful sorry we can't afford a man for each job. I believe Josh will be one of the finest preachers Modesty ever had."

"Hell's fire," Weldon snorted, "we ain't never had nothin' but Barneses before, an' no better preacher than a Barnes never peed through rawhide. But I'll take to your scheme. I b'lieve Josh'll make us a good un. Le's jist privately app'int a committee, here and now, to wait on him when he gits here an' tell 'im the good news."

Weldon, old man Massie, and one of the Lineberrys agreed to see Josh and tell him about his great opportunity as soon as he showed up in the valley. Robin decided, to himself, to see Ellen Cogle and explain the deal to her. He knew Ellen would want Josh to take the post at the church, she being of a religious turn of mind anyway.

Josh Todd did arrive in the valley and kicked like a steer when

he heard what was in store for him. At first he dignifiedly refused; then as he was pressed by both the committee and Ellen,
he asked for a little time to think the matter over. He had seen
Robin the day before, but Robin had given him no inkling of what
the valley was preparing to do to him. Robin told Josh he could
have his horse, pistol, razor, and other things back any time, and
that he dearly appreciated the loan. "In the first place," Josh said,
"the horse wasn't mine, and I'm afraid you'd get in trouble trying
to give him back to the army. As for the other things, I want you
to keep them forever and always remember me with the same affection I hold for you, whenever you use them." With arms
twined over each other's shoulders, they went to the back of the
store and toasted each other in some spirits Walt poured from a
large wooden barrel.

Just then, Lanthus' ox team creaked and groaned to a stop at
the rear of the store, and Lanthus Cedric unloaded a small shipment to supplement Robin's meagre stocks. He pocketed payment, ran a practiced eye around the store. "It ain't," he pronounced, "a very big stock, but it's mighty complete when you
consider what they is to buy. Now, gimme about two fingers in a
wash tub an' I'll be moseyin' on to Mollie's to spend th' night."
He turned to Walt, "Young feller, I reckon it mought do you good
to go that fur with me."

"Thanks, but I don't think I will," Walt answered. Then,
half-timidly, he told them about his one visit to Mollie's. Told it
straightforwardly, without trimmings, or lack of detail. When he
had finished Todd was chuckling softly, and Robin was half dou-
bled up in laughter. Seeing the memory was in no way funny to
Walt, Robin straightened his face as best he could and withheld
comment.

Lanthus nodded gravely. "That's Mollie, all right. Allus
as good as the next un, expectin' to take her turn when the time
comes. No sirree, you can't slight Mollie an' git away with it, not
even for her own gals. She aims to be the queen bee as long's she
c'n git in an' outen th' bed. Young feller, what you done was
plumb bad. She'll hold it agin yuh as long as they's water in that

there creek, unless yuh do somethin' about it. Come, git yo'r hat, and go alongst with me, whilst I put in a good word for yuh. As long's yuh live in the valley you're gonna be a-needin' Mollie more'n she'll be a-needin' yuh. Trip to Mollie's tones yuh up like a spring tonic, knocks the meanness outen yo'r soul, and puts sweet thoughts in yo'r heart. Makes yuh humble and thankful for th' many things th' Good Lord put on this earth for His chil-lun to enjoy. Git clumb aboard my wagon. Them steers o' mine'll walk over there in no time."

Walt told Lanthus he really appreciated his generosity, but he didn't believe he could make it that day. "Well," Lanthus advised him seriously, "it can't be nothin' but free goods as would keep a young, healthy single man away fr'm a high-class place like Mollie's. Let me tell yuh somethin', you mought have free stuff behind every bush in this here valley, but yuh can always remember I told yuh, free goods don't lead to nothin' but killin' an' sich-like, whilst at Mollie's they ain't never nothin' but peace an' good will."

A few minutes later they could hear Lanthus swearing beautifully to his oxen above the noise of the wagon's heavy rumblings.

CHAPTER THIRTY-FOUR

THE NEXT MORNING THE SUN WAS BARELY POPPING A RED EYE over the top of East Ridge when Josh Todd came into the store. His face was stormy, his greeting stiff. Robin was alone in the store, and Josh got right to the point. "Your unofficial committee came to see me last evening," he told Robin without preliminaries. "Don't try and say you didn't send them. I know better. I could see your face at the beginning of every sentence they uttered. You sicked Ellen on me, too. I thought, until now, we were such good friends you would let me run my business like I mean to let you operate yours."

"Now wait a minute, Josh," Robin pleaded. "Maybe I did have something to do with it. I understand the valley can't afford to pay the cost of both a preacher and a teacher, so I stuck my big mouth in and said there was only one man in the world could do justice to both jobs and that you were that man. I still believe that, but if you don't want to do it, then that's your business. I was trying to let them know what I think of Josh Todd's ability to do anything. That you wouldn't be willing to do it for Modesty Valley and Ellen never occured to me. I'm sorry if I've hurt you, but I won't take back what I just said, that you are the only man I can think of who can do an adequate job in both positions."

"I haven't said I won't do it," Josh said, slightly mollified. "It's like this: I've never even thought of preaching. I like to teach, but preaching's another thing. Besides, I've always been a Methodist, and Modesty Church, while it calls itself nonsectarian, is really about as Presbyterian as they come. I don't know that they would like my brand of preaching, if I should try it on them."

"Shucks," Robin answered, "that's no reason at all for not preaching in Modesty. You love the Good Lord. Practically everybody in Modesty does, or so they claim. You just get up and tell them about His Goodness. They'll understand that. Hell, Josh, that's what this valley needs right now in the way of preaching more than anything else. Just preach and stay out of Scriptural arguments with your members, and I'll personally guarantee we'll have the most popular preacher in Crinshaw County. I can't think of anything that would thrill Ellen as much as having you as pastor of her church. You know that, Josh."

"I think," Josh said, musingly, "I might try it for a while. If I find I can't handle the preaching, they will leave me alone with the school and find another preacher. My mind's still not made up, but I might, just might, try it that way."

"Dammit, Josh," Robin exulted, "nothing could be fairer than that for all concerned. Let me handle it from this end and I'll see that you get what you want."

"You mean what you want," Josh answered, his voice soft but short, as he turned, walked out of the store.

Walt was still out and Robin was idly turning the pages of a lawbook when Cessie came breezing in, breathing rapidly, excited. She pulled a seat next to his and sat down. "I hurried coming up from the house," she told Robin. "I have a Yankee soldier friend I hope will be stopping by here in a little while."

"Who?" Robin asked.

"I don't know his name." She laughed tinklingly. "But I saw him first around Malvina's, then just now he passed the house riding up the creek road with two other soldiers. You've got to do something to make him stop here on the way back to town."

"Do you want me to go outside, waylay him, and drag him in, if that's what it takes to stop him as he comes back by?"

"That would be all right with me, if there's no other way to get him in here so he can learn who I am," she said dreamily. "I wish I had just a little paint for my cheeks like they use in the city."

"You're a hussy," Robin told her, without emphasis.

"Yes," she answered, getting up and beginning to prowl restlessly around the store, poking under the counter, peeking at the shelves.

"Look all you want," Robin told her, "but don't mess with those boxes of goods I got from Pettyman. They're not to be fooled with until I learn more about what Pettyman's game is. I'll let you know when I do; then you and Sallie will have first pick."

They heard horses stamping in front. A moment later Robin rose and went toward the door to meet a dapper Union cavalry sergeant, who was coming in. Through the open door he could glimpse two privates sitting their horses in the bored manner cavalry at rest have always sat their horses. The sergeant, who looked to be about twenty-two, flashed a bright smile from under a struggling mustache. He was well set up, of medium size, and almost as blond as Cessie. He held out a hand to Robin. "I am," he said brightly, "Sergeant John Littlebow." His eyes shifted to Cessie's face, "but you can call me Little Bo-Peep. I just dropped in for two yards of reveille."

"We're plumb sold out," Robin told him, seriously, "but I can spare two quarts of retreat."

"Can't use it. Makes me sick. Tried it several times and never did get to where I liked the stuff." He was speaking to Robin, but his eyes kept shifting to Cessie's face. Robin murmured, "Sergeant Littlebow," and introduced him to Cessie.

The sergeant went to the door and looked out at his men, shook his head. One of them laughed, called out, "Go on, you said you would." Littlebow turned back toward them, his face muscles hardened. "I've been given to understand, Mr. Arvane," he said harshly, "that you've got a large shipment of smuggled goods, silks and such, out here. Really, I hope you haven't, for it will mean a term in the penitentiary for you if it's true. I'll have to look around and see."

Robin let it sink in. His first thought was that Pettyman was framing him. He turned the thought over and his anger boiled up. "Got a warrant?"

"Don't need any," the sergeant replied. "Man, don't you know I am the United States Army?"

"If you were General Grant, you couldn't search my place of business without a warrant, except over my dead body," Robin said, and moved slightly forward.

"Come, come, my good man," the sergeant said, authoritatively, "will you show me the goods, or do I have to call my men in to search the place? If I have to do that it will mean, of course, more time in jail for you." He shrugged lightly.

At that moment Robin saw, from the corner of his eye, Cessie behind the counter. In a flash her hand dropped to the cubbyhole where he kept his pistol. In another flash, holding the gun in both hands, she shot the sergeant in the meaty part of his left arm. The sergeant sat down quickly on the floor and pulled his sleeve tight in an effort to stop the flow of blood. As the powder smoke cleared, curling toward the ceiling, Robin saw the sergeant's companions coming through the door, their pistols at ready. One of them pointed his gun at Robin, the other squatted by the sergeant.

"What happened, Johnny Reb?" the soldier who was covering Robin wanted to know.

"I shot him. Don't you see?" Robin answered, heatedly. "God dammit, put me under arrest, and let's get it over with."

"He did no such thing," Cessie cried, facing the soldier. "I shot him. I'm glad I did. I'd do it again."

"Which one's lying, Sarge?" The soldier turned to his sergeant. Robin could tell, from the spreading blood, it was only a snig-shot. It might bleed pretty freely for a while, but it was nothing to worry about.

"I shot myself," the sergeant said and laughed shortly. "I was examining that big pistol and it went off accidentally. I can assure you it was purely accidental on my part."

"Now we know somebody's lyin'," the soldier who still held

his pistol in his hand, said. "Th' cap'n's gonna want to know the truth. He'll make us sign a report."

"The cap'n's a clabberhead," the sergeant stated from his seat on the floor. "I said I shot myself, and that's the way it's going to be reported. You didn't see a thing and he'll have to take my word. These people are old friends of mine. I came in and tried to tease them a bit about some cloth they bought from old man Pettyman, but they caught on right away. I was trying to toss the gun up and catch it, and it went off. That's all. To show you these are my friends, I'll bet you ten dollars they're planning to take me home with them and doctor me up while you ride into town and report to Clabberhead."

They helped Littlebow to his feet, but he staggered against the counter, gasping weakly. "Sorry, boys; must've lost more blood than I thought. You've got to help me."

The two privates made a cat saddle of their hands and Littlebow seated himself on it. They walked down the road to the Arvane home with Robin showing the way, while Cessie ran ahead to get a bed ready for the wounded sergeant. As the two soldiers were leaving, Littlebow told Robin, "Sorry, it was all my fault. Joke looked too good to pass up, until I saw your sister; then I didn't want to go through with it, but the others sort of called my hand, made me. I want to apologize to your sister and pay whatever you say for the time I'm here."

Robin laughed heartily. "Apologies accepted, pay rejected. Now you lie still and rest while I get some things together to kind of clean up that little snig-shot you've got, and first thing you know you'll be as good as ever. I'll have to slip a probe through to be sure you haven't any cloth inside, that the bullet might have taken in; then I'll wash it out with some whiskey, put some of Ma's best salve on it, and you'll find it well in a day or so."

Littlebow slung his feet on the floor. "I'll help you," he said. "I wasn't weakened any. I just wanted a chance to come home with you, and at the same time I got a good joke on those lug-brains by making them tote me all the way. I could get up and

run a mile right now." Just then Cessie came into the room
with a basin of water, some white cloth, and other things for fixing up Littlebow's wound. He heard her light step in the hall
and fell back on the bed, groaning weakly.

It was the next morning before Captain Clabberd, with an
army doctor in tow, showed up. The doctor looked at the wound.
"Probably has you a little weak right now from bleeding, but it's
nothing to worry about." He handed Cessie some black salve
with an evil odor. "Change the bandage once a day and put on
this salve. Keep him in for a week and he'll be as good as new."

"Now, Sergeant Littlebow," the captain said sarcastically, "since
you're not going to die, I'd like to ask you one question, and I
want a truthful answer. Did you, or did you not, wrap a toad in
lettuce leaves and put it in my lunch kit when I went fishing
yesterday?"

"Did anyone tell you they saw me do a thing like that?" Littlebow asked, horrified.

"You know damn well nobody told me. But you are the only
man in my command low enough to do a thing like that in the
name of a joke."

"Then, of course, if you feel that way about me, I didn't do
it," Littlebow said.

"Would you take an oath to that effect?" the captain pursued
the subject.

"Put it this way, Sir," the sergeant evaded mildly. "You didn't
see me. Nobody else saw me. And the toad, up to this moment
refuses to talk. Speaking as a man who someday will be one of
the great lawyers in this nation, I'd say you haven't got a shred
of evidence that would stand up in court."

The captain was getting angrier by the minute. He forgot he
was in the presence of civilians. "It has come to my attention," he
stormed, "that you habitually refer to me as 'Clabberhead.'" I
don't like that, either. Is that true?"

"I always did admire clabber," the sergeant said, placatingly.
"It's a noble and refreshing beverage in its place. Did you ever
taste clabber, Captain?"

"I want to know," the captain shouted, hoarsely, "if you ever, at any time, referred to me as 'Clabberhead.' "

The sergeant moved his head sideways and back and forth, as though he were thinking deeply. "I wouldn't take oath either way," he finally said. "If you should prove I ever called you 'clabberhead,' I would prove it was done out of admiration and affection because I'm so fond of clabber."

"Littlebow," the captain thundered, his face getting redder, "I'm sick of your jokes, your idea of fun. The order for your discharge came through yesterday. You're to be discharged right here in North Carolina just as soon as I think I can spare you. Since I've got some discharge blanks in my pocket, I have a mind to write yours at this minute, and then write out a report showing that your present injury was brought about by your own carelessness and not caused by any military duties. How would you like that?"

"That, Sir, is up to you. I can take anything you're man enough to dish out. Miss Cessie, will you bring the captain a pen, and we'll see if he's man enough to do what he just threatened." Littlebow scowled at the captain, then turned a beatific smile toward Cessie.

For a few minutes the room was quiet except for the scratching of the pen as the discharge was being filled in and a pay voucher drawn. The captain handed them to Littlebow. "You are," he pronounced, "no longer a member of my command, and I can assure you I'm quite happy to say so."

Littlebow took the discharge, folded it neatly, tossed it to Cessie. "Take care of that. It might come in handy someday when I'm running for Congress and want to prove I was an enlisted man. Who knows but what they may be paying veterans pensions someday?" He leaped off the bed, seized Cessie around the waist, took her through a few fast dance steps, while he whistled the tune himself. Then, to the astounded captain, "Thank you, Clabberhead. I'd kiss you if it were not for ruining my meals for a few weeks. Don't make so much noise as you exit." The door slammed mightily as the captain departed.

"Now, Cessie," he went on, "if you'll just let me clean up a bit, we'll go and ask your father if he can stand having me in the family, after he's had a chance to check up on my folks. Shoo, gal. Go don your prettiest dress while I get myself shaved and slicked, so I'll look as presentable as possible when I ask Mr. Arvane to give me his life's blood."

With Cessie gone, Littlebow told Robin, "I suppose you knew I was possuming, but, gracious, man, who wouldn't lie around and pretend to be an invalid if he had Cessie to wait on him? I'm going to marry that girl, unless you shoot me first. But I do have a few things I'd like to tell you about."

"I'm listening," Robin said.

"Back home, in Littlebow, Iowa, I was always the leading practical joker in the county." He was talking seriously. "I not only couldn't pass up a chance to play a joke, but I'd go far out of my way to create opportunities. Cessie already knows this, but I want you to hear it. A joke is fun, but when it's liable to hurt someone it becomes cruelty. Cessie made me see that. I learned when we first came South about old Pettyman having some silks and satins, and I figured they must have been smuggled, though I couldn't have proved it to save my life. I don't know if having them, even though they were smuggled in, is against the law. Pettyman, I knew, wouldn't know either, so I decided to have some fun." He paused and chuckled.

"I'm listening," Robin reminded.

"Yes, sure. I dropped in on Pettyman, told him I had been detailed to learn who in the county possessed a large shipment of smuggled goods. Told him I had been detailed to find out. That having them on hand carried a penalty of up to ten years in prison. I could tell he was scared stiff, but still he swore he knew of no one who would handle smuggled goods. He even promised to help me in catching the culprit. I went back every day and pushed him a little harder, just enough to keep his nerves jumpy. I could tell he wasn't sleeping any too well, and I got scared he might destroy his merchandise, so I decided not to let the joke go any further. Yesterday I went in his store, meaning to tell him

all about it and have a good laugh with him. Well, Sir, Mr. Pettyman saw me coming, came down the midde of the floor to meet
me like he was actually glad to see me." He paused for a moment.

"I'm still listening," Robin again reminded him.

"As soon as I got inside, Pettyman locked the door and then
informed me he had located the man with the smuggled goods.
He said not to mention his name, but if I would search your store,
I'd find them. He hadn't, he swore, actually seen them, but he
could describe them well enough for me to be sure when I found
them. I think this is what happened; you can put me right if it
isn't. Pettyman unloaded the goods on you, thinking it was illegal
stuff; then he wanted you to be caught with them on hand. Man,
he was mad when I told him I'd been joking all the time and
there wasn't a thing I could do about it. He was boiling. Swore
he'd have the law on somebody. I pointed out it was good enough
for him, the way he thought he was sticking you. He calmed
down then and tried to get me to say I'd see you and try to buy
the stuff back for him at three hundred dollars. I told him he'd
have to handle any transaction he had with you himself."

"Then what?" Robin asked.

"Well, I thought I'd have a little fun with you and then tell
you the straight of things, but it seems the joke backfired. I got
a swift kick in the britches, which I admit I deserved, but I'll
also admit I'm glad it came my way."

"Thanks for explaining," Robin said. "Don't tell Pettyman
you saw me. I'll keep the goods back a little while longer and see
what happens. Of course I wouldn't let him have them back for
any amount. This is one year the ladies of Modesty Valley will
wear silks and satins."

"That isn't all I want to tell you," Littlebow went on. "As I
said, I want to marry your sister. My folks are decent people,
back in Iowa. They sent me to college, and I'm going to study
law as soon as Cessie and I are married. We've got a section of
black Iowa land to make sure we won't ever starve, completely.
I'll promise to cut out the joke-playing and get down to the business of making Cessie happy, if I can get you and your father to

agree to our marriage. What do you think?" The last was spoken seriously.

"It's not for me to think. The Arvanes don't do business that way. If Cessie wants you, she'll know if you're any good before she goes through with it," Robin told the sergeant.

"You mean I don't have to ask your father?"

"I didn't say that. I say he won't interfere if Cessie thinks you're decent. You'd still owe him the courtesy of asking. Pa doesn't believe in interfering with his children's lives as long as they keep themselves clean. He'll tell you if it's what she wants, then it's what he wants. He may try to get you to stay here in the valley. Why don't you consider settling down here? I'm studying law, too. We could be partners, perhaps."

"Can't be done," Littlebow argued. "I've got my eye on being a congressman from Iowa one of these days."

"If you live that long," Robin laughed. "Her aim might be better next time."

"Huh," Littlebow snorted. "She only shoots to protect a thing she loves." Then, fondly, "Man, what a protection that girl's going to be for me when I get into a hot political race."

Sallie and Cessie were chattering in the kitchen. Cessie moved over to Littlebow, and they stood each with an arm around the other's waist while Robin mixed their drinks. Cessie trilled, "Robin, isn't it wonderful? He's all I ever dreamed of in a man, and a million times more."

"I thought you said," Robin reminded teasingly, "that you were looking forward to a regular rockslide of beaux as soon as all the men get back from the war. Now you grab the very first one comes after you. Seems to me like you got caught powerfully easy."

"He wasn't after me," Cessie said. "I had to shoot him on the wing. I almost faint when I think what could have happened if I'd missed." She began to cry softly.

"Well," Robin bantered, "I'll bet on one thing. You'll never know what your husband will do next."

"He isn't very damn predictable, is he?" Cessie said.

The two girls looked at each other and giggled mysteriously.

CHAPTER THIRTY-FIVE

THE NEXT MORNING LITTLEBOW WAS OUT OF BED EARLY, MAKING preparations to take Cessie and Pamela to Iowa to meet his people. "You can," he told Pamela, "amuse yourself by the hour just listening to my mother talk Iowa language with a Swedish accent. She'll enjoy listening to your sugary Southern drawl. You'll take to each other."

When Robin reached the store that morning, he found Levi Pettyman seated on the steps, nursing a large black cigar. Pettyman followed him inside, where Walt was unpacking a new shipment of calico, took a seat, and looked appraisingly around the store. He gazed intently at his cigar, which was beginning to burn unevenly on one side, for a moment; then, "Well," he slapped his palms together, "it's like this: last night I couldn't sleep for thinking about you and this store."

His voice was dripping with unctious solicitude. "I finally woke up my wife and said, 'Pettyman should be ashamed of himself. Him, with a whole lifetime of experience, knowing all there is to know about running a store, letting that poor innocent country boy, from 'way back in the mountains, get himself drowned in the sad sea of inexperience, when just a few words of advice from Pettyman could, maybe, save him from bankruptcy, keep him in business.' That's what I said to my wife, and she gave me hell. She says I'll never change. Always wanting to help other people when she ain't hardly got enough clothes to keep from showing her own nakedness, and not enough food to keep from being hungry half the time. She told me I was about to be soft-hearted again. She thinks I ought to let you go on and lose all you've got so my business would be that much better."

"You came out to help me, Mr. Pettyman?" Robin asked, anxiety in his voice.

"That I did, my boy. I'm always helping other people get ahead. That's probably the reason Pettyman is not a rich man today." His tone was modest.

Robin kept a straight face, laid a bolt of calico on the counter, pushed it toward Pettyman. "How is that price for this kind of goods?" he asked Pettyman.

Pettyman felt the fabric, moistened his finger and thumb, examined it more closely a second time. After a moment's hesitation, "Mighty shoddy, mighty shoddy. Very cheapest shoddy," he said dolefully. "My friend, you'll do well to get six cents a yard for this shoddy, fourth-rate piece of goods. I see you have it priced sixteen cents. You will do well to change it down to six, and you might sell it for that to people who don't know much about quality. Pettyman would sell the same goods for four cents a yard, if anything of such low quality should happen to get into our store. Pettyman don't buy shoddy. You know that, Mr. Arvane."

"But I paid ten cents for that cloth," Robin remonstrated.

"Ah-h-h-h," Pettyman sighed. "Inexperience, it is, again. The poor boy, cheated out of his eyeballs by sharpers who don't want nothing but to unload their worst shoddy at the biggest price they can get. My boy, my boy, I came out to try to show you how to price your goods, how to buy, and how to run a store, if I could. I see without going no further that you would need several years of experience before you could run a store and make it pay. My little friend, just to show you old Pettyman is as soft in the head as he is in the heart, I'm going to take this stock off your hands to save you from bankruptcy. Now, that don't mean I can pay you what it cost you, for like I said, they cheated your eyeballs out when you let 'em sell you the goods in the first place. Pettyman don't lie about such things. You believe that, don't you?"

"Well," Robin answered, in a flat, toneless voice. "Let's put it this way: I don't believe you would tell me a complete lie. To be a complete lie the listener would have to believe what he hears. And I don't believe a damn word you've uttered."

Pettyman's face flushed in anger for a moment, but only for a moment; then it cleared. "All right," he said blandly, "let's talk about the goods you bought from me. I'm going to tell you the truth about them, and if you don't believe me you can send out and get a stack of Bibles as high as the moon, and Pettyman will climb on top of them and swear if you keep them fine silks and they catch you with them, you'll go to the penitentiary for about ten years. I got that straight from the United States Army."

"Is that so?" Robin asked, showing interest.

"Yes, that's so," Pettyman said, quickly. "I'm going to explain things to you; then if you still want to be bullheaded, the bad luck'll be on you. I didn't know it was against the law to sell smuggled goods at the time I let you have them. Then, after you was gone with 'em, and I learned they was illegal, I thought to myself, 'Well, maybe they won't catch him before he sells them.' Y'see, it was like this," he lowered his voice, "that sergeant who is looking for these goods heard, some way or another, that you had them, so I'm afraid he's on your trail. So, I got to thinking about it, and I said to myself, 'Pettyman, you can't let that young man suffer for your mistake.' That's why I'm willing to buy them back and take them off somewhere and burn them. You get your money back, and we both get in the clear. Y'understand?"

"Look here, Mr. Pettyman," Robin said sternly. "You know the only thing wrong with those goods is they are a little soiled from the dirty trick you tried to pull, but that kind of soil doesn't show. However, to show you I'm not one who goes out to get revenge for dirty tricks played on me, I'm going to allow you to return the forty dollars I paid you, and five dollars for my time hauling them."

"Now," Pettyman said, giving his hands a dry wash, "I want to congratulate you for being smart."

"Damn right," Robin agreed. "I'm smart. I'm going to take your forty-five dollars and keep the goods."

Pettyman put his purse back in his pocket. "Not while Petty-man is breathing, you ain't," he said.

"That's up to you, Pettyman," Robin answered. "Sergeant Littlebow has been discharged from the army, and right at this minute he's down at my pa's house. If you can't see your way clear to give me my money back, to sort of reimburse me for the profit I lost by holding them so long while I cleared the title, I'm going to take the sergeant to Anseryille and we'll spread the news far and wide about how you tried to gyp me and wound up making a fool of yourself. Funny thing about it is, folks'll believe me, but they all say, and believe, you are a natural liar. Hurry up, give me my forty-five dollars so we can get back to work."

Pettyman counted out the money in United States currency. "Pettyman," he groaned sadly, "has learned a lesson. It don't never pay to be soft-hearted."

As he started to turn away Robin dropped the roll of currency into Pettyman's coat pocket. Pettyman paused, took the money out, wet his thumb and counted it.

"I told my wife," he said, "that young feller won't take advantage of an old man twice his age. He wants to do what's right. She said, 'Pettyman, there you go, thinkin' ever'body's like you, always wantin' to give back somethin' to keep people from thinkin' bad about you.' I knowed you was jokin' all the time. Suppose we don't say nothin' to nobody about it, huh?"

"Mr. Pettyman," Robin said, "I have a witness that I gave you that money. He knows all about the transaction. If you'll agree to talk us up, tell what fine people we are, how honest and fair-dealing we are in business every time you get a chance, Walt and I will agree not to tell a soul in Crinshaw County how you got roped in, and how you came around crying on our shoulder, and how we gave you back your money. You do just that and we won't make everybody laugh at you for getting yourself out-foxed."

"I will boost you if you just don't say nothin' at all about Pettyman."

"That will be fine," Robin said, walking away.

After Pettyman got out the door, Walt said, "I don't know all about what you and Levi Pettyman were jawing about, but I hope you feel honest."

"About the honestest I ever felt," said Robin. "Pettyman won't dare open his trap against us now, nor resort to any kind of dirty competition for a while. His kind had rather be known as a smart crook for two dollars than a dumb gentleman for a hundred. We could make him look pretty silly, the way he sees things.

"Say, let's change the subject. It's time to decide how the manager of this store wants to work. Do you want to be a full working partner, with a monthly draw, or had you rather work for straight wages?"

"I think that's up to you. I'll work either way you want me to, but you know as well as I do that I have very little more knowledge about storekeeping than I had when we first opened, which is next to nothing," Walt answered after a minute of deliberation.

"Shucks, you needn't try to hand me that. You know all there is to know You know how to work, treat folks right, and keep yourself honest. The way I've got it figured out, that's all there is to know about it. So, if you will accept the proposition, beginning with the day we opened, you get half the profits, if there is any, and of course a small drawing account to apply against your earnings from profits. I think I got you in a bind there, Walt. That way you'll be working like hell, trying to show big profits, while I take it easy. I got you so the more you make for yourself, the more you make for me. I think that's just dandy, don't you?"

"Well," Walt admitted, "it beats walking behind a plow on a peg leg. So, I'm game to try it if you are. Of course, I'm going to expect you to take the final say in anything that comes up of any importance."

"That'll be all right with me, if I happen to be around. But the first time you duck a decision of any importance because you can't find me for an opinion will be the day we dissolve this partnership. Now, Mr. Manager, where do you think we would stow this new plowline rope?"

CHAPTER THIRTY-SIX

THAT SUMMER OF 1865 WAS KIND TO MODESTY VALLEY. THE weather was perfect for crops and farm prices were high. Robin could see they were going to make more money by far than he had dared hope. Thus, when he had an opportunity to purchase them, he presented Pless with a pair of fine mules and took the horses off farm work. He also acquired a red-wheeled buggy, which served to remind him of the awful condition of the roads. The latter condition Robin improved by organizing Volunteer Citizens Working Parties, who agreed to give more than the usual five days a year to road upkeep. He didn't get perfect highways, but a man could take a horse over them with less danger of its breaking a leg.

By the time he reached his twenty-first birthday, Robin Arvane was the recognized community leader in Modesty Valley. Pless confided in Sallie, "I don't know whether to be proud or worried about Robin. It looks like he's driving mighty fast for a man as young as he is. You know, wearing boiled shirts on weekdays and keeping shaved up like a city preacher might someday turn some of the valley folks against him. Every time I see him he seems to have his nose buried in a lawbook or some other kind of reading matter, which, of course, is all right, only it just doesn't seem like Robin that way. Big thing I fear is, he'll get so much learning he'll haul off and leave the valley like so many Arvanes have done in the past. Learning is a wonderful thing, if you've got a place to use it, but here in the valley it's something you've got, and which you're mighty proud of, but you can't admit in public it belongs to you."

"Speaking of leaving the valley, I assure you Robin has no intention of ever doing that," Sallie said.

"I hope not," Pless said. "I lost Minter in the war, for always, and now since Cessie and her ma came back from visiting the Littlebows in Iowa, it looks like I'm losing Cessie for part time. When I'm gone, there won't be many Arvane men of our family in North Carolina. That's why I'm saying I would hate for Robin to be so successful he'd leave the State," Pless concluded.

"Don't worry, Daddy Pless, about his leaving the State. Robin's not going anywhere without me, and I'm not going. Understand. That's a solemn promise."

Pless reached over, patted her hand. "You're one of the finest daughters a man ever had," he said with a slight catch in his voice, "and I truly thank the Good Lord for you." He picked up his hat and started out.

"Wait a minute," Sallie called. She crossed the room to Pless, threw her arms around his neck, kissed him lightly on the cheek. "That," she said, "is because I love you as the finest father a girl could have, and because I want you to help me play a little joke on Robin. Will you?"

Pless grinned happily. "Anything you say, honey."

She giggled in her throat. Then, "Go right now and tell that Mr. Smarty Britches I've been building you a grandchild for almost three months." She giggled again. "You can also tell him he thought it was all in fun, but I was serious all the time."

Pless found Robin alone in the store when he walked in a few minutes later, bursting with the big news about Sallie. Robin could tell Pless had something so good on his mind he couldn't keep it. "What is it, Pa?" he asked, grinning broadly.

"Well, Robin, Sallie wants me to tell you that a few weeks ago when you thought you were having so much fun, she was playing for keeps. She says she's going to be busy for the next six months, and a little more, building a grandchild for Pamela and me. If Zack's or Minter's wife had ever confided a thing like that in me, it would have seemed unladylike and embarrassing. But from Sallie it sounded just like the word of God Himself."

Robin stopped his work, walked to the counter, perched on it. A wide, soft smile gradually spread over his face. He breathed a slow tune, in a soft whistle. "The little devil. And she hadn't even told me. Since Sallie's not here for me to kiss, I'm going to hug you, Pa. Sallie loves you a lot; you know that, don't you, you old he-goat!"

"Sallie loves everything in the world that's worth loving. And those things not worth loving, she pities," Pless told Robin, seriously.

Robin went to the whiskey barrel, drew a couple of drinks, and sat down with Pless to enjoy them and debate the greater desirability of a boy or a girl. "Whichever it is, I'll be disappointed if it doesn't look exactly like Sallie."

"That's exactly the way you should feel," Pless agreed. "As for me, and Pamela, we're praying the Good Lord to send you plenty of boys and girls."

Robin laughed again. "Remind the Good Lord," he said with a slight chuckle, "I'll be doing my part right along."

They were still feeling good over the news Pless brought, still talking and half-planning, sort of open-house daydreaming, as it were, when a stranger of ample girth and florid face walked in. He looked around, searchingly, at the layout of the store. Finally he cleared his throat, after the usual preliminary greetings. "If you," he said to Robin, "are Mr. Robin Arvane, and I understand that's right, I would like a few words in private with you."

"This is my pa," Robin told the stranger. "I have no secrets as far as he's concerned. You'll have to speak in his presence. And, by the way, you haven't told us your name yet."

"That, Mr. Arvane," the stranger said blandly, "is of no importance. But it just happens to be Jones. Plain old Jones. I represent the sovereign State of Kentucky. Actually, I work for the Pinkerton organization, but we're doing a bit of special investigation for the State of Kentucky. I believe, from what I can learn, that you passed through that state about the time the Belton gang was wiped out. In fact, you traveled from the scene where they lost their lives in this direction, bringing with you the Bassett girl, who I believe is some kin of the man who owned the farm where the massacre took place. We got that much information from a man named Hembree. That's all he could, or would, tell us. Whoever rid the world of the Beltons is due a sizable reward from the State of Kentucky. Can you throw any light on the circumstances of their demise?"

"Let's see your papers," Robin said.

The portly man apologized and fished from his coat's inside pocket some legal looking documents bearing the seal of the State of Kentucky. Robin studied them, decided they were authentic.

"Yes," he told his visitor, "I might be able to give you some information. Again, I might not. You'd have to give me some first. It's true I passed by the Bassett farm, found Miss Bassett there, scared to death of the Beltons. Afraid they'd come back and do to her what they had already done to her kinsman. They had killed him some time before. He's buried out in the woods, back of the house.

"We wondered why we couldn't find any trace of the old man. Thought, perhaps, he might be a member of the gang, maybe double-crossed them in some way. I'm glad to get that information. You are, I believe, married to Miss Bassett now?"

"Now," said Robin, "it's my time to ask a question, or two. Where did you get your first information? If you don't feel like telling me, you can consider our interview closed."

"It came in a letter from the State of Ohio. The writer asked that his name not be divulged. He said he got his information from the relatives of the Beltons up in that state. So far as we can check, we have found the information he gave us correct. Your wife is chiefly the one I'd like to question. Can we go see her now?"

"Not now, or ever," Robin answered, quickly. "I won't have her disturbed. You may ask me all the questions you wish."

"In that case," said the portly man imperturbably, "let me go back to the beginning. My agency theorized that you set a trap for them with a gunpowder-loaded jug. That somebody did is easily provable by what was found on the scene, and in the bodies of the dead men. We believe that, after they were all dead, you took what gold they had on them and left the scene, taking Miss Bassett with you. Please understand, we're not holding that against you. We think, up to that point, it was fine work. Now here's the rub. Kentucky long since declared the Beltons outlaws with individual prices on the heads of all. The total of the rewards for killing them is exactly ten thousand, five hundred dollars. All you have to do to collect that reward is to admit you killed them, and I have authority to hand you a draft on the State of Kentucky for the entire amount. We have enough evidence to support your word if you want the reward."

"Suppose I should admit I did it, which I haven't, so far, what about the money you say your people think I took off them?" Robin asked.

"That's the rub I was speaking of," Jones told Robin. "You see, since they had been officially declared outlaws, anything they owned, or had on their persons at the time of their death, would automatically revert to the state. That isn't the way I'd like to handle it, but it happens to be the law."

"Put it this way," Robin argued. "Suppose I should admit the killing of the Beltons but said I didn't take any money from their bodies. What then?"

"Young man," the portly one said, blandly, "we can almost prove you killed the Beltons. We would have a hard time proving you robbed them afterwards. We would know we were being cheated, but we'd pay the reward."

"Let's put it this way, then," said Robin. "I don't want any reward for ridding the world of the Beltons. I'm not saying, either way, whether I got any money off them. But, if you'll give me your draft on the treasury of Kentucky, I'll endorse it back to them, and you can close the case. Another feather in the cap of the Pinkertons."

"That, my friend, I consider eminently fair," Jones said, with a broad smile, as he produced a draft and filled in Robin's name, handed it to him.

Robin endorsed the draft, "Payable to the Treasurer, State of Kentucky," signed his name, and returned it to the Pinkerton man, who folded it carefully and put it in his pocket. "Mr. Arvane," he said, "this will clear the case for the State of Kentucky, and, of course, add something to the reputation of the Pinkertons. Your cooperation is greatly appreciated. While I am not at liberty to tell you who sent the letter that put us on your trail, I can tell you the man who wrote it said he'd known you all your life, and that, in his opinion, you were a member of the Belton gang and had been since you were supposedly captured by the Union Army. He said you had very probably double-crossed them, taken all the money in sight, and skedaddled back to Modesty Valley. I shall leave it to you to figure out who he might be. A very good day, and thank you, Sir." He turned and walked out of the store.

"That low son-of-a-bitch," Robin murmured angrily, to himself.

"Seemed like a powerful nice fellow to me." Pless spoke up.

"I didn't mean him," Robin told his pa. "I was talking to myself about Phil Cogle."

That night, as Robin and Sallie lay talking in bed after the manner of young people in love everywhere, Robin told Sallie he would have to hurry and finish his law studies so he could have his license to practice by the time the baby was born. "It will probably look like you," he told Sallie, teasingly, "and people will swear it can't be mine because it will be so beautiful. I want to be able to take such gossip into court and make anyone who passes out that kind of slander eat his words." Sallie giggled and told him to shut up.

Then she told him about her talk with Pless that afternoon. "What did Daddy Pless mean, Robin, when he said education is something to own and use, but not to show?" she asked.

"Well," Robin explained, "it's like this. You and I know you've got the loveliest figure in the world. Everybody in Modesty

Valley, or anywhere else you've been seen in a tight dress, knows it. But the minute you take off your clothes, start waving that figure around to prove the point, everybody will say you're a dirty low-down wanton."

"I believe," she whispered humbly, "I know what you mean." She snuggled closer to him.

" I know you do," Robin whispered back, his lips brushing her cheek. "Another thing I want you to know is I'm powerfully glad that man from Kentucky came along today and made an honest man of your husband."

CHAPTER THIRTY-SEVEN

T HE LAZY DAYS OF AUGUST WERE DOING THEIR BEST, WITH A beaming sun by day and cool clear nights, to spread a pall of indolence over the green-clad hills and field-patched valleys of Western North Carolina that Sunday in 1865 when Cecily Arvane became Cecily Littlebow.

John Littlebow and Cessie stayed in church for the sermon, as was the custom in Modesty, then departed for Iowa.

It had been during Josh Todd's sermon, after the wedding, that a stranger came in. At least, Robin thought at first it was a stranger, but after a second look he realized Phil Cogle had come home. Phil was dressed in the same cut and quality of clothes one would expect to see on one of New York's foppiest dudes. When the sermon was over and the congregation started to file out of the church, Phil stepped outside and stood waiting by the side of the steps. Most of the congregation paused for a moment, shook his hand in welcome, told him they were glad he was back, then went on their way. Some of the others nodded politely, but distantly, while a few passed, acting as though Phil didn't exist. Old Jonathan Weldon, in his vinegary twang, and without offering to shake hands, said, "Well, Phil, you're shore dressed up fit to kill; only most of us know you ain't."

Phil arched his brows with a glint of temper in his eyes; "I'm not what? I don't know exactly what you mean."

"I mean," Jake answered sourly, "that getup on your back in Modesty Valley, it makes you look like a mangy hound what's had chicken manure daubed on him, then had a lot of fine feathers stuck in it to try to hide what's underneath. When I say you ain't fit to kill, I mean you ain't worth it, less'n a man didn't have nothin' else to do that day. I hope you know I don't mean nothin' by my little jokes." Weldon sniggered maliciously and walked off. Robin, who knew how much Jonathan Weldon disliked Phil, was glad when Weldon left. He knew the crotchety old man would as soon stick a knife into Phil Cogle as anything he could think of.

After having his Sunday dinner, Robin reopened the store. He was reading up on torts when Phil walked in. He greeted Walt shortly and strode across the floor to Robin's office. Without a word, he took the extra seat by Robin's desk. Robin marked the page in his book, leaned his chair back, said, "Well, Phil?"

Phil crossed one well-tailored leg over the other, contemplated his glitteringly shined shoes for a moment. "Arvane," he said, in an officer-to-private tone, "I want to talk to you."

"Well," Robin told him, placatingly, "I don't know of anything to stop you from talking to me as long as you don't say the wrong words."

"We both know," Phil came back, "that the night I left for the army you had threatened to kill me the next morning. I couldn't afford to harm you with the difference in ages what it was. You and I know that, but does the valley know it? Would you be willing to tell them now that I didn't leave because of any fear of you? Well, would you?"

"Why," Robin wanted to know, "should I go tell them you didn't leave because you knew I would kill you if you didn't, when I have never told anyone but Walt in the first place? I haven't mentioned it, and if you want to live long and do well, you won't either."

"No," Phil answered hastily, "if you haven't mentioned it I don't see why we shouldn't let sleeping dogs lie. I understood that you were just a boy, and that you would be trying hard next morning to forget it. The truth is, I had already made my plans to leave that night."

"Wait a minute, Phil," Robin commanded, harshly. "I didn't

ask you to come to me and rake this thing up. I meant to try to forget it, if I could. But you don't seem to want it that way. For your information, I would have very likely killed you that morning, just as I promised. I had a gun, and I was looking for you. If you don't believe that, call Walt in and ask him. I think I could have killed you, because we both know damn well I'm a better and quicker shot than you are, unless you showed a hell of a heap of improvement in the army. If you came in to try and stir up something, you've come to the right place. I'm easy to stir that way."

"I came on an entirely different mission." Phil toned his voice down. "It was really a business call. I just wanted to get a few things straightened out in your mind. As for starting anything with me, I'm here to tell you, I no longer believe in trying to settle a difference between two men with guns. Too damned uncivilized. If you should start on a fight with me, I would insist that it be like a couple of gentlemen, fist and skull, a fair fight to the finish, and let the best man win."

"Balderdash," Robin said. "You weigh in the neighborhood of two hundreds pounds. I'd do well to push the scales up to one-fifty. If we ever tangle, and I haven't got my gun with me, I'll do my damnedest to push my knife deep into you. But because I won't fight you fist and skull does not mean you're going to get away with any big talk with me, either. Always remember a few things when you want to start anything with me. If I have my gun with me, I'll shoot you. If I don't have it, I'll knife you. If, for some reason, you catch me without either, then I'll try to kill you with anything I can get my hands on. Goodbye, Phil. Come back to see me sometime, say about a hundred years from now." Robin stood up.

Phil kept his seat, gave a short, sarcastic laugh. "Keep your shirt on, Robin. I was joking you. Just seeing if you had the same old Arvane temper." He laughed again. "I see you have. I did, really, come on a business matter."

Robin sat back down. "Let's hear what you consider business;

but remember, I haven't much time for palavering. I've got work
to do."

"Here's what it is, and I'll guarantee you'll admit I'm your
friend when I tell you this. I heard about a gang of outlaws operating in Kentucky, while I was in Ohio, before I was mustered
out. So, the other day, on the way home, I stopped off in Frankfort to see if any rewards of any consequence were out for them.
I thought, if there were, I might try for them. This will surprise
you: I learned that the entire gang had been wiped out, and that
all trails to the one who did it lead to your door. But they didn't
say they were going to come down here to try and do anything
about it, mainly because they think it wouldn't do them much
good. They think you'd deny it and that would be the end of
the whole thing. Now it's like this: I also learned there are dead
or alive rewards out for the gang that was killed totaling ten
thousand and five hundred dollars. I didn't let them know I knew
you, but I hurried on down to Modesty to put you wise. The
thing for you to do is to write to them, claim the rewards, then go
pick them up; that is, if you can prove you did the Beltons in.
Naturally, as your friend who put you wise to the deal, I would
expect you to split with me. I would think that fair, wouldn't
you?"

Robin seemingly pondered what Phil had said for a few moments. "Phil," he said, "I don't know how to figure you. How
your mind works. It's all far beyond me. You're a genius, no
doubt about it, but in the wrong direction. Here's the way I see
it. You can correct me if I'm wrong on some minor points. You
read in the paper that the Beltons had departed this earth in sort
of a hurry, and that it all happened on the place of a man named
Bassett, who had disappeared along with his niece, Miss Sallie
Bassett. A little later your ma wrote you I had returned from the
war, bringing a new wife from Kentucky named Sallie Bassett.
And since I had made no secret of coming home through the section of Kentucky where the Beltons stopped breathing, you put
two and two together; so as soon as you heard I came home from
the war with enough money to open a store and extend credit to

the valley, you wrote the authorities in Kentucky that letter telling them you knew I did it and that you were in touch with some kin of the Beltons who had given you the information. If you had known at that time there was a reward out for the Beltons, you'd have never said a word about it. Instead, you'd have beat it home and told me right away, hoping to horn in on it in some way. You showed a little intelligence in your analysis of the situation, but you didn't know until now that Kentucky had already sent a man here to interview me, and that he had authority to pay the reward on the spot."

"In that event," Phil said, "you'll still have to admit, if your story is true, that I did have a lot to do with your getting the reward, no matter how I might have figured it. It seems to me that, under the circumstances, you should make some division with me."

"Phil," Robin laughed, "my old friend, I will be glad to give you exactly half of what I got of the reward; namely, nothing. I endorsed the check payable to the Treasurer of the State of Kentucky and gave it back to the Pinkerton man who brought it here. I, of course, wouldn't expect a low son-of-a-bitch to understand that."

Phil Cogle leaned back in his chair, stunned for a moment; then he leaped to his feet. "Arvane, don't tell me you were that kind of damn fool. If you're telling the truth, which I doubt, you're more kinds of a dolt than I thought, and that would be going some. Don't you know you can't trust those Pinkerton's? If you actually did a fool thing like that, I'll bet you any amount the State of Kentucky never sees any part of it."

"I can't take just any amount, Phil," Robin said, "but I'll take a bet up to five thousand the check reached the right people. Put up, or shut up."

Cogle sat, with his chin resting on his palm. He had a disgusted look in his eyes, and his brow was puckered in thought. "Oh, hell," he breathed as much to himself as to Robin, "I'd about as well tell you. I'm completely disgusted with this damn little backwoods valley. Here I come home from four years of hard fighting in the war, and what do I find? I've given my life, up until now, for this valley, and when I come back to it, what do I find? I mean, what do I find that's worth any man's while? Everyone I've met, so far, has acted like I just left on a weekend visit and they hadn't missed me at all. I find my beloved sister married to that damn Yankee, Josh Todd, a man I never thought was good enough to lick the boots of a Cogle. Not only do I find her married to him, but I find him actually preaching in the church I learned to love as a small child, and which I carried as a bright jewel in my memory through four long years of campaigning.

"My own brother, as he always has, frankly shows he's jealous of me. Ellen says she was engaged to Todd when the war started, yet she never told me, her own blood brother. I chided her for it this morning and she plainly told me she had never thought her actions were any of my business. Well, I mean to make them some of my business. You wait; I'll run this Todd out of the valley before I quit. Wait and see. Oh, hell, I should have known what to expect in the backwoods and stayed in Ohio, where a man can get things done in a big way."

Robin shrugged his shoulders lightly. "I don't see any chains on your legs," he told Phil. "Why don't you go back to Ohio? Better for you, maybe. Damn sight better for Modesty Valley."

"Oh, I'll be going, sooner or later," Phil answered truculently. "Only reason I came home was I lost my mustering out pay in a a little game that was rigged against me. I came back to sell my share in the place to Pa. I know he's got the money to buy me out, hidden away somewhere, but he swears he's completely strapped. I should walk out and leave them all in the lurch. I know this little valley isn't big enough to hold me and Josh Todd at the same time. You know, by rights of being the eldest son, and the only one with any education to speak of, I should be managing all the business affairs of the Cogle family, running everything, but with Alan and Ellen against me, and with this Todd coming up as reinforcements, I haven't got a chance."

"If you're so damned eager to help manage things for the

Cogle family, I don't imagine you'll have too hard a time getting your pa to give you that mule he's been managing up and down corn rows all summer. That mule can give you some real farm management experience," Robin told Phil.

Phil Cogle jumped to his feet. "I'll fix Josh Todd's wagon wheel. Just watch me."

Walt, who had been unable, if he had tried, to keep from hearing the conversation, stuck his head in the door. "You so much as harm one hair on Josh Todd's head," he gritted at Phil, "and it's not done in a fair and square way, I'll fix you quick."

Phil gave a short laugh. "You and your peg leg; what could you do?"

"Dammit, I can shoot as well as ever. Don't be fool enough to forget that," Walt squalled back.

"There'll be no more talk of shooting around here," Robin warned. "Perhaps I shot my mouth off too much about it a while ago. If so, I'm sorry. I'll tell you what, Phil; if Josh runs you out of the valley, and you have a little something for security, I'll let you have the money to get back to Ohio. I think every man has the right to live where he wants to live. Fact is, if I had any way of knowing you'd stay away from the valley forever, I'd give you the money to leave on."

Phil strode toward the door. "Remember what I said," he warned as he went out.

"What's wrong with the damn fool?" Walt asked.

"Sore because he ran out of money and had to come home. Sorer still because when he got here he didn't find his pa in position to dish him out a little something for his wallet, like he used to. Disappointed because he didn't get a hero's welcome. I'm afraid," Robin said, solemnly, "he's going to talk himself into making trouble for Josh." He turned back to his lawbook.

CHAPTER THIRTY-EIGHT

T HAT EVENING JOSH WAS IN FINE FETTLE AND PREACHED ONE OF his nondoctrinal sermons, more of a lecture on humanity's debt to the Good Lord than an effort to prove a point of any kind. Josh went through the rise and fall of the Roman Empire, drawing a parallel, connected those early days with the present, proved that human nature, in the main, is unchangeable. Robin thought it was good and was with the many who crowed around Josh to tell him how much they enjoyed his sermon.

As the crowd turned and started out of the church, Phil Cogle stepped forward, faced Josh: "As a member of Modesty Church, Todd, I want to tell you I think what you said tonight was about the most asinine collection of meaningless words I ever heard. If these people knew enough to understand how idiotic you really sound, trying to preach, they'd run you out of the valley so fast your shoe heels would catch fire. I'm serving notice that, as a member of Modesty Church and as a citizen of Modesty Valley, who has done about as much as the next one for the community, I'm inviting you to resign and get out of the neighborhood as soon as possible. Please understand I make no threats in the house of the Lord, but as soon as I can catch you elsewhere I can't make any promises as to what I might do." He turned quickly on his heel and left the church.

For a minute Todd stood white-faced, trembling with surprise and anger, but holding his tongue. Robin gathered from the buzz of the conversation around him that Phil Cogle was in for trouble if he tried to harm the preacher. Real trouble, trouble that he

would remember for a long time, if he lived to remember anything. Sallie caught Josh's arm. "Come go home with us, Professor," she coaxed. "That way you won't have a chance to see Phil
tonight, and he'll have an opportunity to simmer down by morning. He might have been drinking. There's plenty of room down
at Daddy Pless's, you know."

"I don't care whether or not he ever simmers down," Ellen
spoke up to Robin. "All I want is to get my hands on him. He's
always had more of his way, more of everything, than the rest of
us. He was sent to the University until he had to leave because he
wouldn't study, and has made trouble wherever he went. When
he came home from school, he wanted them to fire Josh and let
him take his place. The fact that nobody wanted him to teach
their children only made him hate Josh that much more. He's
just mean, that's what. He didn't join the Union Army because
he cared one way or the other about the causes of the war. He
joined because we showed a little pride in Alan when he went
away and joined up with the South. For his own good, he'd better
not harm one tiny little hair on Joshua Todd's head."

"Come on, darling," Josh touched his wife's arm. "I think
we'd better take Sallie's advice. After all, I am a minister, you
know, and by your choosing."

Ellen was still belligerent. "All right," she said, "I'll do it, but
I'm not ever truckling to Phil Cogle again, no matter what."

As the four of them walked away from the church, Robin
wondered what manner of man Phil Cogle could be to engender
so much hatred for himself in his sister, a woman ordinarily so
gentle as Ellen.

The moon was riding so high and beautifully across the top
of the sky that they couldn't resist the temptation to stop at the
store and sit on the steps for a while talking, airing their hopes
and plans for the valley's future, their hopes for the country. They
carefully skirted around any reference to Phil's outburst. Robin
told Josh he thought he would be able to take his bar examination within another six months, asked Josh's advice on some classi-
cal reading. Josh offered some suggestions. Robin made mental

notes. They were discussing the Union League, which Josh at that time thought was fine, and which Robin distrusted in the same degree that he distrusted Will Holden, the turncoat who was heading toward a State dictatorship, when they heard two voices coming nearer and nearer, rising and falling in hot argument.

"It's Phil and Alan," Ellen said, quietly. Nobody else spoke again until the two came through the moonlight and stood before them.

Phil, spreading his legs slightly, stood over Josh. "Todd," he snarled, "I should have known you'd run out. I waited at the house for you to bring Ellen home, so we could step down to the pasture. I didn't want her to have to see what I'm going to do to you. So when you didn't show up, I came looking for you. Do you want to step down the road, or do you want to do business right here in front of Ellen? Personally, I don't give a damn, at this moment. Tonight I'm going to give you a chance to fight a fist and skull fight, but, after tonight, if you still want to stick around Modesty Valley, I don't make any promises."

"Phil," Josh said, breathing heavily, "you're making it hard on me, a minister of the Gospel, and your brother-in-law. However . . . ." He was removing his coat.

"Stay out of this, Professor," Alan shouted, as he hit his brother in the mouth.

Phil was thirty to forty pounds heavier than Alan, but the fury of Alan's attack made up the difference in the first flurry of blows. Then, they stood toe-to-toe, slugging it out, until Phil's superior strength and weight began to tell. He landed on Alan's jaw. Alan staggered. Phil hit him again and he went down, lay still for a minute, then sat up, his sides heaving, his throat whistling for breath. Phil stood over Alan, a foot drawn back. "Try to get up," he screamed, "damn you, try to get up, so I can kick your brains out, like I'm going to do to the next son-of-a-bitch."

Just then Robin noticed Ellen had darted across the road, was coming back, approaching Phil. He saw the rock in her hands and smiled satisfiedly to himself. He saw the rock as it thudded back of Phil's left ear against his head. He saw Phil crumple, fall, and lie still. A moment later Ellen was crying hysterically in her husband's arms. Walt, who had been in the back of the store going over the books, came clumping out on the porch. "How come?" he asked.

"Let Robin tell you in a minute," Sallie butted in on Walt. "I'm going to take the Professor and Ellen on down to the house and let you and Robin handle the situation here. I hope seeing all this won't affect coming events. Gosh, Robin, Mrs. Cogle must have watched a hard fight about six months before Ellen was born."

"She must have," Robin grinned. "Of course, if it's a boy, I'll want him to be a little bit belligerent, but a girl—well, I want my daughters to be ladies and faint like their mother every time they see anything that looks like a little violence!"

"If I wasn't pregnant, and liable to have a baby any time after the next six months, I'd throw a rock at you, Mr. Arvane," Sallie giggled as she went up the creek road with the Todds.

There was quiet assurance in Robin's voice as he ran a finger along Phil's head and mashed hard against the rapidly swelling lump back of the ear. "He's all right. Skull's not cracked, I fear," he said. He brought a bucket of water from the store and told Alan to clean up his face and then let Walt mosey home with him. He wanted to stay and talk with Phil. Alan and Walt were out of sight when Phil started coming around. Finally, groaning, he sat up. "Arvane," he asked, "did you slug me from behind?"

"No," Robin answered, quietly, "I didn't. Your loving sister did, for which I thank the Good Lord. She won my undying admiration and respect when she tapped you with that rock." He reached down and helped Phil to his feet. "Come on in the store," he said. "I'm going to do you a big favor, I hope."

Phil, on wobbly legs, followed Robin into the store where, grinning wryly through busted lips, he said, "If you do me a favor it will be the first time anyone ever did in Modesty Valley." He sat down weakly.

"I've been thinking," Robin told Phil, "and I've come to the conclusion that I wouldn't blame you if you left the valley and never set foot in it again. I not only think you'll never have any more peace here, but it might be dangerous for you to stay."

"I told you," Phil interrupted, "I'm broke. And Pa won't let me have any money; claims he hasn't got it."

"Well," Robin said, "I don't think he has. If he had any money, I would think he'd break an arm taking it out of his pocket to give to you in order to help you get away. I'll tell you what," Robin continued, mildly, "if you have something I can hold until you can pay me back, I might be able to scrape up enough for you to get on your way."

Phil dropped his head, thinking. "I've got," he said slowly, "two very fine, matched, gold-mounted pistols, a solid gold watch, and that expensive shotgun Pa gave me when I was twenty-one. I would be glad to let you hold the shotgun and the watch, but I don't see how I can get along without my pistols."

"You'll need the watch more than you will the pistols," Robin answered. "Go bring me the pistols and the shotgun, right now, and I'll lend you a hundred and fifty dollars on them. That is, if you promise to leave the valley before tomorrow night and not start anything with anybody before you go. If you break your promise to me about this, provided you decide to take me up, so help me God, Phil, I'll shoot you on sight."

Phil studied for a moment. "I'll do it," he agreed.

In a few minutes he was back with the pistols and shotgun, which he turned over to Robin, and then counted the money Robin handed him. Again he suggested that Robin take the watch and leave him his pistols. "No, Phil," Robin explained, "I don't want the watch. Give me a bill of sale dated ninety days from now, so if you don't pay up the guns will be mine."

"I'm footing it in to Anserville to spend the night there. I'd appreciate it if you'll get the Todds, and that brother of mine, away from the place when I come back tomorrow with a rig to get my things. I don't intend to ever spend another night under Pa's roof, and that's final. Fix me a bottle to take with me, will you, Arvane? Need a little spirits to make that walk to Anserville on."

"I never sell it on Sundays," said Robin. "I hope you like it wherever you land better than you do here."

The next day being Monday, it was quiet in the store. Robin was studying while Walt puttered. A tall, handsome, auburn-haired young woman, dressed in sleazy calico, came up to Robin and said, "Mr. Phil Cogle wants to see you out front, please," and walked out.

Robin was at first nettled by the girl's crude manners and Phil's presumptuousness, but after a minute he thought better of it, closed the book, and went out to the front. Phil and the girl were seated in a livery-stable buggy behind a bony horse. A huge carpet bag was strapped to the back of the rig and other luggage piled on every inch of available space. Phil got right to the point. "I saw Malvina on the street in Anserville this morning," he told Robin, "as I was on the way to pick up this rig. She's back here for good. It seems the man she married turned out to have another wife. She said tell you she'd like to see you as soon as you can get a chance to come to Anserville." He laughed nastily. "I reckon Malvina's mess will give these sanctimonious bastards something to talk about besides losing the war."

"They'll be sorry for her, but they won't hold anything against her. She didn't know the man was married. You know that, and I know it, and all the valley knows it. Anyway, I'm glad you told me, though it does sadden me to hear of Malvina's bad luck."

"The thing I stopped for, "Phil said, "is to put a notice on your bulletin board that Mr. Philip Cogle and Miss Duchess Regnar were married today in Anserville, for that's exactly what's going to happen as soon as this old crow bait can stagger that far. I want my damn family, and the remainder of the Modesty Valley hypocrites, to chew over that one for a while. I'm going to make a lady out of Duchess, and someday, when we've made our fortune, I'll bring her back and show her up and down the valley like a circus parade. Go ahead, Robin, congratulate the lady."

"No," Robin answered him, "the lady's to be pitied. But I do congratulate you on winning the hand of a lady who is so far above you." He turned away, heartsick in the knowledge of how Ellen and the other Cogles would suffer.

That night in their bed, Robin mused to Sallie: "Poor little innocent country whore, getting herself tangled up with a polecat like Phil Cogle. He wanted to hurt his folks and shame the valley. He's done it, even more than he's capable of knowing. Of course, the girl will be back with her ma in a few weeks, or months, but she'll never be the same again. She will either have her tail between her legs or her nose in the air. In either case, from what I know about Mollie Regnar, she'll be run off the place."

"What do you know, for sure, about Mollie Regnar?" Sallie was serious.

"Not a damn thing," Robin answered, "except that she was too decent once to let a sixteen-year-old boy inside her front door. That's decent enough, to my way of thinking, for her kind of folks."

CHAPTER THIRTY-NINE

W HEN ROBIN INFORMED WALT THAT MALVINA WAS BACK, AND explained why, Walt was all for loading his gun and going Schweitzer-hunting.

"Don't you think," Robin asked, "we'd better talk with her and learn more of the details before you start shooting?" After all, this gives her a chance to return to Crinshaw County and the man she loves best."

"I'll swear, Robin, I don't understand you. She's our kin, you know," Walt said.

"She's no kin of yours at all, and she's kin of mine only by a previous marriage. If it was an honest mistake, there's nothing we can do. If it was Schweitzer's fault, we'll try to put him in the penitentiary."

"Somehow, what you say seems convincing, but at the same time confusing." Walt shook his head sadly while small worry wrinkles spread across his wide brow.

"The trouble with you," Robin came back, "and Malvina, too, is you're in love with each other, and neither has enough sense to do anything about it."

"I asked her once," Walt confessed. "She acted so flustered I upped and walked away."

"Then," rejoined Robin, "you're mostly to blame for what happened later. Why didn't you keep on asking?"

"Well," lamely, "she seemed to think I was asking her out of sympathy."

"So, your self-respect wouldn't let you go any further if she

thought that? Self-respect, hell!" Robin snorted. "When it inter-
feres with the love of a good man for his woman, it becomes a
smothering blanket of self-deceit for the proud, ignorant, and
cowardly to crawl under and hide. I must have read that somewhere," he added, half-apologetically. "What's wrong with feeling great sympathy for those you love the most?

"Speaking of the devil—" surprisedly, as Malvina walked in.
Hanging to her hand was little Minter, whose face so much resembled big Minter's it caused a twinge of pain in Robin's chest.

Malvina took the chair Walt brought and sat for a few moments catching her breath before she offered any explanation.

"I had to come back to Modesty," she laughed lightly, but with
a touch of bitterness underneath. "I came because I wanted to,
and because I couldn't stay another day in Daddy's house. Daddy's
new wife told me she couldn't afford to be seen in my company.
She said my old friends wouldn't speak to me, and if she appeared in public with me they wouldn't speak to her again.

"Last night Daddy went to one of those Union League meetings that he's up to his neck in all the time, and she started in on
me. I told her she was nothing at all in my sight but a damned
old trouble-making, gossipy hypocrite, not fit to even lick my
shoes, and if she opened her mouth again, yapping at me, or little
Minter, I would take her by the hair and the seat of her filthy
drawers and pitch her out into the street. I said a lot of other
things.

"When I finished she screamed, something about the shame of
it; then she pretended to faint. I got up about two o'clock, put on
my clothes, dressed Minter, and here we are."

"Good for you," Walt approved.

"So, Robin, if you'll send for my things, I'll take my house
back and try to make a living for Minter and myself, out here
in Modesty Valley where we belong."

"I'm using your house and the rent's paid in advance," Robin
explained. "But here's what you should do: since Cessie's married there's nobody in our big place but Ma, Pa, Sallie, and me.
Sallie's pregnant, and Ma's real puny, so why not come and stay

with us? We've got room to spare, and Ma and Sallie need some
help with their piddling. Now, would it make you feel any better,
honey, to tell us all that happened?"

"Things better be right, or I'll make them right, with
Schweitzer," Walt butted in.

Malvina studied a bit. "I don't," she said, slowly, "think anyone was particularly to blame, except myself. I couldn't get the
man I wanted, so I took what I thought was next best. Maybe
it was a matter of pride, or perhaps it was a case of being so much
a woman I thought I couldn't stand to go through life acting like
a virtuous old maid who thinks all men are monsters.

"I was, you know, the luckiest girl in the world when Minter
Arvane came courting me. I was lucky, and I was honest with
Minter. I didn't make him ask me the second time for anything
he wanted. We ran away the very day he asked me. I'm not
making a confession. But I do want you to understand what
caused me to make the fool of myself I did, taking off with Gustave and all. I want you both to promise to keep me going in the
right direction from here on out."

"We're with you all the way. I swear it," Walt cried.

"Going back to Gustave Schweitzer," Malvina picked up. "He
told me he had been married and that his wife had divorced him
for adultery. She had the right, he said. He had been sent a notice
of the suit while he was in the field in Virginia, but since he was
not contesting it he had thrown the papers away and forgotten
it. No alimony was asked for and the divorce was to be absolute."
She paused for a moment, thinking. "Our marriage was quite a
jumped-up affair. It was like this: We were sitting around in the
family room one day, right after Robin came home, when he
came to see me on business. In the course of talking with Robin
I let him know I was growing fond of Gustave, and he got the
idea I should marry the man if I got the chance. In fact, he ...."

"Wait a minute," Robin interjected, "I don't think it's fair to
Walt for us to discuss that part of the situation in his presence."

"Pshaw," she said, lightly, "I'd trust Walt with any personal
secret just as far as I would you, Mr. Arvane, perhaps further. I

have no secrets from Walt, and you know it. I'm going to tell everything just as it was!"

Robin eyed her askance for a moment. Her face was serene, apparently untroubled, guileless. "All right," he said, "go ahead. It won't leave any splinters in my bottom."

"Starting over," Malvina said, "and this is strictly for your information, Walt, I confided in Robin, while we were in the kitchen discussing renting my house, that Gustave had asked me to marry him and that I hadn't made up my mind. I thought I was in love with Gustave, second to another. I thought I might marry him later. Robin told me that if I wanted the (I won't say what he called Gustave), to say the word, and he would fix it quickly. He might have been joking. I don't know yet. Anyway, Gustave was green with jealousy because I had left him alone to talk with Robin. As a result, he insulted Robin and they went to the back yard to fight. Pretty soon three of Gustave's men came in, toting Gustave, whom Robin had knocked unconscious. Seeing him lying there, helpless, made my heart melt, and when he came to, I, like a fool, told him I would marry him any time he wanted. So, in a way, you might say Robin pushed us together when he slugged Gustave." Her eyes looked innocently into Robin's.

Robin turned to see how Walt was taking it. Walt's eyes were beginning to clear and the same look of worship was creeping over his face that was there that day Malvina and Schweitzer came to call, the morning after she thought she had legally married the lieutenant.

Robin told Malvina, "I'm mighty sorry I had anything to do with your decision to marry the Yankee. I'll be kicking myself until I'm convinced you'd have married him anyway, come what might."

"Yes, that's what I'd have done, eventually," Malvina put in hastily. "What you did only hastened my making a fool of myself."

"I suppose," Robin joked to ease the tension, "you began by being supremely happy, then brokenhearted when you learned the truth."

THIRTY-NINE 271

"You're wrong there, in a big way," she came back. "It was a mess from the very start. I soon learned he was incapable of loving anyone but himself. Selfish and arrogant, he had no faith in anything but his own destiny in the United States Army. At one time I liked him well enough to think I could learn to love him, but actually, as I got to know him, I found him repulsive. I knew by then he had happened along when I was lonely and depressed, ready to fall into the arms of the first man to shake the tree.

"I know it's hard for a man to understand that sort of feeling in a woman, but I would bet my soul Sallie, or Cessie, would know what I'm talking about. Mother Arvane would too, but she'd never admit it.

"He wanted to leave Minter behind," she continued. "That almost did it, when I told him to go ahead and leave me, too. He was ordered straight from here to join a cavalry regiment in Fort DuMont, Kansas. Right after we got there he was drinking, lost his temper, and slapped Minter flat. I picked up his pistol and tried to shoot him but he grabbed the gun away. I told him, then and there, if he ever so much as laid a hand on Minter again, in anger, I would most certainly kill him. I think he believed it. He never spoke to Minter again, which was all right. The boy hates Gustave."

"Good for Minter," Walt said, approvingly.

"I detested that post like Preacher Barnes used to hate the devil," she went on. "I never learned why a lieutenant's wife was a notch lower than a captain's, nor why a major's wife was better than a captain's, nor why they were all supposed to look up to the colonel's old lady.

"About the time I had decided I couldn't stand it any longer with Gustave, a new captain was sent to the fort. Captain Stanleigh was a cousin of Gustave's first wife. He told us she had failed to go through with the divorce because she learned she was pregnant. He had been instructed to let Gustave know she wanted to come back to him. He said if Gustave wouldn't go and explain the situation to the colonel, then he would. Gustave said it was all a horrible mistake, that the captain's idea would ruin his career. Stanleigh said to hell with whom it might hurt, he was going to protect the interests and honor of his cousin, and that was that.

"I saw it all as my chance to get out, quickly and easily, and I was happy about it. I told Captain Stanleigh our marriage had been an innocent mistake, with nobody to blame, but I would no longer be a party to such a situation; that I was going straightway to the colonel, tell him the whole story, and ask his help in leaving the post.

"There wasn't anything else for Gustave to do but go with me; which he did, that very evening. The colonel was well along in his cups; however, not so far as to keep him from raving and ranting about the honor of the service and the duties of an officer and gentleman. In five minutes his cussing had Gustave reduced to a blubbering object of pity. That is, he seemed pitiful to me. The colonel swore that he, personally, would see that Gustave was thrown out of the army in disgrace and sent to jail for bigamy. Gustave sat wiping his eyes, sobbing and not saying a word."

"Kind of a wilting weed when the chips were down," Robin observed mildly. "His kind always wilts when the sun gets hot."

"I explained," she said, "that the whole episode was an honest and innocent mistake with no special blame to be attached to anyone. I asked the colonel if I might spend the night at his house and leave the post by the next day's stage. I lied and said I was willing to give up my happiness to right an honest mistake, and I thought the army should be willing to be as charitable. Finally the colonel agreed to have Gustave transferred to a post in California before his wife joined him. Later it would be easy to say he had divorced me and remarried his first wife.

"Think what you please of me," Malvina said, after a pause. "I was very glad when I learned I wasn't actually married to Gustave, sin or no sin. Do you think I did anything dishonorable, Robin?"

"I can't say," Robin told her. "I've never given honor much thought when I was dealing with a rattlesnake. So, if I'd been in your place, I think I would have done exactly as you did, only more so."

"Well, that's a mighty fine answer," Malvina laughed, shakily. "I don't know what you think now any more than I did before I asked.

"As soon as I got home I realized how hard it would be to live in the house with Daddy's new wife, who can't stand children, according to her own words."

"I don't know the estimable lady," Robin spoke up, "but I have her down as a mean, and common, old sow."

"She talked so much about me around town until all the ladies I've known most of my life are not speaking."

"Another swinish trick," Robin said, softly.

She turned to Walt. "In a way, I'm sorry I put you through this, Walt. I wanted you and Robin to know, since you two are the only ones I've got to advise me now."

"Nope," Robin said, emphatically, "not any more."

"What do you mean?"

"Because," Robin spoke slowly, "as of this minute I'm turning the Malvina advising department over to Mr. Walter Cedric." He paused, looked questioningly at each.

"Walt has confessed to me that he loves you very deeply, Malvina. Unless I'm the biggest liar in Crinshaw County, you once told me you felt the same way about him. You remember telling me," Robin lied valiantly, "that if Walt hadn't been sensitive, and you so suspicious of his sympathy, you'd have been married long ago. Somebody stop me if I'm saying anything to embarrass."

Robin paused again. Malvina was blushing, and her eyes showed puzzlement. Walt, Robin could see, was embarrassed, but pleased. "Being kin to you both, I don't see why I can't make a suggestion when it's for the good of all. Walt, why don't you just take Malvina in your arms, right this second, and see what she does about it?"

Malvina stood, her face red as a beet, while tears coursed down her cheeks. Walt didn't move. His face was drained white. He was trembling, paralyzed. Malvina spoke first. Her voice came quaveringly, through a suppressed sob. "Walt, you fool, don't just stand there."

In a twinkling she was in Walt's arms, sobbing. The next moment he was kissing her. Robin saw Malvina warming to Walt's kisses, saw her arms tighten in honest passion as she clung to him. With a feeling of both guilt and elation, Robin went out and sat on the front steps, whistling softly to himself.

CHAPTER FORTY

T HE WINTER OF 1865-1866 WAS CLOSING IN OVER THE MOUNTAIN country, with a wild wind out of the northwest whipping the leaves from the hardwoods and swinging the dark green of the resinous trees back and forth in grumbling, swishing sighs that bespoke colder weather yet to come. Robin sat in Colonel Bower's office in Anserville while the judge put him through his paces in a rapid oral quiz on the law. It was during these quiz sessions that Robin learned, for certain, that he had a prodigious memory for things he read.

Colonel Bower had not yet regained his right to appear before a North Carolina court. "I don't have to practice law," he told Robin. "I have small amounts of property here and there, and I can still advise others regarding the law. I don't have to be a member of the bar to do that. What I would like," he went on, "would be to join up, in a partnership of some kind, with you as soon as you pass the bar. You can take cases before judges and juries and I can advise with you to the best of my ability. We'd hook up as full partners from the first, and when I get my license back I believe it would mean quite a bit toward helping you along. What do you think?"

"Frankly, I'm more than just pleased," Robin answered. "I'm astonished at your wonderful generosity. I don't think I would actually be competent to handle my share of a full partnership with you for many years yet, but if you want it that way, I'd be a fool to turn it down."

"I think," the colonel mused, "it won't be too long. Many are getting their licenses back now; those who are willing to play ball with Mr. Holden. I can afford to wait because I know, as well as I know the Good Lord made little knotty sour apples, Will can't go on too long.

"Old Will is busy getting the Heroes of America and the Red Strings merged into the Union League. The big idea he's pitching is that the League will work for the upbuilding of the State and exert itself in trying to get North Carolina back into the Union on a full basis of statehood. I've been told that here in the mountains he's drawing a big membership from our most decent people. But in the flat country, where the war hurt them most, the strength of the League is made up largely of riffraff. They think if they get some guns they will be allowed to act as a sort of super-militia, keeping their guns at home, drilling on paid time, and lording it over everyone who doesn't give way to them. I don't think Washington will issue the guns."

"Most of the men in the valley have become members of the League, I understand," Robin put in. "I hear practically everyone who sided with the North has joined up. I also hear that joining is about as far as it's gone with them."

"It might be good political strategy on your part to join."

"Shucks," Robin laughed easily. "Modesty folks don't care a tinker's damn about things like that. They are great believers in a man having any kind of doctrine he wants as long as he attends to his own business."

"I hope you're right," the colonel sighed heavily. "Let's get you into practice as soon as possible. I'll be standing by to see that you don't do anything too foolish."

Robin stood up, held out his hand to the colonel. "I'm with you," he said. "I'll want you to go to Raleigh with me and stand by while I take the test. Will you?"

"I think we should now repair to the Golden Glove and lift a cup or so to King Arthur and the Knights of the Round Table," the colonel answered.

The colonel slipped into his slightly faded, but still dignified, Jim Swinger coat, picked up his gold-headed cane, and even though there were some slight frays in his clean white shirt, he made a grand appearance as he and Robin walked with high heads up the sidewalk toward the Golden Glove saloon.

It had seemed funny to the people of Crinshaw County when a representative of the Freedmen's Bureau came to Anserville and rented office space, while keeping silent about his business until he was all set. Then he posted a notice on the courthouse bulletin board inviting the colored folks in the county to report to his office so that he might look after, and protect, their interests. His name was Higgis, and he was evidently dedicated to helping his colored brethren, for he squalled like a wounded panther when he was informed there were no Negroes in the county, and as far as anyone knew, never had been. He said he didn't believe it and made dire threats against those who so informed him. He said they were refusing to cooperate with the United States government and he, for one, wouldn't stand for it, not for even one minute. He would show them he knew there were some colored people in the county who needed his help, and by gollies, they were going to get it.

They did, too. For Mr. Higgis was a man of action who wouldn't, and couldn't, be stopped by puny and pettifogging obstacles. He journeyed to Chafferton, picked two large Negro families, and at government expense moved them to Anserville into a couple of shacks. He protected their interests by appearing each afternoon at the Golden Glove with his freedmen in tow. After buying them each a drink of rotgut, he gave them a public lecture. After all, wasn't he taking them into a white man's saloon and buying them drinks out of his own pocket, just to impress people with the fact that they were the true salt of the earth?

Robin, who knew something about Higgis' manipulations and had laughed with everybody else about it, only glanced up when Higgis came in with his charges. After all, the United States government was feeding the Negroes all over the South, so Robin could see no reason why anyone in Anserville should object if it wanted to bring some to their town for their nourishments. More business for local people, and it cost about the same in one place as it did in another.

Colonel Bower wanted his own particular murderous concoction. It was brandy, rum, and whiskey stirred together in a glass of weak cream. The colonel called it a rattlesnake's kiss. He said women and small children had been known to faint dead away when they came into a room where it was being put together.

"I'll take the same," Higgis spoke up, as the barman turned away. When Higgis was given his drink, he ordered two slugs of the cheapest spirits for his wards, and while they waited for him to finish his drink, after they had slurped theirs down, he started his daily lecture, pointing out how much he was doing for them and how little they appreciated it. Through his bombast, Robin could hear the Negroes mumbling between themselves in disgruntled tones.

"Ax 'im," Robin heard one of them say, "das all. Hit's plumb time to ax 'im do he, or do he don't."

The other darky turned to the bureau man. "Cap'n Wite Man, do us git dat mule and dat forty, dis week, lack yuh done said?"

Higgis picked up his drink, sipped and turned it in his hand, studied it for a moment; then answered. "Damn it, don't call me 'Captain White Man,' ever any more. Do you understand? My name isn't White Man. Call me Mr. Higgis. I'm working my fingers to the bone for you benighted people and you don't appreciate it."

"Us do," the black came back, doggedly, "but us done gittin' moughty weary ob waitin'. Us wants to see us selfs a-drivin' us own mule down de road to us own wagon. Us can't hitch no 'gonna git' to no plow to work dat forty yuh done promised."

Robin set his glass down, turned toward the two black men. "You all," he said, "ought to be living in Hanby County. I heard they're promising their freedmen two mules and eighty acres out there in the cotton country. I don't know how true it is, but somebody told me that's the promise they're making."

The smaller of the colored men snapped his fingers. "I done knowed hit. I knowed hit. Jes yuh listen to de man, Cap'n Wite

Man. Listen at w'at he say. I'se gwine find dis Hanby County, agin all dem mules be gone an' dey ain't no eighties lef." He laughed loudly, danced a little jig.

Higgis' face reddened to a purplish tinge all over. He scowled at Robin but spoke to the two freedmen. "Don't be a pair of damn fools, rushing after every promise some damn Yankee carpetbagger makes. There ain't nobody can give more than forty acres and one mule. I know what the big man said. You'd better stay here, where a promise means something, or I'll see that you don't get anything. You fool around with me and I'll turn your names in to the head man."

One of the freedmen addressed Robin. "Kin he turn us name in an' knock us out ob dem mules and dat forty, Mr. Cap'n?"

"He can't knock you out of them any more than he can give them to you. No more, no less," Robin told the freedman, while his elbow nudged the colonel, who turned and looked blandly at Higgis but said nothing.

The larger of the freedmen spoke up again, to Higgis. "Do us git um mules today? An' some feed f'r um. Us ain't gwine wait no longer."

Higgis lowered his head, leaned forward, whispered confidentially to the two freedmen, gesticulating and talking earnestly, while the two men listened, leaning forward with an air of patience. When Higgis had finished, the smaller of the two freedmen studied a second, then slapped the bar with the palm of his hand. "No suh, Cap'n Wite Man. Dat ain't what yuh tole us. Us don' want no mules yuh gonna take away fr'm de wite folks. Dey'd jes come an' take um right back ag'in, an' yuh knows it. Us is gonna leave for Hanby County right dis minute, does yuh don't git us dem mules right now, jes as soon as we c'n walk outen dis place."

Higgis' face took on a look of sadness. "That," he said, "would be too bad. I meant to tell you, I learned only this morning it will be at least a month, maybe a little more, before you'll get your mules. If you can't wait and trust me," he shrugged, "then it's just your own hard luck. I've been working mighty hard for you, and you know it."

"Yes-suh," he was told, "but den w'en us gits um, hit won't be but one mule. Hanby County, hit's two. An' hits eighty acres, not forty. Sides dat, man can raise cotton in Hanby, I spect, an' dats more better nor in dese hyar hills. Man with a heap o' chilluns like us'n needs a heap o' cotton f'r dem chilluns to work in. Jes cause you rid us'n up here don't mean us'n can't walk back. Us'n don't b'lieve yuh no more. Us is leavin' jes soon's us can find some tote sacks for us'n stuff." With this pronouncement, they turned and shambled out of the saloon.

Higgis turned belligerently to Robin. "Now you've played hell," he roared. "I don't know who you are, but I'm going to have you arrested for interfering with the duties of a Federal official in his constituted duties, if those men try to leave Anserville before I give my permission. It's up to you to get busy and stop them."

"It seems to me," Robin said mildly, "they're acting like free men, going and coming as they please." He laughed in Higgis' face.

Higgis' voice was excited, but intense. "Want to bet I don't have you in jail before tonight, if those people leave Anserville?"

Robin smiled thoughtfully in Higgis' face for a moment, then turned to the colonel. "Was it two weeks ago we sent in that report they wanted?"

The colonel puckered his brow in thought. "No, it was about ten days ago; not more, anyway," he answered, catching on.

Robin extracted his leather pouch, laid some gold coins on the counter, said to Higgis, "I'll take any bet you want that you won't have me arrested, and bet you an extra hundred, on the side, that you won't be in Anserville tomorrow night."

Robin picked up a coin, clanged it on the bar, gazed into Higgis' face. Higgis dropped his eyes, wavered, turned toward the door, walking rapidly.

The bartender polished glasses and chuckled. "What was the report you made on him, Robin?" he asked.

Robin laughed. "Report?" he said, still laughing. "I haven't reported anything. It wouldn't be any of my business, but I had him figured to be the kind who always runs just before the shooting starts, so I made a little experiment. Those freedmen were getting fed up with Higgis' pretenses and promises. Right now, they're happy, looking forward to a brand new set of dreams that they hope will be pushed at them over in Hanby, along with some free rations, of course."

"That's pitifully close to the truth," the colonel answered. "I heard it straight that a Yankee came south to one of the Eastern Carolina communities, made a few speeches to the Negroes, then sold all of them a new kind of soap he had which was guaranteed to turn them white and take the kinks out of their hair in thirty days. Charged a dollar a cake for the soap, too. When the thirty days were up, the seller was gone. Hasn't been heard from since. My informant told me one of the duties of the Freedmen's Bureau was to prevent just such things happening, and, he believed, they would have, too, if the peddler hadn't split his profits with their head man. If the Negroes were getting all they are being promised, two-thirds of the white men in the State would be sitting up nights painting themselves black. Let's step out to the edge of town and see if our black friends are actually going to leave as soon as they said."

They didn't have long to wait. In a short time the two Negro families, carrying their meager belongings in tote sacks, varying in heft according to the size of the carrier, came along. Robin hailed them. "When you all get to Hanby County, don't pay any attention to a promise from anybody until you have it in your hands. You'll be able to find work out there, which is more than you'd ever be able to do here. Most of our people do their own work. In Hanby County you'll at least have a chance to be with other colored people, and you'll be in the cotton country where you'll know what you're doing."

The Negroes grinned. "Yes suh, Cap'n Boss Man," one of them said. "Das right. Us is pyore down cotton fiel' hans. Us'll be pyore glad to git back to de cotton kentry."

The freedmen shouldered their sacks and started down the road. As they were leaving, the colonel glanced up toward Anserville, then skittered into a convenient clump of laurel, motioning Robin, urgently, to follow. As Robin sat down in the thicket, he could hear the clanking of harness, and a minute later a one-horse wagon carrying Higgis and his wife came by. Just beyond them, Higgis overtook the walking brigade of freedmen. As he passed, one of the men hailed him with, "Cap'n Wite Man, us grown folks c'n walk fr'm now to jedgment day, but us got some little chilluns gonna be moughty foot-weary time us gits to Chafferton. Could yuh-all, please sir, let dese little chilluns kind o' scrunge up on dem stuffs yuh got in de back o' yuh waggin?"

Higgis stopped for a moment, gave a short and bitter laugh. "Hell, no," he told them, vehemently, "you can everyone walk all the way to hell and back as far as I'm concerned. I'm going back to Worcester, and I hope I never have to smell another God-damn nigger." He clucked the horse into a slow jog trot.

As Robin and Bower strolled back toward town, the colonel mused, "You know, Robin, I never believed slavery was right. Every shot I fired, every charge I led, was never in defense of slavery, as such. I was fighting for the sovereign rights of North Carolina as I saw them. I was wrong, and I see it now. I was defending a lesser right in support of a greater wrong. Were it to do over, I would stay completely out. I don't think, and never did, that slavery has any place anywhere in the world, and I'm sure it would have been only a matter of time until they'd have been freed. Now I'm bothered about who's going to protect the Negroes from their protectors. The good Negroes are in a hell of a fix.

"However," the colonel went on, "I'm happy all this happened today. I had a chance to see you in action, thinking on your feet as you went along. I'm more convinced than ever you should hurry and stand that bar examination. I'd be willing to trust you in any courtroom right now. I'm itching all over to welcome you into the firm of Bower and Arvane."

CHAPTER FORTY-ONE

THE FULL REALIZATION OF ROBIN'S LOVE FOR SALLIE HAD BROUGHT him to the very edge of full adulthood. It had caused him to search more carefully into the future, to study ways and means of making a personal success of his life because he believed that would be pleasing to her. For the past few months he had planned with an eye to exerting himself to the best of his ability toward the development of the valley and his law practice.

With this conclusion a great peace came into his soul. Robin Arvane would sit in the game and play according to his lights. Play hard to win. But win, lose, or draw, he meant to let the world know he had been in the fight.

Riding home from Anserville, Robin sensed a newness in his method of thinking. He felt a broadening of his soul, more than a greater ability to reason. He knew that he was facing a crisis in his life—one that was taking place within his innermost being—a crisis that had been created not so much by outside shock as by sudden clarification of thought, which heretofore had been only hazy and dreamlike. He remembered other crises in his life and it seemed to him that he had come through them wiser, stronger, and a better man.

As Robin crossed the bridge, the comedy of his and the colonel's encounter with Higgis began to bubble in his consciousness, and he was half-laughing to himself as he rode up to the store.

There was a handsome horse harnessed to a handsome rig in front of the store. Inside, a handsome red-haired girl, with a generous amount of black silk stocking displayed above a fine shoe, sat on the counter palavering with Walt. And, although there was too much rouge on her cheeks, too much carmine on her lips, and too much of her breasts bulging over the top of her dress, Robin had to admit to himself that she wore her clothing beautifully, and he knew it was of the finest silks obtainable, cut to the latest fashion lines. Her head bobbed animatedly, quivering a rich red feather in the breeze, over a velvet hat. In a moment Robin recognized her as Duchess Cogle, nee Regnar, drunk as a Saturday night corporal and talking a blue streak. She tilted her head to one side studying Robin, swung it back and forth quizzically. "I know you," she said; "you're the one Phil says is a piss ant. He says you own this little bitty old store. Tell me, Mister, how come you didn't have but two dozen bottles of laudanum. That ain't—why, that ain't no laudanum a-tall where I come from." She dropped to the floor and stood weaving and swaying for a few seconds.

"We don't sell but one bottle to a customer, and then only when we know he needs it. Meant to tell you that, Walt, when it came in the other day. That stuff's dangerous. One bottle at the time, and not too often to the same person."

"She came in," Walt said, "and asked for all we had, and I let her have the entire twenty-four bottles. She paid and put it in her reticule, after she took a drink with some brandy she had on her. Maybe she'll give it back."

"Like hell, I will," Duchess shouted. "Like hell! It's mine now. You've got your money. I've got the laudanum. Let me tell you, it's the finest stuff in the world. Try mixin' a couple of doses of it with some licker and see how you can get up and fly around among the treetops just like a bird. Before God, I swear it'll make you do just that, and a whole lot more. Gotta have my laudanum." Her eyes closed briefly, then she jerked them open, looked slowly around. "Too much laudanum, by itself, will put you off into a nice sleep, but a dose, just right, with some whiskey, will help you do some powerful noble things and keep you wide awake. Lord, the men I've been with, and enjoyed, just because I had my dose of laudanum and whiskey before we went to bed. It's wonderful!" she cried, and wept momentarily.

"So, Phil Cogle taught you to lap up laudanum before he sent you back to Molly," Robin observed.

"No," she screamed, "he didn't. And he didn't send me back. He come with me. A gal in St. Louis learned me to take laudanum while Phil was off making a lot of money gamblin' up an' down the river between there and New Orleans. He didn't learn me how to do nothin'. If any learnin' was done, I learned him. He don't use laudanum hisself, but he says it's a good thing for me. He's out at Ma's right now, gittin' over a spell of malarial fever he caught on the river. He's got money, great big gamblin' money, Phil has. An' I want you to know he don't owe no thanks to this pinch-penny valley that he's got it."

"At least," Robin said, "if he's got money, he doesn't owe any of it to me. I didn't give him any."

"I know you didn't," she screamed at Robin. "You took his guns an' kept 'em. You didn't care how late he had to sit up at night, nor how hard he had to work dealin' cards. You didn't give a damn if we went broke in Ohio, and Phil had to go out and hustle up some men for me so's we'd have enough money to git to St. Louis on. But, I'm here to tell you, the joke's on Modesty. After we got to St. Louis, we got a room in a fine hotel, right up close to the river, where I was working practically all night every night. It wasn't long, I can tell you, before Phil had enough money to get his start, and with no thanks to Modesty Valley."

"Good Lord from Heaven," Walt exclaimed. "The lowdown polecat!"

"Polecat, your own black-assed self!" Duchess shouted, turning on Walt. "Phil's got money, an' that's more'n you can say. Oh, them was good days for me. I bought and bought all kinds of fine duds like I got on. First he was dealin' in a gamblin' place; then, when he had enough for a start, he rode the river. O' course, he told 'em he was a big Carolina planter out that way, just a hellin' around for fun, an' they all made like they believed

it, except maybe the boat captains, who once in a while insinerat-
ed they thought he was another river gambler; not that they
seemed to give a damn. But finally, somebody must have com-
plained, because it got to where he couldn't ride a boat. The
cap'ns was a-sayin' Phil was playin' it crooked. One told him to
his face he was a common crooked gambler and I was a common
two-bit whore. I fixed him for that, though, when I said I was a
whore, but I wasn't the two-bit kind, and I wasn't common, an'
if he had the price I could prove it."

"I'm sure glad Phil didn't do anything crooked," Robin interjected, sarcastically.

She paused, studied Robin for an instant. "Whatta you know
about it, Mister Smarty? Of course he was crooked. One of the
finest ever hit old St. Louis. How do you think he won all that
money—dealing right off the top and guessin' what the other
feller had? Phil's got sense when it comes to money. He came
down with his sickness about the time we couldn't git on the river
no more. He was real bad with chills and fevers. He wasn't
much better when two fellers come to the hotel and I told 'em he
was so sick I couldn't let 'em in to see him. They started in a-cussin' Phil, said he owed them half of all he'd won. Said they taught
him how to play to win, then staked him for halvers. Said they
done it because they thought he would play fair, because they
couldn't go on the river any more theirselves. They both swore
if he didn't hurry and pay them, when he got able to get out of
bed they was going to put so much lead in him it would take a
yoke of oxen to haul off his body."

"Too bad they didn't," Robin mused aloud.

Duchess paid no heed to Robin's observation but went on,
"When I told Phil about what the men said, he said we'd have to
leave that very night, sick or not. So we slipped out of the hotel
the back way and come to Ma's. You should see him now," she
said, pridefully. "He's up, an' a-settin' around the house a-jawin'
an' a-cussin' with Ma. He's done give her more money than she
ever knowed was in this world, but that don't cut much ice with
Ma. She's all put out because I take a teeny little bit of laudanum

once in a while. Ma's already told him she was a-workin' on some plan to git rid of him; but shucks, she don't scare Phil none."

"I've heard your ma's a mighty smart woman," Robin observed.

"Yeah, but she ain't as smart as Phil. He could make ten plans to git rid of her, if he wanted to, while she was a-gittin' started on the first to git him." She laughed drunkenly. "He's got plans all right. Done told them to me. Soon's he gets his full strength back he's gonna give this damn valley plenty to talk about. He says he's gonna beat the very livin' hell outen that fiesty brother of his'n. Tear him right down to a short nub." Her gaze settled waveringly on Robin. "He says he's gonna kill you, do you give him the littlest excuse. He says they's a peg-legged bastard in the valley he's gonna cuckold good and proper. Honey," her eyes shifted to Walt, "ain't you a peg-legged bastard? Ain't you the one he was a-talkin' about?"

Alan Cogle, who had come into the store several minutes before, and stood listening to the conversation, caught Walt's arm as he was lifting a one-pound scale pea over her head. Robin seized Duchess by the shoulder and the seat of her dress, as though she were a man, and hustled her out of the store and into her rig. Throwing her reticule in after her, he told her, "Don't come back. I don't like getting rough with a woman, no matter how low she is, but you mustn't come back in this store, ever. Please go somewhere else to buy your God-damn laudanum from now on." Robin went back into the store, where he found Walt sitting white and trembling on the counter, while Alan walked up and down the floor, pounding his right fist into his left palm.

"I'll kill him! I'll kill him! I'll kill him!" Walt croaked, over and over again. "I'll kill him."

Robin leaned a chair against the wall by the fireplace, sat quietly until Alan finished walking and Walt calmed down. "You know," he told them, quietly, "being insane must be a terrible disease. Any man who acts the way Phil Cogle does has to be crazy. There can't be any other answer. It's possible that Walt,

or I, will have to kill Phil Cogle, or get killed by him. I'll shoot
him if I have to, but I'll hate to think I killed a sick man. It isn't
like killing a mad dog, which we know will die anyway. So far
he hasn't done anything but talk to his laudanum-soaked woman,
and she could be lying. Walt, let's wait until he makes his next
move. As for me, I aim to do my waiting with a loaded pistol in
my pocket."

"I'll promise not to go looking for him, but I won't promise
not to shoot him if he comes poking around in Modesty Valley,"
Walt said tersely.

"As far as I'm concerned, it's all right if you kill him on sight,"
Alan Cogle spoke to Walt. "I know he's my brother, but I guarantee you won't find me in your way when you get ready to start
to work on him. And that goes for you too, Robin."

"I wouldn't be thinking of you if I had to kill him," Robin
said to Alan. "It's your ma and pa, and all of Modesty Valley.
No matter what Phil may do, let's try to see he gets a fair trial
in court, if he breaks the law. If you'll think back, we've never
had any really big-time killings in Modesty Valley. At least, not
since Peter Gherkim, anyway. I'd like to keep the valley that
way, so let's wait and see what Phil's actually got in mind. One
thing we know, he's such a damn liar that what he says, and what
he thinks, are two entirely different things."

The other two agreed, reluctantly, and Alan went home.

The next morning Robin took his big army Colt out a short
distance in the apple orchard and tested its firing. He found it
perfect, mechanically. Then, before he left for work, he loaded
and holstered it below his left armpit under his coat.

Days went by and they saw naught of Phil Cogle, but they
heard he was still holed up at Molly Regnar's, recovering from
malaria. Robin still carried his pistol with the same religious reg-
ularity a priest carries his crucifix. He cautioned Walt against
leaving his at home. Nobody knew, he told Walt, when Phil
might get lickered up and come down the road off West Ridge
looking for trouble.

Most of the crops were in and all of those raised for the market sold, with the exception of tobacco, which would be auctioned off in the latter part of December. Almost everyone who had gone in debt to Arvane's had paid out. The first few months of operation had been a sensational success.

CHAPTER FORTY-TWO

Early in January, 1866, snow lay deep in the valley and was followed by a dry freeze in which the wind stirred only enough to keep a stubborn leaf that had held out against the changing seasons barely moving, until it had the appearance of a lone and ragged sentinel against the backdrop of blue sky. Then it gave up the ghost and fell, with no more than a weak flutter, seeking its mates lying damply on the ground and already giving forth that brisk, potashy smell of mineral-carrying vegetation in process of being transformed into a rich mulch which brings back to Mother Earth the wealth she loaned in the creation of the leaves.

Robin had handled a few cases of a more-or-less minor nature in Crinshaw County Superior Court; many more, of practically no importance, before township magistrates; and a blessed few in other counties around the Western Carolina circuit. Colonel Bower had declared that, for a young lawyer just starting out, his practice was coming along famously.

It was during that winter that Robin had his first encounter with the Holden machine. Despite the fact that Zack Arvane had told everyone he had no desire to sit in the State legislature, the County Democratic Convention had nominated him for that office. Although Zack was a member of the Union League, Holden and his henchmen did not want him in the legislature. He was too much of an Arvane, known to be too hard-headed in his thinking when judging right and wrong. As a result, word had come down the line that the State's heads of the Union League didn't like Zack. They wanted him defeated. Robin made several speeches in Zack's behalf, in Anserville and Modesty. He told the voters that although he, personally, did not belong to the League, nearly all the decent voters in the county did, Zack among them, and although the over-all ideals of the League seemed to be high, he didn't believe the people of Crinshaw would stand for the League, or anyone else down in Raleigh, telling them how to vote. He praisingly mentioned Zack's war record and scathingly sneered at his opponent's. Zack was elected by an overwhelming majority.

Holden soon let everyone in the mountain section know who was head man in North Carolina. Zack was summoned to Raleigh to show how he qualified to seek a seat in the legislature, in view of his past record. At first Zack vowed he wouldn't go. "I'll write them and tell them where they can stick their little office," he told Robin. "I'll tell the bastards I didn't seek the job. I haven't spent one penny of my own money on it, and I don't intend to spend my own money going to Raleigh trying to prove anything to Will Holden."

When they had talked it over and Robin had offered to pay Zack's expenses to Raleigh and accompany him to back-scotch, Zack agreed to go. "Under the law," Robin told Zack, "you're in the clear. I don't see how they can keep from seating you."

They sat in an office in the Statehouse before what Robin was pleased to call Holden's qualifications commission. He stood up and told them his brother was as well qualifed by his loyalty to his country, his honesty and intelligence, to serve his State in its legislature as any man present. He was a loyal member of the Union League, with only two political ideals, to help the State back on its feet and to get it readmitted to full statehood in the Union.

The other side had a lawyer, too, one Philemon Banther. In fact, they had a whole battery of them. They waved Robin down, told him there was no need for speech-making. That if Zack could, and would, answer a few simple questions, his fitness for the position could be decided quickly and without prejudice. They admitted they believed Mr. Arvane a truthful man and they would be willing to pass him if he could answer a few questions to their satisfaction.

Then Banther took over. "Mr. Arvane," he said, "we haven't the slightest doubt that you want North Carolina back in its former position of full statehood; that you want the State to go ahead and prosper just as we do. The question I'm going to put to you I would be willing to ask my brother, and your answer will decide as to how we handle your case. Mr. Arvane, do you ever feel a deep sense of guilt, shame, and humiliation, when you remember you once volunteered for service in the Confederate Army, fought against and probably killed some of your fellow-countrymen in a war of traitorous rebellion?"

Robin looked at Zack, saw his face draining of blood with the exception of the veins on his forehead, which were standing out in pulsing ridges. It was several minutes before Zack spoke; then, "If I heard you right," Zack said, "you're asking me if I think I was a double-dyed son-of-a-bitch all my life, up until lately." He got up and bowed. "Sir, I consider it an honor not to serve with any organization that enjoys your company. Sir, if you will choose any alley in the city, and oblige me by entering it at one end, I shall enter it at the other and meet you halfway, where I promise to do my duty to society by shooting you in as many vital places as possible."

Banther's face turned purplish. His hand stole toward the front of his coat. Robin stood up, looked him in the eyes. His hand fell away from his coat. Robin bowed toward him. "Thank you," he said, "thank you! You are showing good judgment by keeping your hands away from your coat. We shall now bid you gentlemen good day. We will, of course, back from the room. So that you may understand why, we'd like for you to know that we're afraid to turn our backs to you."

The two Arvanes walked slowly toward the railroad station. They were almost there before either spoke. Then Zack gave a short laugh. "It was humiliating, but I'm glad I came. I learned more about Scallawag politics today than I'd have learned in the next ten years."

FORTY-TWO 293

"Go ahead and wait for me in the station," Robin answered Zack. "I'm going back to the Statehouse for a minute. Something I just thought of."

"I'll go with you," Zack said. "What's the idea?"

Robin laughed. "I want a list. Tell you why after we get it." They retraced their steps, and Robin found an information center where he asked one of the clerks to give him a complete list of the credentials group they had just appeared before. "The one that fellow Banther is on."

The clerk copied down the roster of Banther's group, handed it to Robin with a questioning look in his eyes. "Tell them for me, please, Sir," Robin said to the clerk, "that you gave this list to the Arvanes from Crinshaw County. That we are planning a series of barbecues in different parts of the State at some time in the future, and we want to be sure each one of them has a chance to attend the one given in his honor. They'll understand. It's very important." He thanked the clerk and they left.

"What the hell?" Zack asked Robin. "I hope you're not planning some kind of action against those poor bastards of Holden's." Robin took the list out of his pocket, tore it to tiny bits and scattered it to the wind.

"Shucks, it's just a little joke," he laughed. "Those polecats will be looking over their shoulders for years and waking up trembling with fright because they'll think we're the same kind of folks they are. They can't prove a thing from what I said, but they can do plenty of worrying. They're the kind who scare easily."

"Well," Zack told his brother, dubiously, "I wish you hadn't asked for the list. I really had something in mind for them, but now I don't know. What you told that clerk might point a finger straight at us if anything happened to one of those bully boys."

"Since you feel that way," Robin laughed, "I'm glad I did. Probably one way of keeping you out of trouble. A United States Congressman can't run a very good race if he's got a brother in the cemetery from being gently hanged by the neck, or in prison for murder."

"So that's the way the wind blows?" Zack whistled softly to himself, stepping up to a window to ask about the next train west.

Sallie's middle was rounding beautifully, or at least Robin thought so. He felt she was something very fragile, and precious, and for which he experienced a great surge of love and responsibility. Every minute he was with her he endeavored with little attentions to show her how much she, and the coming child, meant to him. Sallie, who was not the least bit fragile, the least bit dependent, nor in any way awed by her pregnancy, put up with it for a while before she finally told him she wasn't made of china and she wouldn't break.

"Off with you," she said. "Get out and make a living for us. I'll look to the bearing of the babies if you'll see to bearing in food to feed 'em." She pushed him lightly out the door.

Robin went on to the store happy in his thoughts about Sallie. There Ben Joe, Axiom, and Penderlow were warming by the fire and gabbing with Walt and Alan Cogle. "I figger," Penderlow said, "we didn't git in more'n two-three days work last month, 'count o' th' bad weather. We done promised Cap'n Robin we wouldn't do no scroungin' ner foragin' whilst we was workin' f'r 'im, but we done jes 'bout figgered out iffen we can't work whilst th' weather's bad, we'll jus hafta scrounge. They ain't no other way to eat when a man ain't got no money comin' in. When we can't work, we ain't workin' f'r nobody, so we was thinkin' iffen we c'd git the borry o' some kind of a critter an' a cart we might kind o' slip over t'wards Chafferton, plumb outen Crinshaw County, an' forage us up a few rations."

"Who told you we didn't pay you when the weather stopped work?" Robin asked Penderlow. "I thought you were working by the month, weather or no weather. You remember you worked nights, and on Sundays, when we got rushed on that hay job last summer. We didn't pay you extra for that, did we?"

Penderlow scratched his head, thought for a moment. "Well,

no," he said, "but we didn't expect no extra pay. We thought things like that was part o' th' job when we hired out."

"They are," Robin answered. "But do you think the Arvanes wouldn't pay you right on when the weather keeps you out of the fields?"

"Never give it no thought, a-tall," Penderlow said. "We never did draw no pay when we was knocked outen work down around Salisbury."

"This isn't down around Salisbury," Robin reminded him. "Walt," he turned to his partner, "will you give these gentlemen their wages for last month. Now, gentlemen," he added, addressing all three, "if I hear any more talk of scrounging, or foraging, no matter what part of the State you may have in mind, our partnership comes to an end. Folks associated with me in business have to be honest, or we split partnership. Remember what I told you when you first went to work? I meant every word of it."

Walt had their wages ready. They took the money and, without counting it, stuffed it into their pockets. Axiom looked at the other two with an "I-told-you-so" glance; then, with an air of great pride, "I done told yuh how it'd be. That there cap'n, I mean that there Robin Arvane, allus he knows how to do th' right thing at th' right time."

"You ain't th' one told us first," Penderlow said to Axiom.

CHAPTER FORTY-THREE

P<small>ENDERLOW</small>, <small>AXIOM</small>, <small>AND</small> <small>BEN</small> <small>JOE</small> <small>WERE</small> <small>LEAVING</small> <small>THE</small> <small>STORE</small> <small>AND</small> shambling up the creek road when Queenie Regnar came into the store, walking off the ridge in the bright morning sun with a shawl tied around her head, a man's heavy greatcoat over her nightgown, and a pair of men's cumbersome brogans on her feet. Queenie wasn't exactly walking. She was propelling herself forward in more of a hurried stumble than a walk, and she was too hysterical to do anything but make pitiful whimpering sounds for several minutes after she came into the store, but Robin and Alan Cogle sat her down, poured some whiskey into her, and gradually she got her story out.

"Ever since that Phil Cogle come back with Duchess," Queenie sobbed out, "he's been cussin' an' abusin' me an' Ma. This mornin' he upped an' started ag'in on Ma. So Ma, who ain't took much offen nobody in her life, upped right back at 'im an' told 'im to git outen her house, an' stay out, right that minute, an' not to come back, never. Phil jus' laughed at Ma an' called her a fat-ass bitchy ol' whore who didn't know her fat behind from a hole in th' ground. He said he'd leave when he got good and ready, an' not before. Ma said he'd leave right then, an' went to her room an' got her pistol an' p'inted it at 'im, cussed 'im, an' told him to git goin'. He jus' set right where he was a-settin', cussed her back, an' dared her to shoot. Ma's bullet struck Phil jus' under his right shoulder, an' I could see, from th' blood, where it come out through his back. Whilst he was a-lyin' there on the floor a-bleedin' like all hell and git-out, Ma leaned over an' was a-takin' aim to shoot 'im ag'in when Duchess come up behind her a-screamin' an' split her head wide open with th' kitchen chop-axe."

She lapsed back into hysterics for a minute; then Robin gave her some more whiskey and got her to talking again. "I could see Ma was deader'n a doornail fr'm th' way her brains was scattered all over th' floor. I got on these clothes an' told Duchess I was a-goin' for some help, but she said no I wasn't. I was gonna help her bury Ma; then I could go f'r a doctor for Phil and we c'd tell folks Ma was gone to Tennessee on a visit. I told her I wasn't gonna tell no lies to nobody. Then she run to th' kitchen an' come back at me with a butcher knife, but I got outen th' door an' run off before she c'd git to me." After that Queenie keeled over in a dead faint.

"Walt," Robin said, "you keep store, and I'll run down and borrow a dress from Sallie, or Ma, for this girl. While I'm doing that, Alan, you get your pa, Josh Todd, and your spring wagon. Walt or I will go with you to take Queenie home and see what can be done. We'd better hurry."

"Let me go for the dress," Walt said. "Then I'll stay here while you go with them to take her back. I don't think Malvina would want me mixed up in a thing like this."

"Anyway you say," Robin told Walt, "but hurry."

By the time Alan got back with the team, Sallie and Malvina had appeared. They had been able to restore Queenie to a walking degree of consciousness and got her into one of Sallie's dresses. It fitted her rather tightly, but it was nevertheless a dress instead of a flimsy nightgown hanging below the tail of the greatcoat. Alan whipped up the pair of wiry little mules, and the light wagon jolted rapidly up the hill and over the ridge toward the Regnars'. Queenie sat in one corner of the wagon shivering and whimpering by turns. Josh tried to comfort her, but she was apparently blind and deaf to his presence. Presently he gave up and sat silently with the others.

Mollie lay on her face with her nightgown crumpled and twisted above her plump thighs. The chop-axe, buried to the eye, protruded from the back of her head. A large pool of blood had eddied and clotted around her face on the floor. "Easy for her," Robin observed to Alan. "She never knew what hit her."

They examined Phil, who was lying close to Mollie, breathing faintly, unconscious. "Bullet went through, all right," Robin observed. "He bled heavily at first, but it's almost stopped now. If the wound's outside the hollow of his chest he'll have a good chance to live. Let's see if we can find some clean rags for bandages and look for some whiskey. I reckon Duchess has taken to the woods; at least I hope so. I hope she has sense enough to keep going. It would be a pity to put her in jail for a crime that can be laid lock, stock, and barrel at Phil's door. But, to jail she'll have to go if we can lay our hands on her. It's not right, but that's the law."

Robin and Josh got Phil's shirt top cut away, poured some whiskey into the wound, then deftly wrapped it with a torn bedsheet. The bandaging finished, Robin held the bottle out toward Josh. Josh shook his head. It was fine rye, and Robin appreciated its taste as he tilted the bottle, looked around, espied Alan, and handed him the bottle. When Alan handed it back, Robin poured some of the fiery liquid into Phil's mouth, rapidly massaging his lower jaws to make him swallow. In a few moments Phil opened his eyes, gazed weakly at Robin; then his lips moved.

"Duchess is in the shed room, I expect. Watch out for her. She's liable to come out and kill us all. My pistol's in that room with her," Phil gasped in labored whispers.

Alan made a dash for the shed room, a tiny cubicle back of the kitchen which they hadn't searched when they first arrived. A moment later he shouted for his pa. Robin and Josh answered the shout with Cogle. Duchess lay across the bed. A dozen empty laudanum bottles were scattered over the floor. Robin felt for her pulse, put an ear over her heart. "She's still warm," he pronounced, "but dead as a last year's cornstalk. I wonder if she was trying to hide from herself or actually meant to commit suicide when she drank all that laudanum." They straightened her out on the bed, smoothed her clothes, put a pillow under her head.

Back in the front room Alan looked at his brother. "I reckon," he said to Robin, with a note of apology in his voice, "we'll have to take Phil home, go for a doctor, and try to pull him through. After all, he is our flesh and blood."

"That's right," Robin agreed. "You can't do anything else."

Josh spoke up. "Alan, will you please get somebody to make a couple of coffins from those poplar boards in your wagon shed for these two poor souls. If none of the ladies from the valley will come up and prepare them for burial, I suppose Robin will help me do it."

"I'll have the coffins made," Alan said, "but I doubt my ability to get a lady from the valley to set foot in this house. Where do you count on burying them?"

"We'll have the funeral tomorrow at three o'clock in the church and bury them in Modesty cemetery, of course."

"You mean," Alan asked seriously, "you are going to have a regular funeral, and everything, for them?"

Josh waited a moment before he answered; then, tiredly, "We're going to hold our regular burial ceremonies in Modesty Church and put them away in a Christian manner in our cemetery. In His sight, certainly, all of God's children are equal."

Robin spoke up, softly. "Reverend Todd, if I never have the privilege again, I am, at this moment, looking in the face of a man of God."

They searched the house, getting Phil's things together. Robin told them, from what he had heard, Phil had a considerable sum of money somewhere around the place. They found his clothing, pistols, and a large supply of laudanum and whiskey, but no money. Robin learned later that the doctor had found Phil was wearing his money in a belt under his clothes.

Alan and his pa left soon, with Phil on a mattress in the light wagon. Alan drove the mules while his pa followed with Phil's horse and rig. After moving Mollie's body to a bed, and mopping up the floor, Josh and Robin sat down to wait. It was almost sundown when the coroner appeared. Walt had sent him word as soon as they left Modesty, and he and the sheriff had been riding

hard to make it while it was still daylight. Robin and Josh had
fixed themselves some food from Mollie's kitchen and polished
off the remainder of the rye. They had completely forgotten
Queenie until the coroner said he would like to talk to her. They
looked and called, but she was nowhere in evidence. Since it was
coming on dark, and he wanted to get back home, the coroner
said it was a plain case of assault, murder, and suicide, and he
didn't really need to talk to Queenie anyway.

Robin grew restless as the night advanced. He worried about
Sallie because he was afraid she was worried about him. He was
thinking of asking Josh to let him run home and see about her,
after which he would come back and relieve him so Josh could
get some sleep, when he heard the crunch and rattle of buggy
wheels approaching. It was Walt, astride the black horse, with
a lantern in his hand. The horse was pulling Robin's buggy, and
Sallie and Malvina were on the seat. As Robin helped the two
ladies to the ground, Sallie looked into his face and said, simply,
"I had to come, Robin. Alan couldn't get anybody else to help
you and Josh, so here we are. Malvina insisted on coming with
me. You understand why I couldn't do anything else, don't you?"

Gently Robin put his arms around her, felt the bulk of their
child between them against his body. He brushed her lips with
his, kissed her lightly on the eyes; then, with an arm around her,
led her into the house and to a chair. As he stood beside her chair,
Robin thought about the fact that in her presence he could feel
humbleness, hopefulness, and pride, all at the same time. He
whispered in her ear, "Every time I look at you I thank God that
He gave us to each other. You're the nearest to an angel . . . . "

"Save that stuff and peddle it at the store, where someone
might be willing to pay for it, Mr. Smarty. Flattery will get you
nothing until after the baby is born." She laughed lightly and
patted his face caressingly, as she would a child.

Malvina, who was excitedly treating the entire affair as though
it were a big picnic, in contrast to Sallie's calm casualness and
Walt's indifferent shyness, took charge. She opened her reticule
and produced a pint bottle. "If one of you gentlemen will make

me a drink, I'll go about getting the bodies in condition to be laid
in the coffins. I never thought my first experience in laying out
the dead would be in a country brothel." She laughed a high-
pitched giggle. "I don't intend to have it said that Josh Todd
out-Christianed Malvina Cedric." She picked up the drink Robin
had fixed for her and tossed it down, made a face, and turned
toward the large bedroom. Sallie got to her feet and turned to
follow. After a moment Malvina called out, "Robin, heat us
some water. We have a lot of washing to do on these people."

"I'll soon have your hot water, but I don't see any reason for
washing them anywhere but on their faces. The winding sheets
will cover everything else," Robin answered.

"Sallie," Malvina commanded, "you go back and sit down.
I'll get Robin and Josh to help me turn them while I wash. I'll
guarantee they're going to be clean on the outside when they go
to their graves. As clean as Mrs. Vanderbilt when they lower her
into hers!" She laughed another high-pitched giggle, and Robin
realized then she might break before she finished, that she was
traveling strictly on her nerve and determination to do the right
thing by the clay left behind when two unfortunate souls departed
it.

A little later, when Alan arrived with the homemade coffins,
and as they were placing the bodies in them and sending home the
nails on their lids, Queenie crept back into the house. She was
cold and whimpering but calm enough to comprehend what was
going on. Since Alan had brought men from the valley to sit up
with the dead, Malvina, after coaxing some food into Queenie,
offered to take her home with her for the night, but Queenie still
had enough dignity to refuse.

The services in Modesty Church for the Regnar dead were
over. Josh had preached a short but powerful sermon. "Let him
who is without sin cast the first stone," his voice had thundered
in the face of a large crowd of curious who had come to the funeral. When the coffins were lowered and the first clods of earth
were thudded on their tops by Penderlow, Axiom, and Ben Joe,
who had prepared the graves, the crowd started dispersing. The

graves had been placed well off to one side, and near the tomb of Peter Gherkim. It occurred to Robin that he was glad he had insisted on Sallie remaining at home and not attending the funeral. Queenie Regnar stood between Josh and Ellen Todd and watched the men patting the mounds smooth with shovels. "You can," Ellen told her, "come home with us and stay the night."

Queenie shook her head. "I would never belittle you that way. I've got to go home an' clean my house an' look after my stock. It'll be hard 'thout Ma, but that's what she'd want."

"I would like," Josh told Queenie, kindly, "to give you some advice with a prayer that you take it seriously. It is, 'Go thou and sin no more.'"

"Thankee, I will," Queenie answered and turned away. They stood and watched her leave the cemetery, over the back fence, and start up the hill through the woods, taking a short cut to her empty house.

CHAPTER FORTY-FOUR

AFTER THE FUNERAL, ROBIN AND SALLIE WERE TALKING. ROBIN had finished describing the last details. "Do you think," Sallie asked, interestedly, "that Queenie will take Mr. Todd's advice?"

"No," Robin answered, "she won't. To her way of thinking, there's no sin in her way of life. In the first place, the Regnars have always made a living for themselves by the sweat of their brows. Their other activities were a way they had worked out to combine business with pleasure. Mollie never taught them anything different. When they were very small they attended Modesty School for a year or two. It never occurred to them that other children shunned them because of anything other than jealousy. Mollie saw to that. She instilled in them a fierce pride in their power to attract men. Of course, as they grew older, they realized the difference but never enough to have a sense of shame to any great extent. She'll keep her front door locked until her grief goes down; then she'll be open for business again. I doubt she will ever be able to handle the rougher element with the ease with which Mollie is said to have handled it."

"What," Sallie wanted to know, "will Phil Cogle do—leave the valley if he ever gets well enough to travel; or will he stay here and try to straighten out?"

"I wouldn't," Robin said, "try to figure Phil. Anything I could say would be at best a random guess. Of one thing I am sure. Phil may act differently, but he won't be any different."

Sallie thought it over for a moment. "I hope," she said, "he gets well and leaves the valley. They say he has lots of money.

If so, he may try to use it here in some kind of business, and, if he's what people say, there's always trouble around him."

"U-m-m-m," said Robin. "Don't let Phil bother you in the least, honey. Let's quit thinking about him and think about us."

"Robin," Sallie hesitated a second, "I do have something I want to discuss with you. How much do we have left of the money you took off the Beltons?"

"All of it, and a little over. Business has been better than I hoped. What with there being such a shortage of everything we raise in Modesty, the markets have been good. Crops, as you know, were also good. Crinshaw County's getting on its feet, money-wise, a whole heap sooner than anybody dared hope. I'm thankful."

"I'm thankful, too. We should be." Then, slowly, "Robin, I wish you would take the Belton money and restore it to the people it was robbed from. I would be happier that way."

"Nothing would please me more, my dear," Robin said. "If I knew how to find the families the Beltons robbed, and had a way to make an honest division, I'd do it right away."

Sallie sat up in bed. "You can find a way if you will use your thick skull."

Robin lay silent for a few moments. "How am I going to find out who the money actually belongs to?"

"I thought of that, too. Just take it to the Governor of the State of Kentucky and deliver it with the proviso in writing that the State will assume the responsibility of finding the people who suffered at the hands of the Beltons and divide the money on a proportionate basis. I'll bet he'll be glad to do that for you."

"I'll do it, but not until after the baby is born. For months I've worried about that money."

Long after Sallie slept, Robin lay thinking. One part of him ached with a tingling pride in his wife, while at the same time his mind tried to work out details for returning the Belton money to its rightful owners. Thinking back, he wished he had taken the reward and turned the money back. The Beltons were outlaws, and under the law of the land, assets they might have had in their possession were subject to confiscation by the State. That wouldn't help those who were the real owners. He resolved that he would have a written agreement with the State of Kentucky that the money would be given to victims of the Beltons before he laid a thin dime on the table. Then, feeling better, he went to sleep.

The next morning he confided in Pless what he had decided. Pless didn't seem much surprised. "I've been expecting something like this," he said. "That's why Zack and I were so all-fired eager to get you paid back. We figgered you'd be needing it as soon as you stopped to think things over."

"Give Sallie most of the credit," Robin told his pa.

"No, Son," Pless said, gently. "You'd have done it anyway, sometime. Sallie and I knew that way back when you first come home and we talked it over. Right then you were so full of gunpowder and vinegar we decided to let you run for a while. We both knew you would wake up and do the right thing. Grandpa Ajax would have believed it was honest, and smart business, to keep it. But you weren't raised that way. We all knew, including Sallie and Walt, from the first, that someday you'd start looking for the people who actually own that money."

"Thank you, Pa," Robin said. "I feel better now."

As the spring of 1866 gave way to summer, Phil Cogle came out of his bed and began getting around the valley. Alan reported that Phil's wound had healed nicely and the malaria had left his body. It was, Alan told Robin, the opinion of the doctor that Phil would be as good as ever after he got his strength back. Phil had even sent Alan to Queenie Regnar with five hundred dollars, but she had refused to take it. It seems Queenie had told Alan to bring her Phil's hide to nail to the barn and she would be happy. She would, she declared to Alan, see Phil in Hell with his back broke before she would take a dime off him.

"I think," Alan said, "Phil's really a changed man, even if it did take standing at death's door to change him. You wouldn't have believed it was Phil lying there, so grateful for everything done for him. He's got lots of money here with him, and deposit

certificates for more in a St. Louis bank. He says when he gets
well he's going to make the valley forget what a low skunk he's
been in the past."

"Has he let you in on what he's planning to do?" Robin
asked.

"Well, no," said Alan. "I don't think he knows himself. He
says first he's going to try and make up to the folks in the valley,
live in such a way as to prove he's not the same man. He wants
to settle down and make folks proud of him instead of wishing
he would leave and stay away. I try to think he really means it.
He even asked Josh to pray for him. Ma and Pa are very happy
about it, now that they think he's going to get well and, at the
same time, try and do better. We all try to believe him and hope
the valley will give him a chance to prove he's made of real stuff.
Won't you and Walt go and see him, Robin?"

Robin hesitated awhile. "Alan, we've been good friends a
long time, and I'd hate for anything to come between our friendship, but I don't intend to have any truck with Phil; not at the
present time, at least. I can't speak for Walt. You can ask him if
you like, but I think he feels the same way I do. I think Phil got
scared and almost died, and now he actually thinks he's reformed.
There's a little piece of doggerel that says, in effect, that if the
devil is sick he tries to be a saint, but it doesn't take long for him
to forget it once he gets well. I'm going to let him be up and
around, see how he acts, before I make up my mind. I'm not
going to forget all the mean little things I know he's capable of,
nor any of the great big mean things he's already done, such as
the way he treated that poor little ignorant mountain whore he
married, along with the rest of her folks. You and I know he
caused the deaths of Duchess and Mollie just as much as if he'd
done the actual killing. The wisest thing he could do would be
to leave the valley as soon as he's able to travel, which, I understand, is right now. I'll bet he hasn't offered your ma a cussed
cent, as much as she could use it. I saw her yesterday. She looks
like she should go to bed herself and rest up from waiting on
Phil."

"No," Alan admitted, "he hasn't offered Ma any money, but
I expect it's because he hasn't thought about it. I think he's going to come through all right. I've never had anything but trouble from him, and I don't hold it against you for feeling the way
you do. Still, he's my own blood kin, and I have to pull for him
as hard as I can for Ma's and Pa's sake, if for no other."

After Alan was gone, Robin told Walt when he came in,
"Mark what I'm saying, Walt. Phil Cogle's going to cause some
more trouble in the valley. He can't help it any more than a polecat can keep from stinking. He doesn't even know how to think
straight, much less go that way. I'm very sorry for all of his
folks."

"All I ask," Walt answered, "is that he stay away from me."

In a few more days the fact that Phil Cogle was up and around
was in evidence as he flashed up and down the valley road in his
brightly painted rig, visiting the valley folks, explaining that he'd
turned over a new leaf, seen the error of his ways, and assuring
people right and left they were talking to a new and reformed
Phil Cogle. A rich Phil Cogle, who meant to do things for the
valley which, he confessed, had long suffered from his very presence. He was pale, thin, and guant, but on the mend. It didn't
sound like Phil Cogle to Robin, and he said so. He believed Phil
had something up his sleeve besides a bony arm. Phil must have
heard about what Robin had to say, for he kept away from Arvane's store, though he passed by again and again. One thing he
proved to Robin: he was a convincing talker and soon had a few
of the valley folks, if not exactly on his side, at least in the notion
to hold judgment in abeyance, pending future developments.
The folks of the valley, Robin knew, were a generous people.
Straightforward in word and deed, usually prone to believe a
body who sounded sincere.

CHAPTER FORTY-FIVE

A FEW DAYS LATER, ALAN REPORTED THAT PHIL WASN'T SATISFIED with his reception in the valley. He wanted, apparently, whole-hearted forgiveness for his past, along with approval and community confidence in his future behavior. He had told Alan, "I've seen and talked to practically every man in the valley, explained how I'm trying to turn over a new leaf, and to tell the truth they were friendly enough, in a way, except for two or three old die-hard Confeds who will never forget we had a war and that I fought with the North. I've done about everything to win people over except to kiss the seat of Robin Arvane's britches. I don't intend to do, or say, anything to Arvane, unless he starts it, but I'll never go around kowtowing to him."

"I haven't said anything about Phil to anyone, except when I've been asked, and then I only said I was waiting to see, and that I had no confidence whatever in his good intentions. If he wants to make friends, let him start by doing something useful for the valley. It's awfully hard to make people forget what happened at Mollie Regnar's. I don't think Phil's talking will do it." Robin was emphatic.

Alan shook his head, dismally. "I'm sorry to say, Robin, I'm beginning to believe you're right. I overheard him telling Ma he's going to have a bunch of sanctimonious hypocrites here eating out of his hand soon. He's leaving for Memphis, he says, very soon on a little business trip to bring back something that'll do more good around here than anything else that could possibly happen. I'm afraid he's going to come back and try to organize

a Ku Klux Klan in Crinshaw County, but I don't know. Ma
thinks he's the answer to a virgin's prayer. He finally talked himself into a lather and started pounding the floor with his cane.
That's when I butted in and told him I was beginning to doubt
his sanity as well as his sincerity. He calmed down then and
begged Ma's and my pardon and began to cry.

"I don't know what to think. He's my brother, and according
to what I've always been taught, we should stand by our folks,
no matter what. I wish he'd stayed away from the valley." Alan
moved slowly toward the door. "Well," he said, "no matter what
Phil does, I have to work for a living."

A few Sundays later Josh preached a powerful sermon, using
as his text, "Vengeance is Mine, Saith the Lord." Josh told the
congregation that God's eye always looks with sympathy on the
struggles of His creatures against the forces of evil. How He
keeps an eye on the fall of a fledgling sparrow from its nest. How
His ear is always receptive to man's sincere supplications for
mercy and forgiveness. He explained that compassion is the only
road to mercy and forgiveness, and that to forgive is divine. For
only in forgiveness, he explained, one took into one's own heart
a peace that passeth understanding. Revenge should be left to God.
It was a moving sermon and many a man surreptitiously took out
his handkerchief, while the women wept openly and honestly.

When the sermon was finished, and the following hymn ended, Josh made an announcement. "I have been," he told the congregation, "requested by Philip Cogle to beg your indulgence
and allow him to make a statement from the floor of the church."

Standing in front of the pulpit, leaning slightly on his cane,
Phil made an imposing figure despite his gaunt frame, pale face,
and sunken eyes. A heavy gold watch chain laced across his chest,
and a large diamond gleamed on his cravat. Robin grudgingly
admitted to himself that Phil, even with his pallid appearance,
cut a fine figure. He was certainly, up until that moment, the
most expensively garbed man who had ever stood on the floor of
Modesty Church. Speaking easily, he began.

"Dear friends and neighbors: that is, I want you to be my

friends more than I ever wanted anything in this world. I'm
praying to the Good Lord to help me in making you my friends.
As you all know, I was baptized in this church many years ago,
but as I grew up I drifted away from its teaching. I listened to
the voice of the devil. He kept telling me to do things that were
wrong, regardless of the consequences. I was heedless of the advice of my beloved parents." He paused to wipe his eyes with a
white silk handkerchief.

"I became more and more arrogant," he went on, "with my
fellow-men. I wanted my way in everything; I was being moved
by the voice and will of Satan. I never knew, myself, exactly
what I did want. I have to confess that now, every night, I spend
hours in prayer that the Good Lord will help me in righting the
wrongs I have done. I sometimes think the hurt and shame of
my past life is more than I can bear. My sorrow for the tears
I've caused my parents, for the wicked treatment I've dealt my
own brother and sister, are indeed a terrible burden on my conscience." Robin had to admit to himself that Phil was playing
his cards very skillfully. Phil uncovered another card.

"During the past ten years I've done only a few things in
which I can take pride. One was joining the Union Army, knowing it would make me unpopular here in Modesty Valley with
some of the people whom I admired and loved very much. In
joining up with the North, I followed the dictates of my conscience. I did what I believed was right. Now I would like to
go forward with the veterans of both sides, work for the good
of Modesty Valley, the State, and the nation. I want to dwell in
peace with those who fought so nobly on both sides, because I
can no longer find room in my heart for prejudice, or hatred.
When love fills a man's heart, there is no room left for hatred.

"I know now how much I love Modesty Valley, its people and
its church. All I want is the right to live the rest of my life here,
giving all the service I can to the valley and the Good Lord and
His works. Whether I stay, or leave, is up to the people. If you
reject me, there's nothing I can do but go elsewhere and try for
a new start. I want to reaffiliate with this church. I'm not ask-

ing approval of my sinful past. I can only ask your forgiveness as I have already asked God's. I want your forgiveness, and I need your prayers to help me keep on the path of righteousness I've set for myself. The happiest moment I ever hope to have will be when I can shake the hand of every man, woman, and child in Modesty Valley in Christian fellowship." He stopped, took out his handkerchief, dabbed at his eyes, and mopped his brow.

Then Seth McCoy was on his feet. "Brother Todd," his high, squeaky voice rang out. "I move that Brother Cogle be asked to stand right where he is while this congregation has a chance to come an' shake his hand in Christian fellowship. It took a heap of grit to do what he just done."

Without waiting to see if there was a second to his motion, Seth moved forward toward Phil in a half-sidewise shuffle, shook his hand, and returned to his seat. The congregation followed Seth's lead, with the front pews going up first and working backward. Robin noticed that many of the women were weeping. He caught himself before he snorted audibly. When they had worked back to their bench, Pless looked at Robin questioningly. Robin sat still, staring straight ahead. Then Pless got up, moved into the aisle, followed closely by Pamela. Malvina pulled at Walt's sleeve, saw he had no intention of moving, rose and hurried up the aisle behind Pless and Pamela. A few minutes later every member of the congregation had shaken Phil's hand with the exception of Robin and Walt. Sallie, being in the last stages of her pregnancy, was not in church.

As they walked slowly and silently home, Robin could see that Pless's face was stormy, so he was not surprised when his pa said, his voice choked in anger, "I want to know how come you refused the hand of fellowship to Phil. That's not the way you were raised. It's not Christian."

"Pa," Robin said, "you know I won't argue with you, but I'll tell you one thing, then I have no more to say. It was because I didn't believe one word the son-of-a-bitch said."

"Son," Pless said, with more sadness than belligerence, "it isn't for you to judge." He turned and strode abruptly ahead.

Robin watched Pless walking in quick angry strides toward the house, turned to Walt. "'Pa's not as young as he used to be, but look at him go when he gets mad. This is one time I wish I had stayed away from Modesty Church. I wonder if Josh could have put Phil up to that little act. I can't believe it, but I'm going to find out if I can.

"The way I have it figured," Robin went on, "Phil hasn't played his best cards yet. He's too good a gambler to do that. We can't tell yet what he's leading up to, but we'll be able to catch the drift by the time he makes about two more plays. One thing we know: Phil's not down the way he wants folks to think. He's down the way you and I know he is—that is, low down. If he were actually in the mood to do anything worth a damn, he'd pry his pappy loose from the plow handles by hiring somebody to take over the mule. If he actually cared anything about his ma, he'd get somebody to help her. He'd buy her some decent clothes. He'd put some kind of decent markers over the graves of his wife and mother-in-law. In the meantime, I intend to watch him. He'll show what's in his mind soon. His kind can't wait."

There was another in Modesty Valley who couldn't wait besides Phil Cogle. When Robin entered the house, his ma told him Sallie said for him to go to their room as soon as he came in. He hurried to her. She was standing before the mirror combing her hair. She turned toward him, touched his face with her hand. "Robin, I have a little secret to tell you. Don't tell anyone for a few minutes, but I think you are about to become a parent." As she spoke, a small grimace of pain showed on her face; then it was smooth again. "The lively little rascal wants out. I think you'd better go for the doctor and that midwife you spoke about. It won't be long now, I think."

Robin rushed out of the room calling his ma. The doctor was out on a call, and it was about four hours before Robin located him and started back hell-for-leather toward Modesty. When they arrived Pamela met them at the door, sssshhhed them, and tiptoed ahead to Sallie's room, where there was a red and wrinkled brand new human resting peacefully in the old family cradle, while his mother slept quietly, breathing softly, her hair spread to frame her face, madonna-like, on the pillow.

"There wasn't much to it," Pamela explained. "Sallie was a big help. Not the least bit afraid. That girl's plenty game, I'll tell you, Mr. Robin Arvane. I think she wanted that boy worse than anything else in the world."

Robin turned and gazed at his son again. "I wanted him too, but I was also afraid," he confessed.

Robin sat quietly by the bedside waiting for Sallie to wake up. When she roused, she blinked to clear her head, then smiled. "Howdy, Mr. Arvane. Fancy meeting you here." After a moment, "I wasn't pregnant when Cessie was married, and she swore she would have one before I did. She said she could tell by looking at him John Littlebow was that way. We must get a letter off to her right away."

"Do you feel all right, darling?" was all Robin could think of to say.

"I could have twins, standing on one foot, for you, darling," she quipped. "All of my female ancestors had babies—old family habit. He was," Sallie observed, "right on schedule, which of course is to be expected of the predictable Arvane men. I'm glad he's here; now you can get about that trip to Kentucky."

"I'll go," Robin told her, "before the end of three months, or just as soon as I know you're completely recovered from this."

"You can go before then," she answered softly. "I want you here when I'm completely recovered, as you say." Her eyes lingered momentarily on his face. There was great promise in them.

CHAPTER FORTY-SIX

Robin INSISTED SALLIE HAD FIRST CHOICE IN NAMING THEIR SON, and immediately she named the boy Ajax. Robin said that was fine, and his middle name would be Bassett. "The name Ajax," Pless told them, "would be all right with Grandpa. He said that by the time the fourth generation came along the community would have time to forget a man's meanness and remember only his best qualities, unless he was an outright rascal."

Immediately after Sallie got out of bed, she began on Robin to start out for Kentucky and soon had him astride the black horse headed for Frankfort. He rode with a rifle in the saddle boot, his pistol strapped outside his coat, and with the gold stowed in his saddlebags. He would have been disgusted, indeed, if he had known that Pless was on the little bay, riding close behind, but careful to keep out of his sight. Pless meant to see that Robin got through to Frankfort without anyone holding him up—at least he meant to see that if anyone did try, he would meet with some unexpected resistance. However, Robin reached Frankfort without incident. He cooled his heels in an outer office for a good two hours before he found himself in the presence of that august official, the Governor of Kentucky.

He was surprised to learn that the Governor knew who he was when he gave his name and where he came from. "You've come," said His Excellency, "to claim the reward for destroying the Belton gang, I take it. I remember, Mr. Arvane, very distinctly what our man reported when he returned from interviewing you at the time you endorsed our draft back to our Treasurer.

At the time I thought we were loser, to a small extent, on the deal, inasmuch as the amount you took from the Beltons was in excess of the reward. We also appreciate the fact that you could have signed an affidavit that you took nothing and collected the reward anyway. You chose to refuse the reward and keep the other sum. Since the Beltons were legally declared outlaws and everything found on them at the time of their deaths belonged, by law, to the State of Kentucky, I don't see how we can revoke our past actions and pay the reward to you, unless you will surrender to us the approximate fourteen thousand dollars in gold we know they had on them. Since we know you have no intention of doing that, we prefer to say the case is closed as far as we are concerned." The Governor stood up. "I'm sorry, Mr. Arvane, that's the way it is. Drop in on us the next time you're in town."

Without rising, Robin looked up into the Governor's face. "Governor," he said easily, "if you ever get into a presuming and supposing contest, you'll win in a walk. I reckon you could suppose yourself into presuming more than any other man living, if what you just said is any example."

The Governor sat back down again. "Will you please explain what you just said, Sir."

"Let's put it this way," Robin said. "Suppose I should admit I still have all the money taken from the bodies of the Belton crowd. Let's presume that such a supposition is correct. After we might verify both the supposition and the presumption, then let's suppose I don't give a happy damn about the reward. Then, knowing I don't want the reward, we would have to presume I would like to return that money to those to whom it rightfully belongs. Do you follow me, Sir?"

"I do," the Governor said, looking more or less puzzled. "Am I to presume that you came to return the money to the State, whether you get the reward or not? In that event, I give you my word I'll see to it that you are paid the ten thousand dollars we offered for the Beltons' scalps. Paying it may stretch a legal point or so, but by golly we'll stretch it anyway."

"There you go again, Governor, presuming so rapidly I can't

keep up. I haven't, that I remember, said anything about giving anything back to the State of Kentucky. I have a legal document, an agreement, if you please, for us to sign, stating that I will turn over the Belton money to your State on the condition that your government will take the responsibility of learning the names of those who suffered loss at the hands of the gang and give the money to them on a proportionate basis. Otherwise, you may presume I never saw any of the Belton gold, and I'll be going back to Modesty Valley in North Carolina as soon as I can leave town."

"Am I," said the Governor, "to presume that you wish to give up the Belton money provided it is used to aid their victims? Don't you see, man, much as I might like to do a thing like that, I couldn't without violating my oath of office. Again, I'll have to remind you that, by law, all Belton assets are to be confiscated, as rapidly as they are uncovered, and turned into the State treasury."

Robin rose from his chair. "Good-bye, Governor. Sorry to have taken up your time. Would you please tell me where the office of your best newspaper is? I would like to drop by and explain to the editor how the State had the good fortune to get rid of the Beltons without it costing a cent, yet it would still like to confiscate the money they had on them, which obviously was robbed from citizens of your State." He turned toward the door. "Good-day, Sir."

Before Robin got to the door, the Governor was on his feet. "Wait a minute, Mr. Arvane," he cried. "The sovereign State of Kentucky has always played fair with its citizens. We may be stretching a legal point, but we'll be glad to sign your agreement as to the distribution of the Belton money. If you'll please delay your departure for a moment, I'll go with you to the newspaper so we can tell the story of your patriotic benevolence together."

They went out together. As they approached the newspaper office, the Governor squeezed Robin's arm. "It just occurred to me," he chortled, "I can make plenty of political hay out of this deal. It will be a feather in the cap of my administration."

"I don't care how much hay you make grow with your own political manure," Robin said. "All I want is to see that the money goes back to those who actually own it."

Robin reckoned wrongly as to how the Governor's hay would affect him. The next morning his name flashed screamingly on the front page of the newspaper.

Robin arrived back in the valley one day behind Pless, and it was months before he learned Pless had followed him to Kentucky. He was both pleased and amused at his pa's concern for his safety and saved Pless embarrassment by never mentioning it before him.

He found his family in a dither when he got home. They had read the papers and were bursting with pride in their hero. Pamela clung briefly to him and wept happily. Zack shook his hand heartily and said nothing. "This," Robin told Sallie, "is the first time I ever felt like a hero in the eyes of my own folks. It's a powerfully good feeling."

There were plenty of other good repercussions. Folks came from all over the country to trade at Arvane's and to see what Robin looked like, some to congratulate him, some to tell him they thought he was nothing less than plain crazy. His law practice started picking up. A man who got all that free publicity had to be smart as all get-out, people figured. In a short time his practice was far enough advanced that he had to give it his full time and get Zack to help out in the store on busy weekends. Colonel Bower had his license to practice restored.

Robin was sitting in his office trying to think about nothing, while at the same time thinking a thousand thoughts, which chased themselves around in his head without coming to focus. He was comfortable in body and mentally content when Seth McCoy walked in, looked around, asked, "Air ye by y'rself, Robin?"

When Robin told Seth he was, Seth took a folded paper from his pocket and stuck it forward. "This," he said, "wuz handed to me down th' street a bit ago. I ain't never seed th' man as give hit to me. He jest stuck hit out an' said, 'Read an' then tear hit up. Don't never tell what's in hit iffen you want to live.' I'd like blamed well to know what's in that air piece o' paper, but ye know I never got around to larnin' to read an' things like that when I was a boy. Do ye think hit'd be safe fer yer to kinda read hit to me an' not never tell nobody ye done hit?"

"Sure, Seth," Robin assured McCoy, "I'll read it and keep it in confidence if you want me to." He unfolded the paper and read aloud. It read:

Dear Sir:

We are giving you the opportunity of a lifetime to serve your community, your country, your State, and the entire South. After you've read this destroy it and never mention having received it to anyone. It will cost you your life if you do. On the other hand, if you are with us, you will destroy this communication and follow these instructions: Leave your home Friday night after dark and proceed to Split Rock Spring on the side of the mountain above the head of Modesty Cove. Take a roundabout way and don't let anyone know where you are going. There you'll meet other brave men who feel the same way you do. Men who are sworn to stamp out carpetbaggers, scallawags, Yankee troops, and nigger rule in the South. It will all be explained at the rendezvous. We have plenty to do right here in Crinshaw County to get rid of dirty politicians, cheaters, and swindlers who are growing rich off honest people's work. It is not our intention to commit any killings, but we will use the lash when it is needed, and in that way effect the reforms we so badly need. Come on, join us in our holy crusade, if you will. If not, then do as this says. Destroy this note and keep your mouth shut about it if you want to go on living. If you want to join us put a cross of sticks in front of your gate and you'll get further instructions.

CRINSHAW COUNTY KU KLUX KLAN

Robin hadn't read very far before he recognized the handwriting, but as recognition dawned he only grunted in disgust and went on reading. When he had heard the last of the note, Seth sat down shakily. "What do hit mean, Robin?" Seth pleaded. "Ye know I ain't got enough education ter onderstan' no sich talk as they's in that air letter."

Robin tore the note into small fragments, tossed them into his wastebasket. "Not a damn thing, Seth," he said. "You go back home and forget you had this note. Don't say a word about it to anyone, and I won't either. Just keep your lips buttoned up, and I'll guarantee you won't be harmed. Please don't say anything, and don't worry."

Robin went into Colonel Bower's office and told him about the letter. "So what do you think, Sir?" he asked.

The colonel thought over the question several moments before he ventured an answer. Finally, "It's bad," he said. "From what I can learn the Klan is actually needed in some places. It's a crude way to achieve justice, and I suspect that more often Klan justice miscarries than not. One thing I do know: we don't need the Ku Klux Klan in Crinshaw County. We need plenty of things here, but the Klan isn't one of them. I think the best course would be to keep hands off and let it run its course, as it will quickly in this part of the State."

"I think," Robin said, "it can be a damned dangerous proposition for a lot of folks if Phil gets control of it. Knowing Phil's the one trying to get it started is in my favor, and I, for one, am going to try to break it up before it gets started. Hell, Colonel, any society pledged to violence behind the anonymity of masks, and operating under Phil's leadership, is no better than a bunch of rattlesnakes with their rattles cut off so they can't give any warning. I'm going to try to be around and learn what I can Friday night."

"Well," the colonel said, "I know better than to try and advise you on that score. Fact is, if I didn't have this rheumatism-stiffened knee, I'd go with you. I am going to ask you to take another good man, one you can trust, with you, just in case."

"I have that man, Walt Cedric."

When Robin explained to Walt what was in the air and told him the plan he had worked out, Walt fell in with the idea enthusiastically. "One thing's certain," Walt said. "This is one time we are going to have a lot of fun with little or no danger of getting hurt. Seems like old times to go on a lark with you, Robin."

CHAPTER FORTY-SEVEN

Robin didn't go to his office Friday morning. Instead, he stayed in the barn with the door tightly closed, boring half-inch holes in corncobs, clipping and rolling strips of old newspapers, gluing them into slender tubes. Before noon he had finished and stopped by Zack's and asked him to watch the store that afternoon, relieving him and Walt at three o'clock. Shortly after three, Robin and Walt mounted on the black and bay horses, and with Robin's saddlebags bulging, rode uphill toward the crest of West Ridge. Each had a Winchester repeater in his saddleboot and two pistols at his belt. After they topped the ridge they rode beyond its crest for a half-mile, then turned south through the heavy timber growth.

They rode slowly along the ridge, dodging cliffs and defiles, until they reached the slope of Acacia where the ridge spilled off the mountainside. Then, circling the head of the ridge, they stopped well above Split Rock Spring, where they tied the horses loosely to saplings in such a way that they could break away and escape if bears came looking for fresh meat. There was an acre of fairly level tableground next to the spring, and Robin knew that was the designated spot for the rendezvous. On the off-side of the spring from the picnic ground there was a mass of rocks, a helter-skelter of boulders from those of medium size to some rearing as high as twenty feet in the air.

It was behind the rocks that Robin had planned to carry out their operation. Knowing Phil, he figured it would never occur to him to post lookouts. Thus, long before the first shades of dusk, Robin and Walt had emptied their saddlebags and had Robin's homemade black powder bombs planted among the rocks. The bombs, which were made of black powder stuffed into bored-out corncobs, were fused in different lengths, with the ends of the fuses meeting at one point so that they could all be lighted at the same time yet cause detonation in series.

There was enough light still remaining in the gathering dusk when the first horseman appeared for them to recognize the daintily stepping little gelding of Phil Cogle's when he rode into the picnic clearing, even though the horse was draped from head to knees in a white sheet and Phil was garbed in a white robe with a hooded mask. Phil had evidently made previous preparations, for he tied his horse, dismounted, and put fire to a pile of firewood already prepared, and in place. Then he walked impatiently up and down in front of the fire until he heard the first of other horsemen approaching. By the time the approaching rider reached the clearing, Phil had remounted his horse, stationed himself back of the fire, where he sat, erect, his arms folded across his chest. The rider pulled up, squinted around. He had a mask similar to Phil's and bed sheets draped over his mount. Phil greeted him, "Remain mounted but pull up alongside me to face the others as they arrive."

Within the next thirty minutes some fifteen or twenty horsemen had ridden into the clearing, were greeted by Phil, and lined up in a column of fours. After waiting for a few minutes to see if any others would show up, Phil rode around to face the assembly. His voice rang out: "The first meeting of the Crinshaw County Klavern of the mighty Invisible Empire, the Ku Klu Klan, is now assembled. There will be no use of names, ever, in communicating with each other. You all, of course, know me, but you're never to use my name. We all know each other, but the same rule is to apply. In designation of tasks, and the issuing of orders, only numbers will be used. In that way, with our never meeting without our masks, never using names, never acknowledging identity, should there ever be any repercussions in court, we can always go on the stand and swear truthfully that we never saw a member of the Klan to know he was such except when he wore a mask. And of course nobody can actually make an identification of anyone wearing the paraphernalia we have on.

"We will thus," he went on, "now count off, beginning with myself and picking it up in the columns. Instead of stopping your count at four and starting over, you will take it right on through until every man here will have a number. I will begin the counting." He shouted, "One." When the count was completed, Phil told them, "We will now have nominations for a leader. Make your nominations by number, and remember, whoever is elected must agree to actually lead us in whatever we think it is our duty to handle and must assume responsibility for whatever supplies we may need, such as guns, ammunition, whips, crosses to burn, and any other more or less costly and necessary things for a successful operation of our plans. If any man feels he is unable to meet the expenses of leadership financially, let him bravely decline the nomination. The meeting is now open to nominations. After we elect a leader, we will go on to the taking of the Ku Klux Klan oath of fealty to the Invisible Empire and discussion of future plans."

A tall man on a short-legged, ruggedly-built horse shouted, "By damn, I nominate Number One for our leader. I know he's got plenty of money; let's see if he'll put his pocketbook where his mouth is. But before I take any oath, I want it understood that Number Fifteen won't take no orders from Number One until th' whole matter is put to a vote. I don't foller nobody without havin' some idee of where I'm goin'."

This out of the way, Number One was promptly elected, and they went straight into business.

"I freely predict," the leader said, "that within a month the Crinshaw Klavern members will be numbered in the hundreds because this small group here is not afraid to fight for the right to uphold honor and put down chicanery wherever those evils may rear their heads among us. There are many tasks ahead of us. We have politicians who are promising and not delivering. We are plagued with merchants who are cheating and swindling their fellow-men. We have crooked lawyers who for a small fee will do anything short of murder. Carpetbaggers and scallawags are living off a land that can scarcely support itself. All this we find it our most honorable duty to eliminate. But, we must always remember, the glorious Ku Klux Klan is not a merchant of murder. We must not resort to killing, except in defense of our own lives, or to preclude identification. On that score, we would kill one of our own members, should he try to become an informer, as quickly as we would a rattlesnake. All who agree with these general rules of operation say 'aye'; others 'no.' " There was a loud rumble of approval.

"Now for the next business. Sunday morning, just before the break of day, we will plant on the courthouse lawn in Anserville a large fiery cross made of wood soaked in oil so that it will blaze for hours and tell sanctimonious hypocrites of this county that the Klan has arrived. Number One wants each member present to bring to the meeting tomorrow night, in this same spot, at this same time, a list of those whom he thinks we should take immediate action against. Grievances will be discussed by the entire Klavern and action decided by a vote of the majority."

"It's time now," Robin whispered to Walt. He stooped, flashed the flint on his tinder box, and fired all fuses at once. A few seconds later the first bomb detonated and sent black smoke swirling skyward. Robin and Walt, then, taking shelter behind the rocks, began shooting their pistols a few feet over the heads of the assembled horsemen. With twenty-four bullets from the four pistols singing over their heads, with the roar of the bombs as they went off, one after the other, terroristic pandemonium took over among the Klansmen. They lay forward over their saddles and with screams of hysterical fright spurred their horses away from the picnic grounds and toward Modesty. Some rode straight through the fire, scattering burning logs in every direction.

The yell went up, "Union Leaguers." "Niggers," screamed another Klansman. "I seen about fifty of 'em standin' on the rocks, a-shootin' at us. Who was killed?"

Nobody seemed to care to stick around to see who was killed, or even wounded. The horsemen crowded, jostled, and fought for front rank riding space in the narrow wagon road. Phil Cogle, who had been in front when they started down the mountain slope, held his position and was soon out of sight of his cohorts. He soon pulled into a game trail to one side of the road and waited to let the others pass, listening to their comments as they went by.

The next morning Alan Cogle stopped at the store on his way to work. He made a small purchase or two, then, "Phil came in last night and locked himself in his room. He's in a big sweat. He told us this morning he was riding by a place last night when he run up on a big bunch of Ku Kluxers."

"Tell us more," said Walt.

"Well," Alan went on, "you know Phil. He may be telling the truth, or he may be telling part of the truth; then again, he may be lying outright."

"What," Robin wanted to know, "was the rest of his story?"

"He said they were all dressed up in robes and masks and when they saw him they told him they were headed for Split Rock Spring for a Konklave and invited him to go along and join. He said when he told them he didn't want any part of their organization they started shooting at him, and since he didn't have his gun with him, there wasn't anything to do but sell out for home, which he did, and outran them down the mountain."

"That hoss of his can run, I know that," Walt said.

"Anyway," Alan went on, "he's lying up in his room with a loaded rifle and won't stick his head out of the house. Afraid some of them will kill him on sight, he claims."

"You know, Alan," Robin interjected, "you can't believe Phil. I'll bet you five dollars here and now we won't ever hear of any Ku Klux activities in Crinshaw County."

"Probably not," Alan conceded. "But I would bet if we ever have one Phil'll be right in the middle of it." He went out.

A little later in the day when Charley Zillern came into the store, toting his deer rifle over his shoulder, Walt thought nothing

of it. But as the day advanced, and several of their Saturday customers appeared carrying rifles, Walt finally observed to one,
"Looks like everybody must be going after deer, or some big varmint, on the same day."

"Nope," was the answer. "Not deer, far's I'm concerned. It's
a two-legged varmint. I hear tell he tolled a bunch o' th' boys up
on th' hill to Split Rock Spring last night, and into a bushwhack-
in' job by a bunch of niggers fr'm th' flat country. When I catch
up with 'im, I'm gonna give the low son-of-a-bitch jest one day
t'git outen Modesty Valley. Do he not go, I'm gonna shoot th'
bastard nex' time I see 'im."

Walt laughed loudly. "Robin said sometime ago Phil couldn't
stay out of trouble to save his life."

"Ain't nothin' gonna save his life do he stay in Modesty Valley. They's a passel of us gunnin' f'r 'im." With a look of indignant righteousness on his face, Zillern marched out of the store.

The next day being Sunday, they decided Walt should ride to
Chafferton and be there when the wholesale places opened Monday morning.

There was a tenseness in the air at Modesty Church on Sunday morning. Robin made it his business to glance into some of
the family wagons in which the majority of the congregation had
reached the place of worship. In all, he noticed eleven wagons
had rifles in them uncovered for anyone to see. Robin whistled
softly under his breath. Phil, he thought, was really in for it
this time. To a small extent he felt remorse that he was instru-
mental in breaking up the meeting and landing Phil in so much
hot water. In a way, he supposed, he and Walt would be partly
responsible if Phil stayed in the valley until he was killed by one
of his angry ex-associates in Klan-forming. On the other hand,
Robin reasoned, he would kill Phil Cogle himself, with his two
bare hands, rather than see the Klan get a start in Crinshaw.

That night Robin couldn't sleep. His thoughts were chasing
themselves around in his head, as he was wont to tell Sallie, like
a puppy dog chasing its tail, making a quick circle but getting

exactly nowhere. Finally, he rolled out of bed, slipped on his clothes, tiptoed from the room without arousing Sallie, and went to the kitchen, where he consumed a large glass of buttermilk, hoping it would make him sleepy. After a little while, since he was still as wide awake as ever, he eased out of the house and headed up the road to the store, where he found a seat on the bench against the wall on the porch. It was after midnight when Robin, sitting in the dark, saw enough of the silhouette of Phil Cogle to recognize his walk, as Phil eased carefully up the creek road. Robin waited until Phil was well out of sight, then he set out to follow, stepping carefully and trailing his quarry by the occasional slight noise Phil's shoes made against the rocks in the road.

Phil lengthened his stride. It was evident he didn't think anyone else would be roaming at that time of night. He fumbled with the front gate latch at Walt's. In a few seconds he was up on the porch, rapping lightly. "So, that's his game, is it?" Robin thought to himself, as he stood concealed behind the corner post of the front-yard fence. Within a few moments a light came on in the house and Robin could see the dim form of Malvina at the door, which she only cracked. For a few minutes the talk between them was in such a low murmur Robin couldn't catch what was being said. Then he could hear Phil's voice raised in pleading.

"Malvina," he said, "you're the only woman in the valley, as I just said, whom I have any respect for, any real affection for. I admire your brains, as well as your beauty. Your sympathy and understanding is something I haven't found in another living soul in Modesty Valley; no, not even among my own flesh and blood. You've got to listen to me. Let me explain a few things."

"You'll have to hurry, then," Malvina said, loud enough for Robin to hear plainly. "It's chilly, and I have to get back to bed. My fire's gone out."

"Malvina, please," Phil went on tremulously, "I'm in great danger of losing my life. Somebody spread the rumor around that I pretended to try to organize a klavern of the Ku Klux Klan, and that I actually set a bushwhackers' trap for a bunch of men from Modesty Valley. They're saying I had a gang of niggers up by Split Rock Spring, lying in wait to shoot men from Modesty when they had a Klan gathering there. It's not true, Malvina. I had nothing to do with it, but that won't save my life."

"I haven't heard any of what you're talking about, and I don't believe you have either."

"It's true," he cried, dramatically. "It's the truth. I swear it. If you'll let me come in and hide in your house until morning, I'll slip away to the woods at daybreak and you can get Alan to bring my horse so I can be on my way, leaving Modesty Valley forever. I'm afraid to stay at my own house tonight. They're looking for me, but they would never think of looking here. Take me in. I give you my word, as a gentleman, I won't harm you, or say anything to hurt you, so help me God."

Robin saw the door slam, but before it was closed he heard Malvina's angry, nervous laugh and her voice in a half-scream, "Good-night, Mr. Cogle, you son-of-a-bitch!"

Phil came slowly out of the yard and turned down the creek road. Robin stepped out into the middle of the road, waiting. As Phil approached close enough to recognize Robin, he whirled slightly as if he were about to take flight, then swung back to face Robin, his pistol out. "Don't move, Arvane," he said tersely. "I'm going to kill you, but I'm going to walk you out of hearing up the cove to do it."

"Oh no, you won't," Robin answered. "I don't think you're game enough to kill me, but if you do, you'll do it right here, so it will be easy to prove who did it. Then, if they catch you right away, they'll lynch you. Lacking that, the law would most surely later break your damn neck. But if you were lucky enough to get away, my folks and Walt would follow you down and kill you in the end. Come on, give me that pistol and let's walk up the road while I explain a few things to you."

Phil hung back when Robin turned and started casually back towards the crossroads. He stopped, called back. "Are you coming, Phil, or will I have to take a rock and knock you down and drag you?"

Phil handed Robin his gun, tagged slowly along with him. Robin said, "Phil, I know a man who was there and saw everything that happened Friday night up at Split Rock Spring. If I were in your shoes, I'd get my horse tonight, as soon as I could, and be on my way out of Modesty Valley. There's at least a dozen men looking for you to kill you. When I tell Walt about tonight, that'll be one more on your trail. For personal reasons, when Walt goes after you, I'll have to join the chase. If you stay in Modesty Valley, Josh will have the pleasure of trying to excuse your soul, before God, at your funeral along about Tuesday."

Phil sneered. "What makes you think I won't get my rifle and kill you before I go?"

"I know you won't," Robin said. "You haven't got the guts to do it and take a chance on the probable consequences."

"You can't run me out of Modesty Valley," Phil told Robin, in a half-scared, half-angry tone.

"I'm not trying to," Robin answered. "I hope you stick around so I can have the pleasure of attending your funeral. Good-night." Robin turned into the Arvane driveway.

"I'll leave the valley when I damn well get ready," Phil boasted as he went on toward the Cogle home.

Monday morning, again on his way to work, Alan stopped in at the store. "Phil, his horse, rig, and everything disappeared last night. He left a note for Ma telling her he is fed up with the valley and its ways, and she needn't expect to ever see him again in Modesty, but someday he might send her some money to visit him when he gets settled."

"Do you think he's gone for good?" Robin asked.

"This time, yes, for good," said Alan.

"Good!" Robin concluded the conversation with one word.

CHAPTER FORTY-EIGHT

S EVERAL TIMES WITHIN THE NEXT FEW WEEKS, ROBIN HEARD THAT different men had reported seeing Phil Cogle's horse and rig hidden from the road in the woods back of Queenie Regnar's house. Some of those so reporting said they had gone in and spent a while with Queenie, some as much as an entire night, but all agreed nobody had seen hide nor hair of Phil himself. The general consensus of opinion seemed to be that Phil had, when he left Modesty, gone to Queenie's, where he had left his horse and rig to be kept against some future date when he might return for it. Others believed he had gone to Queenie's and she had made away with him, keeping his outfit for herself. The rumors persisted until the whole valley was agog with speculation as to what had become of Phil Cogle. Listening to conversation in the store, it seemed to Robin that while folks wanted to know what had happened to Phil, they were, at the same time, hoping for the worst.

Of course, the rumors and counter-rumors had to get to the ears of the Cogle family sooner or later. As a result, Robin was not surprised when Alan told him, one day, he had ridden over to Queenie's the day before, searched the woods below her house, and found Phil's horse and rig there, just as they had heard it was. After ascertaining it was Phil's property, Alan went to Queenie's and asked her directly if she knew where Phil was keeping himself. She had answered, Alan said, just as directly and told him Phil had come by, left his outfit with her with instructions to keep it out of sight until he could send back, or come himself, to take it away. She said Phil had paid her well for looking after his things, and she was satisfied with the arrangement and didn't consider it anybody's business but her own. The word Alan brought back was passed along, and interest in Phil Cogle's disappearance died down to nothing.

One of the things that caused folks to lose interest in Phil Cogle and his doings so rapidly was the fact that everyone in the valley had suddenly become hot and bothered over the issue of securing a post office for Modesty. They said it wasn't fair for as many people as lived in Modesty Valley to have to ride all the way to Anserville for their mail. Modesty, they claimed, could, and would, support a post office. A post office for Modesty was an improvement Robin had to admit ruefully to himself he had never thought of; something that would preclude many a trip to Anserville and keep more trade in the valley for Arvane's. Knowing this, Robin and Walt decided it would be the better part of valor for them, for the time being, to say as little as possible on the subject and let it come to a head of its own accord.

The agitation seethed on until it reached the point of action when a delegation came to the store to ask Robin to draw up a petition, addressed to the Governor, requesting him to use his influence in getting a post office for Modesty and explaining the needs of the valley for such a facility. Robin told the delegation, which was headed by old Charm Newbold, from Upper Modesty, and Kenneth Latterbee, from Lower Modesty, "A petition to Raleigh won't get you anything but a lot of prize compost. You all know we haven't got a single man in Modesty who ever did anything for that crowd. On the other hand, they have several strong supporters in Anserville, headed by Lawyer Crewes."

"We ain't askin' for no post office in Anserville," Charm spoke up, argumentatively. "We need a post office in Modesty. Anserville ain't got nothin' to do with it. Come again, Robin."

"All right," Robin told them. "The first thing Holden's crowd will do is to contact their friends in Anserville to get their opinion as to what political advantage there might be in working for a post office out here in the sticks. The word, then, would go back that Modesty has never done anything for Holden, probably never will, and that a post office out here would hurt Anserville and help the valley. Understand?"

"From what you're saying, Robin," Kenneth drawled out, "it looks like Modesty's post office has done died a-bornin'."

Up until that moment Pless had listened to the conversation without comment, but he now spoke up. "I know how we can get a post office, but not through Raleigh."

There was a general clamor for an explanation.

"It seems to me," Pless told the assembly, "I read somewhere that Cousin Llewellin Rufus Arvane, a damn Yankee U.S. Republican Senator, has something to do with the post office department through a committee he's on. I think if we'll just keep quiet, not let them know what we're up to, send Robin to Washington to see the Senator, we might just steal a post office right out from under their noses. Seems to me that's the only way we'll get it."

"That makes sense," Kenneth cried. "Will you go an' see this here Senator, Robin?"

When Robin gave his name to the Senator's secretary, a tall, anemic-looking young man who sat with his feet on his desk reading a French novel, that worthy jerked his feet down with alacrity and ushered him into the inner sanctum without bothering to announce him; probably, Robin thought, because the young man believed he was some close kin of the Senator's from out in Iowa. The Senator remembered Robin as a little tad back when he had attended the last family reunion in Modesty. It was only after an hour's swapping of family news that Robin was able to get to the matter of a post office for Modesty. He wound up his presentation with, "That's the way it is, Cousin Llewellin. They've got North Carolina by the tail and are dragging it downhill. I really don't think Will's stealing much for himself, but in order to stay in power he's got to let his henchmen steal plenty, or the carpetbaggers, scallawags, and mugwumps would look for a new man to lead them." He explained to the Senator how the Holden crowd kept themselves in power by citing the example of Zack's experience when he had been elected by the people to the legislature.

"Modesty needs this post office very badly," Robin went on. "We believe the only chance we have to get it is to come straight up here to headquarters and deal with someone we know is honest and has the interests of all the country at heart. I don't want you to do anything that might embarrass you later, politically. Nor do we want you to spend a lot of your valuable time getting it for us. But, if you can find it in your heart to slip the good word to the right people, we know Modesty will soon have a post office."

The Senator thought for a moment. "You say you operate Arvane's store at the crossroads between Upper and Lower Modesty; is that right?"

Robin nodded.

"Then," Senator Arvane went on, "I'm to presume that you would, naturally, be the logical man to be the Modesty postmaster. And that, I believe, is as it should be, but it would soon become known that you came up here and asked me to use my influence to fix you up with a job. Don't you think that might hurt you more than it would help in the long run?"

"I'm sure it would," Robin answered, "if it worked out that way. But you see, I couldn't possibly handle a post office. It would interfere with my law practice. I propose to build a room, adjoining Arvane's store, for the post office and leave the selection of the postmaster to you. Rent would be one dollar a year. The folks in Modesty would be satisfied with almost any postmaster you might pick, as long as it's not one of Holden's more vicious thieves."

"If you feel that way about it, I'll see that you have your post office," the Senator declared. "Besides that, I'll let you name the postmaster here and now."

"Thank you, Cousin Llewellin, Sir," Robin said. "That's the kind of thing that makes you a great Senator. I hadn't expected to have anything to do with naming a postmaster, but if I may, I would like to suggest the name of a distant cousin of ours, Ames Cedric. Cousin Ames lost his left arm, and all but one finger and

his thumb on his right, in the first year of the war. Right after
Ames came home from the war he lost his wife, which left him
with nobody but his daughter, Miss Effie, who is now about thirty-
five. Miss Effie's a mighty fine woman and she's been doing all
she can to help Ames make a living, but what with the fact that
she had paralysis when she was small and got a weak leg out of
it, it hasn't been easy for them. The Arvane and Cedric clans
would be glad to help Ames out, except for one thing: he'd be
insulted if we offered. Ames is getting along toward sixty, but
he'd make a splendid postmaster. He would let Effie run it while
he kept on farming as best he could. It would help them out a lot
and make all of Modesty Valley happy to see it worked out that
way."

"And which side did Cousin Ames fight on?" the Senator
asked.

"Confederate, of course," Robin answered. "Does it make a
difference?"

"Not to me." The Senator chuckled softly, almost inaudibly.
"It may mean I'll have to do a little ramming of something down
somebody's throat." He laughed aloud. "I know what will happen when I propose a Confed for a new postmastership. May have
to resort to telling the truth and admitting Ames is a kinsman;
but no matter, you'll get your post office and Cousin Ames will be
running it." He pulled a sheet of paper toward him and began
writing rapidly.

A week after Robin returned to Modesty, he and Colonel
Bower were standing in front of the bar in the Golden Glove
striking, as the colonel said, a couple of sharp blows for freedom,
when Lawyer Crewes came in and lined up with them. After
the usual greeting, Crewes turned to Robin, cleared his throat.
"Arvane," he said, "I have some good news for Modesty Valley.
Thought you might like to hear it."

"Do tell," Robin urged.

Crewes half-drained his glass, set it down. "It's like this; not
long ago some of the folks out your way came to me and asked
me to get in touch with Mr. Holden and try to get a post office

for Modesty. At first I didn't think much of the idea. Fact is, I let them get away thinking I was dead set against it. Later, after thinking it over, I sat down and wrote Will and told him I thought Modesty should have a post office." He paused, picked up his glass, sipped slowly.

"We're listening," Robin said.

"Oh, yes. Well, I didn't get an answer from Will right away, but this morning I did get one from his headquarters saying Modesty's all set for a post office and asking me to recommend a loyal man for postmaster. I shall answer and give them my recommendation when I get back to my office."

"Have you," Robin wanted to know, "talked with any of Modesty's folks as to their preference in naming this man?"

Crewes drained his glass. "Of course not. I know more about who has been loyal than anybody in Modesty, so why should I consult them?" There was a haughty note in Crewes' voice. "For your information, I will be thinking of the valley's good when I make my recommendation. It will be a fine citizen who will bring honor and a new industry to you folks out there. You may know the man. It's Joe Mantry, who has a small licensed still out on Charity Creek. Joe told me today he would be glad to move his business to Modesty and run it along with operating the post office. You'll be getting a good, upstanding citizen, a new business, and a post office for Modesty, all because I wrote one little letter."

"I'm sure the folks will appreciate what you've done for them," Robin murmured.

"Well, they should. I don't know a man out there who ever did a damn thing for our crowd, and I doubt anyone from that neck of the woods ever will, but I can tell you one thing, our people are not the kind to pass up doing a good turn for the people of this State, regardless of their politics. Appreciate your passing the word along, Arvane. Tell 'em not to expect the post office to open too soon. Things take time, you know."

"Yes, Mr. Crewes," Robin said, casually. "I reckon they do take time. If we had to wait until your kind of pirates got us a post office Hell would be frozen over and Heaven would be moved down around us."

Crewes bridled. "Now, Arvane, I don't like your tone. If you don't want a post office because you have to accept it through the good offices of my friends in Raleigh, I think it can be arranged to hold its opening in abeyance until such time as the folks in Modesty are able to see the light."

Robin was tiring of old Crewes. "Listen, Crewes," he said, roughly, "throw your chatter in the slop bucket. For your information, the Raleigh crowd didn't have a damn thing to do with our getting a post office in Modesty. If they've heard about it at all, they're as surprised as you were. It will open just as soon as we can finish the building for it, which will be in a very few days. Another thing I can promise you, the postmaster won't be Mantry, nor anybody else that you, and your gang, might want. The fact is, the postmaster at Modesty is Mr. Ames Cedric."

"Over my dead body, he is," cried Crewes angrily.

"Better lie down and start dying, then, Crewes. I have his warrant of appointment right here in my pocket. You can write Will Holden if he has any objections he might try writing Senator Arvane in Washington. While you're about it, get Will Holden to lie down and die with you, and I'll raise enough to erect a five-thousand-dollar monument over you reading, 'Here Lie Two Double-Dealing Bastards. May They Rest in Hell.'"

For several moments Crewes stood, his hand up with fingers spread. Robin thought he was going to slap his face, but instead, Crewes suddenly dropped his hand, turned away sharply, and departed.

In due time the Modesty post office opened. It had a connecting door with the store.

It was rumored that Lawyer Crewes had found business in Raleigh since the day Colonel Bower spread it around how Robin had outbested him and the bunch he served in the post office maneuver. Wherever Robin went he was stopped and congratulated. Some said Crewes was trying to sell his Anserville property so he could move away permanently. Robin had to admit to himself he was feeling his oats and ready to run, that early morning at the store when, as he was preparing to ride into Anserville and court, Queenie Regnar came down off the ridge bearing bad news a second time.

CHAPTER FORTY-NINE

T HIS TIME QUEENIE WAS FULLY CLOTHED. HER HAIR WAS COMBED neatly, her lips and cheeks glowing with red stuff, her dress immaculate. She came in smiling broadly, spoke a polite greeting to Robin and Walt, then crossed the floor lightly, her silk skirts rustling as she swished toward a chair. Seated, she looked toward the two partners. "Do I look happy?" she said.

"Well," Walt answered, "you certainly don't look sad."

"I ain't sad, you can bet," she said. "Phil's dead."

"Phil Cogle?" Robin and Walt echoed each other.

"Yeah," she answered, laconically. "Dead since a hour ago. I done it, an' if they hang me tomorrow for it, I'll die happy."

"Tell us how it happened," Robin urged.

"Gimme a cigar," she giggled shortly, "an' I'll tell you all about it."

Walt handed her a long black stogie, while Robin brought the small spirit lamp they kept burning for customer-smokers.

Queenie took a long drag on the cigar, inhaled contentedly. "It was like this," she began. "Phil come to my house one Sunday night an' knocked on my door. He got inside before I knowed who he was. He had a big pistol strapped on the outside of his coat, an' he was nervous an' mad as all hell. I told him to get out or I'd kill him, but he jus' pushed right by me an' went into my bedroom, where I kep' my pistol, an' took it an' stuck it in his pocket. Then he cussed me out an' said he'd come to live with me awhile. An' that's what he done."

"You mean he was actually at your house all the time since he left here?" Walt asked.

"Yeah, that he was. He told me to set down an' we'd talk things over. He said he'd done put his hoss up in our old cow shed down in the woods an' he was gonna leave it there. He set down an' I set down, an' we jus' set a-lookin' at each other for a while with me a-hatin' him and a-wantin' to kill him so much I was a-achin' all over. He started in a-layin' the law down to me, an' a-cussin' me, an' all. Then I thought I had a chance, so I grabbed a chunk o' littard wood an' chunked it at him as hard as I could. Straight at his head."

"Knocked him out, I reckon?" Walt asked.

"No, it didn't. He ducked under an' hit me in the face with his fist, an' when I come to he had me stripped nekked in bed an' he was a-settin' on the side of the bed a-wettin' my face with cold water an' a-callin' me a lot of fine an' fancy love names. Soon's I was plumb come to he throwed a coupla hunks of good licker into my belly an' I started gettin' stronger right then, but I wasn't so mad at him any more. It seemed like I didn't want to kill him like I did when he first come in."

"Phil was always good at touching a soft spot if he knew where it was," Robin mused, as though talking to himself.

"He musta knowed where mine was, for he put both hands down on 'em as gentle as a kitten; then he kissed me so hard on the mouth it hurt my lips an' I got to tremblin' all over. The next mornin' he stuck two one-thousand-dollar bills between my breasts, then woke me up by kissin' me to show 'em to me. Then we was a-lyin' there in bed a-talkin', and he was a-tellin' me that the reason he was so mean to me and Ma when he was a-livin' with us before was because he was so much in love with me that he got mad at me an' Ma ever' time we got around him. He said he knowed he was a low-down dog that way, but he jus' couldn't help it, an' he was powerful sorry about it. He said ever' time I come around him it was all he could do to keep from takin' me in his arms, which he knowed he couldn't do because my sister was his wife, so he let his love turn into mad an' then he took it out on me an' Ma."

"Damn good talker, Phil, especially when he was lying," Robin observed to no one in particular.

"Damn right he was a good talker," Queenie went on. "An' I jus' et it up. Nobody hadn't never talked so sweet to me before in my life, an' I was awful lonesome for some sweet talk. When he would start in a-talkin' about how much he loved me I'd jus' quiver like a feather and ache all over with love of him. He shore knowed how to make a woman happy."

"He knew how to get your pantalettes hot, didn't he?" Walt asked with a note of sarcasm.

"Damn right, an' that's why he's dead," she answered emphatically. "You wanta hear the rest, or do you want to light out now to pick up his body?"

"Tell us all about it," Robin urged her. "If he's dead like you say, he can't get any deader in the next few minutes."

"Well, it was like I said," she went on. "I got so in love of Phil that I didn't want another man to touch me, ever again, an' told him so. He said that would be foolish, but if I'd lock the front door an' not answer any knocks for a few days, we'd have us a honeymoon. If they hang me tomorrow I won't never forget them next few days. I jus' plumb went to Heaven. We locked everybody else out an' stayed in the house nekkid as jaybirds except when we had to go outside. I hope the Good Lord took him to Heaven, because he was killed without a chance in this world. An' I hope I'll be able to repent enough before they hang me, so I can go up there an' meet up with him again."

She laughed heartily, and Robin noted her laughter had a peculiar, crackling sound. He thought to himself that she was apparently calm but actually on the verge of wild hysteria. He brought her a stiff drink of Monongahela from the barrel in the back. She swallowed it hungrily and resumed her narrative. "After a while he musta got tired of me, for one day he said he had to go to Tennessee on business but he'd be back in a day or so. I wanted to go with him, but he said he couldn't afford to take me where he had to go, an' that he wanted me to open up the door and receive company while he was gone like I always had. I didn't want to do that an' told him so. It hurt awful bad when he told me not to be a damn fool. Once a whore, always a whore, an' he didn't want me to forget it. He was gone almost two weeks, an' I had about decided he wasn't comin' back when he walked in one night. I already had my clothes off to entertain a man in my room when I heard him come in. He come in an' slipped into the shed room, but I heard him jus' the same an' hustled my company off without doin' nothin' for him by tellin' him that I heard my own man from Tennessee slip in an' he was powerful jealous an' powerful dangerous when he thought I might be messin' around with somebody else."

"Now I've enough to laugh at the rest of my life," Walt said.

"Of course Phil heard it all," Queenie paid no attention to Walt's remark, "an' when my company was plumb out of hearin' he come out of the shed room an' cussed me out for a fare-thee-well. He said he didn't never mean to let me forget what he'd told me before, that once a whore, always a whore. He said if I had some funny idea that I was goin' to lay around an' make him support me the rest of my life, I was crazy as all hell. He said his business had kept him in Tennessee longer'n he'd reckoned for, but he had made a few dollars in a little friendly game an' he'd brought us back five gallons of good Kentucky whiskey. After we took a drink or so he got real friendly-like again an' told me to lock the door an' keep everybody out the rest of the night. I didn't sleep a wink that night I was so achin' happy jus' a-lyin' there a-listenin' to Phil a-snorin' so ca'm an' innocent-like."

"I always knew there was something Phil could do that suggested innocence. It was snoring, and he could only do that in his sleep," Robin interjected.

"Damn right," she said, "he had a real innocent-like snore. The next mornin' he told me he was goin' to leave me that day an' he hoped he'd never see me again as long as he lived. Like a fool, I busted out squallin' an' beggin' him to stay with me. Finally he said he would if I would get back to my business an' let him alone except when he wanted me, an' I said I would.

"Then one day we was a-playin' around the place nekkid when he got mad at me an' started cuffin' me around pretty rough. I got mad, too, an' caught him where it would hurt the most an' snatched down as hard as I could. He screamed like a wounded panther an' fell down on the floor wigglin' around like a snake in hot ashes, all the time he was swearin' to God I'd done killed him. I thought so, too, for the next day he was all swoll-up. I wanted to get him a doctor but he said no, he wasn't gonna have all of Crinshaw County a-laughin' at him. Besides that, he said, nobody was sposed to know he was not long gone from the county. He told me to keep 'em soaked with hot wet towels an' mebbe the swellin' would go down. I done it, an' they went down to regular size in a few days."

Robin heard Walt sputter, then break into uncontrolled laughter, slapping his hands together. "I can't help it," he cried, between guffaws. "That's funny, even if the man is dead."

"It is, ain't it?" Queenie agreed. "When the swellin' left, it took somethin' with it. Phil's manhood was gone, an' it near killed him when he knowed about it. It didn't make me feel no better, neither. It was gone a good while, an' durin' that time he kept the water hot for me a-cussin' an' a-ravin' an' a-sayin' if he didn't get his manhood back soon he was gonna kill me, an' I reckon he would, but after a while it come back an' he was almost as good as ever, though not quite. We was awfully happy—leastwise I was—even if he did make me stay with any man as come by.

"This mornin' when I woke up he was gone from the house, but in a few minutes he drove up in front in his rig, hitched, an' come in. He had already packed all of his stuff an' said he was a-leavin' for good. I started in to beg him to stay, like a damn fool, an' he cussed me out an' said he'd heard of a good thing out in Texas an' he was on his way. He said he hoped he never got tangled up again with another woman as much like a damn slut as I was, an' for me to go an' bring him his pistol an' holster belt from our room while he finished tyin' up his carpetbag. When I got back with the pistol in my hand I told him he wasn't gonna leave me. That I'd kill him first. He said for me to hand him his gun before he knocked my God-damn teeth down my whorish throat; then he drawed back his fist. I shot him, an' th' blood spurted out about three feet from the hole in the top of his belly. As soon as I knowed he was plumb dead, I put on my best glad rags an' drove his rig down here to tell you."

"I believe you've told the truth," Robin said to Queenie. "Suppose you stay here with me while Mr. Cedric drives your rig down to notify the Cogle family."

"You goin' to put me in jail, ain't you?" she asked.

"No, not me," Robin answered. "The sheriff will have to look after that. I will do this gladly: take your case as a lawyer and try to get you off if you will promise to leave Crinshaw County for good. Go far away and never come back."

"Thankee, I will," she said and stood up. Robin heard the noise of the rig as Walt was driving away. At the same time, he noticed she was trembling and twitching, her face drained white. Then with a wild piercing shriek she fell flat, fainted dead away.

CHAPTER FIFTY

Rᴏʙɪɴ sᴇɴᴛ ꜰᴏʀ sᴀʟʟɪᴇ ᴀɴᴅ ᴛʜᴇʏ ᴡᴀɪᴛᴇᴅ ɪɴ ᴛʜᴇ sᴛᴏʀᴇ ᴡɪᴛʜ Queenie until Walt, Alan, and Josh came down the ridge slopes with Phil's body. Then, with Sallie accompanying them, he took Queenie into Anserville and the sheriff's office. All the way to town Queenie sat as though in a trance, answering questions in monosyllables and mumbling to herself. It was evident that her nerves were drawn piano-wire tight and that she was in no condition to discuss the killing rationally but would be more than apt to go off into hysterics at the first push.

However, Robin and Sallie kept drumming it into her not to talk to anyone about the episode any more than to say she killed Phil Cogle; then tell them to see her lawyer. "No matter who asks you, don't say any more than that. Tell them to see Robin. He's your lawyer. Say you'll talk when he says you may. Do you understand, Queenie?" Sallie asked her over and over.

Queenie nodded that she understood, but Robin had doubts about her knowing what was going on. He told himself he could only hope for the best. They went to the jail with the sheriff, where Sallie literally bluffed that gentleman into getting clean bedding for Queenie's cell as well as promising personally to see that she was decently fed and cared for.

On the way home Sallie turned to Robin and cried fiercely, "You've got to get her off, Robin. If ever a man had it coming to him, Phil Cogle was that man. That is, if you believe the story she told you this morning."

"Oh, I'm sure she told the truth to Walt and me. But honey,

men juries have a way of believing that women like Queenie
have to expect to be cuffed around by the opposite sex. The very
same men who have been Queenie's best customers are still convinced that, when she started dispensing for money, as well as
fun, she lost all rights of membership in the human race. I don't
subscribe that to theory, but I may have a hard time convincing
a jury of twelve good men and true that my theory is right. I
promise to do my best. But I'll feel pretty lucky if I can get her
off with a life sentence."

"Oh," Sallie swore, and her words came slowly, hard, metallic,
"men can be such damn low-down polecats in their stiff-necked
arrogance that what's right for them is wrong for a woman!"

"But darling," Robin reasoned, "after all, Queenie is a profes-
sional prostitute, and she did kill Phil Cogle, and I am going to
do my best to get her off."

"Suppose she did kill Phil Cogle. It wasn't half what he deserved. If there were no men like Phil Cogle there wouldn't be
any women like Queenie." Sallie's ire was subsiding, but she was
still angrily indignant.

"I'm trying to figure out a defense line to make my fight on.
And, to tell the truth, I'm finding it hard. Perhaps the colonel
will have some ideas."

"Pshaw," Sallie quipped at him, "if I could practice law, I
would bet the baby's shoes I could get her clear."

"Tell me," Robin said smiling.

"I will. First, I'd forget all legal aspects in this case. I'd just
put Walt Cedric on the stand and let him repeat the story she
told you and him this morning. After that, I'd throw my law-
books out the window and plead her case before the jury as justifiable homicide."

Robin thought Sallie's last statement over for a minute, then
his face broke into a wide grin. He chuckled softly, but audibly.
"Do you know, honey, what you just said?" he asked.

"I don't care," she answered tartly, "what you think of what
I just said. You're like all other damn men. You think women,

like children, should be seen and not heard. You think the power of reason is the exclusive property of the male mind."

Robin chuckled happily, amused at her vehemence. "But Sallie darling, you just told me how to win the case. I'm going to do exactly what you suggested and get Queenie off clean as a whistle. That is, if I can get the prosecution to put Walt on the stand. Wanna bet?"

His eyes were twinkling as he saw the anger drain out of her face; then her eyes softened as she cried, "Robin, I love you!" and rubbed her face hard against his sleeve as she moved closer and clung to his arm.

As they approached the house, Sallie asked Robin, "Have you noticed Mother Pam doesn't look too good these days? I think she's lost quite a lot of weight, for her, and she looks kind of pale. I know she keeps going, but I notice that when she thinks nobody's around she sits down to rest most of the time. She swears she never felt better in her life, but I don't believe a word of it."

"I know," Robin answered, gravely, "and Pa knows it, too. He took her to the doctor last month and the doc gave her that bottle of tonic to build her up. I peeked in the medicine closet the other day and she hasn't taken more than two doses of it. I told Pa, and he said he got after her about it and she told him if the Good Lord didn't see fit to do anything for her, she didn't see how a human doctor could. She told Pa flatly she doesn't intend to take any more of the vile-tasting stuff. Pa asked her if she would take it if it tasted a little better, and she said she would, not because she believed it would help any, but just to please the rest of us. Pa went back the other day and got some that's all syruped up, and he told me last night she's taking it pretty well, according to schedule."

Things happened rapidly in the valley for the next few weeks. When the Cogle family opened Phil's money belt they found several thousand dollars in cash and two deposit receipts from St. Louis banks for seven thousand dollars each. They also found a message, in Phil's handwriting, that said tersely, "In the event of my death, all of my assets are to be turned over to my mother to handle as she sees fit." It was signed, "Philip Cogle."

Alan stopped by the store and told Robin about it and said his mother had gone to Chafferton to meet Philemon Banther, famous lawyer of Raleigh, whom she had engaged to represent her in having Phil's will probated, as well as to assist in the prosecution of Queenie Regnar. "Ma's raving mad at every member of the Arvane and Cedric clans since she heard you're going to be Queenie's lawyer," Alan told Robin. "She says she'll spend every cent Phil left, if necessary, to see that they break Queenie's neck. Man, she's raving! Says Phil was the only child she had with any intelligence, but that the rest of us were so jealous of him we dogged him into trouble. All of us have tried to tell her that sooner or later Phil could have ended up just like he did, and that the best thing that she could do would be to stay completely away from the trial. Let folks forget it as soon as possible.

"But she's rampaging. You know how Ma is when she gets the bit in her teeth and her tail in the air. It would take a regiment of grizzly bears to stop her. I'm afraid, sometimes, that if Ma had been a man, she'd have been pretty much like Phil, and I hate like hell to make that statement," he finished, sadly.

A few days before the Queenie Regnar trial, Anserville began taking on a holiday atmosphere. Banther, a portly, red-faced, wattle-jawed lawyer, in his late fifties, with a snow-white thatch of long thick hair, established an office at the Anserville Inn and began rounding up information for the prosecution's use. He took the case largely out of the hands of district solicitor Harkel, a not-too-bright fetch-and-carry boy in the Holden machine.

Banther ran up on Robin in the Golden Glove. "No reason," he said augustly, lifting a glass, "why two barristers shouldn't be good friends and still fight it out in court. Some of my biggest cases have been won from some of my dearest friends. Personally, I don't much give a damn whether I hang her or not. I suppose about all you're hoping for is to get her off with life, and to tell the truth, I don't care a lot if that's what she gets. Of course, old lady Cogle's going to pass a wildcat if I don't get a hanging sen-

tence, but to hell with that. I didn't make her any guarantee anyway. By the way, Arvane, what are you going to plead for her?"

"Hadn't given it much thought," Robin told Banther. "Fact
is, I was thinking about just letting the jury know the truth and
trusting to their judgment as to right and wrong."

Banther studied Robin's face for a moment; then a thought
struck him. "Look here, young fellow," he said in a fatherly
tone, "don't go trying any of that self-defense stuff on me. I
warn you now, I'm going to remind that Bible-reading bunch
of hillbilly jurymen that the Good Book says, 'Thou Shalt Not
Kill.' I thought perhaps we could strike some kind of a bar-
gain, so that we could let her off with a life sentence; which,
of course, would be a feather in your cap, and wouldn't hurt me,
since I would actually hint to the jury that such a verdict would
satisfy the prosecution. On the other hand, if you want to
gamble with your client's life, gamble it is, and I guarantee to
hang her as high as Haman. Is that what you want?"

Robin laughed. "No, that isn't what I want. I want to send
you scooting back to Raleigh faster than you came out here, with
your little rat tail between your big fat legs. I want to let the folks
in this section know what kind of legal protection they have in
that little nimcompoop of the Holden gang who's your colleague
in this attempt to frustrate justice like you did when my brother
Zack was elected to the legislature. And, most of all, I want to
see Miss Regnar go free and hear everybody give her a round of
hurrahs for doing a good job in dealing Philip Cogle out of the
game. Those are my intentions, Sir. Any other questions?"

Banther bowed with a flourish of his swallowtail. "I accept
the gauntlet you've just thrown, Sir. May I give you my word as
a gentleman that henceforth it's a war to the knife, and the knife
to the hilt, between us? I bid you good day, Sir." With a last
eloquent flourish of his coattails, he bowed again to Robin and
left the saloon.

CHAPTER FIFTY-ONE

T HE DAY OF QUEENIE REGNAR'S TRIAL WAS COOL, CLEAR, AND bright, a gala event in Anserville. It seemed to Robin that half the population of the county was in town, plus a goodly sprinkling from the surrounding counties. Then, of course, there were the usual sensation seekers, the crowd-followers trying to garner a few quick dollars, and newspaper reporters—some from as far away as Washington.

The old courthouse would seat, at best, about two hundred and allow room for as many more standing in the aisles and against the walls. All windows were open so that part of the overflow could tell what was going on inside. Folks were in a gay holiday mood. Peddlers roved the streets selling gewgaws, candy, and fruit. One enterprising farmer built an impromptu kitchen in his wagon and dispensed meals from the tailboard. The saloons stayed crowded. Bottled goods passed from mouth to mouth. Small gyp gambling deals, operated by small-time artists, appeared in a half-dozen locations. One discerning operator offered odds of two to three that Queenie would be condemned to hang, the same odds she would be sent up for life, and ten to one she wouldn't be acquitted. Robin and Walt decided to risk a hundred dollars on the ten-to-one bet.

An itinerant preacher set up an outdoor pulpit in the wagon yard and preached a four-hour sermon on the evils of murder, fornication, adultery, stealing, gambling, wife-beating, cheating, lying, high taxes, politics, and failure to heed the powerful words of the Good Lord's emissaries such as himself. By the

time he finally passed the hat, the licker he had preached so up-
roariously against had everybody, almost, in a generous mood.
The hat-passing was highly rewarding.

The Union League, more for political show than anything
else, furnished scores of special deputies to keep order. There
were only two fights worth mentioning, and they wouldn't have
had any significance except for the fact that they involved two of
the special deputies, who ordered a couple of Cat Cove citizens
out of their way and were rewarded for their efforts in behalf of
law and order by having the doctor sew up some very long ab-
dominal gashes deftly provided by the Cat Covers. After the cutting the Cat Cove boys sought the company of the remainder of
the contingent from out their way, where they all, collectively,
dared the special deputies to mess with them. Colonel Bower,
seeing that a first-class brawl was brewing, talked both sides into
a truce for the day. By the next day the incident was forgotten
except by the deputies, who had to stay at home and nurse sore
bellies. All in all, everybody was having a rip-roaring good time.

Queenie came into court, escorted by a deputy sheriff and wearing handcuffs. She was dressed in a country-style black dress.
When she was seated in the prisoner's box she reached up and
straightened her hair with a gesture that made certain the spec-
tators could see the manacles. Banther knew, from the gesture,
that she had been well coached. The audience growled in disgust, and some low hisses were directed toward the prosecution.
Banther leaned toward Harkel, his face flushed with anger. "Of
all the damn-fool moves I ever saw made in court," he sputtered.
"Have them remove those cuffs, you dumb ox."

Harkel bridled. "As the solicitor I have the right to bring her
into court handcuffed. She is. She'll stay that way until she goes
back to her cell." His lips were prim.

The preliminaries over, and after Harkel had read the indict-
ment, Queenie entered a plea of not guilty.

Banther called the sheriff as his first witness. The sheriff
stated that Queenie had admitted killing Philip Cogle but that
she had refused to give any details. Yes, he said, she had two

thousand dollars which she said Phil had given her. He had visited the scene of the crime. He described the lay of the land, as it was when he arrived.

On cross-examination Robin brought out that they had found two thousand dollars on Phil's body, as well as deposit receipts and other personal property which Queenie had not touched.

As Robin had hoped, the prosecution decided to put Walt on the stand in order to establish a motive. Banther was a skillful trial lawyer and led Walt along as though he had a ring in his nose. He got the exact truth out of Walt. That is, he got the exact truth like pouring cream off the top of the pitcher. The testimony he wanted and got from Walt was that he had heard Queenie admit killing Philip Cogle after living with him for some time and that she owned up to having two thousand dollars in her possession that had once belonged to Phil. He was apparently proving that Queenie killed Philip Cogle deliberately and in cold blood when she learned he was taking himself and his money out of her life. When it became evident that Robin was not going to object to the testimony, Banther was admonished several times by the court for getting testimony out of Walt that was, at best, hearsay. Each time Banther gave the judge a courtly bow, apologized, and murmured something about trying to arrive at the facts in the case.

When Banther had finished with Walt, Robin announced that he would like to call the witness back later for cross-examination. The judge cleared his throat, said that was a little irregular, but, over Banther's objection, allowed the motion.

Robin did object mildly when Banther called Mrs. Cogle to the stand, but it was evident that he was making only token objections. She swore Phil had always been a dutiful and loving son, a brave and loyal soldier for the Union forces, who had risen through gallantry in action from private to lieutenant. She testified Phil's own brother and sister had always been jealous of him because he was born smarter than the rest of the family. There were some others in the valley, she said, who were murderously envious of Phil's superior intelligence and leadership. The reason he had been at Queenie Regnar's at all was that he was hiding out to save his life. Asked who it was that wanted to kill her son, she said she wasn't sure but that, in her opinion, it was Robin Arvane. There were titters in the courtroom, and the judge had to rap for order. When he saw that Robin wasn't going to object, he told the jury to disregard the last statement. Mrs. Cogle then got more and more profuse in her praise of Phil, and Banther ceased only when he realized that the jury was beginning not to take her seriously.

Robin, who had been quietly smiling through Mrs. Cogle's testimony, stood up to begin his cross-examination. The first question he asked Mrs. Cogle was if she could actually prove beyond a shadow of a doubt that her son's military record was what she had said. Heatedly she said she could, as Banther shouted an objection. When the judge overruled the objection, Robin asked, "If I could show you with documentary evidence, secured from the files of the War Department, that Philip Cogle never rose above the rank of a private, that he never heard a gun fired in combat, that the two or three letters you had from him during the war, asking for money, were written from prison, where he carved out his army career for grave infractions of military law, that he had the letters mailed from a Cleveland address by someone else, and that he never revealed to you even his regimental designation, would you then believe you were mistaken about some phases of your son's life?"

Banther was on his feet hollering, telling the witness she didn't have to answer, and when Banther calmed down, the witness shouted at Robin, "You're a liar, Robin Arvane! A liar! A liar!"

Again Banther's roaring objection went up. While the judge began angrily quieting the room, Robin went to the bench and laid a sheaf of papers before him. His honor rattled the papers, looking through them. He was getting angrier by the minute. Angry with both prosecution and defense. He had no intention of allowing mountain justice to run away with dignified court procedure. But, as he read the papers Robin had put in front of him, his expression became more mollified.

Finally the judge turned to the jury: "Gentlemen, while it may be somewhat irregular to make this statement from the bench, I feel that it must, in the interest of justice, be made. It is likewise hard to tear down in any small way the adoration and trust of a mother for her son. However, without casting any aspersions on the divinity of mother-love, I am compelled to tell you, after perusing these documents, that the testimony of the witness now before you is to be utterly ignored, and she is hereby excused by the court from further appearance in this trial."

Banther, dazed, decided he was through with witnesses and must get a conviction by his own masterful oratory.

Robin immediately recalled Walt to the stand.

"Your Honor, some of the testimony of the witness may be a bit off-color for the ears of the ladies present. I would like to suggest that Your Honor extend to those of the fair sex present the privilege of leaving the court, unless they wish to hear the details of a most sordid mess."

The women perked up their ears, but not one offered to leave. Finally, when the judge had explained what Robin said, and made his suggestion, the wives of two ministers got up and tiptoed reluctantly out of court.

Skillfully, Robin led Walt through a complete repetition of the story Queenie had told them when she came to the store an hour or so after the killing. He emphasized the details of the orgies of love-making between Queenie and Phil. He dwelt on how Queenie had fallen madly in love with Phil, despite the fact that he had been indirectly the cause of her mother's and sister's death. He had Walt tell about how Duchess had gone into Arvane's and purchased all the laudanum they had in stock when she and Phil came back to Modesty. When he had finished, the jury knew most of the details of Phil's love life with the Regnar girls.

During the course of Walt's testimony, Banther offered objection after objection; kept repeating that the testimony was no more than hearsay, not admissible in court. Each time Robin reminded him who had been the first to call Mr. Cedric.

Harkel summarized the charge briefly and sat down. By now he wanted to see Banther get his come-uppance.

When Harkel sat down, Banther came storming back. He explained that he had not questioned Cedric further because it was evident he had been too well coached by his legal opponent. "This is not a circus," he said. "Nor is it a tea party. This is a court of law where we are trying a prisoner for the coldest-blooded murder ever perpetrated in this noble State. The prisoner, a proven prostitute of many years' experience, admitted her guilt to the sheriff. She turned over to that officer two thousand-dollar notes which she said were given to her by her victim. Now I ask you: why should Philip Cogle give that much money to a woman he could have for nothing, or at best, a paltry sum? Why, and how, did she come to have two thousand dollars?

"That money is the crux of this whole case. How did she get it? Could it have been that she was willing to kill a man for a sum of money larger than she had ever known existed before? Remember, our Saviour was betrayed for a whole lot less.

"Gentlemen of the Jury, I shall be honest. I personally want that scarlet woman hanged by the neck until she is dead. She deserves to feel, as far as her tarnished and withered soul is able to feel, some of the anguish and sorrow she has brought into the heart of that sainted and beloved mother of Philip Cogle. We are not trying Philip Cogle. We are trying his murderess." There was more, and more, for another hour, when Banther wound up with, "I thank you, Gentlemen. I'm sure the jury will not take long to arrive at a just and Christian verdict of murder in the first degree."

Robin began, in his address to the jury following Banther, by admitting that Queenie was a common harlot. But at that, he argued, she was far better, more honorable, than the man she had killed. He dwelt at length on what Walt had told them. On Phil's treatment of Queenie. On the fact that he had threatened her and was in the act of striking her when she shot. He pointed out that had Queenie not killed Philip Cogle he might have returned at a later date and killed her. It was evident, he thought, that Phil was utterly crazy, and growing worse all the time. He asked for an acquittal on the grounds of justifiable homicide.

The judge's charge was brief. He pointed out there could be no doubt that Philip Cogle came to his death at the hands of Queenie Regnar. He summarized the evidence, not only of the killing, but of the hard feeling between Queenie and Phil, of the fact that she had a gun in her room and had made a threat that she would kill Phil Cogle rather than see him leave her. But, he said, killing was not always murder. There was evidence that Phil had also made threats against Queenie and had made a motion as if he were going to strike her just before she shot. The judge told the jury what the possible verdicts were. "You are not," he said, "too tightly bound to legal gymnastics that you can't allow room for the operation of your conscience. The bailiff will conduct you to the jury room and the court will remain in session until you have a reasonable time to return a verdict."

The jury was back within ten minutes. The verdict, not guilty by reason of self-defense.

The crowd moved out of the courtroom, laughing and joking happily. The show had been worth a half-year's work on one of his rocky hillsides, a tall mountaineer chortled.

There were two resounding plops heard, with a woman's scream between them. Deputies pulled Mrs. Cogle away from Banther. They held her while she screamed anathema at his retreating form. "You low son-of-a-bitch," she yelled, "you promised to hang her for twenty-five hundred dollars. You got half of it, but you'll never get another cent of my Phil's hard-earned money. No, you stinking, polecat bastard, I'll kill you before I pay you anything else."

Robin worked himself loose from the crowd which had gathered round to shake hands, offer congratulations. He moved toward the prisoner's dock where Queenie still sat, not comprehending enough to know she was safe from further molestation. He said to a nearby bailiff, curtly, "Take those damn handcuffs off the woman. She's no longer a prisoner."

From the outside, those still in the courtroom heard Axiom's deep-hooting cry, hoarsened somewhat by alcoholic libations, "Yippee! That's my Cap'n Robin Arvane!"

Next morning Phil Cogle's mother was found dead, swinging from a rafter in the hay barn. It was thus that Phil's money finally removed the shaky, bent, and age-wearied frame of Jarrett Cogle from between the plow handles.

At the inquest, the old man, who seemed neither shocked nor sorry at his wife's suicide, asked Robin to inform Miss Queenie Regnar that Phil Cogle's fine horse and rig belonged to her.

CHAPTER FIFTY-TWO

In THE COMING MONTHS, SALLIE AND ROBIN BEGAN TO GLORY IN THE presence of each other without the wild surges of passion so wont to dominate the first years together of two sexually healthy young people who are madly in love, and deeply in love with love itself.

They were learning to sit with each other quietly, silently, yet in perfect communion. They were learning the joy of exploring each other's intellects in long discussions and finding it good. They happily planned for the future of their son, Ajax, while at the same time Sallie was doing all in her power to start the making of another child for Robin.

"I sometimes feel," Robin said to Sallie, "that we, here in the Southern mountains, are like folks sitting snugly on a protected island while the remainder of the South, particularly the cotton country, is like a huge, surging sea, with storms whipping it into a froth from every which way. Of course, the storms are blowing a lot of filth our way, but we're not catching hell like folks in some parts of the South. We're bound to get some, of course, but it will never be like it is down in Georgia, where so many stiff-necked Crackers are being pushed off the sidewalks by Yankee troops in the daytime and Negroes go out of their way to be especially sassy to their former masters as long as the Yanks are there to back them up. Then, by night, the Crackers ride the roads, in the regalia of the Klan, with every man toting his own artillery and carrying a big lash. The Negroes burn barns, they say, get caught, and are killed by the Klan. The military tries to investigate and some of them are plugged from ambush. I under-stand they have a very efficient underground down that way to help those who do it escape the state and light a shuck for Texas when the Yanks and carpetbaggers get too close on their trail. It looks like government by chaos, but I would be willing to bet a workable organization will come out of it. Still, that won't destroy the bitterness that's being engendered by the fact that too many of the leaders on the side of the North are not satisfied with obedience. They want obeisance. Which, of course, they won't get."

They were building slowly in the South an order that Anglo-Saxon Southerners believed would best serve their beloved land. An order that would have its scales of social justice tipped badly out of line, according to the teachings of Christianity, yet was fully justified in the eyes of its architects by the more compulsive laws of biological expediency. Thus Robin theorized.

"And now," Robin said, "another invisible government is making its way among us here in the mountains. We had no more need for the Union League than a cat has for a camel's sad-dle. It meets, marches, and looks for devilment to stir up. When practically everybody belonged to it there were enough decent men in its ranks to hold it down to practically no harm. Since most of the sensible element has left its ranks, the hoodlums who are running it now are capable of causing trouble. That is, they were right here in Crinshaw up until last night."

"What about last night?" Sallie said. "I heard it was practi-cally entirely through the good work of the Union League that emergency relief supplies were granted to Buncombe, Madison, and some more Western North Carolina counties."

"Union League, pshaw," Robin answered. "Will Holden ap-plied for relief for those counties because he thought it was good political business to do so. They're his boys. They do as Will says."

"What did you mean about up until last night?" Sallie asked.

"It was like this," Robin went on. "The Leaguers were having a big torchlight parade last night in Anserville. They were marching around town, singing, yelling, and drinking, about a hundred of them, generally raising hell. After about three hours some of them got to feeling so patriotic they started shooting off their pistols. For a wonder, nobody shot back at them, but along about midnight a gang of riders dressed in sheets and masks galloped into town. Colonel Bower said they had about thirty men. They rode down the street as silent as ghosts, evidently with pads on their horses' hooves. They rode straight to where the Leaguers were gathered, then lined up in a cavalry charge formation, pulled long lashes out from under their robes, and spurred right into the Leaguers. And as the Leaguers dodged the horses, the robed men lashed out with their whips right and left. I don't think anyone was hurt much. The League boys didn't fight back and nobody, actually, was ridden down."

"They didn't try to actually ride anybody down, then," Sallie opined. "I'll bet I could ride my little bay into an elephant."

"No, they didn't want to hurt anybody," Robin said. "The colonel thinks the League will be laughed dead within a week in Crinshaw County. He doesn't think the riders were members of the regular Klan, just some decent citizens who've gotten tired of the way the League's been carrying on. I hope he's right. We don't need either."

Colonel Bower's opinion proved correct.

As time passed, it left with Robin the realization that the first-year-after-the-war prosperity that had come to Modesty Valley lacked considerable in being a lasting thing. In a manner of speaking, in the rich, wide valleys, like Modesty, where any man with industry and initiative could easily amass the comforts of good living in a more than abundant measure, the people had always been able, up until the war, to raise more than they needed. Here, four years of war economy had taught the people the graces of hardship. Taught them how to make do with things they had formerly scorned, or thrown away. Much false pride had been burned away in the fire of common suffering.

Dr. Saddler, the testy little Yankee doctor who had experienced wife trouble up in New England, along with a nasty hacking cough that hung on, and had come South to start over, and to the mountains in particular to see if his cough would get better, was the only doctor in the county. His practice was practically confined to Crinshaw. The fact that his low-paying patients were almost more in number than he could handle, and that his cough had disappeared, had not helped his disposition. He was still sarcastically testy.

The little doctor was devoted to his calling and never failed to go when asked, regardless of how far back in the hills it might be, how hard it might be to get there, or how little chance he had of ever being paid.

Dr. Saddler and Robin were fond of each other, each recognizing and respecting the other's ability. They enjoyed taking insulting, joking pot shots at the professions of doctoring and lawyering, as they were pleased to call their work.

Thus it was one late afternoon when Robin had come home from his office and was idly sitting his horse watching Sallie and her bay mare tearing down the path by the creek with Red Bud stretched to a mad gallop. Sallie was the only woman they had in the valley who rode a man's saddle, dressed in a divided skirt. She wore no hat, and her hair had been loosed to the wind. Robin knew she was talking the mare into putting everything she had into a frenzied burst of speed.

Just as the pounding of the mare's feet began to reach his ears, Dr. Saddler came out of the house, after a call on Pamela, stood by the side of Robin's horse, and watched the rider as she lifted Red Bud over a ten-rail fence without perceptibly losing a stride, then loped her with a slower gait up to where Robin and the doctor waited.

Sallie's face was flushed, her eyes sparkling with excitement and good health. The mare, with running temporarily worked out of her system, stood tranquilly getting her wind back.

"You are an excellent horsewoman, Mrs. Arvane," the doctor observed. "Do you ride that way very much?"

"Thank you, Sir," Sallie laughed, "I ride miles almost every day and try to let my little pet get in one good run. I think she enjoys it almost as much as I do."

"Have you always ridden that way?" the doctor asked.

"No," Sallie admitted, "I haven't. The first year I lived here in the valley we were starting a family. Then after the baby came there was a long time when his demands were such I didn't have time, but I got back to riding as soon as I could. I don't think anything in the world could make me give it up now.

"An ounce of prevention," the doctor murmured.

Sallie looked from the doctor's face to Robin's and back.

"I'm afraid I don't know what you mean, Doctor," she said calmly.

"Come, come, Mrs. Arvane," a note of testiness had crept into the doctor's tone. "Don't be naive. After all, I'm your family doctor, and your husband is present."

"I am still in the dark as to what you're driving at," Sallie protested.

"So am I," Robin butted in with an undertone of impatience in his voice. "Please explain."

"I will," the doctor told them, condescendingly testy again. "I can almost guarantee if you will ride like that twenty-five days out of every month, your mare will never drop a foal."

"Oh," Sallie laughed. "Red Bud doesn't want any babies. It taxes her ability to look after me."

"And you, Mrs. Arvane," the doctor went on slowly, deliberately, "will have no more babies, either."

Sallie's face paled for a moment. "Help me down gently, Robin; then put Red Bud in her stable and burn that damn saddle!"

CHAPTER FIFTY-THREE

W ITHIN TWO MONTHS AFTER SALLIE DECIDED TO STAY AWAY from her daily ride, she told Robin she thought it was going to work. She told him with a proud, exultant giggle, "I haven't had a letter from Granny in six weeks. Seems like Doctor Saddler knew what he was talking about. Proud, Robin?"

"Yes," Robin admitted, "I'm bursting with gladness and pride, but I can't understand why, when it's you who does all the actual work."

"Come again," Sallie said.

"It sort of seems to me," he said, "nature isn't quite fair in the division of work in child-bearing."

She threw back her head and laughed, a soft, tinkling giggle. "Men," she giggled, "can sometimes be the biggest sentimental old maids in the world. How do you know, Mr. Male, what kind of pleasure a woman gets from the deal? I mean having a child for the man she has a God-given right to believe she owns body and soul, just as she has given herself to him body and soul."

She was waxing eloquent.

"How are you to know how much exalted happiness there is in being a mother? I thank God that I am a woman, and that I have Robin Arvane for a mate, even if he is a sentimental old fool."

She paused, dropped her head against his shoulder, and sat quietly, breathing softly, contentedly.

Then, after a minute. "Darling, I didn't mean to be preaching at you, but I'm glad you gave me a chance to knock out any fool ideas of guilt you might have developed in your huge apple-seed-sized brain!"

Then, again, more seriously. "Darling, I didn't think up all I just said by myself. I learned most of it from Mother Pam, and she, of course, being Mother Pam, couldn't ever bring herself to put it as crudely and bluntly as I did, but that's the way she feels."

"No," Robin agreed. "Ma would never be brash enough to talk like that to Pa. Poor Ma! Honey, I'm afraid Ma's sicker than she admits, or maybe thinks to herself."

"She knows," Sallie told Robin slowly, and he saw tears forming in her eyes. "She told me yesterday she hasn't long and made me promise not to tell her men-folks." She sobbed. "I know its a low thing to break a promise like that, but I knew you would feel awful if I didn't let you share the hurt with me."

After that Robin observed his ma more closely. It was evident she was failing, and the fact that he had not fully realized it until now was painful.

Robin, Zack, and their pa were all resting on the steps of the front porch waiting for Dr. Saddler to come out of the house after a visit to Pamela, who had been growing weaker and weaker lately. When the doctor come out, Zack asked, "What's the verdict, Doctor?"

"I don't know what you mean," the doctor said. "I'm not in direct communication with God, and being only human I can't know anything for certain."

Zack's face reddened, but he held a civil tongue. "I mean, how is she?"

"As a horseback opinion, I'd say she'll die soon." The doctor's tone was matter-of-fact.

The shock of his words left them speechless for several seconds. Then Pless was the first to recover his voice. "Are you sure?"

"Of course not. I said in my opinion."

"Does she suspect it? You didn't tell her?" Robin was asking.

Saddler's voice gentled a little. "I didn't tell her anything. She knew it before I did. She's a very intelligent woman, with an

infinite faith in the Goodness of God. She isn't afraid." With
that, the doctor walked away. "I'll be back in a couple of days.
I'm not sure what's wrong with her, but I think it's advanced
cancer of the liver. If so, and it doesn't spread, it's practically
painless. Her passing may take weeks, maybe months."

His two sons rose, placed their arms over Pless's shoulders.
"Go in and talk to her, Pa," Zack urged. "Then come back and
tell us what you want us to do before we see her."

After some thirty minutes, Pless came out to them. He sat
down. There were tears gathering in his eyes, which he wiped
away impatiently, before he spoke, with a catch in his voice. "She
told me; I didn't hint at anything. Says she's known for two
years, but since there wasn't anything could be done about it, she
didn't want anyone else to worry. Go in and talk to her, but
don't mention her illness unless she brings it up. Let's get word
to Cessie."

Cessie came with her infant daughter and John Littlebow.
They were tired, and the baby was fretful, but Cessie in a short
time managed to recapture part of her old-time vivacity.

Having them around her bed seemed to make Pamela happy.
She frequently managed to make them laugh, despite the weight
of gloom that clung to their shoulders. The fact that she could
make them laugh does not mean that Pamela, all of a sudden,
had developed a sense of humor to any extent, or was any less an
adherent of the accepted ladylike formalities of her day. Her ability to bring smiles to their faces lay in the joyful manner in which
she could remember and describe small details of past family doings.

Day by day she was growing weaker. The doctor explained
that cancer of the liver, considered alone, was deadly, but not
painful. She was, he said, starving to death, although her appe-
tite was fairly good. The disease, he explained, was weakening in
itself, but its chief ravages worked through nonfunctioning of
the liver, causing victims to slowly starve. Pamela's condition
proved the doctor's contention.

She slowly worsened and requested others to cut their visit-

ing time as much as possible so that she might have most of her
last days on earth with Pless. When the import of her request
got through to them, the Arvane brothers, their wives and sisters,
left the house, crossed the road together, and went down to the
creekside where, under the big maple tree, they sat on the worn
hardwood benches old Ajax had built and left behind for their
comfort. After a while, Zack, as the eldest of the clan present,
knelt in front of his seat, while the others fell to their knees with
him. Zack commended their mother to God and prayed for peace
and comfort for her husband and children.

The first hints of the coming dawn were glinting the eastern
sky when Pamela died. The family had been roused an hour before and told she was going, and they had hurried to her bedside,
where after a few minutes she requested, in a weak whisper,
that she be left alone with Pless for her last few minutes. It came
home sharply to Robin how old and alone his pa looked when
Pless came from Pamela's room, his shoulders sagging, his face
drawn.

Pless made his way to the back porch as though sleepwalking,
where he bathed his face, neck, and hands in cold water, combed
his hair. He came back into the family room where his sons,
their wives, Cessie, Malvina, and Walt sat huddled miserably together. Pressing business had returned John Littlebow to Iowa.
"Your ma," Pless said, "wants you all to go with me to watch
the sun rise from Picnic Ledge. She promised to be with us when
the sun comes over East Ridge this morning." He looked critically at Malvina. "I don't know whether you ought to go or not,
Malvina, in your condition. It's a hard climb in several places."

"I'd go if I had to crawl," Malvina said, simply. "Besides,
I'm only six months pregnant. But poor Walt with his bad leg—"

"I'll be with you if I have to walk on my hands," Walt said
to them all.

The break-o'-dawn birds were chirping merrily around Picnic
Ledge when Pless's tall frame silhouetted itself on top of the rock,
against the newborn red fingers of dawn already reaching for the
treetops on East Ridge. Pless, with a lantern in his hand, had led

his flock up the winding family path to the ancient family picnic spot. Walt, swinging another lantern, had brought up the rear. They seated themselves around the ledge on the hewed-out seats in the rocks old Ajax had cut by hand so many years before. Each sat silent, the Arvane boys holding their wives' hands. Malvina clung closely to Walt's arm. Cessie sat by her pa, who dropped an arm around her while she wept silently against his chest.

Soon the first rays of sun came through the mist over the valley, and as it topped East Ridge, Pless rose and faced the east. His clan rose with him.

"Our Father Who Art in Heaven...." Pless' voice was smooth, sweet, and clear. "Thy Kingdom Come...." A chorus from his clan joined in, and the words floated softly out into the half-mist over the valley toward the rising sun.

CHAPTER FIFTY-FOUR

SALLIE HAD PUT LITTLE PAMELA TO BED AND RETURNED TO SIT BY Robin for their before-bedtime talk. Little Pam, who would turn out to be the spitting image of Cessie, was old enough to show a mouthful of sharp little teeth. She was already starting a life of tyranny over Robin, but the day would never come when she could bully her mother.

As usual, their first topic of conversation was the children, to be followed by anything that came to mind. That evening Sallie chose to muse aloud. "I wonder what would happen if you should get into politics; find yourself elected to high office. I wish I knew if you would give it the same amount of thought and hard work you do in trying to get ahead in public law practice."

"I don't think I'd have enough patience to be a big-time politician, and I haven't any desire to be a small one. My biggest interest in politics today is to see Holden's crowd out. The folks in this State have never been as hotheaded about their politics as they are in some of the Southern states, but they won't stand for being walked on too long before something has to give."

Sallie chose that moment to exercise her woman's right to change the subject without warning. "Daddy Pless is in Bassett's room telling your son a bedtime story. That boy has certainly been good for his grandpa. He's absorbing a lot of the affection Pless used to lavish on Mamma Pam."

"He's also having the very old scratch spoiled deep into him by Pa. You take one small grandson, one doting and indulgent grandpa, and it adds up to a lot of warm britches for little boy

later from his own pa, who has to pull up the weeds behind
Grandpa's planting."

Before Sallie could answer, Pless came in and joined them.
He fidgeted a minute, looking glum and unhappy. Robin finally said, "Out with it, Pa. I can see from the outside you got
something on your mind, but I can't see inside well enough to
know what it is."

"All right," Pless answered without further ado. "Your ma
made a request of me a few days before she passed. She asked
me to tell you she wanted you to get married by a preacher in the
presence of a witness. I reckon you're wondering why I didn't
tell you before."

"Yes," Robin said, "I wish you had."

"She asked me not to tell you until she'd been gone long
enough that grief for her wouldn't cause you to rush out and do
it without thinking as to whether it's the right thing for you.
She didn't want it to happen if either of you think it isn't necessary. Her idea was to get Josh to tie the knot in secret with nobody but Ellen as a witness, and for all of you to keep it to yourselves. You know Pam always thought that good, as well as evil,
can sometimes be a case of the least said the better. She said wait
to tell you, and if you didn't feel like doing it, she would understand."

Robin looked into Sallie's eyes. She looked back. They understood each other. "Miss Bassett, will you marry me?"

Sallie pulled his head against her. Tears glistened in her eyes
and her voice was thick as she answered, "Of course I will, you
fool. Once every day and twice on Sundays."

"In that event, I suppose you've got me hooked!" Robin
laughed softly. "It's after eight, slightly late for a call, but I suppose Josh and Ellen are still up. If not, we can wake them. Slip
into one of the dozens of wedding gowns you own, while I hitch
up the horse, and we will journey to Josh Todd's in search of
romance." The words were bantering, but the thickness in his
voice betrayed his feelings.

Ellen met them at the Todds' door. She said Josh and she had been sitting and talking, wishing they had some company. She asked about the children, and when Sallie was answering she noticed tears in Ellen's eyes. Sallie slipped an arm around Ellen's waist. "You can't?" she asked. "No," Ellen answered, dropping her head on Sallie's shoulder and crying softly for a moment or two. Josh says it doesn't make any difference to him, but I know better."

She dried her eyes, forced a smile. "Let's join the gentlemen before we get left out of something good."

Robin didn't mince any words. He began at the beginning and told Josh the entire story of his courtship of Sallie. How they had declared themselves man and wife and always felt that, in the eyes of the Good Lord, it was sufficient ceremony. He was frank to admit that the reason for wanting the ceremony now was to comply with the wish of his ma. They wanted the ceremony performed and nothing said about it to anyone, ever.

Josh could be, when the occasion arose, a bit pontifical. He said, "I will, of course, comply with your wish, as I would the wish of any very dear friend, but I think it would be far better if you could both come to me in sincere penitence."

"I can't, for the life of me, feel a single qualm for any sin I promulgated with Sallie. Fact is, I'm rather proud of myself. Almost as proud of myself as I am of her and those two squalling brats at home, who were so ignominiously born out of wedlock. But I still would like for you to help us do what Ma wanted. If you feel it will, in some way, compromise your conscience, then we can seek elsewhere. I will still consider you one of the best friends I have in the world." Robin was speaking slowly and seriously.

"Possibly you misunderstood me," Josh said quickly. "All I said was I would like for you to be willing to admit some consciousness of guilt. After all, leaving the question of marriage aside, you had to be guilty of something when you, as a young man, took an innocent girl alone with you into such perils as you took Sallie, then in the heat of excitement and the dark of the night, proceeded to seduce . . . ."

"Tush, tush, Josh Todd," Ellen interrupted, "don't be stuffy. I think their marriage is the most romantic thing I ever heard of. Romantic, and certainly as sacred in the eyes of God as any preacher could ever make it. Good Heavens, if you hadn't dashed off to the war the way you did, I was going to ask you to do the very same thing, if I couldn't goad you into asking me, which you, up until that, had been too stuffy to do. I've always regretted we didn't."

Josh sat thinking for several moments; then his face cleared. He turned to Ellen. "You know, dear," he said softly, "on second thought, I'm inclined to think perhaps you're right."

The ceremony was short, but solemn. Afterwards Josh brought out the mixings for a toast to the bride. A little later they felt another toast coming on for the happy couple. It wasn't much longer until it seemed right and fitting they should have one for all of them. By this time they were in a reminiscing mood. An hour later, Sallie and Robin had told them she was the grand-daughter of Peter Gherkim but asked that it be kept a secret be-tween them.

On hearing Sallie's words, Josh jerked himself erect. "You are a descendant of Peter Gherkim?" he asked, as though dis-believing.

"Then," he continued, "I have something for you." He rose, went to another room, returned with a small brass-bound chest, fitted a key into its old-fashioned lock, and took out a sealed pa-per. The chest was lettered, "Property of Modesty Church." He handed the paper to Sallie, who read the inscription on its out-side before she broke the wax seal. It was inscribed in the flowing hand so popular in the days of Ajax Arvane.

"Mrs. Barnes turned that over to me, along with other church documents, after I became pastor. You've noticed it says, 'To be opened by a descendant of Peter Gherkim, and only if such person should come to live in Modesty Valley.' I had no idea it would ever be opened."

He sat back as Sallie read aloud. The document, after the

usual dating and identification of the place where it was written, said:

This day I attended a wedding which I believe cuckolded a good man. It was the marriage of the Widow Cedric and Jarrett Cogle. Most folks wouldn't see it, but I could tell the widow is big with child, a child I don't believe sprang from Cogle's loins. In my opinion, she is carrying the child of one Peter Gherkim, who no longer dwells in the valley but is engaged in following his trade in Salem, from whence he came.

About three months back, the Widow Cedric did approach me with much weeping and wailing, swearing Gherkim stole one of her finest lambs, which he had killed and dressed for his own eating. She said I would find part of the meat and the lamb's skin at Gherkim's house. She likewise showed me some heavy bruises on her thighs where she said Gherkim had beat her when she tried to keep him from taking her sheep. She said she had been promised in marriage to Gherkim, but that lately he had been threatening to break it up. She had, she said, promised to give him a lamb as soon as they got up to eating size.

According to her, he came that night and told her he had never meant to marry her but he still wanted his sheep. When she told him he couldn't have it, he beat her with a stick, picked up a lamb, and went home. She further said she would be willing to forgive Peter Gherkim if he would go through with his word to marry her. I promised to see what I could do, after she asked me to keep the whole thing secret, and sent her away.

When she was gone, I got with Zebulon Cedric and we concocted a scheme because I didn't believe a word she had said, though I knew if she got stretched out she would soon get Gherkim killed.

That night, when me and Zebulon went to see Gherkim, he got mad as all hell at first but sort of calmed down after I talked to him a little more. He said he told her he would pay for the lamb later when she gave it to him. When he went by to pay her, she refused the money and told him she was pregnant by him and they would have to get married. He said he told her he didn't believe it, and if she was, it had as much chance to be Cogle's as his. She cussed him, he said, and then he told her he would just as lief marry a woman out of a brothel as her. Then she made after him, scratching, biting, screaming, and cussing. To give her something else to think about, he turned her over his knee and gave her backside hell with his open hand. Then he put the money for the lamb on the table and went home.

We explained to him that his days on this earth would be numbered if she started talking in the valley. Me and Zebulon thought he would be wise to disappear from Modesty that very night.

Sure enough, next day when the Widow learned Gherkim had disappeared she went out into the highways and byways telling folks how he stole her sheep. Of course, she didn't tell the same tale she told me. It was then I got the idea for the Peter Gherkim tombstone. Me and Zebulon vowed to each other not to ever tell a soul about our part in the Gherkim business, but I would hate to die without leaving something to clear things up if any of Peter Gherkim's descendants ever come to live in the valley. This is being sealed and turned over to Arch Barnes, only to be opened by a descendant of Gherkim who might come to live among us.

The paper was signed by Ajax Arvane.

When she had finished reading, Sallie sat silent for a few moments, with Robin holding her hand tightly in his. Then she flung herself on his lap, buried her head on his shoulder, and wept heartbrokenly for a minute, while he stroked her hair and made little throaty sounds of consolation that only she and he understood.

Sallie was not one to allow herself to weep for long. Soon she was calm, looking toward the lamp, thinking. Robin waited. A decision was coming, and it had to come from her.

Suddenly she rose and said evenly, "The only thing about this affair that gives me a sense of not being quite clean is when I think there is a strong probability that Phil might have inherited some of his mean traits from Grandpa Gherkim. I remember now he had a marked facial resemblance to my mother."

She stepped toward the fireplace where a few embers made a faint glow with tiny flames licking hungrily at them sporadically. With a firm hand she tore the document into fragments, dropped them on the embers, watched them catch and burn.

"Peter Gherkim," she said, casually, "never knew, while he was alive, how much he did for Modesty Valley. The day will come when folks will travel the length and breadth of the country to gaze on Peter Gherkim's tombstone and wonder what manner of men once lived in this valley who would murder a man for stealing a sheep. Thanks, Josh, Robin and I are leaving our family skeleton in your closet."